PRAISE FOR SUSAN SHWARTZ

"Shwartz's understanding of political situations and cultures comes through, making her characters seem even more extraordinary than they already are." —*SF Site*

"Susan Shwartz can evoke a setting immediately." —*Starlog*

"Susan Shwartz is a sorceress surely without peer, weaving her spells of entrapment to the wonder of all." —Dennis L. McKiernan

"With *The Grail of Hearts*, Susan Shwartz spreads her nets very wide and takes on a theme of great complexity and grand scale. She brings it off. She brings it off very well, with careful scholarship and prose that sometimes sings. The scope is broad, the philosophy is intimate, and there is something to reward the reader on every page. I congratulate the author for a stunning achievement." —Morgan Llywelyn

"A book to savor, a power and Power itself, a study of the narrow abyss between shame and pride . . . A delight for those with the intellect, heart, and guts to dig that deep into themselves." —Elizabeth Moon on *Grail of Hearts*

"An enigmatic tale of love, betrayal, and ultimate redemption . . . Shwartz has created a strong, eerie, and often painful world inhabited by a woman difficult to forget." —*Publishers Weekly* on *Grail of Hearts*

"The glory and the gore of the battles are so vividly real that one can almost smell the blood and hear the screams of the dying men." —*Voya* on *Cross and Crescent*

"Shwartz paints vivid and enchanted pictures of life as perhaps it ought to have been lived in far distant, more exotic times." —*Publishers Weekly* on *Shards of Empire*

Tor Books by Susan Shwartz

Cross and Crescent
Empire of the Eagle (with Andre Norton)
The Grail of Hearts
Heritage of Flight
Imperial Lady (with Andre Norton)
Moonsinger's Friends (editor)
Second Chances
Shards of Empire
Silk Roads and Shadows
White Wing (with S. N. Lewitt as "Gordon Kendall")

SECOND CHANCES

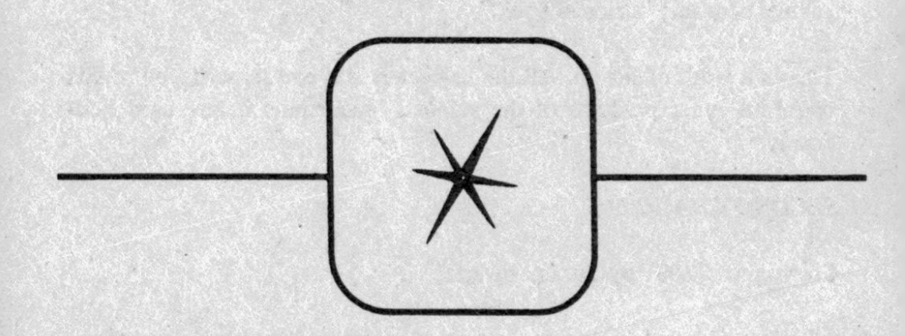

Susan Shwartz

A TOM DOHERTY ASSOCIATES BOOK
NEW YORK

SECOND CHANCES

Edited by Claire Eddy

A Tor Book
Published by Tom Doherty Associates, LLC
175 Fifth Avenue
New York, NY 10010

www.tor.com

ISBN: 0-812-57912-7
Library of Congress Catalog Card Number: 2001027527

First edition: August 2001
First mass market edition: April 2002

Printed in the United States of America

0 9 8 7 6 5 4 3 2 1

For Richard Curtis, whose idea this was

Acknowledgments

Special acknowledgments go to Claire Eddy, who showed remarkable, if characteristic, forbearance when the worlds turned upside down again; to the International Maritime Bureau, part of ICC Commercial Crime Services; and to Captain Cynthia Smith of the U.S. Merchant Marine Academy, King's Point, New York.

And especially to *il miglior fabbro,* Joseph Conrad.

Corporate BioShip *Irian Jaya*

1

Don't let me screw this up, the pilot prayed. A survivor of Alliance's Fleet, he'd been an interloper on the civilian *Irian Jaya* since he'd boarded.

"Three klicks out, same heading." The cybernetics tech raised his voice a careful degree to carry over the hums and beeps of navigation and the rasping breaths of three techs and one pilot trying to pretend they weren't expendable. "That's the worst of it. Better strap in."

Shirtsleeve environment, these civilian riderships were supposed to be, but now the crew sealed their helms, cautious as Alliance spacers who'd survived the Secess' war that had first divided, then almost destroyed, space-faring humanity. The pilot felt his hands sweat, then go cold inside his heavy gloves. He looked beyond the slagged and tangled umbilicals to the adiabatic pods that held a new generation of pioneers for a war-torn world. Let even one of them snap and the recoil could crush the tiny rider, slash through the hull of the corporate bioship, bound on its mission of well-paid mercy, and fling its cargo, men and women sleeping deep in Freeze, beyond this isolated Jump point through the space beyond the No Man's Worlds.

If they were lucky, they'd drift and not even feel the moment centuries from now when their systems failed and Freeze became death. But if their luck failed, they'd be retrieved by pirates. They'd fired on *Jaya* before, prying the light-armed ship away from its convoy until it had two choices: surrender or risk premature Jump.

Jaya had Jumped. By the time it miraculously emerged at a Jump point near its goal, the rough return to normal space sent the damaged umbilicals twisting around the ship's central disk. If they couldn't be stopped, they'd soon exceed their tolerances, and they'd snap, leaving *Jaya* easy prey. He had no confidence that the civilian captain, who'd made him feel like a hired killer since the moment he'd come on board, would blow the ship. Probably he feared to stick his estate—because of course the bastard had a substantial one—with the insurance premiums.

The pilot drew a rough breath. Other Fleet TDYs had complained of claustrophobia on these civ riderships, prompting long, long meetings on how cubic was precisely, absolutely the same as on Fleet riderships. But cubic be damned: matched against *Jaya,* this thing felt fragile as an egg. Matching it against a warship was like going through Jump in a soap bubble. And Fleet didn't give medals for damn foolishness.

He swallowed. Atmosphere display might be nominal, but he still felt he wasn't getting enough air.

Through the suit-comms, he heard a tech cough. Nerves or spacer's throat, whatever: the man fought to suppress it as the pilot edged away from *Jaya*'s central disk toward the worst of the tangled lines. So he wasn't the only one.

The cyberneticist's voice seemed to vibrate in the cramped cabin. "Jim. Did you hear me? Three klicks out. Same heading."

The pilot bent over a jury-rigged display he'd delayed take-off to install. Its yellows, reds, and greens glowed too brightly in the reddish cabin lighting that preserved his night vision.

The tension in the ridership thickened.

"Did you hear me, mister?" the cybernetics tech snapped. He seemed to puff up in his flight suit. Custom-made, no less, not ship's issue. On bioships in particular, cybes were privileged characters, used to people asking "how high" if they so much as murmured "jump."

If Jim remembered it right, this particular cybe was some kind of VIP or VP of R&D groundside. Civilian alphabet soup. The whole chain of command was different.

On *Irian Jaya,* though, this bigshot cybe came under the

orders of Chief Tech Danamon, who reported direct to Captain Heikkonen. Never mind that: for now, this rider was under its pilot's command, and that was Jim.

And if they didn't like it, they could all breathe space.

A Regular service arms officer, Jim was on an expensive and somewhat controversial exchange to the civilian bioship *Irian Jaya*. He wasn't in the corporate chain of command. All the evidence of a six months' tour of duty—at taxpayers' expense, as the captain liked to point out too often at too many meetings—showed he barely understood. From the first day he'd come on board, it had tripped him up. Like the major flap before they got under way for New Amman when he insisted on going through the usual security manual before certifying that *Irian Jaya* was fit for departure. The deadline was tight, and *Jaya* could win a fat bonus if it arrived before it. The captain had tried to "give him guidance" about security. Jim had replied, "Management guidelines be damned," no one was going anywhere until the ship was secure.

So what if they missed a fat performance bonus. The money wasn't going into Jim's account. But if the mission failed, they'd take that out of his hide.

No one in Fleet had ever accused Jim of being arrogant. There, after his rare minor screwups, he'd apologize and make good fast. A career in Fleet with lives riding on his decisions gave him a phenomenal learning curve, and he never made the same mistake twice.

The problem was that he wasn't on their team, they didn't want him on their team, and he had only to breathe to antagonize them. He'd more than breathed; he'd insisted on Fleet levels of security, and they couldn't forgive him.

Especially because he'd been right.

God. Get them through the Secess' war, and now all the civs, especially the corporates, wanted to do was get on with their lives. People like Jim were an unpleasant reminder that not only could fighting break out again, it might break them—and what's worse, any way they sliced it, they'd have to pay.

"Jim!"

The pilot whirled. Blue eyes flashed beneath his gleaming visor. Seeing only the ridership's crew, he made himself relax and turn back to his instruments. Mustn't scare the passengers.

"Three klicks, aye."

Behind him, he heard the techs start to breathe again. *Don't want to stir up combat reflexes, do you? Not when I'm driving.*

"Steady."

After his last wardroom confrontation, Jim had taken to keeping to himself on board *Jaya*. He was actually more shy than aloof, and he thought some of the crew were beginning to see it. But most of the senior staff saw him only as "tin soldier," an expensive line item on the ship's manifest, useful in the kinds of PR that used more spin than a space platform explaining to shareholders how concerned management was to protect their investment. They simply couldn't forgive him for being what they thought he was: a meticulously groomed, polite, stiff-backed recruiting holo of the sort that had lured their brothers and sisters out of secure berths, into the damn Secess' war and the subject lines of messages that began "we regret to inform you."

For a long moment, Jim stared at his passengers, reflected in the glow of the instrument panels. He could see his own reflection staring back at him from their helms, could see what they saw now: a soldier who restrained himself from striking out, whose eyes were bracketed from strain, and who stared at the ship's crewmembers as if they were part of an unquiet dream that distracted him from his instruments.

A pilot's concentration approached trance, sometimes. Even corporate pilots. The story was, all pilots did was eat, sleep, and brag for ninety-eight percent of their time. The other two percent, they earned the exorbitant bonuses and even stock options that helped divide them even further from the rest of the crew.

Stop thinking and drive, Jim told himself.

He sent the ridership gently forward.

JIM SIGHED AS AWARENESS OF HIMSELF AS A BODY CRAMMED into a too-cramped ridership with nervous civilians returned. A moment ago, life had been stars, screens, and the hope, spiky with adrenaline, that debris wouldn't pop out of nowhere and hole them a good one or scavengers didn't choose to emerge from Jump right now.

I'm supposed to protect these people. How can I concentrate with all this chatter going on in back?

Not that he could protect anything right now. The ridership was unarmed. Not even a dead man's switch.

Careful, he warned himself. This wasn't the time for the cybernetics tech to squeal "your tin soldier's trancing out on duty" to the bioship's captain, who'd consider it his duty—as in fact it was—to relay that back to Corporate HQ.

Besides, the meager kilometers between Astro-Pharm's *Irian Jaya* and the fouled umbilicals that mated the bioship to its cargo of eggs, sperm, zygotes, and cryonically frozen shipsicles didn't give him enough time to get a real trance of concentration going.

Lights blinked *white/off, red/off, green/off* on the snarled and damaged tubes. They looked like the landing strips in the rider's docking bay on board *Jaya.*

It's not over yet. This ship, these people, this mission all depend on me, Jim reminded himself again. *I used to dream about being helpful, being necessary, saving lives. I wanted to be a hero. They should have locked me up for a madman instead of letting me enlist. If I could wake far away from here, if I could relive the last twenty years . . .*

If he were back on *Irian Jaya,* or, better yet, if he were young again, innocent of the discipline and the memories of the regs, with no blood on his hands or the kind of dreams that woke you up choking in the night watches, fingers clenched on nothing, as if you were running out of air, he'd damned well dream about life as a groundsider.

But no, he'd had to want the stars, he'd had to dream of glory, of sacrifice, and he'd never factored the blood and the sweat and the fire and the death that the war was really about into the equation. War had become his trade. Now the war was over, and he knew he'd have to learn a new one. Assuming he wasn't too old to learn new tricks.

"Getting restless, are you?" Jim asked his passengers. "I'll send the steward back with drinks."

A grunt and a chuckle told Jim his flippancy had registered.

"Our tax money at work," muttered someone. "Tin soldier's turned into a comedian. Someone tell him to shut up and drive."

Ah, progress.

The war with the Secess' had been long and expensive. There were still some civs who didn't understand why the Secess' couldn't simply turn around and go their merry way. After all, it was a damn big galaxy.

Trouble was, everyone—Secess', Alliance, and the barbarians in between—laid claim to the same real estate, the same planetary systems and Jump points, no one compromised; and everyone had loud and stubborn theories over how to run the show and who was best qualified to run it. Contradict any of them, and they could bring heavy firepower to bear . . . and had.

Manifest destiny, expansionism, *lebensraum,* ethnic cleansing: the Secess' war had been all of the same obscene standbys, but played out at faster-than-light. Jim didn't know about Secess', beyond the fact that they were hell to fight. What he did know was that the ordinary Alliance citizens, who relied on the Fleet for their lives, would probably never forgive it, or the people—the brothers and sisters of a hundred star systems—who shed their identities for a uniform and discipline and emerged as those almost unrecognizable creatures, combat soldiers. Assuming they emerged at all.

The war had been a near thing. In the end, Secess' and Alliance made peace, such as it was, because they couldn't afford to go on killing and being killed, and force humanity to retreat to planet-bound barbarism.

"Lighten up," someone told whoever had come up with the tin soldier remark this time. "He actually made a joke. And I could do with a drink. Yellow."

Jim jerked an elbow at the pac storage compartment: yellow for a jolt of pick-me-up; green for electrolyte balancing; clear for recycled water.

"Living dangerously, are you?"

"On sucrose and caffeine? What about you, Jim? They let you drink on duty? Clear? Well, all right, man, but you know what that stuff really is!" The pac flew at him, a good-natured assault. Jim snagged it without missing a blip on his readout, unsealed his helmet, tugged loose the straw, and sucked down the water, chemically pure despite the jokes about its source. For all corporate crew complained about defense appropriations, their living conditions were a damn sight better than Fleet's.

Just shrug off insults, Jim remembered the briefings that preceded this TDY. Fleet shrinks had cleared him for it, and he'd survived Basic Training years ago; he was pretty sure he could rise above a few insults.

It was the rare civilian who hadn't lost friends or family, who hadn't had her career derailed or his research confiscated. Some civilians, whose homeworlds were near the front, had had to hold the line with armed shuttles and aging ground installations until the Regs could build up to strength and take over. Never mind the fact that before the Secess' struck, Alliance force appropriations had been down to all-time lows. The Fleet was supposed to make bricks without straw, and don't you forget it. Now that the war was over, economics had replaced survival as the bottom line as civilians reckoned up the prices they'd paid to survive and decided that they'd paid far too much.

No good deed goes unpunished. This war wouldn't be the first time in history civilians had turned on their military.

Suck it down, mister. He did, along with a last gulp that

drained the pac—they were right, the recycled water did taste like his idea of stale pee—and hurled the empty into the recycler. Right on target. He didn't want to think of the chaff he'd have taken if he'd missed.

He resealed his helm and cast an eye over the bioship's tangled umbilicals and the pods they still sustained. They all carried scorch marks, but no heavy damage—except for the pod and cable furthest from the ship. That umbilical was all but severed. An energy beam had gnawed a hole in the pod's hull. Its registration number was empty space, and even its stationkeeping lights were dead. The thousand shipsicles in there would never wake. Their hibernacula had become coffins.

The cybernetics tech hissed.

"Captain's not going to like the body count," Chief Tech Danamon muttered. "They'll probably dock his pay."

Was that supposed to be a joke? Jim wondered. *And they complain about* Fleet's *gallows humor?*

Corporate-politics alert, he told himself and kept eyes forward, where they belonged anyway. *Just fly the ship, Jimboy. That's what they're paying you for.*

"Think of your assignment as a chance to build bridges," Fleet psychs had urged him. "Or repair them."

Problem was, "building bridges" had been problematic the day he reported on board. The techs had been wary, still were—but Jann Heikkonen, the corporate bioship's civilian captain, had been downright hostile, and his needling spread down the chain of command.

"I suppose you think we're slack," he'd confronted Jim as he slouched behind his desk in his office.

"Sir, no sir." Jim snapped to attention. His second mistake. Coming aboard had probably been his first.

" 'Sir, no sir,' " the captain had mimicked. "We polish our instruments, not our brass, soldier. You just remember that. Your job is to advise, sit around in your pretty uniform, and collect your pay while we do all the hard work. So let us do

our jobs, all right? Don't touch something you don't have the degrees to understand. You might break it, and we'd have to pay for that too—not that Fleet's ever given a good goddamn about the bottom line."

"Sir, yes sir" would have been the wrong reply. Anything he could have said or done would have been wrong.

And that's how things had stayed: armed stalemate. He occupied a berth. But he wasn't crew on Jaya, *and if the captain had a thing to say about it, he never would be.*

Damn, why didn't he have the brains just to pack up right then and report back to his old CO?

War's over, Jim. You have to make some *contingency plans*. The Old Man thought he was actually doing Jim a favor by sending him on board *Jaya*. He couldn't just go back and say, "Sorry, sir, I don't like it."

So. He was actually following orders . . . wasn't he? A thousand more repetitions, and maybe he'd even believe it.

A ship like *Irian Jaya* with its well-paid corporate crew could be part of his plans if Fleet retired him. Assuming he didn't botch this exchange assignment and learned to fit in with civilian corporate culture. It had its points, his CO had assured him.

Yeah. Most of them would be aimed at his back, if the *Jaya*'s captain had anything to say about it.

Alliance's fleet gave him a name, a rank, a serial number, and a role. No one on *Jaya* threatened to take those things from him, but people's mouths twisted if they were forced to use his military title, so they used his name. His first name, as if he were some hired hand.

And the fact that Jim unfortunately resembled the kind of recruiting holo that civilian scientists thought were the lowest form of propaganda hadn't helped him win friends either. He was fair-haired, spacer-pale, and blue-eyed. Political types in the post-war Alliance Fleet warned him to be diplomatic among civs, so he smiled when he remembered. His grin stripped years from him and made people who'd determined never to trust him want to like him. Trouble was, he hadn't had much to smile at lately.

At the sight of the ruined pod, Jim felt his lips snarl back from his teeth in a way the civs wouldn't have found likable at all. A thousand lives. Scavengers had taken out a thousand lives. Just as well he sat up front with his helm sealed again so they couldn't see his face.

Jim's universe had to be as full of enemies as it was of stars: if not Secess', then scavengers who could kill people who'd had the courage to lie down in those pods, never knowing if they'd wake to save a world or dream forever.

"Prepare to fire braking thrusters." He felt, more than saw, someone swing forward and sink into the seat next to his. The little ridership really didn't need a copilot, but he'd take Tech Danamon's help as evidence he was making progress.

"Got it." Jim nudged the four-person rider closer to the umbilicals. Danamon would need a visual inspection of the surviving pods. "Thrusters engaged."

Firing this close to the umbilicals was tricky. With diagnostics compromised, there was no telling if some last power surge wouldn't make a stray cable break free and slice the ridership in half.

Sweat trickled into his flightsuit's absorbent lining. In the early phases of his service, such as it had been, medical telemetry had given him—and biofeedback training—hell for nerves. Ventilation kicked up in the cabin, dispelling the spoor of fear and tension and too-close quarters, its rhythm like a heartbeat in the womb: persistent, reassuring, life itself.

Jim's face in the back-lit heads-up display, which flickered as navigation's colored lights fountained and subsided, showed him a fierce stranger.

No wonder this crew of softer strangers bristled.

He wished he felt as confident as his out-thrust jaw looked. *God, don't let them catch on,* was his first hope, immediately followed by the real form of the pilots' prayer that had been ancient even before mankind left Earth: *God, don't let me fuck up.*

He glanced at the sensor he'd attached to the console next to the navigation readout—his DEW-trap, he called it—a distant early warning sensor he'd jury-rigged to monitor the mines he'd placed around the ship. He was uplinked to such weapons systems as *Jaya* had. If scavengers Jumped, he'd order fire from here.

Nothing out there but particles and background radiation.

Yet.

Scavengers knew *Irian Jaya* was out here and that she'd taken damage. After all, they'd cut her off from her convoy and forced her into Jump. He had to assume they'd tracked her all the way here. It was what he'd have done.

The best outcome Jim had been able to force was to destroy two ships and drive off a third. No reason, he snorted inwardly, to pin a medal on him. The ships he'd killed had been nearly derelict, thank God. Besides, he'd borrowed his tactics from Conrad Ragozinski's encounter with Abendsterners at Sigma Draconis. Abendstern, one of the capital planets of the Secess', had proved to be an almost unbeatable enemy until Ragozinski, covering the evacuation of the outpost on Xanthus, had used his ship's mass as an anchor for the other ships, as little suited to combat as they'd been.

Ragozinski's victory at Sigma Drac had gotten him promoted to captain at some ungodly young age, "an inspiration to us all," as the saying went until the next person to intone it got thrown out of the wardroom. Even the Abendsterners sent an uplinked commendation, but then they always were weird about honor, or their notions of it.

Jim knew he hadn't won honor with *Irian Jaya*. He'd simply gained a little time. Maybe even enough.

He spared a glance back at the screen showing the bioship's status. Talk about a fat, tempting target.

Irian Jaya was a late-model bioship that melded a heavy transport's hull with the special fittings and tech crew that let it carry immunosuppressants and seed organs, cloned skin for grafts, sperm, ova, and zygotes, to worlds whose populations had been driven below viability by the war. And its specialized equipment, its priceless cargo of genetic material, and its pods with their ten thousand immigrants in cryonic suspension made it too rich a prize for the scavengers not to try again. Ten thousand people was a planet's worth of hostages—or slaves. And the frozen embryos and gametes could be hatched out into little scavengers, expanding their forces and their gene pool.

Or, if they were feeling kind, the scavengers could hold the whole shooting match for ransom. If there was anything Alliance and the Fleet agreed upon, it was the importance of the bioships.

Not that that had made a lot of difference in Jim's present mission. What they needed for proper protection of a ship like *Jaya* was a full convoy, assuming ships and money could be found, which they couldn't.

But New Amman's need was desperate, and it could pay for living freight in rare earths and chemicals that made the R&D people's eyes go all bright and greedy. So *Jaya* flew with only a few companions. Complicating the situation, the best he could say of *Jaya*'s handling capabilities was that she didn't handle; she wallowed. But then, she wasn't built for speed or maneuverability; she was built to endure. She'd have been torn apart in Jump otherwise.

They'd embarked in communications silence, such as it was. Even so, the scavengers had found *Jaya* preparing for Jump and scored her hull near the propulsion scoops before the captain could turn and try to fight back.

Would they be lurking by this Jump point too? Where'd they get their data? And from whom?

Dangerous thinking, Jim my boy.

Even after the scavengers had taken out one of their three convoy vessels, some of the crew had wanted to negotiate, not fight. High-minded of them, Jim thought. Their minds had to be high up their butts, if they thought you could negotiate with scavengers. Scavengers pounced on unwary ships and stole, not just cargo, but whatever they had a mind to. One of the ship's crew looked tempting? She—or he—got hustled onto one of the flying derelicts that the scavengers called home. The ship needed spare parts? Why, then, it stripped its prey, and too damned bad if what it stole was primary life support.

Fleet had zero tolerance toward scavengers. It was practically the one thing on which they agreed one hundred percent with Secess'.

You didn't negotiate with vermin; you burned them, Jim had snarled—and opened fire. He guessed he could give up on the vote for Most Congenial Shipmate.

Still, he had saved the ship. It was his old civilian fantasy, and he'd actually done it.

Congratulations might have been nice. He would have been grateful for a pat on the back; it had been a long time since anyone who wasn't a physician's aide had touched him. But he didn't have time. Jim had driven the scavengers off in search of simpler prey, but *Jaya* was too rich a target for them not to try again. There were improvements in the ship's defenses he could make now, if only he had the time.

What he got instead was an entire war's worth of debriefings. *Irian Jaya*'s Captain Heikkonen might not know how to use ship's weapons like an expert, but he did know the energy consumption and depreciation costs of each weapon he'd fired—and he'd lectured Jim about profit and loss numbers et goddamn cetera while the adrenaline in his blood made him fight not to shiver in the aftermath.

Then, the red lights flashed up an ion storm on the umbilicals' monitors and it was the engineers' turn to justify *their* existence. And Heikkonen's job to see that they did just that. While needling Jim into taking over damage control and surveillance missions like the present one. *Bastard didn't even give me a chance to volunteer.*

So far, the mines he had rigged as another distant early warning system were untouched. His sensors were flatline, his DEW trap empty. No bugs, no signals, and no scavengers.

Behind him, the techs and scientists tensed as they got visual confirmation of the damage to the lines.

"You think the other pods are compromised?" one asked.

"Better hope not," Danamon tossed back over his shoulder.

The most important thing—and the most dangerously tempting—about *Jaya* wasn't the genetic seedcorn she carried. It was that she was rigged to ferry the Linebarger adiabatic pods that trailed out a hundred klicks behind it on complex umbilicals. In the last years of the war and now, too, in the aftermath, when convoys were a luxury no one could afford, ships like *Jaya* resembled those quail or whatever from Old Earth, assuming they hadn't been eaten during the blockade. Jim had studied those birds as part of his fascination with flight. Mother quail, seeing their nests endangered, would leap away and posture, one wing down, as a way of luring predators away and protecting their young. He knew. He'd watched them as a boy.

Not even Frekans, obsessed with genetic engineering as they were, would challenge a bioship, Fleet myth whispered. But Freki had a crazier honor code than even Abendstern. Scavengers had nothing but what they stole.

"If the engines scorch the vents or those exposed housings . . ." whispered a man from Life Support. "We could lose another pod."

Jim glanced from sensors to controls. A touch, practically a caress on his board, accelerated the tiny craft. *Just a touch, you beauty. There. You like that? Want me to do it again? You'll do anything I say, won't you?*

Tech Danamon hissed, demanding caution. "Were you planning to mate up with the pods?"

Jim's fingers paused in their fugue on controls long enough for him to flick a wary glance at Danamon. No pun intended. "This mission's time-sensitive," he reminded the crew. "I want to get in as close as we can. Mr. Banks barely qualified for EVA in the last powered-suit drill."

Jim's words aborted another whispered staff meeting among the civs. Again, he let his glance flicker from DEW sensors to navcomp. On this board, navigation looked a lot like target acquisition on a Fleet rider. Too easy to make a mistake . . .

Perhaps he should not have left weapons control on board *Jaya* to pilot this mission, but he'd already exceeded the time the civ medics thought he should spend on watch. He'd had to bully them into letting him go out.

Tin soldier, they'd whispered disapprovingly. He'd been counting on precisely that reaction.

"While this ship is under my command," Jim said, not bothering to turn his head, "Mr. Banks will go EVA only under tether. *Short* tether."

Cybernetics Tech Banks began a furious protest starting with "No tight-ass . . ."

"Shut up and let the man fly," whispered the maintenance tech. Banks subsided, quelled by her glare. In corporate life, Jim knew, Tech Rourke was Dr. Alanna Rourke, senior technical staff with two earned PhDs—in physics and engineering—and a couple honoraries. On board ship, she might be only a warrant officer—he never could figure out the civ version of ship hierarchies—but she outranked the others morally, at the very least.

Take twenty years off her, put her in uniform, and she reminded Jim of an officer from his first ship. One he'd liked. One years dead.

He raised his head (carefully not looking away from nav-comp as he maneuvered thrusters) so she could see his reflection smile at her.

She snorted. "Is charm school part of our arms deal with Fleet?" she demanded.

His smile widened into a grin.

At least she didn't freeze him out. Not entirely. God, if that little bit of support warmed him, he must be freezing to death inside.

He was coming up on the tubes now. Jim tapped thrusters, edging in. Scavengers might set off his sensors or detonate his mines in the next instant, but these maneuvers were critical.

Damage the bioship's umbilicals and the adiabatic pods they fed lost power. Power loss meant the shipsicles sustained damage, and what was revived at planetfall wouldn't be immigrants, ready and eager to help rebuild New Amman, but freezer burn cases a slagged world couldn't afford to rehabilitate. Might as well simply cast them loose now.

Light glinted on the scorched cerametal tubes, the trailing filaments, and the jeopardized pods. Parsecs beyond, gas trails coiled in immense dragon shapes, the stars of their hoards glittering sapphire and diamond in the darkness.

Forget the poetry, he reminded himself. *Think of what's out there simply as a cosmic version of this wretched snarl of smart machinery—idiot gadgets studying to be morons—that we have to fix before we can power up and escape into the safety of Jump.*

Wouldn't this be one hell of a time for scavengers to pop back in-system?

He glanced at his DEW trap. No activity.

So what if the starscape was beautiful? What he was really looking for—beside a safe halt near the pods—was any flicker of anomalous motion. Besides, his training and his survival had taught him the value of taking a pragmatic view of deep space. That meant that gas clouds were just navigational hazards, and singularities were traps.

Space didn't care whether you lived or died. If you were stupid, you ran into trouble. Usually, you died. If you were really stupid, you died slow and messy. And that was just from space hazards: before Armistice, the Secess' had been far worse. The Abendsterners tended to outplan you; the Tokugawans never gave up; and the Frekans always and invariably attacked like madmen.

Damn, he still didn't know how that misbegotten trio of worlds had agreed to break off from the Alliance, much less how they'd attracted satellite and client worlds. All three were authoritarian as hell. Abendstern and Tokugawa both had hereditary aristocracies, and on Freki, you fought to win your place and keep it. The first hint had come out of the universities, when some of the senior-most scientists had resigned and returned to their homeworlds. If Intel hadn't hacked into the university systems and copied their research, Jim probably wouldn't be sitting in this ridership.

Exposure had prompted formal complaints, then withdrawals. A couple attacks that everyone knew now had been feints.

And then the massed Secess' fleets had come out, driving the Alliance back, always back, until its capital world, old Earth itself, lay imprisoned by a blockade.

They showed all the graduating classes the blockading fleet. *Beyond those ships lies Home,* the CO would say. And just about then, usually, some Frekan fighting star would come out to test the mettle of the new officers. For all he knew, the Frekans thought they were doing them a favor.

It would have made more sense and saved lives not to hold Academy graduation so near the blockade, Jim knew. But it took a far more cynical mind by far than his who didn't see the blockading fleet and pledge, inwardly, to break through and restore Earth to the Alliance, and reclaim the stars. All of them, Alliance and Secess' alike.

The part of him that was still a dreaming boy who'd looked up from the bottom of his lavish safe gravity well at the blue sky of his home and craved starlight still believed that.

He blinked his eyes hard, as if cleansing them of dreams. Even the familiar ergonomic light of the controls hurt his eyes. The wrinkles that bracketed his eyes didn't show any signs of smoothing, and a muscle in one eyelid ticced. He looked fifteen years older, at least, than his age. Mid-thirties—no gray hair yet, but he was getting up there for a combat officer. Had his reflexes slowed yet?

The mines still floated out there untouched, thank God. The DEW trap showed empty. His monitors shone clear. *Just a little longer,* he prayed.

His unlikely crew was shifting in their seats, unsnapping restraints before the all-clear chime.

"As you were," he spoke without bothering to turn. He knew what he heard.

"We're losing time!" Banks snapped. "Energy levels are dropping, or don't you care how many more we lose?"

Think about the mission.

If those umbilicals snapped now, it was his ridership with its limited capabilities that would have to chase them. He'd have to avoid a recoil that could breach its hull, then reconnect them to the bioship. He'd heard that trick described as "crocheting with a hundred kilometers of yarn and an explosive hook." In better times, he'd have liked to try it.

These weren't better times.

Still, a tricky repair job was better than having an umbilical snap while *Irian Jaya* was in transit.

Painstakingly, Jim adjusted a final course vector. He could remember his former officers: there's a right way and a wrong way to do everything. And then there's the Fleet way.

Yes, he knew this wasn't the Fleet. Jim still flushed with anger at Captain Heikkonen's accusation that pulling some of the bioship's engineers off regular duty to improvise mines and upgrade weapons systems had turned them "into goddamned unproductive toymakers!"

Do I hear anger, mister? Angry is stupid. Stupid is dead. And if you screw up here, it will *go on your fitrep.*

He took a deep breath, masked by the rest of the crew's heavy breathing. When a mission turned critical, oxygen consumption always jumped.

Captain Heikkonen wasn't out here. So Jim would conduct this mission according to the Fleet's best practices, or this was one rider that was heading back to *Irian Jaya*'s docking bay. He didn't want to cook those pods any more than Banks wanted him to.

Besides, the investigation would be worse than any possible accident.

One more microburn, and they could maneuver alongside. *Do it neatly, Jim. Make a good impression.*

His fingers danced a last dance on the control, then rested on the console after the infinitesimal course correction. A burn slowed the ship, briefly forcing its inhabitants back against their seats.

"Matching course achieved," he reported. In the silence of the tiny ship, heavy with the tense breathing of four people, he sounded like a priest giving his blessing.

At least the readouts, thank God, were green. As green as the hills of the Earth he'd never walked on.

"Make us proud, son," his father's most recent transmission had ended. He still had all his father's tapes, kept them despite the stringent weight allowance that taught the Fleet to travel light. They were a blockade in their own way, against fear, against loneliness. Jim, at least, had a home he could go back to once he was no longer needed. No Secess' ships had ever gotten through to his homeworld, to scorch it bare or turn it into one of its slave holdings—in that way, war-time Secess' resembled scavengers. Jim liked to think that his efforts had something to do with that.

His father was safe. Somewhere other than in his memories, the stream ran clear across the corner of the acreage he knew would be his own if he survived to come home and claim it. He knew just where the best place would be to build. Assuming that was the life he wanted. It never had been before. Still, the fact that it was still going on in his absence was cause enough for pride.

Jim blinked again, hard, then stared out at the glowing tendrils of red and blue gas that coiled from the binary as it danced about its cosmic axis. He'd put in one dose of drops before he'd left the ship and wished he'd doubled it. One good thing about a corporate ship; *Jaya* had the best pharm-closet he'd ever seen. When Jim thought about how Fleet ships went chronically short, not just on the meds for deep pain or antibiotics, but on the little amenities that could boost performance or prevent it from degrading . . .

You fought off scavengers. What are you doing out here?

He'd already fought this out. *Shut up,* he ordered himself.

Strict chain-of-command would probably say it was no job of the arms officer on loan from Fleet to court burnout. Still, the facts remained: in space—or in the Fleet, there was no such thing as "it's not my job."

So, while Chief Engineer Stuart checked out the hull, lounging by his readouts in Engineering, Jim played driver and nursemaid for ship's biotech maintenance staff, who whispered behind his back or spoke science more often than any language a serving officer like him could understand without advanced degrees.

The time would pass faster if he could check in on the civs he had checking out ship's personal arms. Although standing orders required qualified arms officers and maintenance techs staffing ship's weapons, *Jaya* wasn't just a corporate ship, but a bioship, for which "ship's safety" meant something other than armaments. The *Jaya*'s personal arms had never even been unpacked and tested out. And that wasn't just a dereliction of duty, that was suicide.

That was also when he'd all but charged into Captain Heikkonen's quarters about this violation of standing orders and been told that the standing orders governing self-defense were "low priority." God, he hated terms like "prioritization" when they interfered with his duty. If scavengers had boarded, he'd have had crew firing at them from every lab and cabin. No doubt, that was precisely what Heikkonen wouldn't want, if he'd thought that far. Damage to his expensive ship. No doubt, its owners would have tried to negotiate *Jaya*'s return. Dealing with scavengers. God.

It was easier to negotiate even with Frekans than with scavengers. Frekans would shoot at you, but they didn't "revisit issues" or "put back on the table" problems that he'd thought had long been solved. Not to mention the occasional "misspeaking." And the "feedback." Good God, the feedback.

I wish I knew what they were doing with those sidearms back on board. Just thinking what *Jaya*'s crew could do with active weapons, minimal arms training, and technical ingenuity could give you post-traumatic stress. But he was on communications silence, except for emergencies. Which this wasn't. Not yet. And worrying about it would disrupt his concentration.

The DEW trap was still empty. He already had the mines, and soon he'd have crew EVA.

"Have Tech Rourke go over the checklist on that suit with you," he ordered as the cybernetics tech struggled into EVA gear. The woman wearing engineering insignia bent as close to the cybernetics officer as she could in her bulky EVA suit and whispered. Both scientists laughed.

Jim bit back a sigh. More jokes about his first name, no doubt. His family had pinned it on him before civilians had regarded war or the military as a subject for irony. Before he'd become a straight arrow and the *Jaya*'s resident arms consultant. But to civilians, "Jim" meant straight arrow. "Jim" meant hero. Not a stressed-out refugee from Fleet who wondered what he'd do now that the war was over.

"Aye, Captain." More teasing. He thought it had gotten friendlier since yesterday, when Jim had had to suit up and go EVA to rescue Banks, who'd lost orientation during boost, burned out his fuel, and gone drifting, too stunned by the view to do more than hyperventilate.

Jim hadn't even grimaced when they got Banks inside again and found he'd fouled his suit. He'd seen worse and, for that matter, smelled it. And at least the man was alive. He'd even managed to laugh over his mortification, which was probably more than Jim could have brought himself to do.

"We're coming up on the damaged section," Danamon reported. "Coming up . . . coming up . . . stay on course . . ."

His voice sounded almost hypnotized: on a pilot, that would have been fighting trance. The Abendsterners and Frekans induced it with drugs, Jim had heard . . . They used drugs to augment their pilots' performance and block out fear . . . stop it!

God, don't let the scavengers Jump in-system now, please!

"You can see it now, sir," Danamon told Jim.

"Sir"? Had he actually gotten a "sir" out of the senior tech, who had made it perfectly clear one evening that any of *Jaya*'s senior staff could buy and sell the likes of Jim? Would wonders never cease?

There. Jim was no biotech specialist, but even he could see the discoloration on the umbilical and the way it bent.

The cyberneticist watch bent over his console. Blue and green shadows flickered over his dark face, lit already by the ambient glow of the red lights that kept them from losing time while their eyes adjusted to darkness. Blue, green; a deeper, blinking red.

He hissed under his breath, then swore.

"Well and truly snarled," muttered Danamon. "Auto-correct's burned out. See?" He pointed out the flashing red lights on Jim's screen. *Not* the mines. Not yet.

"Can we get confirmation from the umbilical systems?" Banks asked.

"Burned out. We'll have to replace the whole control panel," Danamon said. "Banks, you can unhelm. You're not going. I am."

He found the case, carefully sealed and time-stamped, counterstamped it, and tenderly lifted the replacement panel from its packing.

"Want me to move in closer so you can grapple?" Jim asked.

"No way I want to use grapplers on that mess," Chief Tech Danamon told him. "I'll EVA. I'm rated satisfactory, without tether," he informed Jim, with a flicker of a smile.

Jim inclined his head ironically. *What do you have to do to win friends around here?*

Rising, Danamon checked his oxygen tanks, inspected his helm seals, and headed for the airlock, pulling on EVA gauntlets as he went.

The white panel slid aside, then whooshed shut.

"Seal."

"Engaged."

"Vent."

"Counting down."

"Ready." Danamon's voice, filtered through helmet comm, sounded tinny.

"Opening."

Depressurization flashed on Jim's board.

A moment later, the outer hatch slid aside. In a ship this small, he felt the jolt.

"EVA initiated, sir."

Another "sir." Well, again, would wonders never cease? He noted Danamon's egress time, although recorders had been live since they'd left *Jaya*.

Give Danamon this, Jim thought, the man could fly. His trajectory out to the damaged umbilical and his landing were as tidy as Fleet could wish.

Bioships demanded first-rate equipment and first-rate crew. Bioships were a bitch to maintain and, because the pods required shielded engines and slow speed, a worse bitch to protect. But nothing was more valuable to a recovering Alliance. The immigrants who clambered of their own free wills into those pods' sterile hibernacula were special, not just by virtue of their genes and their decisions, but because of their courage.

And that, not just restlessness, was why Jim was out here.

He stared at the green of clear readouts till his eyes watered.

His sensors stayed blank.

"READY FOR RETRIEVAL," CAME THE FILTERED VOICE ONE hour point five minutes later.

Jim gestured at an engineer to secure his helm. After the last one, on any mission he flew, no one went EVA without a backup.

"Fuel?"

"Sufficient." An embarrassed pause while Danamon remembered what had happened last time to a panicked colleague.

Let your mission commander decide sufficiency, Jim had snapped and refused to let the man fly again.

"I mean . . . eight point six minutes."

"Sufficient," Jim agreed, consciously letting his voice warm to assure the scientist "no harm done." "Come on home."

Another tidy take-off, economic use of fuel, smooth landing. Man was good enough for Fleet. No doubt he preferred the easier berths, the benefits . . . the safety.

The airlock cycled open and unsealed. The man emerged, cracking his helm open only in the safety of the ridership.

Cautious. Good man. Safe man.

He pulled off his gauntlet and rubbed one hand over dark hair cropped so close to his skull that it looked almost like beard-shadow. Jim's own jaw itched.

"It's seriously ugly out there," he told Jim. "We're going to have to cast off the lines to unsnare them, then hook them up the old-fashioned way."

"By ridership?" Jim asked.

"That's my recommendation."

Jim sighed. By the time the ridership returned to *Jaya* and was checked over, Captain Heikkonen would be offshift. Sleeping, Jim would bet. Corporate officers in the fleets of companies like Astro-Med, Bio-Cosmos, any of the majors, lived more like executives than honest spacers.

If Heikkonen could sleep, maybe Jim could get in a meal, maybe even a session in the gym, a shower, or some sleep. God, his eyes hurt.

But the sensors stayed blank.

2

Docking bay's hatch had barely closed behind the ridership before the alert went off.

Damn, DEW trap said no one'd so much as breathed on the God-bloody mines!

This wasn't scavengers, his frantic glance told him. The alert was coming from inside *Jaya.*

"Status report!" he snapped. "*Jaya,* come in!"

"It's weapons systems." He knew that voice. Tech Ivarr Vingtsson. A pharmacologist, a fair mechanic, and, even more, to Jim's surprise, a man whose groundside hobby was small-arms hunting. But ships' arms weren't projectile weapons.

Damn, had Vingtsson gotten overconfident? He'd seemed steady enough.

"I'm turning up volume," he said. "I'll need you to confirm what I'm hearing."

A faint howling echoed in the background. Jim focused in on it, then glanced at his boards, squinting despite their careful lighting. Three minutes until full pressurization.

He raced through power-down as fast as he dared, skinned out of his suit down to the ship's blue coverall, and waited. He wouldn't be much use if he forced the hatch and leapt out into docking bay before air was pumped back in, now would he?

"We were testing personal arms, like you ordered. Bokassa reloaded, and the damn thing started to howl. Listen: you can hear it heterodyne."

The howl went up a tone and grew louder.

The technical term and Vingtsson's alarm made for a ludicrous combination. But if that charge went off . . . Worse yet, if it set off a chain reaction . . .

"You've got yourself a lethal malf," Jim said flatly.

Keep your voice calm. Don't spook anyone, Jim warned himself.

"The good news is that it seems to be taking its time to reach critical. You can hear the buildup. Patch me through."

He slapped open in-ship comm. "Bokassa, you there, man?" A stupid statement. Where would Bokassa be going? "Eject your sidearm! Use the HazMat dump!"

A pause, then a gabble of explanation.

"If I jettison my sidearm," Bokassa protested, *"they'll dock my pay. Can't we just power this thing down? You're the arms officer."*

Jim suppressed a howl of sheer frustration that would have harmonized with the charge and cost time they couldn't afford. Dammit, he'd given Bokassa a direct order. When you got a direct order, you were supposed to obey, not hold a committee meeting. *He's not used to Command voice,* Jim warned himself. *He's probably fouled himself like Banks. Push him and he'll freeze; that thing will explode, and we'll be lucky if we vent just one compartment into space.*

Bokassa's only chance was if Jim could make him listen. Inspiration, fueled by adrenaline, made him shout, "Deduct the fucking thing from *my* pay, dammit!"

"I don't know, sir," Bokassa said. *"Procedure says . . ."*

Jim suppressed a howl of impatience. The three minutes to full docking bay atmosphere had to be the longest three minutes since the Big Bang. Damn relativity. Damn Bokassa.

The lights were cycling up now. Almost time. He drummed his fingers on the console, counting down. Thirty seconds . . . twenty . . . ten . . .

The lights flashed, then stayed on.

"Pressurization complete," the serene automated voice of ship's system droned from the overhead.

"Move!" Jim pushed past maintenance without proper courtesies, and ran. By reflex, he swiped a hand over his matted hair. A gleaming bulkhead showed sweat had all but turned it brown. Thin, not so tall he couldn't fit in any craft that Fleet maintained, he was very fit, even by Fleet standards, from sessions in *Jaya*'s lavish gym, and he outran the ship's crew as they gasped and pounded after him.

The ship's schematics he'd memorized before he'd ever boarded indicated a drop tube . . . *here!* He flung himself into it before he could wonder if *this* were properly maintained. *Damn, if I make a bloody smear on the deck, I'm going to come back and haunt maintenance,* he thought and dropped, like falling feet-first into a planet's gravity well.

The drop tube's A-grav arrested his fall—*red lights/green lights/white,* rising beneath him as he dropped—and cushioned him to a landing that was . . . too slow! Much too slow!

He hit the deck running and dashed toward arms storage. The bulkheads hadn't been sealed off to isolate the compartment. *And I'd like to know who neglected* that *simple precaution. Probably didn't want Bokassa to think they were writing him off.*

Humane reasoning, but stupid.

The malfunctioning sidearm's charge shrieked, rising in pitch like a child's tantrum.

But this tantrum belonged to one deadly baby. The hatch slid aside. Vingtsson was practically dancing with anxiety and hoarse from arguing. His face lit when he saw Jim.

He gestured toward the viewscreen and the miserable sight of Bokassa, stubborn bastard that he was, his face livid with fear, tinkering with the weapon.

Dear God, would the man really risk blowing arms storage, perhaps the whole damned ship, so he could fix one charge and save some credits?

He'll get us all killed!

"Bokassa, throw it out the HazMat now!" Jim ordered.

Bokassa jumped at the sound of Command voice.

Scientist types didn't like direct orders. Didn't cope with them at all well. Oh God. Oh God.

"But I've almost got this circuit disconnected," he muttered.

Jim overrode the lock, dashed inside, straight-armed him and grabbed the sidearm, palmed the lock on the HazMat chute with its distinctive red hatch, dropped the weapon in, and shouted, "Eject!"

The bulkhead shuddered. Vingtsson lurched against . . . Heller, that was right. He'd seen her before, once or twice. She glanced at Jim, nodded, then accessed damage control.

She thinks on her feet. And she's got legs that don't stop. I think I'm in love.

A whistle shrilled on compconsole.

"Bloody hell, it's Captain Heikkonen!" Vingtsson muttered. "What are you going to tell him, sir?"

Jim's knees went rubbery. "Nice work, mister," he mouthed at Vingtsson. If he hadn't known when to hit the panic button, "Abandon ship!" might be echoing through ship's comm as everyone who survived struggled toward the evacuation pods.

"I'll tell the captain the truth," Jim snapped. "Yes, sir, we've had a malf. Weapons malfunction, sir. Sidearm charge almost blew during weapons inventory, but we ejected it in time. That was the bump you felt. Crew's got everything under control now."

He gestured rapidly for someone to bring him the results from power generation and damage control.

"After we docked, crew called me down to supervise. Yes, sir. Defective weapon. They were unloading weapons. No, not on my initiative, as a matter of fact, sir: we've discussed this. Weapons inventory's even part of civilian ships' standing orders . . . Yes, I'll file a claim. Yes, sir, that's my job. I'll present my report at staff meeting at oh eight . . . very well, sir, as the captain says, ten hundred thirty hours. Night, sir."

And have a nice nap. Sir. Any captain he had ever served with would have been down here—bare-ass with beard-off burning holes in his hide if that was what he was doing when the alarm went off.

The least challenging part of this damned charm-school assignment on a corporate ship was observation of civilian procedures, such as they sometimes were.

The worst of it was trying to deal with Captain Heikkonen. *Managing up,* corporate crew called it. Privately, Jim thought of it as another form of damage control.

When he didn't call it worse.

"Get you a coffee, sir?" They must all have been really scared if civilian crew—especially female civilian crew—offered to wait on him.

He dragged his hand across his hair, dry now, but standing out in cowlicks. One evening, when people were trying to be friendly, he'd taught these scientists and techs how to make proper wardroom coffee, "the strongest stimulant you can get outside a pharmcloset," they called it. A couple of cups would postpone the inevitable shakes until later, when no one could see him curl up into a ball.

What did old-Earth coffee really taste like? With the blockade over, some entrepreneurial soul would start exports soon. *Right, and if you think you can afford it on an exec officer's pay, even if they hand you one of those corporate bonuses at the end of this tour, you're* really *sleep deprived.*

But there was no point in being rude. *Say "thank you" to the kind tech lady, son.*

"Thanks," he said, obedient to familiar, silent commands. "If you're brewing coffee, better bring enough for all of us. Please. We're going to be here for some time."

Forget dinner. He logged into ship's records, pointed at Bokassa, and told him, "Now. You, mister. From the beginning."

ONCE JIM OVERSAW UNPACKING, TEST-FIRING, AND STORAGE of the remaining weapons, cross-checked every witness, edited out the last "uh" or stammer from his taped report, and saved the written version, securing it with his own retinal scan, he was free to go. At least the cyberneticists would take care of the report on the repaired umbilicals. And he could simply replay the flight recorder for his report's segment on real-time events.

Maybe Captain Heikkonen had really set a good example by getting some sleep. Maybe . . . Jim stretched, rubbed his eyes, then flinched and reached for drops. He wasn't tired any more. Adrenaline hangover had hit and hit hard.

So, it looked like he could forget about sleep the rest of this watch. Maybe he could walk off some of the tension before he got the shakes or they got him: it was only a matter of time.

He remembered now. *Hardcastle*—damn, Secess' had blown his first ship out of space years ago—always had a few senior officers doing what they called night patrol, working out the stress. Night patrol was better than tranks, his first exec always said. She was right.

She was also long gone, blown away with *Hardcastle*. The night Jim heard that, he'd gone out, gotten drunk, and damn near been put on report: the only blotch on a stainless record.

He started down a corridor lit for ship's "night."

Jim paced down the corridor, too lavishly enameled in blues and greens from some inner planet or other. The emergency lighting glowed in its track along the deck: ornamental white lights now that might be vital later.

He strode a few meters further, the dimmed lights turning his blue shipsuit gray.

The clean bulkheads of the long, curved corridor elongated his reflection. Glowing screens showed ship's status and discolored the image of his face so he looked like a recruiting poster worked over by a bouncer in the sort of bar that should be off-limits. He walked toward an arch created by a curve in the ship's hull. Seats had been built into it—which you'd never find on board Fleet's ships—and a viewport. Days after their fight with the scavengers, they'd still not lifted its collision shield.

Groundsiders, Jim nodded to himself. Real spacers never got sated on starlight.

The lavish overheated corridor oppressed him. Temptation lured him: override the shield and stare out. Escape. Back on his own ship, when it was safely in Jump and he was off-duty, he would find a port watch as the shimmering dance of particles and the great billows of substance that bore no relationship to anything in known space crested and fumed. He always visualized his ship breasting those waves, sending up spray formed not of brine but of starstuff in fountains light-years high just as the Fleet's blue-water ancestors weathered perilous crossings and storms.

Real space held not just stars, but hazards. But in other-space, he had always seen glory, splendid ghosts from the past when the Fleet of man had blazed up from its blue-water origins on a column of fire into the heavens to touch, like it said in the old poem, the face of God. That was a dream you could die for.

Jim paced on. If he opened a shield to look out, he'd probably set off three alarms.

His reflection matched his pace, human after its fashion. They were all human, weren't they, civ and Regular; Alliance and Secess': humans fighting for human reasons for worlds on which humans could live, but living on parallel courses with creatures who ignored those worlds, those quarrels as unlivable, incomprehensible. The galaxy held sapients other than human, but they went their own way, for which all parties could thank God.

Still, every time a ship went missing, you could hear some mouthbreather whispering that aliens, not scavengers, had stolen it to use its crew for experiments (at worst) or to breed (at best) for First Contact. Fleet gossip and civilian legend both cherished stories about lost ships floating through otherspace: there might even be scientific justification for them. And then, there was the myth that if you listened during the "night" watch, spacers' ghosts would whisper your fortune to you. He paused, sure he could hear something whispering, an unquiet duet with the micro-meteorites exploding against the ship's charged hull. But he heard no fortune.

Jim's boots clicked on the deck. *I wanted aliens. I found enemies instead.*

And now he'd found these strangers. Their quarters and wardrooms were crowded with *things* that Fleet admirals would consider treasures. He had wanted aliens, all right; and he'd got them.

Trouble was, they all looked just like him.

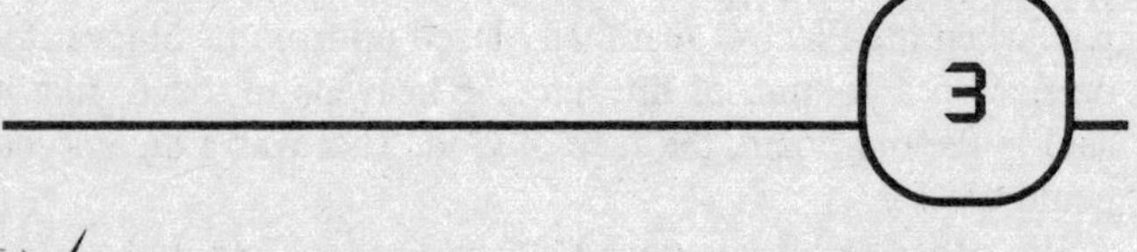

Showered, his face meticulously depilated, and dressed in a dark, sleek Fleet uniform rather than a *Jaya* shipsuit, Jim strode through officer country to Captain Heikkonen's quarters and buzzed for entry.

"Come on in!" Heikkonen ordered in a voice that was intolerably, deliberately cheerful and well-rested for a man whose ship had survived a scavenger attack and a weapons malfunction in the past few ship's days. Like Jim, the captain wore a uniform, not coveralls, for this meeting.

Actually, Heikkonen looked pretty good in it. Granted, he bulged a bit amidships, but that was to be expected in a man putting in the last few years between himself and a prosperous early retirement. Aside from the weight, he looked pretty good: his hair transplant—in an age-appropriate silver—probably cost a good six months of Jim's salary. Not that Jim was surprised: the right appearance was as important for corporate crew as it was in the service. Mid to late fifties, Jim pegged his age. A little old for a spacer. But, then, he wasn't a spacer, not really: *Jaya* was just one more well-paid assignment on his career vector.

I don't understand. If I *were master of a ship like this . . .*

The captain's smile at Jim indicated his official opinion, which he'd put into words more than once: *I don't need fire-eaters on my ship, mister. You'd go a whole lot farther if you could forgodssake relax, get along by going along!*

"Ah, our arms officer. Take a seat, pour yourself some coffee."

The chief engineer raised a hand, made as if to slide the pot down to him.

Jim felt his nostrils quiver. The wardroom was fragrant with decorative plants—conservatory exotics at that, and, more to the point, with honest-to-God groundside coffee, not service brew strong enough to send your eyeballs into Jump. So all right, maybe the coffee didn't come all the way from Earth but from fourth- or fifth-generation stock grown on planets like Aviva or Skolion and a damn sight better brew than anyone below the rank of Admiral was ever likely to see.

"No, thank you, sir." Jim all but clicked his heels before he seated himself, careful not to let his back touch the upholstery of a far-too-comfortable chair. He wondered, just as he always did in here, why a man who lived as if he'd never set foot offworld had decided to go into space at all. Here, too, the viewport that would have revealed the stars was closed. Jim's hand flexed. He wanted to check ship's sensors on the readout glowing on the captain's worktable.

Producing the report chips that had cost him a night's sleep, he inserted them correctly in the conference table's display system, then sat as if he faced a Board of Inquiry.

"God, our very own space cadet," whispered Stuart, the chief engineer. He was a man about Heikkonen's age, artificially tanned under UV the way most senior corpses got. Apparently, the "outdoor" look was a career enhancer, along with the transplants, the compulsive fitness, and the grooming.

"Young blood," Jim bristled as he heard Heikkonen's murmured reply. He'd never see thirty-five again. And no one who had survived the Secess' wars could ever be considered truly young.

By that reckoning, he thought, *I was senile at eighteen.* Far older than *Irian Jaya*'s officers, who lounged in soft chairs at this travesty of a staff meeting, sipping coffee, trading ship and company gossip until it should please the captain to call the meeting to order.

Jim found it hard to sit quietly in their presence. He'd seen civilian crew before. Hell, the crew of the ridership he'd just docked were civ, argumentative, noisy, but they knew their jobs.

Senior staff, however . . . The term "command crew" choked him for this group of corpses.

"Well," Heikkonen said, amiably, "let's get this show on the road, gentlemen. You too, Ty."

The engineering second laughed a polite high-pitched laugh and tossed her hair. *Captain makes a funny; you laugh, mister. Or ma'am.*

He gestured at Engineering Officer Stuart, who finished off his coffee, sat up in his chair, and began to speak.

"Before you go on, Liam," Heikkonen said, "let's make sure you've got all the holoprojections you'll want when we debrief at headquarters."

"Right." Stuart touched controls, and the holomodel of *Jaya* flickered into existence above the conference table.

"Rotate seventy-five degrees," Heikkonen said. "Maybe you want to present repairs in stages as they occurred. You can overlay them sequentially on the same matrix. Cybernetics . . ." he looked over at Chief Tech Danamon, whom Jim had ferried over to the umbilicals.

Danamon's fingers performed a brief keyboard fantasia, calling up not a schematic but a spreadsheet. "Resources expended . . . time measured against optimal completion projections . . . cost per crew-hour . . ."

Heikkonen nodded approvingly.

"I think that should make us look quick enough on response time," he said. "Projections for going fully operational?"

"Fourteen days, sir," Danamon said.

Heikkonen adjusted the position of his coffee mug. Clearly, that wasn't the answer he was looking for.

"This isn't what I'd call a timely basis, gentlemen. It's ten days from here to New Amman. You're talking twenty-four days to port best case. But if we reach New Amman in eighteen days, our performance bonus is a hundred and fifty percent of total comp. I'd like to see us be a little more proactive here."

Meaning he was taking Danamon's best-practices report as a jumping-off point and trying to shave time off of it.

Meaning, if they weren't careful, accidents would happen.

"We've already got half of each watch on scan or weapons," Stuart replied. His face reddened.

"As mandated by ship's security," Jim said and stiffened, as you tended to when you had to quote regs to a senior officer. "Sir, Article . . ."

"We're not at war, Arms Officer!" Stuart said. "Of course, Fleet has such immense crews that I suppose it wouldn't occur to you we don't have people on board to cater to your paranoia. Even though you'd think someone with as few real duties as you would've had time enough on board to understand by now. We staff lean on a civilian ship. Any crew on surveillance is crew off repairs. Fleet standard's a luxury we can't afford now. If we ever could."

Jim bit back a protest. Someone chuckled anyway, and Heikkonen clucked indulgent reproof.

"Nevertheless . . ." Jim persisted. Just as well he wasn't on Heikkonen's team: if some quirks within civilian chain-of-command customs stopped corporate crew from protesting, the same constraints didn't apply to him.

And a damn good thing . . .

"Come now, Arms Officer, aren't you overreacting?" Heikkonen asked, assured, urbane, in control of this meeting. "Or are you telling me you found cleaning up that deep space trash a challenge?"

Those scavengers were good enough to detach us from our convoy and kill one ship. They damaged our umbilicals, scored our hull, and *wrecked one pod,* Jim thought. *And we don't know if they got a message off to other ships in the area.*

"My first responsibility is the safety of this mission, its passengers, cargo, and crew," he recited standing orders.

"Are you implying . . ." Stuart's face turned red, and the man levered himself away from the conference table with its slick black glass surface.

"As you were, Liam. No one's implying anything!" Captain Heikkonen waved a calming hand, oil over troubled water. He poured coffee for his engineering officer and pushed a mug toward Jim. It would have been rudeness itself to refuse the captain's personal hospitality, which probably had the rest of the meeting jealous. He sipped, demonstrating appreciation of the fine coffee. But its caffeine seemed to coil snarling in his belly.

"Gentlemen. Like our resident firebreather here," Heikkonen manufactured a genial laugh, "I have orders to preserve the safety of this ship. Unlike him, but like the rest of you, I have a vested interest . . ." he emphasized the financial pun and basked in the smiles meeting his across the conference table . . . "in ensuring our timely arrival."

Completion bonus, Jim translated. Weren't a thousand lives enough to lose?

"Mr. Engineer," Captain Heikkonen spoke formally now, "will you recalculate for full shifts, watch on watch?"

Jim felt himself rising to his feet.

"As you were," Heikkonen set a hand on the table.

A direct order.

Jim sat. "Begging the captain's pardon."

Heikkonen smiled benignly. But you could count the teeth in the smile.

"We could work watch on watch, shift on shift if we were in Jump, couldn't we?"

"Risk to the crew," said the medical officer. "Have you factored in workers' comp claims?"

"A few months' R&R at the most. I've given the matter quite some thought," Heikkonen expanded. "I made my own estimate of when we might make planetfall."

Now it was Stuart's turn to grimace as the captain pre-empted his job.

"We need full power if we're to reach New Amman under deadline. But hull damage is right where the engine shielding's most needed. Medical's informed me that even if we nurse the engines along, we not only reach New Amman late, we risk cooking the biomass. Right?"

He waved a hand at his medical officer, demanding confirmation. Randolph, a wiry man happier in his Sickbay than in meetings like this, slipped his report into the dataslots. He gave Chief Engineer Stuart a look—*they're both bucking for promotion,* whispered crew gossip, *and likely, only one will get it.*

"What about Jump?" asked Navigation.

"Couldn't advise that either," the medical officer said. "Not till shielding's nominal again, if we want to keep freezer burn to a minimum."

"Thank you, Doctor," Heikkonen said, as if begrudging the words. They weren't, Jim knew, what anyone wanted to hear—especially Stuart. "Now, I don't have to tell you it's to everyone's advantage to deliver as many healthy immigrants as possible. New Amman's, certainly, but we have interests of our own in it. So, right now," the captain went on, "we're dead in space. It's good for our cargo—and our passengers in Freeze, provided nothing else attacks."

"Begging the captain's pardon . . . again," Jim put in, "if the engines are shut down, how many hours would it take to bring them back online in case of attack?"

"Hours?" Engineer Stuart parried.

"My understanding is that it takes three point two hours

to bring engines fully operational from a cold start," Jim spoke formally. "Under optimum conditions. A scavenger attack . . ."

"What about those weapons you're always talking about?" demanded the engineer. "You do your job, and I'll do mine."

"Gentlemen . . ."

"As the captain wishes." Jim checked ship's time and sighed. Meetings were relativistic; they expanded to fill all the time available and then some. He was due on watch after this meeting. So he could forget any petty hopes for workout and a rest, maybe even a chat with those few crewmembers who didn't find talking with him a threat to their career paths or a First Contact situation.

"You know . . ." Ty Parnell, the engineering second, chose her moment and dropped a new idea into the meeting. It was her favorite gambit: let the meeting drag on (which wasn't hard), wait till everyone was half-stupefied, make her point, and rely on exhaustion to carry it. "We could make a hell of a lot more speed if we jettisoned the pods, marked them with a buoy, and went off to make repairs. After all, when we were attacked, we sent out an all-services call. Sooner or later, Relief'll be along to pick us up . . ."

Jim glared at her.

"Assuming worst-case, that is: we stayed in real-space and ran into something our arms officer and his merry men couldn't cope with," she qualified her first remark and planted the barb deep.

"What if they're picked up for salvage?"

"Someone else gets the reward and we lose our bonuses. Company's insurance premiums hit Jump. And review's coming up," Nav Officer Olssen objected. "I'm ten years away from retirement, if you don't mind."

"They'd still get the cargo to New Amman, at least," Life Support observed. "It's not as if we're anywhere near critical on durability. I'd certify the shipsicles to survive at least ten years, and the genetic material's good for longer than that—as long as Freeze holds."

"You're assuming the pods would be taken in tow by another bioship or by the Fleet," Jim pointed out. "We're out in the No Man's Worlds . . ."

"Translation, please, this isn't a military ship, we don't understand Fleet slang . . ."

"This far from the inner sectors," Jim rephrased without having to draw breath, "I do not think we can assume that the pods would be safe. What if they're held for ransom?"

"When I last tapped the Newsnets," Parnell said, with a toss of very non-regulation metallic red hair, "we were at peace with Abendstern and the others. Civilized people. They'd return the pods to us—that is, if they knew what was good for them. Abendstern may care for pedigrees more than genomes, but even they can read a balance sheet."

"I wish the Secess'—the former Secess'—were all we had to worry about," Jim persisted. "What about the possibility that scavengers might simply appropriate the pods and their inhabitants for their very own private labor colony?"

"Oh God, Jim, not your damn pirate havens again," Parnell drawled. The chief medical officer growled. Jim might have an ally there, if the man didn't retreat back into Sickbay.

"I always thought those stories about scavengers were the Fleet's form of job insurance," someone muttered to laughter all around.

Jim flushed until he was almost as ruddy as the civs who dozed off-shift under sunlamps. Just in time, he bit his lip rather than remind them that he had already fought off such job insurance once while on board *Jaya*.

"Why not jettison the pods?" asked Parnell again. "We could mark the place and set out buoys. If we don't bother with bioshielding the engines, we can trim . . . first-approximation estimate would . . . let me see . . . fifteen point two days from estimated planetfall."

"Fine!" Tech Chief Nguyen snarled. He was a geneticist whose three postdoctoral degrees made him bear the designation of warrant officer with less than good grace. "You get a bonus if you reach destination early. If scavengers pick up those pods, I lose my job. Company is socked for catastrophic insurance costs. And the Alliance loses all those people. We could face a class action suit the size of Betelgeuse."

Captain Heikkonen rapped on the table for attention. "Let's wind this up. You've all raised some good ideas. We'll meet again tomorrow to thrash them out the rest of the way.

"About expenses." He turned an eye on Jim. "I still haven't gotten your cost estimates for weapons consumption."

"The captain will have estimates by fourteen-hundred hours." Jim managed not to grit his teeth. There went lunch. "I need to revise, figuring in the results of the arms inspection I conducted once we stood down. By the way, the blaster we jettisoned was a malf. Of the charges we tested, one hundred thirty were nominal."

"Wouldn't it have been more efficient to approximate?"

If I'd approximated, you'd have asked for an exact count.

"Not when crew's lives are at stake, sir," Jim said. *Damn. That sounded too stiff, like a reprimand. Which it was, of course, but there's prudent and there's stupid.* "Or company money. At any rate, the report I'm preparing writes off the blaster we ejected and its costs. I've used the higher Fleet-issue price schedules, so you won't lose out there either. I'll go on record that Astro-Pharm can claim compensation from the supplier."

"That's fine," Heikkonen said, affable for a moment, before he spoiled it by asking, "The crewmember? Any responsibility there?"

And to think he'd been close to bawling Bokassa out for overreacting! I want to get back to the Fleet. I really really want to get back there. These people's priorities are as twisted as those umbilicals we repaired today.

"I certified Mr. Bokassa as qualified on sidearms myself, sir," said Jim. "I am convinced he performed to standard. The weapon was faulty. We are fortunate Mr. Bokassa kept a cool head. If he'd panicked, six lives could have been lost. If the charge had exploded and triggered others, the entire compartment could have been vented."

Heikkonen's eyes had gone glazed. He wasn't listening.

"I've got the incident recorded, sir," Jim said. "I'll send it to you, shall I, sir?"

"You do that," said the captain. "Meanwhile, if there's nothing else . . ."

Chair scrapes across the table told him that Ms. Parnell, Mr. Olssen, and Chief Stuart had risen. The meeting wasn't as much adjourned as escaped from.

A FINAL KEYSTROKE, AND JIM FINISHED THIS LATEST DRAFT of his report on weapons consumption costs, copied it, encrypted the copy for his personal files—and his inevitable report to Fleet, and transmitted the original to the captain. Fleet and the multiplanetaries had one thing in common: the compulsion to play CYA games. The only time CYA broke down in Fleet was during battle, when saving one's ass outranked covering it.

Clearly, things would be different now that they were at peace. More complicated.

" 'Fire at will' is inefficient," Heikkonen had told him the last time he'd lost this particular argument. "*You* get to play with your toys. Then *I* have to account for every item in inventory. Including the ones you've blown away. This isn't a pleasure cruise."

Jim had no sooner programmed in the cost, personnel, and materièl projections on combat scenarios under Jump, at a stop, or waiting for aid, when communications whistled for his attention.

"Arms Officer to the captain . . . Arms Officer, report to the captain . . ."

There was no way Captain Heikkonen could even have scanned the report so soon after Jim had delivered it. Possibly, he wanted to engage Jim in a lengthy discussion of comparative ships' procedures. More probably, he wanted to put a finger, or a whole hand, into Jim's report before it was put on file.

If he's already made up his mind to detach, enter Jump, and make repairs, why rehash the situation? Jim wondered.

"I wanted you to know," Heikkonen came to the point promptly for once. "I've made my decision."

Well, praise God! Maybe they'd be able to achieve Jump before the scavengers achieved them. Maybe they stood a chance of making planetfall, even of getting home.

But then what?

Jim forced himself into his most polite "I'm listening, sir" posture and waited for the captain to announce precisely what he'd decided.

Heikkonen waved him to a chair, ritually adjusted the reports on his desk, and took his time speaking.

Predictably, Heikkonen had elected the most conservative course. The engines would be shut down, the pods detached, the engines repaired, and then *Irian Jaya* would start up again and make planetfall.

Jim tilted his head, eyeing the captain with considerably more respect. There had never been anything wrong with his administrative skills, just his initiative and his emphasis on profit. If concern for the safety of his ship and mission now made him choose the safest course, maybe Jim would have to recalculate.

What a relief it would be to be wrong. Jim nodded respect at the older man as if he'd been his CO.

"I'll step up monitoring the Jump points," he said. "You know, sir," he added cautiously, "if we're being conservative, the safest policy would be to call Fleet for convoy."

Heikkonen glared and breathed hard. His artificially tanned face turned ruddy. "We asked for convoy. What Fleet saw fit to send us was you and a couple light-armed craft that didn't survive our first encounter with these wreckers you're always moaning on about. And now, you're suggesting Fleet convoy. I don't even want to think of what that would cost."

"What about the company, sir?" Jim made himself ask. "Doesn't it want to protect its investment?" The words tasted strange in his mouth.

"You may as well know that Headquarters has told me Astro-Pharm has no spare ships, at least not for an operation where the margins are this low. I'm just as concerned for the safety of this ship as you are, but do your methods have to be so damned labor-intensive? Just having crew standing around by the weapons in case they're needed is simply not cost-effective. What you may not realize is that our mission isn't just to deliver cargo, but to deliver it on a timely basis. It's worth taking a few risks to do that."

" 'Timely basis,' " Jim said, "kills ships."

The captain's face grew even darker. That was the signal to back down.

"Begging the captain's pardon. No insubordination meant. Nor rudeness."

"Not a problem," said Heikkonen. But there was, there was: they had simply deferred it. Captain Heikkonen was a company employee with stock options and a bonus to lose, and he duly regarded Jim's sneer at company policies with extreme disfavor.

But right now, the captain needed him, and a complaint to Fleet from an officer who—for all Heikkonen knew—might be on a fast track was not a thing he cared to consider any more than Jim wanted a downcheck from him.

Heikkonen manufactured a smile and applied it.

"Drink?"

"Thank you, sir, but no. I've got watch coming up."

"Suit yourself." The captain poured, drank, refilled, and began the correct professional and technical gossip appropriate for covering over their quiet warfare and ending what had become another unpleasant session.

Computer signaled. Heikkonen set down his glass on the sleek extruded desk.

"Heikkonen." He slapped the console for privacy mode, then activated Dead-Air mode. Jim saw the captain's eyebrow go up, saw the man eye him.

"You're quite certain?" Heikkonen's lips moved. If he'd any idea that spacers routinely learned to lip-read—after all, suit coms might fail—he'd have turned his back.

Another pause. Jim tried to look as if his eyes weren't focused on the captain's mouth.

"I'll attend to it. Thanks for bringing it to my attention. Out."

The captain turned back to Jim and shifted in his chair—a clear sign Jim should excuse himself. He grinned inwardly, evilly, allowing himself the small vengeance of being a good little officer and waiting until he was dismissed.

"About that call . . ." Heikkonen shifted again and glanced at his spotless desk.

That was the signal Jim had been waiting for.

"I'll take my leave, then, sir," he said, rising. He came to almost-attention and waited for Heikkonen's nod, which meant permission and escape.

Even if he could almost hear the captain's mutter of "damned tin soldier."

4

In the end, Heikkonen had two meetings, one tantrum, and at least ten antacids that Jim counted before he ordered *Irian Jaya*'s own pilots to go out and re-attach the last of the umbilicals.

"Get some rest," he'd ordered Jim, for which small mercy he was duly grateful and for which he wondered if he had Medical's warning or Heikkonen's distrust of him to thank. Even he could admit now that he'd been going watch on watch too long. He was glad enough to shower—real water, even if it was recycled—and cast himself down on his bunk for a few hours of sleep.

Golden leaves shimmered outside his window, as birdsong greeted dawn on a world he had never seen but knew was home as nothing else had ever been. He sighed and stretched and realized: he had waked smiling. . . .

Jim leapt up as his alarm buzzed beside his bunk, one hand reaching for the sidearm he no longer carried. Would he never get over the habit of not so much waking, but scrambling as if his ship were going into battle? His memory snatched at the final wisps of the dream he had had.

Come back, he wished it. *No such luck.*

At least now his eyes felt as if the sand poured into them was room temperature, not superheated.

Why are you doing this? he asked himself as he prowled the silent corridors on one of the patrols he had taken upon himself to do. Even his footfalls were muffled. Two women from hydroponics walked toward him, eyed him, then strode past. If they whispered, especially if they whispered about him, he didn't want to hear.

This was not going to be a quiet ship's "night." Heikkonen had had to rotate the ship to reattach the umbilicals, and he had begrudged every moment of triple-time, not to mention the wear and tear on ships. What was more, the chief medical officer was calling for life-support checks every fifteen minutes and Engineer Stuart was swearing at the medical reports graphing rising radiation levels. As a result, the captain had not been in the happiest of moods, and he had passed his mood along to senior staff.

Another few steps down the corridor. He heard laughter behind him and managed not to flinch.

It had been one hell of a meeting. As if repairs, radiation, and personnel weren't bad enough, *Jaya* had even had a brush with micro-meteorites. Worse yet, mid-range scanners turned up a shower of the wretched things. The suit-maintenance specialists launched an epidemic of damage control and checklists while everyone else stowed loose tools and personal effects against the impact of anything bigger.

Still, Jim's pet monitors shone green. No one, nothing, had detonated his mines. Yet.

We might make it safely into Jump at that, he let himself

think, then made a small, propitiatory gesture he remembered from his childhood.

"I used to ward off bad luck that way too." A voice behind him made him whirl around, then rise from a crouch. "It's not very scientific, is it?"

Jim knew he was flushing, whether at being caught committing a superstition among scientists or at going into combat-ready mode, he didn't know.

The woman laughed. "Didn't know they let you Regulars blush," she said. At least it was Heller, not one of the women who eyed him as if he were some unfathomable, if strangely desirable, alien trophy. Heller had always been courteous. He suspected they were both from Aven, although they'd never gotten around to exchanging homeworld stories. Now she smiled at him, and he liked the warmth in her brown eyes.

"Sir," she asked, going formal on him. "May I show you something?"

"By all means," Jim inclined his head, automatic response to the almost-military courtesy, and followed her down the corridor and into engineering. Admiration of her long legs and the way she held herself boosted his pulse rate for just an instant.

She may not be in your chain of command, but forget about it anyhow, he warned himself. *Probably, when she makes planetfall, she goes to those meetings of disinterested and benevolent societies where they lecture the unwary that Fleet should be cut back or shut down now that nice people don't need it anymore.*

Aven hadn't sent that many into the Service. His family had been proud of him even if most of the people they knew thought he was insane.

"We were cross-training," she said. "Captain Heikkonen said, 'Don't tell that damn tin soldier, but he really does have some good ideas,' " she added. Her eyes lit again, this time with a kind of conspiratorial humor.

"Perhaps indeed you should not have told me," Jim agreed, smiling despite his resolve of a minute ago. She gave him an "are you serious" grin, head on one side, and decided he wasn't. Maybe, when they made planetfall . . . if they ever did . . . he'd try to show her otherwise. *Oh God, a woman from home . . .*

"Now that we have agreed about your indiscretion, what"—no, dammit, you can't ask her 'what else'—"did you want to show me?" he asked. *Civilians call fraternization harassment, and they don't just court-martial you, they fine you. If you don't want to declare bankruptcy when you get out, you'd better think of* Jaya*'s crew as off limits.*

Heller bent over the workstation and tapped a color-coded key, bringing up the results of a prior search.

The ship trembled. Prudently, she reached for a handhold. *Keep one hand for the ship.* He'd learned that on the blue waters of home long before he ever left his first gravity well. Apparently, so had she. *What sorts of small craft did you sail?* The question hovered, unasked, on his lips. They had work to do.

"That's a substantial meteorite shower," Jim remarked. "It would be interesting to see the density of particles per cubic kilometer. Still, we're within shield tolerances."

Heller nodded. The tension in her face did not lighten.

"Here's what I need you to see," the tech said. Was he imagining things, or did Heller's voice shake?

Her screen shifted and colored. A three-dimensional section appeared on it, rotated, then resolved.

Jim froze where he stood.

He shot a glance around the corridor for loose objects. His hand shot out as if thrusting toward the "alert" signal, before he forced it behind his back again.

"That's not micro-meteorites," he confirmed the unspoken question. "We need to signal an ion storm alert." Again, the ship trembled slightly. You could think the trailing edge of a micro-meteorite shower of long duration had just passed if you were stubborn or in denial. But it made more sense to believe that the leading edge of an ion storm would soon engulf them.

If he took down the shields blinding the viewports, he knew he would see the storm's darkness, reaching out to grasp them, its depth lit with colors he knew he could never remember after they faded.

"All labs are secured," she said. "I told the others."

"Before you told your captain?"

"I'm not one of his direct reports."

Jim managed not to snap out an obscenity he'd heard once before a pilot ejected. He leaned over the console and tapped out probability equations.

"Storm's going to hit us hard, isn't it?" Heller asked. "Before we can Jump."

He shrugged. "Your math background's probably better than mine. I'll alert engineering as to when we need the engines back on-line." *Hah,* he thought. *As if Chief Stuart would listen if I told him to move up his schedule.* "And speak to the captain."

She held his eyes, and he nodded reassuringly. "You did right to bring this to me. If you like, I can say I discovered it myself."

The ship trembled a little more strongly than before. He laid a palm against a bulkhead. It was warm. Her skin would have felt warmer.

Lock it down, mister.

"You can already feel the vibrations in the hull," he said. "The storm's coming. I'd recommend we keep all ports and equipment secured as if we were entering Jump. On my recommendation. If anything, they'll think the 'tin soldier' is overreacting again. You can make it sound as if you think so, too."

Heller flashed him a smile and strode off. Even after the curve in the corridor hid her from sight, the lights seemed a little warmer. He knew he had a stupid smile on his face.

Jim knew ion storms. Once they hit, you couldn't Jump; you could only run with them, engines on full, shielding up to protect the vulnerable soft crew from the worst of the buffeting. A ship with hull damage, with engines offline, and trailing adiabatic pod umbilicals . . . he shivered, although life-support kept ship's temperature constant.

An engineer on loan from the Fleet might be able to make himself useful bringing the engines back on-line. But Jim was no engineer, and Chief Stuart was even more intolerant of strangers than engineering's usual clannishness. He headed back toward Command Information Center, planning to call the captain on the bridge.

Passing through the forward observation area, he did not break stride, although the shields were up, revealing the starfield. His gaze swept its beauty, always new, always changing. The ship trembled slightly. He adjusted his balance by instinct, imagining how the very first edge of the ion storm brushed his ship's jeopardized fragile hull. Testing it, while the unfiltered starlight far beyond the ship flickered beyond the storm's reign of terror.

A million voices seemed to whisper in the closed horizon of the passageway:

. . . at such and such a place, the Frekan Stars surrounded us and vaporized the ship before we could scream. . . .

. . . we died starving, choking in the cold and dark. . . .

. . . as the black hole sucked us closer to its horizon, we blew the airlocks. . . .

. . . space grew dark and thick, a tangle of flashes and purple: and the ion storm seized us, shook us like a rat, and bounced us against itself. We tumbled over and over, end over end, until the stabilizers failed and the ship tore apart.

We died. Our names are known, but our bodies were never found.

We died.

He closed the shields protecting the viewports. An ion storm that breached them would destroy the ship, but still, it was a precaution he had to take.

Then, he changed his course, heading not for his duty station in the Command Information Center, but for the bridge itself.

* * *

"AND YOUR RECOMMENDATION?" CAPTAIN HEIKKONEN snapped. He glanced away from Jim to his computer screen. He had another one of his spreadsheets running. Jim read the letters upside down: stock; total holdings; compound rate of return; projections of stock splits; estimated retirement bonus, on top of pension.

Stop playing with your damned investments! He'd have liked to snap that out, but arms officers did not order captains in any service.

"We have several options, sir. Now that we have the umbilicals reconnected, and assuming the CMO approves the engine shielding, prudence would require immediate reentry into Jump."

Jim leaned over, reaching for computer access, then paused. "If the captain would permit. . . ."

He grumbled permission.

He saved the spreadsheet, pushed the keypad toward Jim. "Let's see your numbers."

Jim accessed navcomp and tapped out his proposed course.

"This heading through otherspace would bring us to New Amman through a series of chained Jumps around . . ." his fingers tapped more quickly, very sure now that the moment was upon him. ". . . this 'hot' area to avoid jettisoned gas shells. . . ."

"Yes . . . yes, I had a report about that supernova . . . go on. . . ."

"And bring us in two point four six weeks late."

Captain Heikkonen's eyes flared.

"I would not recommend this," Jim conceded, "if the *Jaya* carried emergency medical supplies. But we cannot restore New Amman's declining population or genetic damage in two point four six weeks."

The captain looked away, his eyes going cool. "What you consistently fail to understand is that this is a business venture. Crews' compensation is calculated to the day. Time overruns bring us into the area of time and a half, double, and triple time, and they compound, very fast indeed. I suspect that the additional comp would be subtracted. . . ."

"Begging the captain's pardon, but the security of the mission . . ."

Forget the damned bonus, Jim wanted to shout. *There's an ion storm out there, and scavengers are probably following to scrounge among the flotsam.*

For wrecks like what might be left of Irian Jaya.

Heikkonen slapped his workstation, clearing the screen.

"Missing deadline's unacceptable. Your next option?"

"Batten down and evade," said Jim. "We'll catch the leading edge of the storm, but if we can ride it out, we'll make planetfall on time and deliver at least the medical supplies."

"At least?"

"I would not give odds, sir, on the pods surviving intact." Jim clasped his hands together so he wouldn't make the warding-off gesture he'd used around Heller.

"Damage claims from survivors . . ." Heikkonen murmured. "And I'm not indemnified by my employment contract."

"I understand, sir. Perhaps even a class-action suit from survivors or heirs of those who did not survive."

Carry battle to the enemy. Use the enemy's tactics. God, why couldn't I simply shoot down scavengers?

Even fighting Secess' would be easier. You called for reinforcements in the face of Frekan Fighting Stars. Against Abendsterners, you massed firepower. You could trust Tokugawans never to retreat. Those were all tactics he understood.

"It would be a nasty lawsuit," he agreed, trying to conciliate, to reassure the captain. "But at least, we'd be alive to face charges. And if you preserved the ship, which represents a considerable capital expenditure, it might be that AstroPharm would help defray legal expenses. You'd know that better than I."

Heikkonen grunted. He turned away once again, calling engineering.

When he veered back, his expression was angry.

"What made you think we wouldn't have full power in time?" he demanded. "Shielding's been approved, and my chief engineer just told me he's ready to bring the engines full on-line when I give the word!"

Sure he is, Jim thought. *He's in the bonus pool, too.*

"Your orders, sir?" he asked. There was no point in prolonging this. God, he was sick of—what did they call it?—managing up?

"Lay in a course for New Amman," snapped Captain Heikkonen. "When I give the word, engines on full. Shields up, in case this storm"—the ship did not so much as tremble this time as lurch once—"is as bad as you seem to think. Honestly, it's no wonder the war's lasted as long as this if our entire military is this risk averse. . . ."

Jim drew himself up to attention, stifling the one-word protest, "Sir!"

He would bring charges himself, he decided, when they reached New Amman.

Assuming the ship survived the ion storm.

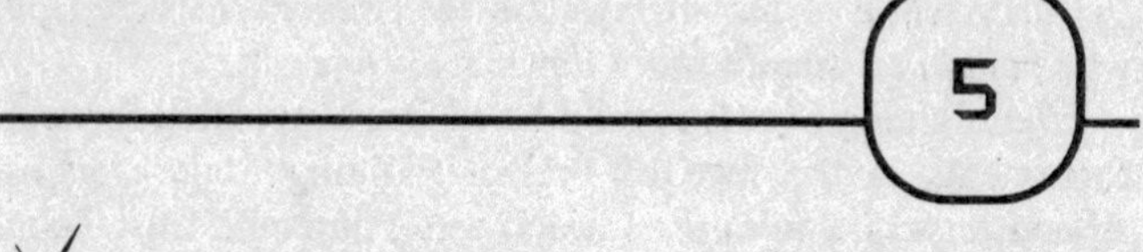

5

"Sir, you've got to wake up, sir, we've got trouble!"

The remnants of his dream played themselves out to their climax.

The warship erupted in a slow-motion splendor of Cherenkov radiation to the rescue of the ambassador, the company president, the prison camp—it hardly mattered which—and now he stood on a reviewing stand. Considering he had just fought hand to hand, he was remarkably clean and in dress uniform, no less. . . .

Again, the shining dreams Jim hated to admit he harbored

had turned exhaustion into pure glory. Some people dreamed of getting laid. Jim dreamed of being a hero.

"Come on, sir, wake up!"

. . . Damn, just when the CinC was about to hang the medal around his neck; he could all but feel the massive gold of the award on his shoulder. . . . Ragozinski himself was rising to salute him.

His father's voice replaced the accolades, *"James, time to wake up now, son,"* and he could smell Aven's seas along with the breakfast he'd eaten, the same thing every day, until he left his homeworld for the Academy. . . .

Adrenaline erupted into red alert. Jim hurled himself from the narrow bunk, twisting away and rolling. He came up in a fighting crouch, only to stop himself at the last moment as motion sensors brought up the cabin's lights.

Tech Heller flinched, crying out in alarm.

"I asked, *'What?'* " he snarled. "Dammit, if you're going to wake me out of a sound sleep, it better be for something good! Now what . . . ?" A good officer wakes up *up,* he told himself. *Coherent. Tidy, if possible.* "Sorry," he made himself mutter.

"Do you need a wakeshot, sir?" Heller's voice, controlled; even analytical.

Jim sighed. It wasn't as if he objected to finding Leigh Heller, in particular, in his quarters, with her chestnut hair and brown eyes and those legs that went on forever, but this wasn't quite how he'd have preferred it.

Don't need a damn thing but more sleep.

Jim shook his head, aware he was weaving from side to side. The tech produced the wakeshot anyhow and came toward him. He waved her away.

"How long till the ion storm's leading edge?" he demanded.

"Three point five hours, sir," she said. "But it's not the storm, sir. It's the scoops."

Jim hurled himself out of bed and at the shipsuit he'd draped neatly over a chair. Heller was too worried by whatever brought her in here to notice he'd slept bare. Or care.

"All right, let's have it," he ordered.

"Captain's in conference with the engineer," Tech Heller said. "And my crew chief's tranked out."

She ran her hand through brown hair matted against her head. How long since she'd showered or slept? Her eyes were reddened, and the tiny muscles along the left eyelid twitched from time to time. He felt his own eyelids jerk in reluctant sympathy.

"I was trying to secure the ship as much as we could before the storm hit. I figured we could get a closer coil on the umbilicals. We'd discussed it in staff meeting, so I went down there, meaning to check out EVA equipment and a flight pack."

EVA, no doubt alone. Gods.

"I've got advanced certification!"

Jim shook his head. "Go on."

"I ran a check on the engine shielding."

If the engineer had taken a short cut and they actually arrived, winning him his precious on-time bonus, New Amman's new arrivals would hatch a crop of lethal mutations, if they were really unlucky.

"Shielding's fine, sir," said Heller. "Nominal, in fact. It was the boost engines."

Used in-system or from a full stop, the boost engines functioned precisely the way their name implied. A modification—perhaps the twelfth generation—of the first Bussard scoops, the boost engines scooped up whatever was available in terms of micro-meteorites, the interstellar medium, or plasma for power and propelled the ship to the near-relativistic speed that was required to make Jump insertion.

"I'm a radiologist, but I've turned maintenance tech for this cruise," Heller said. Probably for a hardship bonus. Probably, downworld, she was Doctor Heller to the likes of him, and he'd better call her ma'am if they were formally introduced. But here, like the rest of them, she was tech crew, rank and file, and as a Fleet officer, he outranked her.

"God knows, I'm no engineer. But we had our orientation briefings, and my memory's almost eidetic, you know. I remember seeing the angle of incidence on the boost engine scoops. It didn't look like the models. So I came in and tried to find Chief Engineer Stuart. He was busy. Talked to one of his staff, who tried a remote reset. . . ."

Cut the chatter, mister! If he'd been on board a proper Fleet ship, he'd have interrupted Heller five minutes ago.

But Heller was a scientist, not real crew. Clearly, she meant to tell her story in all the detail it might take, present all the evidence, *all* of it, together with hypothesis, substantiation, and whatever-deadly-else that could steal life and breath from an honest officer. And from the ship's life, which was going to turn his hair as gray as Heikkonen's if she didn't shut the hell up.

"Cut to the chase, mister," Jim finally did interrupt. "Are you telling me the scoops are frozen?"

"Yes . . . I mean, aye, sir."

Heller picked a fine time to play tin soldier. Jim shut his eyes in deep weariness. Be fair, he scolded himself. She was playing a game that had turned deadly, and, under the circumstances, not doing too badly. She had identified a serious problem. The scoops weren't just efficient, they were hyperefficient, able to extract every iota of power from the infinitesimal amounts of matter they absorbed. Ordinarily, that was all the matter they could find. But an ion storm was raw power, and swirling in its wake came more matter than a fully deployed scoopfield could deal with. If the scoops could not be furled or retracted altogether, the engines would explode from sheer abundance.

As deaths went, it was at least fast.

"The engineer's mate you spoke with. Hasn't he the authority to EVA and proximity-reset the scoops?"

"He didn't take me seriously. Regular ship's crew's like that. Once I could finally get him to run diagnostics and the remote-reset failed, he said the tolerances were borderline, sir! And that he was too busy to go EVA because his priority was getting the Jump engines back on-line before the storm."

Jim suppressed the impulse to put his head in his hands or bang it on the bulkhead. "Relying on borderline tolerances being borderline is damn sloppy," he said. "Someone's got to go out there and reset them manually. If that's not his priority, whose is it? Did he say?"

"He said he'd refer it up the line. And make a note in the log."

Jim glanced at his chronometer. The storm was too close at hand for chain-of-command games, cover-your-ass, or just plain gutlessness.

"I'll take the matter up with the engineer, Heller," he said. "You get some rest."

"But, sir, the engineer's with the captain!"

"Then I'll take it up with your friend and his crew chief. You don't want to rest?" He eyed her. Too worked up to sleep, probably. "Come along, then, to Engineering. I may need another pair of eyes, and you've proven yours are sharp."

Eidetic, in fact. He had no reason to doubt her word.

He strode ahead of her, deliberately paying no attention to her moan after the fact that "This is seriously going to fuck up my evaluation." Whether it did or not, Heller was a scientist, a real one, and she'd told the truth as she saw it. Maybe, he was far enough away from anyone's chain of command that they'd listen to him.

At the very least, he could, as corporate officers droned on et endless cetera, make his own determination.

Jim erupted into Engineering, trailed by Heller, brushed past a warrant officer and reached for controls. Punching up the scoop schematics, he checked status against the nominal profile.

They were close enough that someone with a mind to could have dismissed her report.

He factored in hypothetical damage levels from a Force Six ion storm and grimaced.

"What are you doing here?" Ty Parnell, the engineering second-in-command demanded.

"Thought you were in a meeting."

"I was. Your meddling dragged me out."

"Scoops are frozen, Parnell. Now, are you going to do something about it, or do I have to take over?"

That crossed the line. If he took over, it was damned close to mutiny.

The woman glanced at Heller—a witness. Her glance turned poisonous, but she swallowed once and edged in before the workstation. Her hands raced over the touchpads, fingers racing like a patrol in retreat.

"Damn!" she whispered. "Reset *is* frozen."

"Automatic retract?" Jim demanded. Parnell shook her head.

"I told you!" Heller whispered.

"Can you perform manual override?"

She shot him a what-do-you-think-I-am look. "I'm trying, sir," she said.

So, he was *sir* now, and he knew what Parnell was.

Damned scared.

She pounded on the console as if somehow, the impact would communicate itself to the fatally stuck scoops.

Jim took a deep breath. This was the dream. This was his chance. Someone—he himself—would have to go out there on the hull, in the teeth of the ion storm, and reset the scoops or, failing that, blow them away.

"Log this in, mister," he ordered. "Time-stamp it. I'll leave retinal scan and thumbprint ID if you like. 'On my own initiative, I have decided to go EVA and manually reset the scoops.' "

He waited for Engineering Second Parnell to volunteer to go herself. Then, he glared. "If I were you, I'd go back into that meeting and report this."

"I have to get back in there. I'll refer the matter to the bridge."

Jim felt his lips twist in disgust. Probably, she was looking forward to stock options herself.

He turned his back and strode out of Engineering toward the nearest emergency airlock. To his surprise, Heller trailed after him. "You'll need help getting into that thing and getting out the airlock."

There were manual systems, he knew, and you could—in an emergency—clamber into EVA gear alone. Having help made matters safer, and faster.

He checked the signoffs on the EVA equipment. That was his thumbprint on the inspection seal of this suit.

"Get the helm," he ordered, pulling on the leggings and pulling the heavy harness up over his head. The shoulder fastenings hung around his neck like a yoke. Heller came forward with the helmet. She was too short to get it over his head, its fastenings in the correct slots: he knelt to accommodate her, an unlikely knight before a stressed-out lady.

They could have been deep-sea fishing on Aven. Damn shame they weren't.

"Sir," she asked, her voice husky, "do you think we'll have to jettison the pods? Or"—her voice broke on the unthinkable—"abandon ship?"

"Not if I have a thing to say about it," he told her. "If I have to, I'll blast them free." That was a line straight out of his most youthful dreams, but it won a flush of hope from Heller. Maybe, when he returned. . . .

So, Jim's most familiar dream, How I Saved the Ship, was now on re-run. It had two main scenarios. In the good one, Jim ventured out and walked the hull in the trailing edge of the ion storm. He returned to the applause of the crew, their recognition that he had been misjudged, the captain's slap on his back, the commendations of topmost management and the Fleet. He liked that version.

Then, there was the other scenario, the downer in which he died trying and then, his dreaming self had to watch his parents stand, burning-eyed and decorous at the memorial as they handed his mother that anachronism of a flag that persisted in the Alliance even now.

Belay fantasies, mister, he told himself, almost grinning at the ludicrous command. *You need your concentration focused real time.*

Heller secured the EVA suit's helmet, shutting him away from the world.

"You all right in there?" she mouthed.

He nodded as emphatically as he could. The suit was cumbersome in gravity, weightless outside, like an ancient underwater pressure suit. He flexed clammy hands in the sandwich-thick composite gauntlets and glanced down at the suit gauges. Suit integrity: nominal. Suit air: one hundred and twenty TSE—Terran Standard Equivalent—minutes.

Long enough to get out there, fix the problem and get back.

He nodded again and lumbered toward the airlock. Heller slapped a wall control and the thing gaped open. Dark. Dark. Dark against the blaze of stars. The suit's internal lights rose about him: blue and green, for a well-maintained suit in good order, for a suit-wearer in good health. He could hear his breath in the massive helm, feel the blood pounding in his temples—so little plastic and metal and oxygen against that emptiness.

Good luck, sir! He could see her lips twist on the words. He tapped the side of his helmet, the old signal for her to activate communications. Then, an even older signal, he gestured: thumbs up.

The airlock cycled. The air whooshed out, ice forming at the edges of the hull.

Jim floated out of the airlock, then activated the magnetic plates on the soles of his boots. He could not hear them click home: he felt the impact, felt the plates stick and hold, then disengage as he took the next step.

And the next. The next. The next. Across the hull.

Hard to imagine space actually darkening, but so it was. The gaseous clouds stirred up by the ion storm swirled hundreds of thousands of kilometers away. The storm's leading edge might hit them sooner than he expected. He paid out a belaying line. Even if he came loose, he would call for help, and Heller or some other rescuer could emerge from the airlock and play him, like a gasping unwieldy fish, back into safety.

Safety? With that impersonal savagery of ions out there?

"Sir," Heller's voice was soft, alarmed. *"I'm picking up cross-chat."*

He nudged open communications with his chin, punched a heavy button on his suit's chest console with his thick gauntlets. "Pipe it through, then shut down," he ordered.

"I'm EVA. Used the Auxiliary lock . . . Captain, you're sure?" Engineer Stuart's voice, filtered by suitcoms.

"He's one man. Not one of ours. If we tell Fleet he died in the line of duty. . . ." That voice belonged to First Officer Harriman.

A long pause.

Finally, a voice spoke. Jim broke into a sweat that dried, pasting the shipsuit nastily to his body. Captain Heikkonen.

"We'll offer to cover the pension. Hell, I could practically cover it out of ship's credit, without touching company funds. Or our P&I club will cover it. Insurance claims, you know. Load the drugs and zygotes on board the gig; they mass the least. The pods are salvage. We'll mark them like good little spacers, precautions in case we have to abandon them temporarily. If all goes well, we ride out the storm, deliver the most urgent biosupplies, and come back. Then we collect. Well?"

"What if scavengers salvage Jaya *first?"* from the engineer.

"We'll slap a tracer on her and come back armed," Heikkonen replied. *"And* not *with our galactic hero."*

The engineer laughed, almost a growl. *"I'm with you, Captain. So's Ty."*

"You'd better check on our steadfast tin soldier," said Heikkonen. *"He's dying to be a hero."*

"Let's give him a hand," the exec said.

Jim shuddered at the man's laugh. *"My pleasure."*

"Well enough, then." Clearly, Heikkonen, having decided on murder, was making an Executive Decision. *"We'll get the gig out and overfly you. Pick you up from the hull, if you don't mind jumping for it."*

"Aye, sir."

A wonder the title of respect didn't stick in the bastard's throat. Jim heard his own growl in the confines of the helm. He glanced down at his belt. There was a knife among his tools. A knife and a cutter. He hadn't expected to need a sidearm. Not to protect himself from his own crew!

But the truth was, he had no "own crew" on *Jaya*. Unless you counted tech crew like Heller and Vingtsson and Bokassa and Chief Danamon and the others who wouldn't be just dead, but betrayed and abandoned if the captain had his way. Somewhere along the line, they had become as valuable to him as the people he'd trained with, the officers he'd served under.

As his comrades, living and dead.

So many more dead than alive, now.

The suit seemed to tingle around him—his mind supplying sensations as radiation seduced its way through the treated "sandwich" of the armor and its soft, movable joints. Micrometeorites pinged minutely against his air tanks. He glanced at the O_2 gauge.

Time enough. Sixty-five minutes.

Pick up one foot. Click. Set it down. Pick up the other. Hurry. Not *that* fast, fool. Not unless you wanted inertia to rip you free, sending you starfishing into the endless dark.

Was there something wrong with his air? Was his oxygen supply compromised by the coming storm? He forced himself not to hyperventilate. His eyes would bulge; his hands would tear at the helm's fastenings; he would hurl himself forward and faint, suspended only by gravity boots.

The voices of the captain and the engineer had long since fallen silent.

Jaya's officers were preparing their escape, abandoning the techs, even the rest of their own crew. They'd be in the gig's launch bay by now. Except for the engineer—he'd be on the hull looking to give Jim one good push.

When the mist of horror that shipmate would kill shipmate cleared from his eyes, he saw he had clambered up the curve of the ship and now stood right below the scoops. He leaned forward, unable to perceive damage. The joints were reinforced. Perhaps they would yield to manipulation.

Jim pushed forward. His clumsy gloves faltered on the manual controls below the scoops. The panel slid aside. He punched the thick buttons. No movement. He hammered them with his fists. Firing might weld them into place not forever, but for what few minutes remained.

The leading edge of the ion storm seemed closer, a palpable, dark thing; a closer darkness overhead, blank but for one light. The gig!

"Sir, someone's joining you. It's . . . Chief Engineer Stuart. . . ."

"I see, Heller," said Jim. "I see." Superfluous words. But he did see. Better than Heller did. And God forbid her sight of things like this improve!

He drew the cutter. Worst-case—blast the scoops free. The ship wouldn't go anywhere, but if they could keep it edge-on to the storm, they could ride it out. Maybe. It would add new meaning to the term "turbulence," but they'd survive, even if the pods didn't. Even if the ship took heavy damage.

He saw the engineer, raising his hand as if in greeting. He made himself respond, a man relieved and happy at finding unexpected help. Damn the man, was that a sidearm he was holding? It had more power than the cutter, the better to blast through metal housings.

The engineer raised his hand as if to fire on the frozen scoops. Used to people not knowing what the hell he was up to, wasn't he? Used to being smarter, stronger, faster, and deadlier than almost anyone on board?

He could save that for the civilians.

As the gig hovered overhead, Jim leaned forward, as if

urging the engineer toward the scoops. He made as if to turn his back, an idiot rushing on his fate.

The engineer's fingers, thickened by the gauntlets, tightened visibly. Now! Jim grasped the man's wrist and turned his hand before he could fire at Jim.

The blast hit the man's faceplate full on.

Jim glanced away. He could hear his breath rasp. He gagged, gurgled, and swallowed. You could aspirate if you puked in your suit. If that didn't kill you, the crew chief would.

Forcing himself not to look at the seared horror that had once been a man and a traitor, Jim plucked the sidearm out of its slow descent toward the hull. He turned it on the scoops. Focused energy raved out, directed fire, expertly focused.

The scoops began to close.

"Well done, man! We see you. Get clear. Get clear. At my signal, release plates and jump. Harriman's suited up in the airlock. He'll retrieve you."

"Sir . . . sir . . ." Heller's voice cut in.

Don't answer Heller or you'll give it away, Jim warned himself. The gig was armed.

He started back toward the airlock. He could feel the pinging, the tingling, a sort of oppression rising up around him. The storm was very near.

His eyes felt like they were drying out. He gasped for air.

The air gauge jittered on the line, then crossed decisively into red. An alarm began whistling in his suit, enough to wake a man from a trance of anoxia.

The gig's airlock yawned as the small ship maneuvered. It was closer than the airlock. You wouldn't even have to be particularly skilled at EVA to make it: just detach and leap straight up.

He could smell his own sweat, taste his own bile. He was breathing his own waste. It might poison him before anoxia claimed him. Before the storm hit.

The exec in the airlock waved overhead, paid out a tether, motioned at Jim. . . .

His eyes blurred. His head spun. Click. Click. He walked faster and faster. His breath turned into ragged gasps.

His boots released.

His gauntlet caught the line, and he stared at his hand as if it belonged to someone else. A moment of panic, and he had abandoned the vulnerable bioship he should have given his life to protect. His survival instinct had betrayed him.

They hauled him into the gig. The airlock cycled closed. He felt, rather than heard the clang. He lay gasping on deck, while they tore off his helm, patting at his arms and legs, offering profane reassurances as the gig veered away from the *Irian Jaya,* its miniature boosters attempting to take them into Jump before the storm's leading edge struck.

Harriman pried off his helm as the captain steered away from the abandoned bioship. Jim lay wheezing, head down, until they turned him over.

The first officer's face chilled. In the bluish lights of the airlock, he looked like something that had been too long dead.

You wanted me dead, Jim thought. *I'm worse than dead.*

He laid his head on his arm, bracing himself for attack. Harriman had plotted murder and worse. But the contempt in the first officer's eyes made Jim realize he'd have traded the soul he had just lost for passage back to *Jaya,* where he might have died but would have kept his honor.

The gig shuddered as the ion storm approached. He knew past instinct that they were doomed to survive it.

6

Station Five One Niner, Alliance Space

As the medtech steering me got me through the tense crowd on Station Five One Niner's upper level, whispers made me regret my decision to sit in on the trial.

"That's *her,*" the medtech pried a path for me through the

reluctant crowd. "That's *Marlow.* Remember when that prospector brought her in? No shipsicle's ever been resurrected after twenty years in Freeze. At least, not without serious freezer burn. . . ."

Or worse culture shock, I realized. That was giving me worse shakes than revival and the drugs they'd pumped into me. Twenty years in Freeze, and even here in Havilland Roads, where refit facilities nursed the remnants of Alliance's space-faring capability as carefully as . . . they restored me, my birthspeech had turned unfamiliar. Strangest of all, the war was over, and my former enemies walked the station's decks.

Twenty years ago, the decks of Station Five One Niner had been quieter—and in better shape. They'd been tense with action, not sullen revolt. Odd: I could sense the emotions from the crowd that milled about me as a threat, in the abstract, but I couldn't feel it. I was protected not just by Medtech Ankeny, but by a kind of psychic Freeze akin to the years I had spent near absolute zero. Too many people, and too much ice. . . .

I reeled, and Ankeny steadied me. "Think you can make it?" he asked for the fifth time since I'd ventured from MedCenter's Critical Care unit at the station's core.

I might say I was too old for a nursemaid—mid-fifties in actual years, if I hadn't spent those twenty years in Freeze. Still, I was also only a week out of resurrection. So, the best terms I could get from the mob of physicians that hovered over me were that I either came up here under escort, or I stayed where they could monitor their prize research subject.

For the first time in my life, I was too valuable to risk.

"Just past this docking bay, Commander Marlow," the medtech murmured, hand warm at my elbow. *Ankeny, Thomas:* tarnished letters glinted on the breast of the deep blue, Class B uniform tunic he wore instead of the utilitarian short-sleeved MedCenter issue. I could see us both reflected in the metal reflectors, somewhat battered now, that allowed a few depleted gardens to multiply into a rain forest. Carefully placed lights struck mirrors and plants alike, resembling not just sunshine, but the light of Earth's yellow home star: yes, another fine summer day on-station. Assuming life support held out or nothing ruptured the hull.

Ankeny's touch seemed to reach through the heavy cloth of my own uniform. The official tailors had delivered it just this morning, station-time, and its newness stood out against the cleanly shabbiness of the other uniforms I'd seen. "The Commodore said you could go into the courtroom and sit down before. . . ."

"Before all hell breaks loose?" I asked. "My compliments to the Commodore, please, and my thanks, but I cannot allow what could be construed as favoritism. Especially not now."

I pushed past Ankeny toward the improvised courtroom. The entire station showed signs of makeshift plans, makeshift accommodations—everything but vital systems, which, albeit old, were the choicest they could find. The station had outlived itself, that was for certain. They should have built a new one five years ago.

I moved too fast. My head spun, my vision darkened. Dammit, this was no place for a memory vivid as a waking dream.

I remembered now.

RAGOZINSKI, MY OLD CLASSMATE, MY OLD FRIEND, AND looking a damn sight older now than I did, had dropped by MedCenter to see me shortly after I was revived. My fingers still tingled, remembering how he had taken my hand and held it, the warmth of human, remembered flesh carrying more healing than all the heatlamps and drugs.

"Cam," he said. "Caroline Marlow. I've got you back!" Never taking his eyes off me, he'd dropped into the chair by my bed. To my surprise, he'd leaned past a thicket of sensors and brushed my face with his fingertips—warm! So very warm. His eyes grew wet.

"Didn't know you cared," I managed to get the joke, as weak as I felt, through a dry mouth. It was the first joke I'd made since I'd been thawed. My own eyes burned. I had forgotten how warm tears were. And how salty. I put my tongue out to taste them, and that was the first taste I'd savored since resurrection.

"Neither did I." He laughed. "Not many of us left now, Cam. You slept right through the war, while I fought Secess'. And when I look at you—even though you're still young, so goddamned young! I think I got the better of the deal."

His once—dark hair was a lot thinner and going gray, his waist thicker than I remembered from when we were ensigns together.

I shook my head and sighed—for different reasons now. A sensor erupted, along with a whole battery of lights.

"Damn," Conrad said. "We'll have the whole MedCenter in here soon."

I shut my eyes, suddenly very tired, leaving Conrad to cope with the physicians. His hand felt so good.

"Sir, you have to cut this visit short. . . ." they told him.

"But she's awake, now!" Conrad protested. "She knew me!"

The voices counterattacked with "Commodore, she's not even stabilized. . . ."

Commodore? Who was "Commodore"? We'd been mids together, then ensigns, Conrad Ragozinski and I. . . .

I let my eyes drift back open again. I'd been frozen at age thirty-three. He'd matured. Progressed. I'd simply *stopped.*

His warm hand had made me feel stronger. Allies again as we'd been through training, we glared away the medical staff, then turned back to look at each other, abruptly as shy as ensigns in front of their first CO.

"It's good to see you," I'd said in the whisper which was all the voice I could muster at the time. I tried to call him "sir," but he shook his head.

"The others?" I got the question out. Glad to see my nerve survived Freeze.

His eyes filled up again.

"We're the last of our class, Cam. Sorry."

I let myself sink back. If I could just shut my eyes, I could drift back to the ice, the whiteness, the Freeze without dreams. . . . Still, it was good to see him: old rival, old lover. Old friend.

"Cam, there's a crisis and I need your help!" His voice grew urgent, pulling me back from dreams. From the Freeze. And then he told me the rest.

By the time Conrad finished, tears were running down my face, and medstaff were all but tugging the gold braid off his sleeve to pry him away. I half agreed with them. I *was* just out of Freeze! The coward's whine clamored to be let out, but I clamped lips on it. But to be what I was, rescued after long abandonment, and sit through a treacherous shipmate's trial: to serve as a living reproach to a man who ran away.

I knew I was going to do it. But I hated it.

And Jim, of all people! If you'd asked me who, of all the people I'd ever served with, would flee a damaged ship rather than fight to save it—I wouldn't have said any of us was capable of sinking that low.

God, what did this mean for the peace with Secess'? They had discovered an Alliance officer betraying his own. It would be like them to start fighting again, disgusted at being treaty-bound to a Fleet who could tolerate this kind of disgrace. Not to mention how our own civilians might react.

I made myself breathe deeply and opened my eyes. I had the shakes but good, just as I had about the time they'd finally chased Ragozinksi away from MedCenter. He went obediently, mission accomplished, walking like a man bleeding inside.

"COMMANDER? COMMANDER?" ANKENY HAD HIS DAMN scanners out, monitoring blood pressure and brainwaves. And the way I'd gone blank was clearly something he didn't like at all.

"You sure you want to go through with this?" he asked again.

"I'm sure," I told him. Of course, I was lying through my

teeth. I focused on the stripes of blue and green on an ornamental light panel that had once been an advertisement.

They'd already been making noises about "retirement on disability." I didn't want to give them more ammunition than they had.

"I wish you'd take the Commodore up on his offer of VIP seating. After all, this is the first time you've been out since . . ." Tactfully, my own private nursemaid fell silent.

"Since my resurrection?" I asked. "It's all right, Tom. Really. I understand. I just can't accept the favor. Look at that crowd, why don't you? Those civs are angry. Think about this trial they've come to see," I ordered Ankeny. "Now," I demanded, "you tell me. Do you really tell me they'd understand preferential treatment for anyone in Fleet blue? Even the worlds' oldest shipsicle?"

Looking at the crowd of protesters made my hands shake. Granted, the outer rings of stations tended to be chilly. After twenty years in Freeze, I thought I qualified as an expert in temperatures below zero—considerably below. But that murmuring, growling crowd turned me colder yet.

I could smell the battle tension in the crowd along with their sweat, the cheap dye of synthetic clothes, the reek of spiced food and drink, the sudden surge forward, blotting out the signs and the attempt at decoration.

I started to shrink back, hating myself for it. Damn, had I lost my guts along with the last twenty years of my life?

"Get down!" Ankeny pushed me down beneath him onto the deck. Its metal smelled of industrial oils and whatever they'd used to scrub it down. My head slammed up against something hard: damn fake-tropical plant they'd put in here to pretty the place up and make this giant tin can livable.

Light roared up, white dimming to the reddish womblike glow of MedCenter's heat lamps, then winking out. Firebomb. On a sealed station.

Good thing it was a small one, or there'd have been no return from resurrection this time for me, or anyone else on deck.

Sprays of fire-suppressant at zero extinguished the reek of the explosive, reducing the stink of blood to a memory of shipboard deaths.

I shivered against this new assault of cold. The medtech's body shook against mine—evidently, he'd joined up too late to see much action, lucky man. I reached up to pat him on the back. I had forgotten how good it felt to be close to another body. He hugged me, then let go.

"Beg your pardon, ma'am. Sir."

Don't cling, Marlow, I warned myself. *You're old enough to be his mother.*

And I could have been, if I'd lived through the past twenty years.

"Not much of a bang," I tried to make a joke of it.

Ankeny shook his head. His eyes were a little glazed. I realized the explosion and the screams of the crowd had left him deaf for the moment. Spacers had a fix for that. I moved my head to let him lip-read as if we stood on a ship's hull, helmet to helmet.

"If they were going to set off a real bomb . . ." I mouthed, exaggerating my lip motions so he'd get them.

He shuddered, then scrambled to his feet and pulled me up. Very carefully. This soon out of Freeze, I bruised easily. "Sorry to push you down like that, Commander. And for forgetting myself. Let's see now . . ."

Out came his pet scanner again. So much for the commands of the team of Alliance Fleet surgeons and two civilians from a biotech consortium who had revived me that I was not to overexert myself! I'd be mottled and sore all over from the fall tomorrow. My cardiovascular system couldn't quite manage yet on its own, and I got these weird spikes in body temp that could prove fatal. Which wasn't bad for Alliance's oldest shipsicle, assuming I could heal the rest of the way.

Shrill whistles and amplified orders told me Security had found whoever threw the firebomb. Shouts of disgust told me that what they'd really found was an angry mob's leftovers.

"This wasn't the wakeup call I expected," I muttered. "Let's keep moving toward the courtroom. Talk to me. Explain what else is going on. For example, who're the well-dressed screamers near the viewports?"

"Outraged shareholders," said Ankeny. His reddish hair was tumbled and his pale skin, all the paler for living and working in a sealed environment, looked a little green. He too was shivering, though he tried not to show it in front of me. "They're threatening a . . . a proxy fight, they call it, on account of the charge *Irian Jaya*'s owners are making against earnings due to the lawsuits coming up. And they're seriously pissed—excuse me, sir, very angry—that *Jaya*'s captain and the others got away. So that's why the crowd wants to take it out on *him.*"

A jerk of his chin indicated the courtroom and today's defendant. The years I'd known him before he'd transferred off *Hardcastle,* years when I'd had the training of him, he'd been anything but a coward. A dreamer, yes, but not a coward. Jim had been one of us, one with us. I'd have expected him to blow up with his ship, not desert it. Good thing this wasn't combat, or he'd face capital charges.

"He's under guard since they brought *Irian Jaya* in. And," Ankeny added after a pause, "suicide watch."

Maybe he'd prefer a death sentence. I shook my head with sudden, absolute assurance. "If he hasn't died yet, it's because he thinks living's a worse punishment."

That is, if he were still the man I remembered.

God, what a world I'd been waked to. The Secess' war, which had been all I had ever known, was over. People felt actually safe enough to protest a budget line item. Or set off bombs because of a court case.

Which was worse? Freeze or culture shock and the knowledge that I'd outlived my ship, my captain, my crew? Conrad was a mourning stranger, astonishingly old. The only one left was Jim. The coward. Anger warmed me, then grew too hot. I fumbled at my tunic's high collar, then let my hand drop.

How could he do this to us? I had to blink away the blur in my eyes. At least, our captain hadn't lived to see this. I'd seen the pain, the disgust in Conrad's eyes when he'd asked for my deposition, his horror that I had had only good to report of Jim when he was my shipmate, and he'd never served with Jim.

"There she is! Ms. Marlow! Commander!" One of the reporters shouted, pointing at me, and the whole scavenging pack turned. "It's the shipsicle!"

Ankeny cast his eyes up to the heavens or, in this case, station's viewports. His hand on my elbow hastened me along, and I heard him grumbling about "rankers who exploit my patients."

"Come on, Commander, let's get you through weapons-check and into the courtroom. Once we're inside, the news can't make that much of a nuisance of themselves," he said and pushed past to the head of the line. Two civilians protested, and Ankeny simply gestured. They fell back. One reached out as if to shake hands, but Ankeny edged between us. I hadn't realized my image was that well known on-station.

So much for trying to avoid special treatment. If I got trapped in a crowd, let alone a crowd of journalists, and my adrenaline spiked up, God only knew what would happen to my system.

"You promise they'll leave me alone, do you?" I asked.

Ankeny answered my grin with one of his own. "You can always go back to MedCenter."

"Lead on," I told him.

My knees were wobbling although I'd only taken the lift and walked perhaps a hundred meters. Still, I tried not to lean on the medtech, at least not so any of the civs could see, as he led me toward Security outside the courtroom they'd set up on the loading dock.

I stood away from the tech and held out my arms for the metal detector. Lights paused, confirming retina and palm patterns, flashing over each piece of metal I was officially entitled to carry. I'd been surprised at the array of medals I'd apparently won. Posthumous, of course. Would they make me give them back now that I'd been resurrected? They could deduct the cost from back pay. I had a lot of that coming.

Yes, and you'll need every bit of it for when you're retired on disability, came the usual unwelcome thought. Usually, it waited till station's night to ambush me.

I heard shouting outside and shouted orders, followed by thuds and minor crashes.

The female security officer—Montez, I remembered her name, an old command habit I hoped I'd need again—patted me down and laughed sharply. "We turned the slickies on the rioters, Commander. It'll be a good long time before they can do anything but slide on their butts. Good to see you back," she added. She patted my shoulder, welcoming me back to the world of the living and the thawed.

"Tired?" Ankeny asked me as he led me to a seat down front.

"I've got to push myself, or I'll never recover," I told him.

"If the Commodore calls you to testify, I've got one dose—one—of epinephrine. Pick your moment, Commander. You're only getting the one shot. The CMO will have both ears and my tail if you collapse on my watch."

I was damned if I was going to collapse. Still, I sank into the chair Ankeny held a good bit faster than I'd have preferred. For a moment, I did my breathing exercises, content to sit in this hard chair near the front of the room, looking out at Havilland Roads and the stars beyond. The refit facility was less crowded than I remembered. Still, since this was my first view of anything much but MedCenter since the ice had blocked my eyes, I was thrilled to be seeing anything.

Irian Jaya was out there too. They'd towed it so we could see it from the courtroom, a mute witness, its station-keeping lights an additional, silent reproach.

A "suitable room" was all that regulations ordered for a court-martial. Dismantling some bulkheads—you could see the scars where they'd cut them free of the too-well-polished decks—and lugging in tables, chairs, and computers had turned the loading dock on Station Five One Niner's outer rim into a room big enough to accommodate the crowds, both official and curious.

In a highly unfortunate attempt at spit and polish, some officious souls had hung Fleet insignia over the three-story-high observation panels. I thought I could see it twist with the faint draft. Swinging in the breeze, was it? The draft was heavy with damp and metal and heavy oils, alive with the crackle of power. If the firebomb had been any bigger . . .

"Being in the same room with Secess' makes me queasy, too," said the man on the other side of me. He wore civilian clothing—another feral shareholder? "You see the man over there? Youngish, tall, pale, looks like he wants to bite? Ever see a Frekan before?"

Not outside their ships. Certainly not this close. Much too close for my liking.

Frekans were feared even among the Secess' as fighters who flew in teams of six and seemed to specialize in controlled berserker episodes. It had been a Frekan Fighting Star that had blasted *Hardcastle.*

"Tension's thick enough you could cut it with a knife," I brought out the commonplace, old before I went into Freeze. "Assuming you could sneak a knife through Security."

The civilian chuckled. "Metal detectors." He patted the breast of his tunic, far better cut than my uniform. "Even state-of-the-art detectors are useless on Lethe eggs or super-hardened glass. Fleet hasn't got a monopoly on being prepared."

Ankeny stiffened. I laid a hand on his arm, tightened it, and relaxed only when he did. Someone beckoned to the civ from across the room, and, to my relief, he moved. One of the last things I wanted was to sit next to a well-off fool. A well-off armed fool.

Was calling Security on him worth the risks of inciting another riot? I didn't think I had the strength for it.

Light and sound erupted again, striking reflections in the shabby polished metal of what had been a loading dock and was now a courtroom.

I jumped, but managed just in time not to hit the deck. I didn't want people to think Fleet had spawned a coward. *Two* cowards. Station Security pressed reluctantly close to the defendant, leading him past the raving horde of journalists, their mouths open, demanding anything they could get. The very blankness of the guards' faces showed how much they wished they could throw Jim to reporters, then escape. Abandoning a ship, and leaving thousands of lives and potential lives to die in space aren't precisely character traits that win loyalty from Security.

"That man's too young and . . . and clean to desert a bioship," the civilian behind me gasped. "He can't be a coward."

I got a glimpse of fair hair, a face I thought I remembered. A rush of compassion threatened to swamp me. I remembered someone barely out of eager boyhood, remembered a smile, a willingness to help: the accused had been a good shipmate, if not a friend.

He braced himself, then glanced around the room as if looking at the place he'd been brought to die. His eyes actually met mine, his face began to come alive, to warm with—

I don't want your recognition, I thought at him. *I don't want your relief I'm alive. I don't* know *you.* I turned my head, and saw, out of the corner of my eye, how he flushed like a boy at the snub.

My metabolism went switchback on me, spiking from cold to so hot my sweat drenched my undertunic. How, after what he'd done, could Jim be so happy I'd survived? He looked so young, so injured. I hardened my heart.

He would have abandoned you to Freeze and worse—the way he abandoned his entire ship. A bioship, *no less.*

And on top of everything else, the ship, so important to the survival of an Alliance planet, had been rescued by Secess', some of whom were sitting in this very room, witness to my Fleet's dishonor.

If the firebomb had killed or injured them, my old shipmate might well have not just the distinction of deserting a bioship, but of restarting the war that had almost wiped out humanity out as a spacefaring species.

The presiding officer entered the room. Twenty years ago, he hadn't won nearly that many decorations. Now, he wore them like battle armor, or camouflage. In the days since he had come to MedCenter and held my hand, my old friend Conrad had transformed himself into this remote, older man I could barely reconcile with the one I'd known. He was not Conrad now, but the Commodore, obviously practicing for when he became admiral.

As he stood, foursquare, before his chair, every officer in the echoing courtroom rose. Including the Secess'. I struggled to my feet, ignoring Ankeny's arm. After a moment, the civilians got the idea and scrambled up—some of them more reluctantly than others.

The Commodore glowered as he studied the room. From the way he reddened, I could see that his temper was reaching Jump velocity. He might have to make this trial public; he did not have to like it, and, clearly, he did not.

I caught his eye, nodded, and fought an unaccustomed blush of my own.

Hello again, old friend.

I remembered more now. . . .

A last spatter of shouts, a flash of light, a few shouted complaints about who shoved whom, and a bark from Conrad Ragozinski that daunted even the self-proclaimed experts at the back of the room.

My VIP seat gave me a chance to study Jim up close. Damn, didn't he look just like a recruiting holo for Alliance's fleet in our glory days before the war with Secess' bled out?

His face still wore that open, earnest look I remembered, but his mouth had tightened, and the blue eyes looked pained, perplexed. I remembered him as little more than a boy, though we all grew up fast during the war. He'd survived the past twenty years and was the same age as I now. Maybe even a little older.

Dammit, Jim had no right to look so fine in that uniform!

I wore its match, as I had when we served on board *Hardcastle.*

I tried to summon the anger I knew the psychs expected me to feel, the anger I'd felt short moments ago. I ran over my reasons—after all, he had abandoned people in Freeze like me, but all I could do was suppress another damn shiver. The madness that had made him abandon his ship seemed to have passed. They'd stuck him in protective custody, under suicide watch, rather than into the brig. No one worried he'd disappear like the captain and exec of *Irian Jaya.* His face was too well known.

My old shipmate, as promising a young officer as I'd ever helped train up, was what they used to call a marked man.

The regs give the presiding officer the option of closing the trial to the public. But in this case, Conrad, with his instinct for the political move, the career-builder, even the right move, knew he didn't dare. Confidence in the Fleet was already as low as confidence in our future. And what the Secess' on station thought . . .

Don't bristle at them, Marlow. We're at peace, remember? Just reading about the Armistice had sent my vital signs into a tailspin. *Give yourself time—after all, you've lost two decades—to get used to the idea.*

Behind me, I could hear the spectators hissing out more scandal. Command training doesn't give you eyes in the back of your head, but it does wonders for your ears and peripheral vision, even if you haven't used either for twenty years. One thing that hadn't changed: the amount of misinformation enthusiastic spectators could present in tones of utter assurance.

"They say he abandoned his ship. . . ." The man who spoke was thin, intense, with an accent I couldn't place. "A *bioship.*" His voice lowered in horror.

"That can't be right, I don't know, but it had to have been a mutiny. . . ." A civilian woman, the one who'd commented on the defendant's youth, began to explain, but was promptly interrupted.

"Not a chance. Scavengers made them evacuate. You know

they'd taken a hit from them and stopped to make repairs."

" 'Improper hazarding of vessel,' they say the charge is. It should be desertion. That's a capital crime."

I'd heard chaplains sound less dogmatic than that deep voice with its prosperous, misinformed inner-world nasals. I turned to get an eyeful of this particular expert.

"*Ssssh.* She's looking at you. The blond woman sitting up with the other officers. The one in the *new* uniform. I'm surprised she's here. That's *Marlow.* She's not just fresh out of MedCenter; she's fresh out of resurrection, oldest revival on record. A prospector brought her in. She only thawed last week."

Damn, they were pointing. I could feel Ankeny bristle in his seat beside me.

The expert subsided in a flurry of whispers about ". . . shipsicle . . ." "They say she served with him. . . ." From a corporate type, I heard the beginnings of a lecture about "physiological challenges" that I really didn't need to hear.

Still, the gabble in the room was one step better than misinformation about this trial. I glared. It was high time they shut up and let Ragozinski open this case up and then, mercifully for everyone, shut it down.

The torrent of misinformation and abuse continued.

Far too much speculation on the Secess' in the room, but fear soon quelled that. And: "High and mighty. Fleet's always gotten special treatment. And now you see what a load of nothing it buys us in return."

We all could have done without that remark. Or that attitude. If I had to live with the loss of faith it represented, maybe I should be sorry that prospector had detected my pod's dying beacon and pulled me out of Freeze instead of letting me drift halfway to the next galaxy or into the nearest star.

I'd at least have died warm.

I wasn't just going through denial, regardless of what the psychs said. I still found the very idea of Jim on trial—and on charges of abandoning a civilian vessel—hard to believe.

He should have been just fine. He had been one with us. He had been one of us.

But the record was damningly clear. Depositions from the rescue ships and from the *Irian Jaya*'s technical crew indicated Jim had panicked.

"If he'd thought the ship was doomed," a graying petty officer seated near me muttered, "he should have blown it up rather than let it fall into . . ."

"Peacetime, remember? Secess' even helped tow it in."

"Wasn't thinking of Secess'. It's scavengers that stick in my throat. They could have claimed the whole bioship as salvage, then brought the colonists up as slaves."

That was the crux of the matter. Ships got lost—not often, but they do disappear, and when survivors—*if* survivors turn up, they're welcomed home. No one would have thought to doubt a survivor's story of a doomed ship, an evacuation, an ion storm. They'd even treated Jim and the *Jaya*'s civilian officers as heroes when they'd first arrived here. No one thought to doubt the story Captain Heikkonen told—until *Irian Jaya* herself came in, ferried by our former enemies, which only made things worse.

Under the circumstances, everyone on the station was astonished when Jim had demanded not just to stand his trial, but to stand it in public. He'd even claimed the right to act as his own defense counsel though he might have had civilian counsel, with their plausible fantasias of diminished capacity and stress and oxygen deprivation, if he could pay for it, or military counsel if he'd requested. Conrad would have commandeered some poor soul to sit beside him and try to explain away the unthinkable.

As the Court seated itself, the damned journalists' playpen started flashing like a miniature firefight.

I turned toward the observation ports for a sight of clean space rather than the spacer-pale faces in the courtroom. Beyond the ships keeping station in Havilland Roads, stars glittered.

Stars like ice . . . ice crystals . . . *Don't panic, Marlow . . .*

my God, they're blinding me, walling me off from the universe . . . I can feel them in my veins!

The flashback that had been lying in wait for me reared, showing its icy fangs.

Get a grip, Cam. Try.

Medtech Ankeny eyed me, and I shook my head. *I'm just fine, dammit.*

Liar.

One of the observation ports blurred. Someone gasped. If the field collapsed, we'd be breathing vacuum unless the shields could close. A minute, ninety seconds, maybe two or three minutes for the hardiest among us, which I wasn't, and this time, there'd be no second resurrection for me.

The port stabilized. Looked as if we had a new lease on life.

The plague of journalists turned their attention from Jim to the Secess' in the audience. Some had already given depositions as I had, freeing us—strange, so strange to be "us" with Secess'—to attend the trial.

I was getting tired now, even after so short a time out of MedCenter, and it was getting hard to keep from drifting off into dreams.

I used to dream of a captain's berth. But, by the time I met Jim on *Hardcastle*, I focused simply on surviving and carrying out my duties. It was better that way.

Again, the flashback struck, too fast for me to evade.

The starscape beyond the Station blurred. I was back on board Hardcastle, *young and fit and scared.*

We'd fought our way out-system. Just when we thought we might live to fight another day, we ran into three Frekan Fighting Stars. Each Star, we'd learned, consisted of six cloned pilots, genetically built as killing machines, hyped on loyalty and drugs, and isolated from anything that might distract them from war. One was bad enough. We faced three.

I had my safety restraints strapped across my chair. Even so, the Stars' assault hurled me forward and I damn near broke my nose on my controls. Morton lay across his chair, torn apart by a chunk of scrap from a bulkhead that had been peeled away from the deck.

"Those damned Fighting Stars are ripping us apart!" Navigation shouted. His panels crackled and fat sparks jumped from them. He recoiled, clutching his hands against himself, fighting not to cry with the pain.

The air went foul with smoke and blood and sweat and shit. For the first time, I thought it: We're going to lose. We're going to die.

Captain sat like a rock. "Prepare to abandon ship!" he ordered.

"Sir, no!" It's easier to protest if you're not coughing your lungs up. I'd remember that. If I lived.

"Move, dammit!" I couldn't disobey that tone if I tried. I rose and spent a millisecond saluting. Captain nodded where he sat.

"At least, let me stay and help," I started to plead. "Let's try to ride this out."

"Move your butt, Marlow!"

By the time I heard my pod's hatch seal behind me, I understood.

The captain never meant to eject. . . .

Disobedient now, at the very last, I tried to push the hatch aside, but the goddamned pod would not re-open; computer was counting down ten, nine, eight to ejection . . .

The explosion that thrust it out into space sent me reeling against a hibernaculum that yawned open like a fresh grave.

"All hands secure for Freeze," came the recorded command we'd been drilled to obey. I heard the other two who shared the pod scramble for their hibernacula. I flung myself into mine and waited.

A rush of air, a spray of something pungent, soporific . . .

I shut my eyes, felt the needles and the cold that might be forever . . .

Red lights, heat, blurs that solidified into faces, buzzes that became words. I was alive.

I sighed and shook myself, flushing with relief.

"Flashback?" Ankeny asked me and gestured at his belt. I shook my head, no. No adrenaline, at least not yet.

I'd picked one hell of a time for flashbacks.

I was the only one in my survival pod they could revive, and even I had freezer burn.

I was cold. That had to be what provoked the flashback. Maintenance kept creche level and MedCenter hotter than the rest of Five One Niner, with heat lamps and wired thermal blankets maintaining body temp till my sluggish system could learn how again all by itself.

Up there in the dock, Jim shivered. He was in a Freeze all his own, that was for certain. It had to be insulating him from the hatred, the contempt that smoldered in this too-chilly makeshift courtroom. Otherwise, the people keeping suicide watch on him would have had something to do, long before this.

I rubbed my arms in the shoddy grandeur of my dress uniform and tried to remember decades-old training in biofeedback. The tailoring might be bad, the insignia garish, thinly plated metal on crude shapes of plastic, no doubt recycled from more important components past their useful life, but it kept me warm.

I wondered what I'd have looked like if Deep Freeze hadn't kept me at chrono age thirty-three. I could see myself in the polished, battered deck: shortish, deceptively sturdy; almost fair-haired, eyes the pale blue of ice. Eyes that, if the truth be told, looked rather shocked and uncertain.

God knows, I was no great beauty. I never had been. Even after twenty years on ice, I still preserved the layer of penalty weight that made me look stocky in uniform and had probably been what kept me alive so long in Freeze.

"This court will come to order," Commodore Ragozinski announced. That wasn't Command voice. That was a voice of pure doom.

We stood until allowed to sit, the Secess' moving with a pride that had nothing to do with deference to an Alliance senior officer. Did I truly have to like that? To shake them by the hands, bloody with my ship's, my captain's life? Actually drink with them in the renamed Joint Forces Club that Station Five One Niner had cobbled up? Station had space enough to spare so each service could have had its own place, but the psychs and bureaucrats had decreed we had to learn to play nice with the people whose tails we had tried to blast as assiduously as they'd tried to blast ours, rather than go off and brood over our nasty private military rituals. After all, we were all friends, now, weren't we? The very damned best of damnable friends.

Get used to it, Marlow.

Some freezer burn case flashed lights around the echoing, artificial "courtroom." A shout, quickly suppressed, of protest erupted from the audience.

"Quiet!" Ragozinski ordered. "If you can't keep discipline, I'll order the courtroom cleared. And if you don't clear it fast enough . . ."

He'd send in Security, and the best we could hope for was another riot. Oh joy.

Conrad, this is your world now, not mine. I hope you know what you're doing.

My eyes dazzled. For a moment, I saw the veins in them like a holoimage seared onto my eyelids. *Shut your eyes,* the emergency drills warned us, *you'll be fast-frozen, but shut your eyes the instant you feel the drugs so the blood vessels don't rupture and you wake up blind.*

When I opened my eyes and wiped them, I saw Jim wiping at his eyes too. So. His Freeze had melted. He knows what he did. Serve him right.

Dammit, man, haven't you disgraced us enough already without breaking down in public? He had damn good reason to cry. We all did. Why had he insisted on this trial? He could have died. He could have disappeared, as the other *Jaya* fugitives already had. But instead, he'd had to insist on His Day in Court. If this was his idea of atonement, he was the one who needed medical attention, not I.

So far, I'd managed to at least look as if I were eyes-front, while actually studying the loading dock, the audience, the board itself, and the observation ports. I turned my attention in earnest on Commodore Ragozinski. He was introducing the court now. We'd all have our jolly moment on the newsnets, whether we liked it or not.

Those idiot lights exploded again as my old friend Conrad finished introductions. He glared as if he wished all those newscasters had one neck and he had a cleaver. I wanted to tell him: *they're doing us a favor, letting us show Fleet's outrage and how it acts to cauterize the infection among its own.*

You could say journalists serve their purpose just as scavengers did on Old Earth: cleaning up carrion. But I'm going to insist on a distinction between journalists, who may be a necessary evil, and scavengers, who are just plain bad.

Today's scavengers don't scour the worlds for carrion; they harass the living. Most aren't really pirates, I suppose. The distinction's pretty narrow. Both of them live by taking what they want. Some—you could call these the real pirates—operate in fleets. There's always rumors of whole planets that serve as havens for them, and I for one don't know enough to dismiss those tales as lies.

Others are petty thieves just as they've always been. Leave cargo unguarded on a dock, and it disappears. Supplies vanish, even if they've been logged in. And the occasional ship's been stopped in real-space by craft that are heavier armed than ships of their size have a right to be, demanding—what? Food, spare parts, the occasional key technician or physician or whatever. Sometimes, though, they want backup systems, and if your life support happens to be on their shopping list, you'd better be able to go into Freeze then and there. Or perfect the art of breathing vacuum real damn fast.

"The defendant will rise," Conrad said, sinking himself into his role.

Jim rose as if he were a robot in some unquiet precise dream. He gazed past Ragozinski at the Fleet insignia, then past them out the viewports, at the ships awaiting repair or cargo or salvage operations. At the *Irian Jaya* he'd abandoned. He never even flinched.

"I so swear," the oath ended. Jim said it with never a catch in his voice.

"Can't trust a word he says," came a catcall from the rear of the courtroom.

"Eject that man," ordered the Commodore. Mercifully, the scuffle didn't last long and didn't spread. Even the angriest in the audience were quiet now, intent on their prey.

The questioning began.

"Answer the court," Ragozinski ordered Jim.

He drew a breath that seemed to shudder within him. No words came out, or if they did, he spoke in a kind of croak.

"Spacer's throat," muttered Ankeny, seated beside me. In the sealed environments of ships or stations where all water—and I do mean *all*—is recycled, your throat can dry out fast, offering squatters' rights to germ cultures. Some of them are just damn painful, while others can kill you, especially if no one knows the treatment regimen. You learn to drink a lot of water.

Courtesy of the court mandated filled glasses at each place. No one, however, had filled Jim's. He blinked at the omission, tilted his head in apology—a gesture as incongruous under the circumstances as it would have been charming anyplace else—then poured for himself, and drank.

At the presiding officer's table, Ragozinski pushed his glass away. Perhaps the motion was involuntary; certainly, he moved the heavy glass only the length of his hand, but the other officers imitated him. You could hear the sound as they slid across the metal of the tables.

Jim could drink if he must, but no one would join him.

He flushed, looking so young and guiltless that I wanted to hit him, and drained his glass. Then, he set down his glass hard, cleared his throat, and, in a low, clear voice, began to speak.

7

Captain Heikkonen, Jim told the court, took the tiny craft through the edge of the storm and into three closely chained Jumps—about a week's travel, real-time, to Five One Niner, the nearest human settlement.

The trip must have been a transit of hell.

They'd pulled him on board, Jim said, and he'd lain gasping on the deck of the airlock while they secured it.

"I think I almost wished," he said, "the lock would cycle once again and throw me out into space above the *Irian Jaya*'s hull."

His eyes glazed, as if he had spent too long staring out into otherspace. His voice was calm, remote, as if he spoke from the depths of an endless, unquiet dream.

Boots kicked at the glossy armor of Jim's EVA suit. "So, for all your fine talk about the good of the service, you're no better than the rest of us, are you? If you're what we've paid taxes for, maybe we should cut a deal with Secess' fast." He recognized the voice: First Officer Harriman, who'd expected to pick up Chief Engineer Stuart while Jim's corpse drifted in space.

"So now you want to fight? As you *were,* mister!" Heikkonen had said. "You can't go all holy on us. Never again. Where's Stuart? I suppose you killed him so you could take his place?"

He stared at the captain and the exec's eyes, glittering in the darkness of the airlock, and set one hand to the cutter at his belt in case the others attacked.

The gig shuddered and pitched, forcing them to grab handholds. The leading edge of the ion storm approached. Heller, Vingtsson, Bokassa, Danamon—the techs who might even have started to be friends or at least shipmates—all trapped back there on *Jaya*, along with the bioship's precious, irreplaceable cargo. If he could have grabbed a flight harness and jumped back that very moment, he would have thanked God. But you got no second chances.

The strange thing was, he couldn't even remember the exact instant he'd betrayed his ship, his crew, his whole life. One moment, he stood on *Jaya*'s hull. The next . . .

"Captain"—Jim wondered how the exec didn't gag on the title—"if we're planning to get out of here, we'd better move fast."

"Come on, hero." Captain Heikkonen gestured at Jim. "We're stuck with you. But you'd better not be too high and mighty to work for your passage."

ALL THAT TRIP, JIM BARELY SLEPT. DURING THE GIG'S "nights," he would lean against his workstation, his eyes half-closed, straining to hear the whispers among the people who hated him, who knew he held their secret—as they held his disgrace—but who needed his skilled hands on controls to spell theirs. The storm that picked the gig up and tossed it about was the least of his fears now.

Before the gig made the first Jump, Jim tried to scan for the *Jaya,* questing with eyes and instruments and straining to find out if the ship had ridden out the storm.

Time after time, he convinced himself it couldn't possibly have survived. He wanted to believe that.

Over and over, he replayed the moment when he had lost control and hurled himself up off the *Irian Jaya*'s hull and into the gig's yawning airlock. Even with his oxygen depleted, he ought to have thought of some other way. He ought to have thought. Surely, once the scoops were freed and he had taken out the engineer—his mind shrank from the decompressed horror that had been a mortal enemy—he could have flung himself back through the ship's airlock. Surely,

Heller would have known enough, would have been fast enough to get his helmet off now and drag him to Engineering. He could have overwhelmed section personnel, taken command of the crew. . . .

And been a hero, just as he had dreamed. He laughed harshly. Heikkonen and the exec went white under the gig's ghastly lights, which brought him another fear. What if they killed him as a madman and a walking danger?

It never occurred to him to escape the torment of his thoughts by retreating into Freeze. The gig carried hibernacula. Still, he didn't dare. It would have been so easy—a simple "adjustment" of a seal rather than the stake through the heart with which monsters used to be punished.

A waking eternity later, captain, exec, second engineer, and military advisor in their battered gig reached Station Five One Niner. Heikkonen was taciturn, the exec protective as they were led to MedCenter through the mandatory plague of journalists. Jim followed as if standing guard, thin, strained, white of lips, and red-eyed from sleeplessness and anguish he refused to discuss. MedCenter thought he was playing soldier and treated him to endless kind persuasions and diagnoses of Post-Traumatic Stress Disorder.

He accepted the ministrations, the compassion, even the admiration of Five One Niner because it was unthinkable to tell the truth and because this new fraud was just another part of his incomprehensible self-imposed punishment, if you could call it that.

Heikkonen and his crew vanished one night, disappearing, no doubt, into the human flotsam found in the lowest rings of stations. Having no place to jump to this time, Jim stayed, waiting for discovery.

He was seated in the observation deck watching the ships' lights in Havilland Road when *Divine Wind* brought in *Irian Jaya*. Bad enough the ship survived: but to see a ship Jim thought had died towed in like that, trailing its adiabatic survivors like some monstrous deepspace jellyfish—Jim had begun to laugh. The tears he could not shed before ran down his face. He laughed, he hooted, he bellowed till his voice cracked. He convulsed, knees rising to his chest.

The cool whisper of a trank spray was the last thing he heard before he collapsed.

AFTER SECESS' HAD BROUGHT IN THE *Jaya,* Jim had waked, he told the court, in the out-of-the-way MedCenter bunk they had given him, not to protect his privacy but to shield others from the sight of him. A thermal blanket was warm about him—but not warm enough to shield him from the absolute zero he saw in people's eyes.

While he had been out cold, his entire universe had changed. As soon as he showed himself to be coherent, military police arrested him. Taking his word he would not try to escape—where would he go?—because to restrain him would mean they had to touch him, they led him back to a Fleet that received him only because it must.

He could have died. He could have run. But he stayed.

Because it was his duty to admit his action and stand trial.

And, probably, because it was the worst punishment he could think of.

Yet, I thought as I watched him and brushed aside the solicitude of my medtech escort, Jim was still one of us. That was what put the angry disgust, the fear even in the faces of the officers of the court, though they tried to hide it.

If he could betray his charge, any one of us could turn traitor. Any of us. That, not the criminal charges, was why he was kept under guard. Never mind that he could not forgive himself: that was what we could not forgive in him.

Or in ourselves.

THE DOCKING BAY TURNED COURTROOM WAS DRY NOW, CONserving precious moisture. Jim's voice had thinned to a dry rasp. He reached for his glass and gulped thirstily. The room was so quiet you could hear him swallow.

I licked my lips. I should drink too, I knew, to prevent spacer's throat. I had only recently been let off rehydration treatments, and, so soon out of Freeze, my immune system was compromised. An infection might be fatal.

But even though I knew Jim, even though my heart ached for the thing he had made himself into, I could not bring myself to drink with him.

Jim stared at his empty glass as if it held the judgment of the court.

8

As Ragozinski turned to call the next witness, light bloomed beyond Havilland Roads. A ship erupted from Jump, shedding billows of rainbows. Last time I'd seen a ship exit Jump, it had released red-and-black-patterned Fighting Stars, and I'd lost my captain, my ship, and twenty years.

My training clicked in. I didn't need computer access to calculate speed and mass displacement as that ship emerged. It was dumping V too fast.

Someone in the audience cried out and pointed. That, of course, interrupted the trial though the Commodore bellowed for it to resume. Half the people in the room jumped up. Ragozinski gestured, sending junior officers up and down the rows of seats, making be-calm, stay-seated noises that actually worked. We couldn't afford a panic. Some idiot would get trampled, and Fleet would only have another scandal to manage.

"Too fast," whispered someone with as many service ribbons as I. Could the incoming ship brake before it hit the station? Or would it break apart and, quite literally, hit the station in pieces?

Twenty years of nightmares went to afterburners.

"Brake," I wasn't the only one to mutter. "Come on, brother, slow down . . . slow down . . ."

And still that rainbow light sluiced from the hull as if a sharp prow sliced shallow water.

The Tokugawan sitting off to himself raised an eyebrow at the spectacle. I could practically see him come to the conclusion that made sense for him: suicide mission, although computer breakdown or a madman at the helm made as much sense. He drew a deep breath and—there's no other way to describe it—went into himself, meditating. He might die, but he would not die afraid, or disgracing himself by losing his composure.

How *had* we managed to achieve even a truce of equals with these people, anyhow?

"Damned thing's a derelict!" came a shout.

"It's going to blow!"

Hull tolerances finally exceeded, the ship tore apart as if twisted between monstrous hands.

Klaxons began to bray. *No, it's not "abandon ship!"* I reassured myself. Station lights flashed red and white, followed by that damnable, deliberately calm computer voice that we've all been conditioned to obey, directing nonessential personnel to take shelter, station officials to report to battle stations, and all others to rejoin their ships. Shields slid over the observation ports. Five One Niner braced for impact.

The *reddish/whitish/dark* strobing of the light could provoke seizures. "Don't look!" Ankeny ordered me. Instead, I looked at Jim.

The instant the alert had sounded he had leapt to his feet, as if looking for something that needed doing. Damn him, why couldn't he have cared that way on *Irian Jaya*? Security shook his head, barring Jim's way. He sat back down.

"I'll be all right here," I hissed at Medtech Ankeny. "You get to station! No, don't waste the epinephrine on me. You may need to revive some other poor bastard."

He cast a desperate look at me, wanting to believe my promise, and took off.

I waited long enough so he wouldn't look like an idiot when they asked, "Why did you leave her?"

Then I ran for all I was worth, which wasn't much. *Toward* the danger.

I could feel the faint shudders as ships launched from Five One Niner's docking bays. The decks rumbled as weapons techs readied the station's arms.

Make yourself useful, Marlow.

I had no duty station.

Still, when a station's compromised, you always need people to suit up and check the seals. Or I could do weapons backup. At worst, I could act as a searcher before the emergency bulkheads closed.

The duty officer would know. I ran toward him as fast as I could.

And collapsed not twenty meters later onto my knees, failing to make it to a bench nearby. They'd warned me that my aerobic capacity was way down, and that my heart wasn't up to any heavy lifting yet. How could I have guessed that "heavy lifting" included lugging my own weight? "Dead weight" took on a whole new meaning.

Useless. So damned useless.

I toppled wheezing onto hands as well as knees, managed to creep to the bench but not to haul myself up on it. I would have vomited, only my muscles lacked the strength to force out any of the pap I'd been fed. I gasped until I gagged, my mouth dryer than a disinfected cargo bay. Streaks of red and white light exploded behind my eyes, and a copper taste filled my mouth. My uniform went sodden from my sweat, and the cheap dye stank, but I was freezing.

The dream reached out for me again.

When you feel the Freeze drugs take hold, close your eyes.

I closed them and rested my face on the cool synthetic stone of the bench.

Nothing happened. Not resurrection in the womblike heat of a MedCenter with faces staring down at me. Just the *whoop/whoop/whoop* of those disaster-alert klaxons, and boots pounding as people lucky enough to be useful ran toward their duty stations. I heard measured footprints and froze. Certainly, in the shape I was in, I'd be an easy kill.

The Tokugawan I'd seen compose himself for death in the courtroom stalked by and paused beside me. I met his eyes, aware that I must look like a disgrace to my uniform.

You going to finish me off, mister? It was cold comfort that I must look too weak to be worth killing.

Besides, that's the wrong question, Marlow. War's over. Remember?

The Tokugawan officer raised an imperious hand, then moved on, the black and red of the robe he wore over his uniform flowing. Probably, he would try to assist someone, as I'd have done if my body had not betrayed me.

At this rate, I wasn't likely to pass the medical exams to go back into the Fleet, was I?

Cam Marlow, as good a candidate for command as any in her year. Cam Marlow, washed out from freezer burn, at how old was I really? Fifty-two? Three? I felt like five hundred now. Maybe the Blue Helms, or the relief workers, would hire me and let me fly a nice safe desk. In my day, they'd always been suckers for walking wounded.

Something warm fell about my shoulders where strong hands anchored it. I brought up a shaking hand to touch a jacket of finer fabric and tailoring than anything I'd been issued. It was forest green, the color itself reassuring me.

"Commander Marlow?" The youngster who greeted me and laid his expensive jacket over my shoulders had barely worked up a sweat. He looked a lot like the Tokugawan—thin, golden-skinned, his brows and eyelids arched. A first cousin, maybe, or a tenth?

"Hashimoto-sama said to look out for you."

My head spun, and for a moment, this unstained boy had three heads, each with a useless yammering mouth opening red in its center. *Whoop/whoop/whoop,* the klaxons still screamed, but the rush of footsteps had died.

I wondered if the fighter ships could blast whatever was

incoming or if Five One Niner's own weapons would have to be brought into play.

"Get me to a monitor," I rasped.

"Never mind that. You're going back to MedCenter."

"Damn you, not that kind of monitor!" Short of breath or not, I could still use Command voice.

The youngster helped me rise. "I'll get you to a monitor," he said. "But I don't think you can walk that far alone. Here." He slung my arm across his back where equipment rode in a fancy harness.

"You're news," I said with almost as much loathing as I'd have accused him of scavenging. But I didn't have the strength to pull away. "Not supposed to talk to press. How'd you know my name?"

He shot me a give-me-strength look. "I was on the ship that picked you up," he said. "PR mission with the Secess'. The Tokugawans think I'm sort of a long-lost cousin. Name's Ryutaro Jones. Now, you get a choice. Let me get you to your damn monitor or lie here till you puke. Damn, who was the idiot who let you out alone?"

I started to stammer a defense of Ankeny. Lack of breath and language problems shut me up. I was too old, too tired to fight. Besides, Jones' anger was somehow comforting.

Even a week out of resurrection, I'd heard of him. Some of his stories were in the hypnopedic reorientations I'd gotten, never mind the real-time study I'd never catch up on.

For a boy-wonder journalist, he had a reputation as a straight arrow. He played fair—if you said something was off the record, he kept it off, and I'd heard rumors he'd been caught actually doing research rather than cosmetic surgery. Plus, he listened, or he couldn't have sounded as much like Fleet as he had just managed. I couldn't help chuckling. "Learn something on board, did you?"

Young Jones nodded. I caught his move in peripheral vision. My real attention was directed to my feet, keeping one ahead of the other without weaving too much.

He got me to a duty station, talked his way past Security

as if he'd had plenty of practice blindsiding them, and dumped me into an observer's chair. Comm crackled overhead. *"We've found evacuation modules."*

"Going in for pickup."

A rusty cheer went up around me. I'd have joined in if I'd had breath enough. So it wasn't mercs: just some poor bastards whose old ship had finally given out and gone derelict as they emerged from Jump.

"Damn lucky," muttered Jones.

"What do you think you know about it?" I had breath enough left to snarl at him.

You get trapped in Jump: there's no death there, sure, but also no life, no time. You're trapped conscious in there, while the tides of otherspace roil about you, till your systems fail, and you had better pray they fail quickly.

"I listen for a living, dammit!" he snapped.

I watched until the last fighter pilot sliced up the big chunks of debris—no point letting it impact the station's skin. The Blue Helms picked up the pods, an art almost as tricky as steering Linebarger adiabatic pods through Jump.

Jones handed me a cup of recycled water. It was flat, but tasted clean enough even though I knew where it had come from.

"C'mon, Commander," he said. "Show's over. I'll get you back to MedCenter now." He caught my glare.

"With your permission, of course, Commander," he added demurely. Put him in uniform, and wouldn't he just be the perfect ensign?

"Oh shove it," I muttered to myself. The idea of hiding in a warm bed, basking under the heat lamps, sounded better than a hundred shore leaves or full pension, but damned if I'd give this pup the satisfaction of knowing he'd read my mind.

"Get me to the wardroom. The All-Services Club," I explained, "and I'll buy you a drink." *I had to have some money, didn't I, after twenty years of accrued pay? Let Records sort that out.*

Disabilities and Pensions would be likelier to have my file, I realized with a pang.

Better yet, I could see him realize, if he did what I wanted, he'd have a legitimate right to poke around and listen in.

At least, somebody would profit from this mess. Even if it had to be a journalist.

As I tried hard not to lean on Jones, I saw Ankeny leaning against the bulkhead—*let's not panic the patient*—facing the observation ports that turned the long corridor leading to the wardroom into a gallery.

You really expect me to believe that you just happened *by?* I thought.

"Why am I not surprised you lied to me?" The medtech didn't even bother to sound shocked.

"You were needed for the duration," I told him.

"You needed me, too. Ship Second Hashimoto told me you seemed to be in some sort of distress during the Alert," the medtech said. "He was most impressed to find you running *toward* the trouble before you made a full recovery."

Damn the Tokugawan! Just because of Jim, did he expect every officer in the Alliance to run the other way? Or was that what he was hoping for? God, had we ever lost face. Good thing the war was over.

He gestured, and a woman with Greek-letter tabs on her collar came up. One of the Fleet psychs. He handed me over with a lame excuse, clearly relieved.

She flicked a glance at Jones. *Are you out of your mind, bringing* him *in here?* she seemed to want to ask, but even a military psych would be more tactful.

"Your Hashimoto-sama's been busy," I told Jones. Then I turned to the psych. "Apparently, Doctor, he told Ryutaro here where to find me. I offered to bring Mr. Jones here for a drink to thank him before . . ."*before you even ask, I'll go quietly* . . . "I report back to MedCenter."

The woman glared impartially at Jones and me.

"You're still on meds," she warned me. "Even one drink

now that we've just finally gotten your fluid levels adjusted . . ."

"I'll stick to fruit juice," I promised with exaggerated patience now that I'd won the engagement. "Or whatever reconstituted gunk they call fruit juice here. Why not come and watch a family reunion between Jones here and the Tokugawans? Save me having to be polite all by myself."

This time, Jones glared at me. Pinned in the crossfire between medical officer and journalist, I tried to look perfectly at ease. At least the vise around my heart and lungs seemed to have relaxed.

"If you're not back in an hour, I'll call Security," the psych told me.

"You do that," I said. What could she do—put me on report for insubordination? I waited till she turned, then gestured Jones past the guard and into the wardroom.

Before the truce, wardrooms tended to be bright with the seals and trophies of a hundred worlds, the prizes of the Fleet units in residence. With the war over, some optimist had renamed the place for all the services, left the Fleet insignia, but removed the more conspicuous trophies. You could see the places on the bulkheads, less weathered than the rest of the space, where they had been fastened.

So now, the place looked less like a wardroom or an O-club than an economy-class passengers' lounge in a low-rent spaceport. Another optimist of a morale officer had tried to make amends by hanging up some local artists' works. Bright daubs and rough holos about as amateurish as the kids' work in the creche livened up the steel-gray walls, which showed unweathered spots where the heraldry of a hundred Alliance outfits had been removed.

For the rest, people were trying hard to make it look as if we were still officers and gentlefolk. But the cloths laid out on the tables and counters were yellowed, mended, and the snacks looked—and smelled—like freeze-dried crud, algae, and reconstituted tofu even if, by God, the serving platters were still silver, and the glasses were the familiar triangular-shaped crystal of Fleet's pattern, its insignia still intact.

"Commander Marlow!" an older man, his hair silvered at a receding hairline, called out and headed toward me. He wore civilian clothing, old, but of better fabric than my uniform, and he carried himself as erect as any admiral. His skin was weathered, as if he'd spent years planetside.

"I am Abram Becker," he introduced himself.

"Honored, sir!" I came to attention with no more than three major twinges.

"And this is . . . ?"

He had to know Ryutaro Jones from the holocasts that had made his reputation, but I performed introductions anyhow. Jones smiled charmingly. Those teeth must have made him a fortune.

"Marshal Emeritus," Jones began.

"I'm afraid I've been recalled to active duty, sir," the marshal said. "I keep trying to retire, and they keep dragging me back to service. I'm here strictly as an observer."

I returned his grin. Even before I was frozen, Federal Security Marshal Becker had been perennially close to retirement. I'd heard rumors about some last-ditch strategies he'd come up with when it looked as if we might lose the Secess' war or it might knock us below viability thresholds. He was the man who'd come up with Operation Seedcorn, seeding distant planets with colonists to make sure that something of humanity would live even if we blew the rest of it into a black hole or something. One day, we'd get those worlds back, he'd said. Funny thing was, people believed him and still do. Which is why Marshal Becker is always just *about* to retire.

Jones had clearly heard the same stories. He was standing straight as a midshipman, his eyes bright, and saying, "A great honor, sir. Perhaps, I could ask you . . ."

Becker waved Jones away. "Later, if you don't mind. Perhaps you could ask Freiherr von Leinigen if he'd be kind enough to come over here for a word before you start practicing, as I know you will, your languages on the Tokugawan contingent."

I was not surprised when Jones went quietly. Or when he returned, looking almost like a one-man honor guard for the very tall, blade-thin Abendsterner whose thinning, fair hair shone above the decorations on his sleek gray shipsuit. He looked as if he had been born at attention, and I'd have wagered a year's pay that those chiseled features were natural, not genetically engineered *in utero* or surgically altered.

"Ah, Freiherr," Becker said. "Did I not promise to present you to Commander Marlow?"

The Abendsterner stiffened to attention and by-God clicked his heels. He inclined his head formally to me though he probably outranked me by thirty years and at least three grades. Not to mention the "von" in his name. "Von" was archaic in the Alliance—but still meant something considerable to Secess' from Abendstern.

"An honor, Commander, to meet an officer of your endurance."

Tactfully put. When you don't know what to say, incline your head and make Ritual Response number four. "Sir, you honor me."

"It is good that there is honor to be found," the Abendsterner said.

"The Freiherr was on board the *Divine Wind* as an observer with the Tokugawans," Becker offered. "*Wind* was short of crew, so he stood watch on *Irian Jaya* while they brought her in."

What did Becker expect me to say? It was hard enough talking about Jim to friends, let alone Abendsterners.

"Madam, I share your most justifiable outrage," von Leinigen said. "This failure of spirit, this breach of discipline . . ."

Becker must have felt me bristle; he set a hand on my arm.

The Freiherr eyed me approvingly. "I too would be enraged," he said. As if he liked me better for going into threat display, such as it was.

"The Freiherr's going to testify tomorrow," the marshal said.

"I know what I saw and what I think of it," the Abendsterner cut in.

"—But," Marshall Becker retrieved the conversational initiative, "he forgets that the accused is under Fleet authority, and, under Alliance jurisdiction, a man's innocent till proven guilty."

The Abendsterner's carved nostrils flared, and he snorted in contempt. "Even the most junior officer—which this man was not—must be above suspicion. An example needs to be made. One wonders why he lives to face exposure. One does not do such a thing and survive it. Had I been mad enough to forsake my duty, I know that I would not."

Becker snaked out a long arm and retrieved two drinks, handing one to the Abendsterner and one to me. Freiherr von Leinigen clicked his heels and toasted me. This time, I managed more of a bow before I drank something that very possibly had been recycled by way of HazMat. Fruit juice? Not a chance. Tears rushed to my eyes, and I decided it wouldn't be hard at all to abstain, not if all post-war liquor tasted as bad as this.

I managed to swallow it all, the way you do when giving toasts. I also managed not to list to one side. Doing really *well,* Marlow.

"I've seen stranger," Becker said. He had somehow acquired a third drink. "Freiherr, Commander? To your health!" he raised his glass and poured the pallid liquor down his throat, swallowed hard, then coughed. "Take the case of the commanding officer of one of my Seedcorn colonies. She actually demanded to stand trial for genocide. Amory Eliot Neave presided."

"Ah, indeed," von Leinigen said, inclining his head with more than politeness. Even I had heard of Neave, a former senator now helping to restore order to the worlds. "And this officer of yours?"

"Captain Yeager? If we speak literally, she was innocent.

The native culture managed to survive its exposure to humanity. But it was 'intent' on which she denounced herself. Ultimately, we shifted jurisdiction to the indigenes, which even she thought was punishment enough."

"Enough? What punishment can be enough for such betrayal?"

"In these days, we can afford neither damnation nor such pride, Freiherr," the marshal said. "In war, people do hideous things in the name of survival. But the war is over now. I want to hear this young man's testimony. I would call his anoxia a mitigating circumstance. So, it seems to me that he might be—*might,* I say—none so bad that with a period of reflection, counseling, retraining . . ." Becker shook his head.

The Abendsterner and I exchanged glances, reassuring ourselves that we agreed about Becker's cluelessness.

Becker smiled. "Ah, but you think, 'He is a civilian and an old man at that; he has earned the luxury of being charitable.' I will not belabor the point, but, instead—Commodore Ragozinski! Have you met two of your witnesses yet?" he called.

"Sir," I said, coming to attention before my old classmate. We'd keep the moment in MedCenter private, of course.

"Cam, when was it ever 'sir' before?" he asked. His hands went out as if he wanted to grab my shoulders, then dropped. "Can't prejudice the trial, now, can I?" His smile emerged from the gloom that had wrapped him in the courtroom. It was bright, young, and too quick.

He clicked his heels Abendstern-fashion at the Freiherr. Conrad never could put a foot wrong. "I have known this officer—this lady—since Academy days," he told von Leinigen, who attempted to look pleasantly surprised.

"Cam, I can't tell you how glad I am you survived Freeze and resurrection. And that you were willing to be an expert witness. I know that you and . . . the defendant served together, but surely, after twenty years on ice . . ."

Jones' laughter rose over the crowd's conversations. Another point to me for social skill: my guest was a graceful youngster, born to a rich Earth family, but taken offworld right before the war. He could have gone back now that the blockade was lifted, but so far, he hadn't. For a moment, I hated young Jones for his talents, his drive, his ready laugh, his future, when my old shipmate Jim had no future left at all.

"When two old friends and comrades meet," Freiherr von Leinigen said, "it is simply courtesy to take oneself elsewhere. Sir and Marshal, if you would care to accompany me?"

"Don't influence the witness, Commodore," Becker said. "We've got enough trouble without that. And appeals take time and money."

Commodore Ragozinski laughed politely.

He watched Becker steer the Abendsterner through the crowd. Various Fleet officers returned formal nods, but the mood of the room felt strained, wounded. A Tokugawan had pressed charges; an Abendsterner witnessed Fleet's disgrace.

My old classmate looked me over. "How's it going?" he asked me.

"Just because I wasn't awake doesn't mean I don't feel my age," I said. "It's been a long day."

"You don't look it. Tell me. Is it decided that you'll come back in?"

I looked down at my boots. Damn things pinched. "Freezer burn," I muttered the unbearable truth.

The pause drew out like a hangman's rope.

"As bad as all that?" he asked. "Rehab can do marvels these days. After the trial, we'll talk." Ragozinski turned back to me. "Cam, perhaps you'd consider having dinner with me then. To talk over old times."

"As long as we're not compromising the trial," I told him.

"It'll be over in a day or two. And then . . ."

He put his hand on my shoulder and clasped it before he turned away. I felt the cold in him through my thick uniform tunic. It really was past time to retreat to MedCenter and the comfort of its heatlamps.

If there was any comfort to be had at all.

9

The crash actually closed Havilland Roads to commercial ship traffic for three days. Because the perimeter hold where Jim's trial had been held was crammed now with debris and investigators, they had to shift the trial.

So, we—judges, witnesses, spectators, and the occasional protester before security spotted and ejected her—crammed ourselves into an inner and much smaller room near the Station's core. Its bulkheads bore the scars of multiple uses. Maybe it wasn't desirable enough to be staked out as someone's territory, but space on a station is always at a premium, so it was too valuable to waste—and too small to use as a barracks for the survivors for whom Command was trying to squeeze berths from already-crowded cubic.

Life support, taxed by the presence of so many agitated bodies, produced an odd chorus of sounds as well as heat that had people wiping their foreheads and surreptitiously fingering their tight collars. God forbid they let reporters, civilians, or ex-Secess' comment on the breakdown in discipline.

The room should have been warm enough for me, what with life support working overtime and the press of uniformed bodies in the room. I should have been soothed by the uterine thrum of station generators trembling at the threshold of awareness, and the watchful red lights that recorded and scanned for weapons, retina modification, and God only knows what else. But I couldn't stop shaking.

Only Sickbay with its auxiliary power, heat lights, and controlled environment, still came close to being warm enough for me, and Sickbay was filled now with crash survivors and trauma flashbacks. I'd been evicted to what felt like a closet with a bunk, half of it filled with medical telemetry. I was off Sickbay's premises, but not out of its clutches. That was great if my biosigns glitched, but, in terms of any future I might have in space, not at all encouraging.

This improvised courtroom, unlike the last one, had no viewports or even a screen. That focused attention relentlessly on Jim's trial, which moved from witness to witness as if it were a warship painstakingly targeting, then blasting, rescue shuttles out of existence one by one.

I had shut my eyes when I went into Freeze. Now, I couldn't look away from this stately progress toward the disgrace Jim had earned.

For God's sake, get on with it! I wanted to shout, and knew that the medics would sedate me the instant I opened my mouth. The numbers on the glowing chrono panel on the bulkhead that vied with various shabby banners as the room's sole ornaments clicked with almost relativistic slowness toward the blessed moment when Commodore Ragozinski might reasonably dismiss the board for the station's "day." Staring at it was a breach of protocol, but as inevitable as the trial itself. We were counting down toward a dishonor that was inevitable. And I was ashamed I found myself regretting it.

Jim sat alone at his table, isolated by space that was as much moral as physical. After the first day, he had not touched his water as if he, like the officers who judged him, refused to drink with himself. The lightpanels, admirably calibrated to let us bask in full-spectrum light (Earth normal, they said, though few of us had ever stood under Earth's sun), shone on hair slicked back neat enough for review by an Inspector General. And even after all his years in space, he didn't show so much as a hint of gray.

Damn the man, how could he look like such an insider, with that shining hair and a face that looked like it wanted to smile and be smiled back on, yet abandon his ship—and a bioship at that?

He hadn't just dishonored us all; he had betrayed us, and

with the discovery of *Irian Jaya* by a Tokugawan ship, he had exposed us all to our former enemies. We were all disgraced.

Now, there he sat, awaiting judgment that couldn't be enough, no matter what it was: well-groomed, erect, attentive—and terrifying. After all, if a man like Jim could cut and run, how about the rest of us?

How many of us can prove our courage beyond doubt? Everyone goes through the training that tries to cast out fear; everyone talks of what they'll do—what they hope they'll do, and everyone, if we're honest enough to admit it, wakes in the night fearing that the moment has come, we've failed at the test, and *everybody knows*.

Ragozinksi's eyes flicked from Jim to some inward calibration of his own morality, while junior officers shifted in their seats. Jim's very existence questioned our courage.

I had sterling credentials right now as Alliance's Oldest Surviving Shipsicle, but I hadn't done anything: simply followed my captain's orders (notwithstanding my first protest at leaving him), closed my eyes, and gasped until the drugs took hold.

My real test had begun the instant the ice had melted, brain activity started up again, my body temp returned to normal, and I knew I'd drifted through twenty years and one war that had damn near blasted us back to before the space age. For me, the test of my courage wasn't having lived through the war, because I really hadn't. My test was how I was going to survive the peace. And so far, I had no answers. I'd always been out and doing: I couldn't see myself as a pensioner downworld, and, until Sickbay cleared me and my cranky lifesigns, I probably wasn't going anywhere.

If Jim could break, I could break. Any of us could. That was the truth, and it was a harder truth to face than Jim's . . . aberration.

Conrad Ragozinski turned toward Jim, wet his lips, and turned away as if studying another slow-motion catastrophe. The days had stamped stress lines and brackets on his face, as crude as the cheap imitations of medals they'd given me to wear. Only his uniform and his will seemed to hold him at attention.

Ryutaro Jones leaned over me with that damned outsiders' solicitude that made me feel about the age of the Big Bang.

"I heard you checked out of Sickbay, Commander. Was that wise?"

"They needed the berth," I said, managing at the last instant not to add "you idiot" at the youngster. Jones' eyes lit with a very un-reporter-like admiration.

Idiot probably thought I was being altruistic. Fleet could use a little altruism around here, so I said it anyway. Besides, it was true. For some inexplicable reason, Jones had taken a liking to me. He wasn't one of us the way Jim was, but you couldn't help liking him back. But then, I'd liked Jim, too. . . .

"I had an entire ward to myself before the crash," I told him. "It's hotbunked now: two borderline cardiac transplants, three broken legs, a couple cases of trampling as people tried to get to the pods; the usual number of post-traumatic stress disorder nightmares, and one man who's catatonic because all he could reach in time was a survival bubble, not a pod, and he was agoraphobic."

Jones nodded. Little bastard probably had interviewed them all already. *Including* the catatonic.

Wasn't it about time for him to finish up here and start on his next project? Someone should suggest it to him. His long-lost cousin Hashimoto had departed on *Divine Wind,* leaving Jones with an invitation to visit Tokugawa any time, the first time any Alliance citizen had been so welcomed since the War. Hell, he'd be able to beat Marshall Emeritus Becker into the sector; assuming he had a mind to go.

But no, Jones had to stick around, recording our particular disaster.

"I heard Astro-Pharm's trying to slap an injunction on Fleet to recover its bioship," he said.

Right. And New Amman was sending an ambassador to demand that *Irian Jaya* be sent on its way to deliver its cargo, as if the people in Freeze were cattle delayed en route to market. I'd heard that from Marshal Becker at dinner. To my surprise, more than Medstaff wanted my company. For once in my life, I was a social asset. No word from Conrad, though, but then there wouldn't be, seeing that I had an interest in this ordeal and he was presiding.

Either way, I'd put any money the Pensions board said I had on my bet that Jones wouldn't be going back to Earth to pick up his inheritance any time soon. Damn that boy. He was the sort who could fall into a recycling vat and come up smelling like roses, whatever they were. Not like my old shipmate Jim. Or his judge.

Ryutaro Jones slipped me an insulated flask that warmed my hands. "Calories," he said. "That coffee's real, and so's the sugar. Drink up. Don't worry about it. I'm making new sales now that the Terra blockade's over. You need it. By the way, Tom Ankeny says, crowding be damned, you can call him if your meds need adjusting. And you can rely on me."

You've already got my story, boy. Or do you think I've got another one in me? If that meant I had a future, I'd take the spoiled little newspuke's flask and welcome.

The coffee was hot and sweet, worth the godawful price Jones must have paid for the real thing. It warmed me all the way down, and the caffeine had enough of a kick, like adrenaline to a dying heart, to jolt me into an awareness I'd have preferred to do without.

But the chrono barely seemed to have budged from the last time I looked at it. Percussive maintenance, I thought. Someone hit the damn thing. Someone hit *something*.

"Look at this new witness," Jones whispered at me. "This Heller. You think there's anything personal there worth an interview?"

"Quiet!" For another moment, I hated the bright, glossy youngster with his golden skin and his sharp eyes. Damn him, he was so observant he was cruel.

Heller had been tech crew on board the *Irian Jaya* and a research scientist when she was on groundside rotation.

Pretty, I thought. Glossy hair, fresh skin, a downsider's way of moving. Not as young as she looked, which was probably lost on every man in the room. After all, *she* wasn't the Worlds' Oldest Corpsicle.

"Drugs, sir?" Heller tilted her head at Conrad Ragozinski after he cleared his throat, reminding her he was waiting. "He barely accessed his pharm card. Sure, he drank coffee. A lot of coffee. Said you did that in Fleet. He even showed us how to make it right. If you call that stuff right. How you all don't get ulcers . . ."

I had another sip from Jones' flask. I hated to admit it, but it was much better than Fleet coffee. A ripple of amusement went around the room, and Ragozinski gestured. *Get back to the story.*

She shook her head. "He was always so calm. When Mr. Bokassa's weapon malfunctioned, he practically ran the length of the ship and threw it in the HazMat chute himself. That's why . . ." Deep brown eyes traveled reluctantly over to Jim, clung, then released, even more reluctantly. "Why he did what he did? It wasn't drugs, sir. I don't know what it was. We're both Aveners, so we got along. Aven doesn't tend to produce terribly excitable people. I'm not a psych, but I can't think of any reason for what he did except . . . it was the war, it had to be. He just snapped. He's only human, and humans make mistakes. Please, sir, can't you see that he gets the therapy he needs?" Heller's eyes filled.

"Thank you, Doctor," Ragozinski interrupted before she could distract the court again. His eyes rested on her—so fresh, so untouched by *Jaya*'s ordeal, so alien in her thoughts—as if she were one of her own lab specimens.

He flicked a glance at Jim, who shook his head as he had at every witness since the trial began.

Jones made a sound like a cat's hunting reflex, and I hoped to hell Heller could get out of there before Jones got through to her.

Move, I wished the chrono. *For God's sake move, so we can get out of here.*

The red lights no more blinked than the ones on the security cameras. One of the LEDs was broken. Even if the chrono was working, how could I be sure it was accurate?

"No questions?" Ragozinsky asked. The question was ritual: Jim had declined to cross-examine any of the witnesses so far.

Jim looked down.

"Very well then, Doctor. You are dismissed."

She nodded, tried to get Jim to meet her eyes, then shook her head. Her glossy helmet of chestnut hair swung at chin length. Then, she turned and left the room, slowly, as if a funeral had just ended.

"Commodore Ragozinski looks like hell," Jones murmured to himself. I didn't want to look at any of them. Astonishing: the chrono had actually ticked down one more minute.

Conrad rose and struck the bell. "This court will recess for fifteen minutes," he proclaimed, and strode to the door that led to whatever spare closet they'd set up as judge's chambers.

Outside, I was jumped by two reporters, whom Jones could sandbag, and a shrink, trying to sandbag me. Evasive action engulfed my attention. Anything I said could be used against me—to make me sound like a senile fool on every known Alliance 'Net and some of the bootleg ones, or to retire me—or commit me permanently. My enemies weren't Secess' any more; they were my damned well-wishers.

No, I matched the psych's earnestness and false candor with fake sincerity of my own. I didn't agree I was being morbid in attending my old shipmate's trial. I was there at the request of Commodore Ragozinski and—inspiration struck, and I produced the worst officialese of my soon-to-be-curtailed career—I was attempting to "engage myself in the here and now."

Behind her back, Jones, overhearing, rolled his eyes at me. He hadn't started out after Heller. I was touched. Maybe all his stories about liking me weren't just a ploy to get me to spill my guts.

The psych pronounced her benediction on my psychobabble—talk about using the enemy's tactics! Another light flashed, and I got to extricate myself just as the trial was about to start again.

Staying in Freeze would have been a whole lot easier.

I SLIPPED BACK INTO MY CHAIR. RANK HATH ITS PRIVILEGE. No one on station would dare plant his butt in the seat reserved for Cam Marlow.

A newcomer, tall and thin and dressed in gray, not Fleet blue, entered the witness box. Jones hissed. *Better work on your control, boy, if you're going to Tokugawa.*

The witness was familiar to me. It was that Freiherr von Leinigen I'd met at the All-Services Club, the death-before-dishonor aristocrat from Abendstern. A very hostile witness indeed.

The Abendsterner inclined his head, clicked his heels, then stood at attention as he affirmed his willingness to testify. "My life answers for my truth," he added, with some sort of ritual gesture that I suppose people on Abendstern understand. He couldn't be touching a knife. Security had seen to that.

Visibly, the Freiherr tolerated the litany of questions Ragozinski asked as the people in the room devoured him with their eyes: an Abendsterner here. An Abendsterner, who will not shoot at us. An Abendsterner whose presence here is a reflection on us. An Abendsterner who just stood as if on review, permitting the stares.

Finally, he held up an imperious hand.

"Sir, I am of Abendstern. What I understand is discipline, the discipline that your distinguished record—sometimes against my kinsmen"—Ragozinski met his stately head inclination with one of his own—"shows that you understand. It is not just the ability to stand fire and return it. Discipline protects us from the thoughts that surface during the dark watches of ship's night. The weak despair; the disciplined hold their faith."

"Well, yes," Ragozinski said. "But, Freiherr, may we ask

what you were doing on board *Divine Wind*?"

Von Leinigen raised two pale brows in a face that, although unlined, was hollowed at the temples and beneath sharp cheekbones: he looked too fastidious to be the fighting man he probably still was. With his bone structure and the genetic engineering that Abendstern was famous—or notorious—for, he could have been anywhere from forty to eighty-five.

I wonder if they cloned him. His descendants might have been the Fighting Star that took out Hardcastle. *No, they were Frekans.* The memory lapse made me sweat.

"You could say I was on a fact-finding mission."

A murmur heated the crowded room.

"I have given my oath," von Leinigen reminded the murmurers.

Ragozinski nodded. "The courtroom will observe courtesy or I will clear it. Tell me, Freiherr, how did your connection with *Irian Jaya* come about?"

"*Divine Wind*'s scanners picked up its distress signal. The *Jaya* was running, but slowly. Its scoops had sustained damage in an ion storm and, upon visual confirmation of sensor evidence, we ferried over a repair crew, security, and duty officers."

"Did you think that this might be a trap? A decoy?"

The Abendsterner's face grew remote. "It would have been a highly dishonorable trap, using a bioship as bait. And yet"—he glanced around the room, his nostrils flaring as his glance fell briefly on Jim—"we have seen such things done."

Damn, was that chronometer broken?

"Although you were concerned that it might be a trap, you stayed with *Jaya* when *Divine Wind* took it in tow, is that right?"

"*Divine Wind*'s officers had duties of their own. It was my duty, as I saw it, to assist them. And, when I saw that we relieved a bioship, it became my honor to restore hope to New Hope."

The aristocrat smiled thinly. Some recess of my brain

thawed, producing the knowledge that Amman meant hope in one of the languages of Old Earth.

"Why a bioship more than any other type of ship, sir?"

"Commodore, Abendstern breeds its sons and daughters to duty. Chief of all duties, as we see it, is the coding in our genes. A man may disobey orders." The Freiherr's voice went chill with contempt. "He may prove to be a coward. In either case, the law exacts its rightful penalties. But to abandon the genetic material of one's race, to violate the trust to preserve it—how one can do this, I do not understand."

"So you stood watch on *Irian Jaya,* not knowing whether or not her crew would turn on you?"

"Civilian crew," von Leinigen said. "The doctor who spoke last told how their . . . arms officer . . . attempted to train them. I did not expect opposition there."

"And scavengers? Ms. Vartanesyan from the shipyards has testified that *Irian Jaya* was in no condition to fight when you brought her in."

"Scavengers are undisciplined scum," the Abendsterner said. "From time to time, they may overpower a better ship through sheer ferocity. But it is one's duty to oppose them, even for the ship of an enemy. A former enemy," he corrected himself with a slight bow.

"He probably has a script," whispered Ryutaro Jones.

"You'd be the clever one who knows that," I told him. "Hashimoto-sama probably told you."

"Why is that?" Ragozinski practically needed a tractor beam to pull out those words.

"Sooner or later, some orders cannot be followed, some duties cannot be shirked. Beyond the laws, there are unwritten laws. Including not abandoning a ship—any ship—in such distress as your *Irian Jaya.* If mine was the misfortune to do so," again, a skeptical lift of one fastidious eyebrow, "I should not survive it."

The prosecution had no questions.

"Questions?" The Board offered the Freiherr to Jim.

Again, he shook his head.

"Are you planning to offer no defense?" Ragozinski demanded. "Even at this stage of your examination, you know you can request counsel."

Was that pleading I heard in Ragozinski's hoarse voice? Jim was—had been—one of us: why didn't he put up a fight?

Probably for the same reason he fled *Irian Jaya*.

Maybe he just didn't know. Or maybe the worst punishment he could think of was sitting and watching his disgrace tick nearer and nearer to him with every flash of that damned chronometer as his former crew spoke, and his former enemy studied him as if he were a particularly disgusting lab specimen.

"A reminder, Commodore," von Leinigen's cool tenor cut across the room. "I hardly think that the defendant has any questions to ask that I would understand. Nevertheless, I assure you I accept it as my duty to comply. . . ."

Contempt for what was still a member of the Fleet by a former enemy hung in the room. Von Leinigen watched: would anyone be such a fool as to challenge him—over what we all believed, even though it was an Abendsterner saying it?

"Indeed? I thought not."

"Dismissed, Freiherr. This court thanks you for your courtesy. And your service to the *Irian Jaya*." You'd have thought a tractor beam had pulled the gratitude out of him.

Someone seemed to have applied the same tractor beam to the chrono. Almost quitting time. Almost. Thank God.

"Sir." The Abendsterner drew himself up and bowed stiffly, with the faintest clicking of his heels. He stalked down the length of the courtroom, his measured footsteps seeming to crush half the air and all the honor in the room.

Jones let out his breath in a long sigh of relief. "Hashimoto-sama says the Freiherr is one tough bastard."

"Hashimoto-sama never used language like that. Or questioned an ally's parentage."

"Not among strangers," Jones told me with a grin. "I'm family."

"God help you," I retorted. We shouldn't have been talking—Conrad had enough problems—but it took up time.

The Board of Inquiry muttered, back and forth along its long table.

Adjourn the court. Adjourn it. Please.

Ragozinski rose, struck the archaic brass bell across from his place. Story was, it had come all the way from Earth. It glowed, polished by untold generations of ensigns, reflecting the room. Distorting everything in its field.

"This court will be adjourned until oh-nine-hundred tomorrow," he announced.

There's a story that was old even before the first ships left Earth: once a year, out of mercy, Judas is let out of hell and goes and sits on an iceberg. That's what adjournment felt like that day.

"Well." Ryutaro Jones raised a hand. He even succeeded in being breezy. "I'm going to file today's story. You'll probably be able to hear my editor screaming through the interstellar medium when he gets the message I'm not going back to Earth."

I paused, not precisely sure why.

"You all right, Commander?"

"Follow-up story, Jones?" I asked.

"Hold your fire, ma'am!" he laughed. "No, no follow-up story. An inquiry, as they always told me, about a lady's health."

"Well, this lady's a free woman."

Wasn't as if I had dinner plans either. Last night's dinner with the Marshall Emeritus had been worse than being on review. I'd hinted about getting cleared to return to the service; he'd hinted about the Relief Service, and I'd bitten my tongue before I could blurt out that light blue wasn't my color. I had no objections to my uniform; just to putting on a Blue Helm as a consolation prize. If I ventured out by myself to any of the station's "good" restaurants, I might run into the likes of him or even—Freeze the thought—von Leinigen. But I didn't want to sit in my cabin, knowing that the station was crammed, but the Famous Shipsicle rated a room all to herself.

Jones, I'd heard, could be pleasant enough company. *Come to dinner:* the invitation trembled on my tongue. What would he make of it?

"Incoming." Jones gestured at the shiny young officer coming up to me and standing at my shoulder as if a noisier announcement of her presence would have caused her uniform to catch fire. INDIRA CHANDANANI, her badge said. The cording on her shoulder told me she was a staff officer, a junior aide.

"Commander?" she asked. The fabric of her uniform still reeked from the dye. As new as mine—and as cheap. "Begging the Commander's pardon, but Commodore Ragozinski's compliments, and if you could spare him a few moments of your time?"

Another chronometer hung overhead in the corridor.

"Back in there?" I gestured with my chin at the impromptu courtroom. Jones was treating me to a wide grin I definitely didn't need. I turned my back on him.

"The judge's chambers, ma'am. If you will follow me . . ."

"I'll call you later," Jones shouted after me. He even managed not to make it sound like a threat, and I could almost believe it.

"Lead on, Ms. Chandanani," I said.

10

"Lieutenant Commander Marlow, sir." Polite young woman, this Chandanani. Her complexion should have been ruddy brown, but corridor lighting turned it gray, tacking years onto her apparent age.

Ragozinski had always insisted on working with the best. She led me past the courtroom and through another door. I tried to remember this station's schematics. Apparently, judge's chambers weren't the temporary closet I'd expected, but a private room near the All-Services Club. Trust Conrad to make the best of things.

"Good to see you, Cam," said my old friend. "Dismissed, Indira."

The ensign let the door slide closed, effacing herself. As the door sealed, lights flickered *orange/yellow/red,* and I heard a faint whir. The room came equipped with its own sound system, which didn't just suppress noise, but transmitted a stream of non-controversial, easily decrypted babble to potential eavesdroppers.

"State secrets?" I asked as he rose from his chair to greet me. His hands went out as if to clasp my shoulders, then dropped. Which one of us needed the support?

I'd waked to see my old classmate, inexplicably twenty years older than I remembered. I'd seen the Commodore in the courtroom, brass and polish holding together on sheer nerve. Now, as Conrad's face flushed, I took a step back. How long out of Freeze was I? Long enough to see two riots, a crash, and now, a senior officer losing it.

"Cam, tell me," Ragozinski demanded. "You served with the idiot. What the fuck does he think he's doing?" The words came out in a bellow that echoed off the walls.

"Which idiot does the Commodore mean?" I asked.

"Oh hell, Cam. Sit down. And I'm still Conrad to you, at least in private. Let's start over. Your friend Jim. No, don't bristle at me. You think I don't know what sitting and watching the man hang himself this past week has cost you?"

Are you projecting, sir? If I had to ask questions like that, I'd been spending too much time with the shrinks. I tried out a smile on Conrad, hoping he'd scramble himself back together somehow.

"Here, let me get us some coffee."

A silver pot steamed on the heat element inset in the desk. He poured into blue and silver Fleet china, chipped now, but there was no time or funds for amenities.

"Sugar?" he asked. "It'll kill the taste. Pot was on this morning when I left the place."

You didn't so much drink the stuff as wrestle it into your gut, where, no doubt, it would do things that would make Sickbay flinch.

Conrad looked as if he'd been doing a lot of wrestling. And losing.

"That'll warm you," he said. "Those shivers are psychosomatic, that's what the doctors told me. Your body still thinks it's cold." And how, dammit, did he get the medics to talk to him?

He steadied my hand around the archaic design of cup and saucer. His fingers were hot and dry.

"Sit down, Cam. Let's start over," he said, watching me settle into a chair padded in some nappy synsilk in Fleet blue. "Any idea what this idiot thinks he's doing?"

"Jones thinks Jim's punishing himself," I said.

"Why don't we get youngsters like Jones in Fleet anymore?" Ragozinksi said. "I'd like to've had the training of this one. He's too damn smart for our own good. Still, he seems to like you, which is about the only piece of luck we've got right now. Do you agree with him?"

I nodded. "I also think since Jim . . . left *Jaya,* he's been in a kind of Freeze state too. As if he's done something that has absolutely destroyed every image he's ever had about himself, everything he's ever believed in. He can't believe that he's being accused of desertion because he can't believe he did it."

"Those things cancel each other out."

"Just the way that idiotic leap he took cancels out everything he ever stood for. You heard that woman Heller. He was doing a damn good job, doing what they paid him to do, in the face of some pretty nasty opposition from *Jaya*'s captain. He was starting to make a place for himself. And then, this. . . ." I shook my head and fought down another sip of the thick coffee. Where was Jones and his flask when I needed them? The sugar, gray from sealed storage, only made the Fleet coffee worse.

"Jim can't believe it." I couldn't believe I'd used his name.

"He didn't just abandon ship and crew," Ragozinski said. "But if he'd thought out his whole life how to humiliate Fleet, how to shoot everything we stand for out an airlock in its underwear, he couldn't be doing a better job. And in front of men like Jones and that damned Abendsterner who stands there with his heel clicks and his talk about honor, and you just know he's planning what he'll say in his report to his Autarchs. Probably saying, 'Why'd we make peace with these people, when we could just sit tight and watch them fall apart all by themselves?' "

"The Autarchs sealed the agreement?" I couldn't help making it sound like a question. "If they think like he does, they'll make good on their word." I shook my head, surprised to hear myself defending something that had shaken my world on wakeup.

Ragozinski began to slam his fist down on the table, then brought it down more gently. *Doesn't do to traumatize your best public relations asset, does it, Conrad? Not to mention antagonizing an old friend.*

"Sorry, Cam. I hate to dump all this on you after . . ."

"Hey, I've had twenty years' leave; about time I earned my pay," I said.

"You should be all right," he said. "Pension and Disability's squabbling with Records even as we speak. If you need a loan to tide you over . . ."

That was Conrad as I remembered him. Always sure he was in charge of everyone else's well-being. Always finding out what was none of his business, except that he made it so—out of the best possible motives. Conrad Knew Best. That damnable assumption.

It had driven us into shouting matches at the Academy. For that matter, it had meant, beyond a shared leave or two, that when it came time to leave him for my ship, I hadn't hesitated.

I'd sent a gift when he married Leesa—don't know if they got it, but if they did, he probably knew to a fraction what it cost. I remembered Leesa from the Academy. Outdoors-looking for a spacer, very fit and well-adjusted. She'd been a decent sort of officer, the kind who spends an entire career as a lieutenant or maybe lieutenant commander if she's lucky. Conrad had chosen well: she was the sort of woman who could put up with a one-career, two-person partnership. Rest her soul, I'd heard she'd died in the defense of Santayana, tougher, at the end of her life, than anyone had thought she could be. I wrote, but didn't know if he'd gotten the transmission. That was when Conrad switched to afterburners on his career track.

And then *Hardcastle* took the hits that Froze me.

I saw Conrad's face. Twenty years of thinking he was responsible for everyone and twenty years of watching them die. Not being able to protect Leesa or anyone else. And now Jim. And me.

"Thanks, old friend," I said. "I'll be all right." I put my hand on his arm and felt its sturdiness.

"You always were," he said, and turned away. "I heard you had dinner with Marshal Becker. Has he started to recruit you for the Blue Helms yet?"

I shrugged. "Damn, Conrad, did you have that poor old man wired for sound or just the station?"

"Small station," he said. "People get to know other people's business. And you . . ."

I found myself laughing as I parried. "These days, I guess I'm everybody's business. Just as Jim is."

Counterthrust, Conrad. What will you do with it?

"If I can't stay in Fleet, I'd rather do relief work than fly a desk, wouldn't you? What I really want would be for Medical to clear me to return to active duty."

This is a test, I thought. Is *this a test? Do I want it to be?*

I could see his back tense through the dress uniform tunic. "They . . . they could. If they were approached correctly. Officers with the real training, the full four years that we got, are rare. The last years of the war, they were graduating them after eighteen months, sometimes less."

You've already offered me a loan. What are you offering me now? Besides a chance to hang onto the only home I've known?

"What do you want of me, Conrad?" I hadn't slept through the past twenty years to sip bad coffee and dance around facts, when the fact was that my oldest surviving friend had just tried to bribe me. "You must want it pretty bad if you're prepared to scuttle the ethics of a lifetime."

He didn't so much as flinch. He turned and paced about the conference room. From the back, he wasn't Conrad; he was the Commodore, responsible not just for the friends he took on, but for ships and their thousands of crew.

"We're limping along, Cam. I don't know if you've had time to brief yourself, but we came out of this war on our knees, and all that's saved us is that the Secess' were in just as bad shape.

"Appropriations are down, and Alliance is looking for ways to cut them further. All we've got is our reputation for decency, for protecting our people. Then, here comes this damned fool who deserts a bioship, for God's sake. Now, we could explain away an atrocity more easily. People go berserk in combat all the time, and what you do is get them away, punish or heal them or write them off—whatever, for the good of the service."

He whirled, and I saw his face age twenty more years before my eyes. "What I've got to be concerned about is Fleet's overall reputation. Decades of service, of endurance, of trust—once that's broken, there's no going back. And that bastard on trial is killing us."

Now, I could see how tension knotted his muscles. A word to the physicians . . . get him declared unfit for duty.

"Spit it out, Conrad," I said in a voice I scarcely recognized.

"I'm getting some pressure to put you on the stand," Conrad told me.

I snorted. "So people can look at me or hear me, not an Abendsterner, talk about duty, honor, homeworld? They haven't thought the whole thing through. It would backfire."

Conrad watched me levelly. *Take the stand. Make nice for the reporters. And what then? The next ship? What if I came up damaged in some way the medics hadn't been able to find yet?*

"You used to know better than this, Conrad. If I'm sworn in, I've got to answer truthfully. Jim wasn't half-bad on the *Hardcastle*. You really want me to be a character witness for him? I can't believe you'd want me to lie."

Conrad laughed. "God forbid," he said. "You know, you had it easy. Drifting through the war, unconscious. Now, you have the luxury of keeping your hands clean while—"

I held up a hand. A clean hand. "The Conrad Ragozinski I knew twenty years ago didn't think clean hands were a luxury."

I lowered my eyes to my half-empty cup. Cooling oil seemed to turn the coffee's surface iridescent, and I set the unpalatable stuff aside to face the unpalatable truth. For the past twenty years I'd been drifting, outside human contact, outside human references. And now I was back, but those twenty years had put me outside the bounds. I was safe, the way confessors or therapists are safe. And, unless I figured out my own moves, I was a piece to be moved on other people's chessboards.

Including my oldest friend's. If Conrad turned against me, there would be no one I knew from before Freeze. Except Jim, and he was less than no one.

I was getting the shakes again. Conrad had called them psychosomatic. Now, I had reason to shiver. I shut my eyes before the ice could hit them once again.

Walking wounded, I told myself. *You're freezing and he's burnt out.*

"We shouldn't be having this talk, and you know it," I said. "I'm going to forget everything you said. Except, of course, the fact that you were concerned I might need help, for which

I thank you. As you say, I've got money. And I can make it into the Blue Helms all by myself, Conrad, and once I do, D&P can sit on my retirement until . . . well, they can sit on it and rotate."

"You're tired," Conrad said, rising. His face was tight, expressionless. "I should let you go rest. Promise you'll call MedCenter."

Again, Conrad Knew Best.

My face twisted into a grimace that approximated a smile accurately enough to convince him. "I'll go commune with the telemetry they left in my cell. Takes up half the cubic."

I saluted my old friend, then retreated.

SOME COMPASSIONATE TECH HAD JIGGERED THE LIFE-support setting in my cabin. It wasn't just warm, it was tropical by station standards, and the water—real water, if recycled—in the attached head ran hot and unmetered: no timer on this shower.

Once I'd dripped dry and wrapped myself in two layers of shipsuits, I hitched myself up to the monitors Tom Ankeny had set up for me and taught me to use. *Mirror, mirror on the wall . . .*

Telemetry said I was in perfect shape for someone who'd spent the last twenty years in cryonic suspension. I plucked off the leads. Apparently, I was going to live, even if living felt a whole lot like Freeze.

The question was, what else was I going to do?

Catch up, I supposed, and so I turned to what seemed like the endless stack of taped briefings Psych was wetting itself to provide. It was like being back at the Academy: spending my nights studying. As I fed the wafers into my headset, stacking them for quicker feed and processing, a pounding on my door brought me around. I reached for the sidearm I no longer owned and glanced at the Station Status Monitor. SSM didn't show any kind of alert.

Why would anyone pound on my door when . . .

Messages would be recorded. Messages could be retrieved.

In the shape I was in, I was no match for anyone on station. I opened the door to the unlikely spectacle of Conrad glancing down the corridor as he tried to make his considerable bulk appear no more than a speck upon a drab bulkhead.

His "I've got to talk with you" collided with my "I take it this is off the record" as he slipped into my cabin, and I closed the door behind him. I had two chairs, one piled with various relics from Sickbay, and my bunk. He sank down on the chair, setting his elbows on my small table, and leaned forward in "let's deal" mode.

"I meant what I told you earlier," he said.

I let my lips thin. "You told me a lot of things. Which do you mean? Sorry. I'd offer you a drink, but they're keeping me sober. Water all right?"

He waved aside my offer.

"About Jim, dammit," he said.

"I can't be a hostile witness," I said. "I told you. My experience of him . . . at the most, all I can do is sit up there and be an object lesson. And every reporter on the station will know that you're grandstanding. Is that what you want?"

"I want him to disappear, dammit," Conrad said. He took the glass of water I handed him and drained it as if he wished it were a hell of a lot stronger.

I took a deep breath and borrowed Ryutaro Jones' flippant tone. "If you're getting up your nerve to tell me, a week out of Freeze and still wobbly, you want me to turn assassin, you can forget it!" It was so preposterous, it forced a laugh from him.

"I'm serious, Cam. His presence—this goddamned trial—is killing us. Look: the other *Jaya* senior officers cut and ran. If Jim can abandon a bioship, why wouldn't he run out on his trial? He should never have insisted on it in the first place. We've got to get him out of here, Cam."

I blinked at him. Either he took it for encouragement, or, more likely, he was so intent on his tactics that he forgot anyone else was in the room. "I've got computer techs who can engineer the fund transfer from my own retirement account, set up a new ID." Conrad rose and paced, energy flowing back into his movements. "We'll get him off-station, to someplace quiet where he can . . . I don't know how people do these things. Change his name. Dye his hair. Hide for the rest of his life, and let us clean this mess up."

A lifetime's service and it came to this: Jim had chosen to jump. Ragozinski, faced with that decision, dreamed of suborning Fleet justice for the good of the service.

"And if this gets out?" I asked. "What then? Your reputation gets sunk lower than Jim's—nothing's worse than a war hero gone bad, and now they've lost me, too—their prize shipsicle, melted into a dirty puddle. So everyone's worse off than we were. Doesn't sound like good tactics to me."

Conrad sunk visibly into his chair, sighing as the strength went out of him. I managed not to wrap my arms around myself to hold in the warmth of my shipsuit. And then I fought not to wrap my arms around my friend, my oldest friend, my only friend, who was as cold as I and in more pain. The air circulating in the tiny cabin whispered to us of cold and loneliness and an answer to them.

"Look: Fleet's got a vested interest in seeing this is cleared up. We'd get him safely away, and—"

"And then what?" How far would he go? For that matter, how far had he gone?

"You could get him away yourself, maybe, on your own ship. . . ."

The Blue Helms were planning to offer me my own ship? I must have dazzled Becker at dinner. Or would Conrad's bribes extend to returning me to active duty?

I'd been spending too much time with the medics, that was for sure. What was his blood pressure like now? What would the psychs think of Conrad's state of mind?

I could stop this right now, I thought. I sat on my bunk, opposite Conrad. All I had to do was press the panic button, and the medics would come.

But you won't, the air whispered to me.

Conrad might hint, he might try—ineptly—to bribe. But he was my friend and he had come to me with this scheme of his because he trusted me and because, even though the war had left him as hollow as I was cold, he still cared. Or fought to care.

Just as I did.

"Cam, you know I'm right," he said and smiled at me—the remnants of the enthusiastic grin I remembered from a midshipman who'd gotten gloriously, gaudily drunk and proclaimed, "Give me a place to stand, and I will save the worlds."

Close your eyes, Cam. Don't let him see how they fill. In a little while, the tears will freeze, and then you'll be safe again.

"Once this is through, I'm heading back to Earth. I've more than earned my passage Home. Hell, maybe I'll write my memoirs." He even managed a brief grin. His eyes met mine, then fell. He shifted, as if trying to ease the aches that years of tension had twisted into his shoulders. What would his shoulders feel like under my hands? At one time, I knew.

"Send me a copy." I tried to match his tone. We had steered this course before, after all, and gone our separate ways.

"Hell, you can buy one. Pensions and Disability says you're getting interest on all your back pay. Compounded over twenty years. And if you go back in . . ."

"We don't know that," I reminded Conrad. "We don't know if Jim would even cooperate."

"Ask him, Cam," he urged. "Promise me you'll ask him. Of all the people on this station, I can't think of a person likelier to influence him than you." He reached out and captured my hands. He did trust me. And his hands were warm.

"And if he won't go?" I asked gently. "Or he won't go till after the trial's over."

Conrad lowered his head. "We still have to get him away. Somewhere. Cam . . . you're shaking again."

"I don't have a whole lot of reserves, Conrad," I said. My voice broke, and I hated myself for it.

"I know," he said. And came to sit beside me on the bunk. His arms went around me.

"My God, Cam, you're freezing! Do you want me to call the medics?"

A voice I didn't recognize as my own broke as it said, "Just hold me." His tunic was coarse against my face, but his arms around me were more real than anything I'd felt since I waked.

"You need to be warm," he muttered. "Let me warm you. Please."

I ran my hands down his back. Tight muscles loosened, and he pressed against me, seeking comfort. Our clothing felt coarse, intrusive under our hands, so we shed it.

"Cam, you're so young!" he said, and stroked my cheek.

After all these years, I was almost afraid to look at him. My own newly restored body was enough of a mystery to me. His was over twenty years older than I remembered it, and the years hadn't been kind to him. I could feel weariness flow out of him as he pulled me close. His hands trembled. I dimmed the lights.

For awhile, his body moving over mine held all the warmth in all the worlds. I clasped him tightly to me, whispering, encouraging him, hoping for more, but it was not enough. It just wasn't going to work.

"Cam," he whispered. "I'm sorry. I just don't know what to say. This damn trial . . ."

He tried to push away from me, but I pulled him back.

"It doesn't matter," I told him. "Stay with me. This is enough," I told him. And hoped he believed me. Hoped it sounded like the truth.

He tried again. For a while longer, his hands and lips and arms warmed me. For all I know, my touch warmed him too. Then he rolled away, only back against the pillow, but it felt like lightyears.

I heard him urge me to sleep, his lips moving against my

shoulder. Tenderness, he could summon, if not passion. Well, I would take it and be glad.

I whispered, "Aye, sir," felt, as much as heard, him chuckle, and slept.

I did not dream.

When I woke, he was gone. And I was not surprised.

My message light glowed steadily. Becker, inviting me to breakfast. Damn near a direct order. Conrad's information, as always, had been good. But, over the past twenty years, his execution had fallen apart. If he juggled files to get me back into the service, the time might come when I, like Jim, faced a board and the fervent curses of Fleet. The Blue Helms were preferable by far. If I had to leave Fleet, I'd leave with clean hands.

And hands that were warmer than they'd been since I woke up.

11

I'd arranged to sit with the Marshal Emeritus when Jim's sentence was announced. Even though I still wore Fleet uniform, Jones raised his eyebrows and flashed me a good-luck sign, and I knew he'd be calibrating the ratings consequences of "Shipsicle Joins Blue Helms" with "Bioship Deserter Expelled from Fleet" on the various Nets that published him. Ragozinski, entering with his board, saw me too.

And looked away. We had not spoken since he had left me while I slept. We had barely glanced at each other across the courtroom.

Beside me, the Marshal cleared his throat. He was going to be my CO once my discharge took effect: I owed him my attention.

"About your young friend's sentence," Abram Becker began. He had to be one of the oldest people on active duty in the Alliance, and he could make a secret surrender itself even faster than Conrad. More to the point, he could do so without making it betray himself.

"Can't we at least wait till sentence is pronounced?" I muttered. Blue Helms didn't just guard the law like Fleet; they came in and swept up after it.

I glanced over at Jim: still groomed, still wrapped in what the shrinks would call denial. *This can't be happening to* me. Becker chuckled. "You must be the one person here who still cares about that. Good for you, Commander. Cam, if I may."

"I feel like I'm watching a man being killed."

"Precisely. And everyone else is watching to see if he'll flinch from the death blow."

"And you, sir?"

"Me? I want to see that too. He is an interesting case, your young friend," mused Becker. Spatulate, age-spotted fingers came up and massaged his temples. "Will he go up, or will he come down?"

Briefly, I reconsidered a career in the Blue Helms. Becker was pondering a question the answer to which seemed obvious. A man broken from Fleet for desertion and cowardice had only one trajectory left: down, and never mind the fact that there is no local vertical in space. It was inevitable. Even if I had gone on the witness stand and begged. Even if I had taken Conrad's suggestion and tried to convince Jim to disappear.

For awhile, the remnants of Jim's membership in human society—his *belongingness,* we could call it—would protect him. But ultimately, wherever he went, he'd face exposure, trial by a thousand thousand pair of accusing eyes, and he would retreat to find himself sucked into enterprises of lower and lower worth the way a derelict falls into a gravity well, is drawn into atmosphere, and is consumed to ash.

That could have happened to *Irian Jaya* when Jim abandoned it, and here I was practically mourning him. Even now, he was still one of us. Would he end up as victim or victimizer? "You ask as if there could be any question, sir," I said. Ragozinksi was straightening his documents, his shoulders, the order of his Board. The sentence was only moments away.

"There are always questions. As I said before, an interesting man, your friend. Soiled past use for some purposes; still good enough for others; and far too good for many," Becker added. "I think the scavenger who tried to play upon his anger would be very surprised. In fact, I think there's morality in your Jim yet. Certainly, there are enterprises for which I might well seek out a man like him, now that he has leapt the stone wall between illusion and his actual fate. . . ."

"The stone wall?" I asked. It had overtones of one of Becker's longer speeches.

"Later. See, the Commodore is rising."

Jim rose too. Wearing his glossy, inquiet illusion along with the uniform he was told he no longer had a right to, Jim stood and heard himself proclaimed derelict, coward, and deserter. Heard himself sentenced to death, but that sentence commuted in light of clause . . . however many clauses . . . in the armistice between Alliance and Secess'.

At least Freiherr von Leinigen, with a kind of bleak mercy, had stayed away, perhaps to spare the rest of us. We didn't know where to put our eyes. We were all complicit. And Jim, who'd actually abandoned that ship, listened to the words that damned him and didn't so much as flush.

The Commodore struck the bell and pronounced the proceedings ended, and people shuffled out, half-ashamed. I was halfway down the corridor when a man cried out, "That's *her*!" dropped his poster protesting something or other, probably war crimes, and raced toward me.

My reflexes glitched long enough for a leg muscle to cramp, and I stumbled, bringing up against someone who shoved me viciously aside.

"Can't you even wait till I get downstation or even downbelow to jump me?" came Jim's voice, angry for the first time in all those long, demoralizing days. "What do you think you're doing? I might have been thrown out of Fleet, but I can still—"

"Jim," I said. My leg tensed up again, and I could feel myself about to topple. And in public, too. Damn, if I didn't watch it, the Blue Helms wouldn't want me either. Not to mention the damage that an enraged man could do to systems that weren't quite nominal. Twenty years since I'd felt any pain beyond cold or stress on lungs and heart taxed past their limits.

"Jim, it's me, Cam Marlow." I put the bridge-commander's snap into my name. Another instant and those hands, which I'd watched rest passive during his trial, would reach out and if he wanted to take out the frustration, the humiliation, and the rage a normal man would feel at such a time on me, he could. "Belay this right now, man! That's an order."

"I'm not in Fleet anymore, Commander," Jim said with a laugh that hurt worse than the Freeze. "I know perfectly well who you are. What I don't know is why you hit me. I didn't abandon *you*."

"My leg cramped," I explained, not that he deserved any explanation. "Freezer burn. I got a bad case of it. I'm not in Fleet anymore either, Jim. Now, stand down, mister. What in hell were you thinking of?"

"I thought someone struck me. Big man, picking on the outsider. But you . . ." He flushed with shame this time, a red I hadn't seen for years. "I remember when *Hardcastle* blew. I was on *White Cliffs* by then. Gunnery. Damn, it's good to see you again!"

He laughed, this time a sound of pure happiness. Had he forgotten for the moment who and what he was, and who and what I was?

Apparently. But in the next, he remembered it, and the hands that had come out to grab my shoulders and whirl me around fell to his sides again.

"Your pardon, Commander," he spoke formally. "You cannot wish my company. If you will excuse me . . ."

"Jim," I sent my most persuasive voice after him, "I was rescued. You didn't abandon *me.*"

He stopped, the uniform he no longer had a right to stiffer even than his posture.

"Come on, now, mister. Shipmate to shipmate. Let me buy you dinner."

He paused.

"I'd do the same thing for any shipmate down on his luck," I said.

And God knows, he couldn't get much more down on his luck than he was.

He wouldn't want to eat at the All-Services Club, any more than its members would want him around. But the station boasted many food courts and even one or two civilian eateries that weren't too bad, all in all. Some even used natural preparations, rather than synthetic.

With luck, Security would have done its job and given us both breathing room from reporters, gawkers, and—for Jim—would-be avengers. Maybe, we could find a place that would give us a table out of the flow of passers-by, a table where the shadows would enfold us and where two old shipmates could talk for as long as they needed. If we were very fortunate, we would not be noticed at all, and the incongruity of our dining together would pass unseen. "Come on," I said and tugged once at his arm. Fabric over muscle: he felt no different from anyone else.

"Any problem with that?" I asked, pointing. He shrugged.

We took the back corridors to the restaurant, which, unlike most of the station's grade-A eateries, overlooked not the stars but the ten-level drop to the hydroponics and botany labs. When some station areas were privatized, some business genius had converted the various levels and platforms above the labs to hospitality areas. Grotto was one such. You walked through some fine holosims of forests into rock enclosures, gleaming with crystals that looked real. Each tiny cave held one table, which looked out and down over the beds of plants and trees from a hundred different worlds for which this segment of the station was known and loved. People swore the air was fresher here.

Tiny lights set into the poured rock glinted off the crystals manufactured to retain light and emit it in a kind of low-level glow. Tiny luminescent white spheres glowed on the table, hiding any scars on its surface or the marks of wear on the cloth napkins live attendants unfolded for us, an earnest attempt at pre-war luxury. The lights cast a comforting glow on Jim's face: he looked less drawn here, away from the bright lights of a station that knew who and what he was. He even managed not to flinch away from the attendant, who either didn't know who he was or pretended superbly. Grotto made a point of hiring waiters fresh from Rehab, offering them easy jobs and a chance to make a stake for themselves from patrons' tips. *There but for the grace of* . . . I promised myself I'd tip this one well.

Jim refused wine or anything stronger, though I offered, and matched me glass for glass of the water that tasted fresher here than anywhere else on the station. When salads—probably plucked from the gardens below—arrived, he ate hungrily. Oddly enough, his appetite quickened mine.

The doctors insisted I was dehydrated, although personally, I felt I was scurrying to the head every time I got up. And it was still hard to eat what they considered enough. Jim polished off his salad and attacked the bread. He hadn't had much of an appetite either since he'd abandoned ship, I imagined.

"The condemned man ate a hearty last meal," he said between bites of something that the menu inset in the stone table said was a specialty of Aven, his homeworld.

I held up a hand.

"Sorry, I'll play nice," he said. "I'm at least capable of that. I want to thank—"

"Never mind that," I said. "We were shipmates and besides . . ." Ragozinski's proposals solidified in my mind. If I couldn't bring myself to persuade Jim to abandon his trial as he'd abandoned ship, I could at least help him disappear now.

"Eat," I said. "Afterward, we'll talk."

Doubt flashed across his face, shadowy in the play of the Grotto's subtle lighting, but he nodded and went on with dinner.

A small light beside the menu flashed. I had used that light to summon a server.

"A gentleman wishes to speak with you, Commander," the server said. His eyes flicked from me to the comforting embrace of the "rock" caves. A recovering agoraphobic, at a bet. He set down an ID disk that flashed as I touched it.

I craned around the nearest stalagmite, brushing past the flowers (courtesy of the first-level gardens) set into a cut in the rock. There Jones stood. Damn the man; how'd he sniffed us out?

He saw me looking at him, raised a slanted eyebrow, and half-sketched a civilian version of a salute. The shifting lights made his features look . . . devilish, was the old Earth word. Hey, I was doing better, if I could remember the old allusions. Terran airs and graces were becoming fashionable again, Becker had told me with some humor.

"Damn," I hissed under my breath. Just when I was coming to like the young journalist, he had to try to intrude on my dinner with the last person in the worlds I needed to be seen with. If his editor was still pissed at him for not returning Home, this was a perfect way to soften the bastard up and he could take off for Tokugawa or the No Man's Worlds with everyone's blessing.

I was surprised, though, by how disappointed I was. I'd expected more humanity from Jones. I beckoned to the attendant.

"My compliments to Mr. Jones," the old military locution popped out before I could blurt something I'd regret, "that I . . ." I didn't regret, I was disappointed and angry, and when I got my hands on Ryutaro Jones, cub reporter for the starways, he was going to be . . .

"Wait." Jim held up a hand. "Commander, not on my account. In fact, if I might ask a favor, I would say let him join us."

Damn Jim, too. Did he have to turn a dinner invitation into part of his own personal ordeal? Still, he was my guest. I sighed, surrendered, and beckoned to Jones. A moment later, escorted by the attendant who managed not to limp too badly, he was seated at our table.

Spotting where we were in our meal, he declined food, but accepted glazed fruits and coffee, and settled in. Jim eyed him nervously, but Jones met his glance with that damnable charm of his and a comment about the assorted fruits. He was going to pull it off again, turn a hostile subject into an admirer: I just knew it. I wanted to slap him. Instead, I sat back, sipping water, and listened to the banter between the two men—the two "young" men, I almost said. Jones was young; and Jim, though he had to be in his thirties by now, and the trial had left him drawn and sallow, still seemed haunted by the eager teenaged ensign I remembered. They made me feel older than the Big Bang as they bantered back and forth, laughing as they fenced.

Apparently, Jim came to some sort of decision, because he drew a breath and began, "I suppose you want to know—"

"Actually, what I wanted to know isn't a matter of public record," said Jones. "I gathered that one reason your ship was in the path of the ion storm was that you'd come out of Jump damaged. Run into scavengers, did you?"

"Nasty customers," Jim agreed. "You've dodged around from station to station and downworld, so you probably know that most scavengers aren't much more than space-based muggers. Leave something at a docking bay—components, foodpacs, maybe the oddlooking vacuum container—and chances are, it's going to disappear. You seal your ship. Hell, if you're sleeping out of it, you seal your quarters and carry your ID and sidearms and any other valuables—not that Fleet mostly has much worth stealing beyond equipment—with you. Some stations, you go two by two, and there are some places you just don't go."

Jones nodded. "A long and honorable tradition, I've heard," he said. "Way back, on Earth, for all the stories about blue-water piracy, I've heard things weren't much different."

Jim laughed, only a ghost of a laugh, but a laugh nonetheless. "I've read some of those stories. Pirate fleets, weren't there supposed to be? Commanded by Bluebeard, or some other scourge, with one leg, or one eye, or a prosthetic hook? Or by a woman with a grudge against a local magnate? They all had heroic pasts and fabulous bases in hidden islands where the water was always blue, the weather hot, and the women . . ."

He laughed again, then collected himself, remembering not just the place, but his place within it. Disgraced cowards do not make jokes about women, especially not before reporters and in the presence of their host, who happened, in this case, to be female.

"Well, I remember those stories about pirate bases. And some of them did turn out to be seriously nasty customers. Now, we were running *Jaya* to New Amman—"

"You'd have thought New Amman could have requested convoy from Fleet," Jones' murmur cut in, a leading question. "Or Astro-Pharm could have provided security."

"*You'd* have thought," Jim scoffed. "Sure. Where I was on the food chain, only crumbs of information sprinkle down every so often. What I heard was that Amman could barely cover A-P's bill, let alone a special security assessment. And A-P's suits did a 'probability assessment' "—his voice went pedantic and cynical, and I felt myself nod in agreement—"that claimed we had as much chance of running into an ion storm as we did of running into scavengers."

"And they were right about both!" Jones said, timing his words with a boy's malice to Jim's sip of coffee.

He gasped, fought against spraying the table, and gulped. "Damn you, you did that on purpose!" he said.

They laughed, young men's casual laughter, and I wondered what in hell Jones thought he was up to.

"Look," said Jim. "I hate to destroy your dessert, but—

here." A slice of green melon became a gassy cluster. A large berry became the *Irian Jaya,* its hull and stem becoming, in both men's imaginations, the umbilicals and adiabatic pods of the bioship. "Now, imagine ships—small, fast ones—scavengers are getting materièl from somewhere, but we—I mean, Fleet—hasn't been able to find out yet—coming in at . . ." He pushed over his untouched wineglass and arranged a small bunch of hothouse grapes over its rim, set another berry or two on a plate and a piece of bread to show their attitudes. "You'll have to take my word for it, but they were trying to englobe us."

Jones picked off one of the "scavenger ships," popping it in his mouth as Jim maneuvered his edible fleet, talking more animatedly than I'd ever heard him.

"Scavenger ships are fast. They're not heavily armed, but if you aren't prepared, they can pack quite a punch. I was arms officer, but Captain Heikkonen"—his face twisted as memory suddenly ambushed him.

"It's all right," said Jones. "Tell me." His voice was damned near seductive with the promise of sympathy, someone-who'll-understand, the chance to justify himself.

"He didn't take my recommendations. I could have filed a formal protest. I did, in fact, for all the good that does when you're practically in the No Man's Worlds, but all I could do was put myself watch on watch so I'd be in the Command Information Center when the sludge hit the life support.

"Little bastards," he said, shaking his head. "Some scavengers are so pathetic you damned near want to give them a shower and a good meal before they go off into the big dark again. Others, though, are ugly customers who'll strip your ship of life-support systems even if you're on backup. What we ran into was a goddamned fleet. Organized. Audacious. Brave, even, to tackle a bioship. They sent cutters to blast their way in. Here: I'll show you." A golden apple became *Irian Jaya,* menaced by fruit knives, coring their way in.

"They attacked the CIC?" I couldn't help asking. On a

Fleet ship, there'd be marines guarding the Command center, and we'd all be armed. But on a bioship . . .

"Figured it would be senior officers there, fat, corporate types," Jim said. "They weren't wrong. They started to cut their way in, and we got some fumes. But I was there too, with some of the security I'd gotten through to. We sealed the area, tossed out O_2 masks and drove them back. I even managed to stop some of the bridge officers from ejecting."

Ejecting. Leaving the ship leaderless, the long, fragile chain of adiabatic pods, like bladders in seaweed, drifting, the hope contained in its genetic material abandoned to scavengers for God knows what reason.

"Sounds like quite a fight," Jones said. I wasn't imagining the admiration in his voice. "Two fights, seeing as you had internal . . . problems with personnel."

Jim waved a hand, dismissing it. "It went well," he said. Abruptly, he withdrew. He'd been animated, hopeful as he described the successful engagement leading up to his downfall. Now, he withdrew, drawing the quiet, agonized dream that he had lived in during his trial about him like camouflage.

"You didn't say anything about this at the trial," Jones observed. No judge could have been more dispassionate.

"No," said Jim. "It's in ship's records, I suppose."

Assuming Astro-Pharm would do anything but seal those records now that everyone had their scapegoat, who was sitting beside me now, munching fruit. Any sort of new evidence mitigating his absolute guilt was hardly a thing A-P would want.

Still, the case could have been made that Jim had been injured. That he was stressed out from fighting not just scavengers, but his own chain of command. That he'd been put in an impossible position by Fleet. An appeal would not—and should not—restore him to Fleet, but his discharge could be laundered, giving him some benefits and less of a blood mark on his records.

"You didn't bring this up at your trial," Jones said. "Man, you could appeal."

"No."

Abruptly, I was furious. I could feel pulse and respiration spiking way up. To my surprise, my monitoring telemetry didn't squeak and queep its idiot head off: I must be getting better. Guess even this anger was good for my cardiovascular system.

"Of course he wouldn't," I interrupted. "What sort of idiot do you think you are?" I demanded of Jim. "I'm the one with freezer burn, not you, but you—you're talking about Old Earth pirates and history. Let me give you some more examples." Adrenaline drove my words like afterburners. "Don Quixote, tilting at windmills. Or Lawrence, punishing himself after Arabia his whole damned life. You made a bad call, Jim. I'll go further. You couldn't have made a worse one if you'd tried. But you've stood your trial, you're taking your punishment. Why make matters worse?"

He shook his head. This too was part of his self-imposed sentence. Not just to stand his trial, but to tell people who might even be in a position to help him of even slender mitigating circumstances, then refuse to allow them to act.

"It makes no difference," he said.

Jones hissed.

"You know it won't," Jim said. "Where can I disappear to? The worlds already know my face. You're too good at your job."

So now what? All this talk of scavengers had given me something else to worry about besides the dreams I still wasn't talking to the shrinks about: What would become of Jim? For all the competence he'd just so infuriatingly displayed to Jones, Jim was a walking target, lasers glowing on his back in a kind of "shoot here" pattern.

I have no doubt that if Heikkonen had been a decent man and captain, Jim would have helped bring *Irian Jaya* into the Port of New Amman, and I'd have spent my rehab reading about a world restored to health, celebrations, and an old shipmate's promotion upon his return from detached civilian duty.

But Heikkonen had been a coward and a thief. He wasn't

the only one. The spaceways were full of people who preyed on fools whose actions had plunged them to the bottom and whose consciences forbade them to fight to win. People like Jim wound up impressed, snatched from cheap bars in the parts of stations where sensible people don't go; sold off the decks of the only ships willing to sign on crew with pasts they won't talk about, maybe sent to those worlds that are run by scavengers where they'd have taken the *Jaya*'s shipsicles and thawed them out to be helots, bred to their tasks.

Scavengers, though, had purpose and motive.

There were worse things in No Man's Space than scavengers. There were wreckers, who destroyed not for principles, not for orders, not for greed, but for the sheer lust to destroy. Scavengers would use shipsicles. Wreckers would shatter people sleeping in Freeze with one blow of a rifle. Would Jim ultimately sink so low that they would seek him out—or would he seek them?

Jones glanced over at me, put a hand on my arm that I flung off, and shook his head at him. *Now-see-what-you've-done!*

"I'm fine," I told him. "He's the one who needs help!"

Give him credit, Jones made the attempt, protesting, "Dammit, man, you can't throw away your future for one rotten call! Get over it!

"Jim!" Jones grabbed him by the shoulders—not the brightest move with a combat-trained officer who thought he had nothing to lose. "At least, think of what you're doing to her!"

A polite, attentive look directed at me. I hadn't planned to present Conrad's plans like this, but I found myself blurting them out: loans, new papers, recommendations for work, and all. I barely had time to put what the likes of Jones would call "spin" on them so that they sounded like a notable senior officer's taking pity on an unfortunate, not the bribe I knew them to be. "What's more," I added, coming up for air and beaching myself on the much safer ground of Marshal Emeritus Becker, "you won't know this, but the Marshal Emeritus and I have been talking. It's agreed I'm joining the Relief forces. He's followed your trial, and he's a decent man, he understands that . . ." *Evasive action, Marlow, you're losing him.* "I'm sure, that if you spoke to him—"

Anguish flashed across Jim's face. "Why would the likes of Abram Becker, who's rescued ten worlds if he's saved a single life, even want to breathe the same air as someone who . . ." he drew a breath like a gasp, or a sob, ". . . did what I did?"

"Maybe because he agrees with Ryutaro here, that one rotten act shouldn't damn a man for his whole life?"

"Mr. Jones will pardon my saying it," Jim replied gently, "but Mr. Jones is very young, and, celebrated as he is, all Alliance does not have to agree with Mr. Jones. I may have betrayed my principles, but I at least remember what they were."

And a damn sight higher than any reporter's seemed to tremble in the ten levels of open air beyond Grotto. For the first time I wondered whether Jones and I could stop Jim if he decided to make a dash for the railing and hurl himself over it.

Again, he gave us that aloof look. "I appreciate the Commodore's suggestions, and I'll take them under advisement."

Which was Fleet-formal for "no fucking way."

Jim began to rise. "I want to thank you for the dinner, Commander," he said. "Mr. Jones, it was . . . interesting to meet you."

And he was gone. Just like that.

He didn't even go near the railing. Didn't even look at it.

I closed my eyes and practiced my deep breathing. I felt as if I'd run a marathon. On a heavy-G world.

"I think we could both use something," said Ryutaro Jones. "Allow me."

He was scrolling through the menu, accessing the wine list, ordering. Just as well the boy had independent means; you didn't buy vintages with prices like that on salary alone.

The server cleared Jim's place, drew the tablecloth, provided fresh glasses, and presented the venerable dessert wine with ceremony to Jones. "I know you drink, Commander," he said, going from callow reporter to grand gentleman with a flick of his superbly trained voice. "Will you honor me by tasting this?"

Delicious. Like spending twenty years in Freeze, then waking up in a country garden. My eyes filled. I wanted to go home. Problem was: I hadn't gotten one.

I sipped again, admiring the almost amethyst luster of the wine in the table lights, glinting in the facets of its glass. No home. And I was twenty years out of time.

Another sip. The wine seemed to be thawing an inner Freeze.

"Jones," I said, "you've lived through the past twenty years. What do you make of all—" I ran out of words and substituted a hand wave. Mercifully, my hand didn't shake.

"He's retreating," Jones said. "Fleet takes them away from their families and homes, makes them over in its own image, and then, when something like this happens, they've already changed and can't change back. They just don't have any resilience left," he explained from the vast certitude of his lack of years and experience.

"I watched him during the trial," he went on. "I saw him do it again tonight, retreat within some sort of shelter within himself."

"Do you think he'll ever come out?" I had another sip of wine, pleased at my success in interrogating the interrogator.

"Hard to say. I think he's a very good sort of man, basically, for all that he's done. And that's going to make it harder. If his standards had started out lower, or if he were more pragmatic—he's a towering idealist, I think."

"I'd noticed," I put in dryly.

"A coarser personality would simply get over it. Men like him withdraw. If things get too bad, they make themselves die."

"Like von Leinigen said? Or did Hashimoto-sama tell you all this over whatever it is they drink on Tokugawa?"

"Sake," Jones supplied, and poured another glass of wine, waving the waiter aside. "Hashimoto-sama would have died in protest of his orders, perhaps. He would not have lived to make Jim's initial mistake."

I hadn't processed ideas this quickly or this logically since my resurrection, and more and more were cascading into my thoughts. So, I thought I hadn't a home, friends? Hashimoto reached out from the other side of a long war to claim Jones as kin. Even now, there were—there must be—people for whom my life had a meaning.

Conrad, for instance. Now that the trial was over, there was no reason we couldn't get back in touch. Jim had even refused to consider Conrad's offers. We were safe.

"Will you excuse me?" I asked Ryutaro Jones. "Least I can do is thank Commodore Ragozinski for thinking of . . ." I gestured with my chin and had another sip of wine. "And tell him his plans won't be needed."

"Table's got a comm unit," Jones volunteered.

"I don't think so." I smiled at him, meeting Jones' pretense of innocence with a pretense of my own. Maybe Jones was right. Conrad and I were both older, scarred now. And after that one night, we owed each other more than to just drift away.

I slipped into an alcove hollowed into the artificial rock. Tiny stalactites provided light enough for me to access Conrad's code. The system cycled, then flashed on a fleet sigil: "Commodore Ragozinski is unavailable. If this is a Fleet emergency, please contact Havilland Station's CIC. If this is not an emergency, please leave a message at the bell."

I grimaced at the machine voice, waited for the tone—chime of an archaic ship's bell like the one that had closed Jim's trial—and spoke softly: "Conrad, I spoke with Jim. He's not interested. I'm joining Blue Helms; it's all settled. And we need to talk." I even managed not to laugh. Twenty years on ice, and all I could come up with was the old boy-and-girl clichés that were no less embarrassing and no less painful for being true.

When I returned to the table, Jones had his own comm out and was hunching over it the way you do when you're hearing things you don't want to make any mistakes about. Usually the news is bad.

Seeing me, he ended transmission and rose. "You'd better sit down," he said. "I just heard from—"

So he had a source in Security. What did I care? But, the deliberate gentleness of his voice, the care in his hands as he eased me into my seat filled me with a cold worse than Freeze.

"Commodore Ragozinski was an old friend of yours, wasn't he?" Jones asked.

Was.

I began to shrug, then nodded.

"Security's just reported. The Commodore went to one of the maintenance airlocks, left a report for his staff, put his insignia and his will on top of it, and cycled out into space. Security's recovering his body now."

My hands were on the table, pressing it as if I could push Conrad back. I could imagine it: cold hands, total resolve, and a mind screaming protests inside. A quick death, if a horrible one. Those hands, which had tried to rub warmth back into my body and make it sing. If we had succeeded . . .

I wanted to weep. At least the tears would be warm. But I'd been warned; after so long in Freeze, I could expect to be dehydrated for some weeks yet. Conrad: my old friend in my old life; my first friend in this new life that wasn't shaping up all that well. Who knew? It might be that Conrad, for once, did know better.

"Here, you need this," Jones said, picking up my hand and my wineglass and attempting to wrap the first around the second. The vivid grape scent turned me sick. Sun on the vines; sun in the wine; living things, and light. Conrad had no light, only the cold, the air exploding from lungs as they froze, and the long, frozen night.

I lurched up from my seat.

"Absent friends." I forced the words out and threw the

costly, wasted wine against the bulkhead with its phony textured rocks. They'd just have to bill me for the broken glass, wouldn't they?

JONES WAS WAITING FOR ME AT THE AIRLOCK WITH A SMALL riot of other reporters who thrust their vidcams at me as if they were presenting arms. If Jones had a camera about him, he'd mercifully hidden it. He took my arm as if he were a friend of the family and attempted to escort me on board Conrad's gig. I stared at his hand and at mine, pale against the blue of the dress uniform I was wearing for the last time, with the band of mourning black on the sleeve. The Arvies—the Relief services I planned to join—had retrieved Conrad the day before, and now we would send him back into space, ejecting him into his last orbit, a decaying one around Havilland Roads' star.

At least Conrad could get warm again. They hadn't bothered to thaw him when they retrieved him from outside the airlock.

Damn the man. Damn which man? The boy who was alive, or the man who was dead?

I clenched my jaw. This would be my first flight since I'd been thawed. Jones inclined his head and murmured sympathetic concern. When had the intrusive brat decided I was chief mourner?

Security stopped Jones at the airlock. "Sorry, sir. No reporters. The Commodore left very detailed instructions." The guard's face was white, strained. He looked twenty years older than he should. Jones jogged my elbow: what if I asked to bring him on board?

"Sorry, Jones," I said, disgusted with myself for how my voice faltered. And for how relieved I was. The day I couldn't face down reporters . . .

That day had come for Conrad and he was dead.

A tape of bosun's pipes that must have come all the way from Earth shrilled out, wailing on two notes, as I boarded.

So. Conrad had left very detailed instructions. Did they include being piped on board?

"Gig" was a misnomer. The ship was too big to be called that, bigger, even, than a shuttle. Its metal and enamel gleamed, while the colors of its computer displays glowed like the holos of stained glass I'd seen so many years ago.

A canister draped with the Alliance flag waited on a bier, constructed for the occasion. In death, Conrad was guarded by two young officers standing at parade rest. In dress uniforms. Gloved, even. Expressionless, in a trance of concentration and formality. The funerals I'd seen on board ship—the last time I'd seen death. My captain, ordering me to abandon *Hardcastle,* the ice sheathing my eyes, flowing into my veins. . . .

I fought not to shiver.

A faint nudge was all that told me that we'd come ungrappled and were heading out, well past the station, to a point where the canister could be launched on an easy trajectory into the sun. The viewscreen went live. We were under way, but too slowly for me to see the stars move. They glowed, waiting, and I caught my breath. I had forgotten how beautiful they were.

Conrad, you son of a bitch.

In death, he'd done me a kindness. I was in space again. And again, I found it beautiful, timeless, serene, despite what I knew it could do. What I'd seen it do. What it had done to Conrad. The starfield off Havilland Roads glittered like the medals Conrad had kept in his brag case.

I looked around: no reporters; senior officers—I recognized several from Jim's trial. Abram Becker moved unselfconsciously to my side.

"He asked me to conduct his memorial," Becker said. He looked not so much old—he *was* old—but used up. "I got the message from him about the same time that he—" His face twisted. "Why couldn't he have asked for my help? I knew he was in pain, but . . ."

A slight jolt.

"Ah," Becker said. "We've reached parking orbit."

Leaving me, he took up his station before the burial canister, his face furrowed and pale in the starlight.

Becker held a black-bound book in his hands, an old one I'd seen in Conrad's quarters before the wars. He did not open it. Instead, staring over our heads, he seemed to draw the words from as far off as Earth and as long ago as when fleets sailed the waters, not the stars. The words Becker spoke were not the words of the Fleet burial service. They were older. They had been old before ever humanity had left Earth.

"We therefore commit his body to the deeps of space to be turned into light, looking for the resurrection of the body (when the Stars shall give up their dead) and the life of the world to come, through Our Lord Jesus Christ, who at His coming shall change our vile body—" Becker's voice roughened, then went ruthlessly on, "that it may be like His glorious body, according to the mighty working, whereby He is able to subdue all things to Himself."

As Conrad had not been able.

How long had Conrad brooded over these words, planned for them to be spoken after his death?

Becker closed his eyes again.

He gave a nod to the officer of the day. The canister shuddered as the guards lifted it, then loaded it into a firing tube.

One nodded at the other.

"Prepare to eject," came the word.

The other tensed.

"Fire." Both men stiffened to attention, and the pipes wailed farewell. I braced along with every officer on deck.

The ship jolted.

The pipes ceased: the ship's master had left.

We turned back from the starlight toward Havilland Roads and its docking bay with its glare of artificial light.

Jones was waiting for us. As the airlock gaped open, he too stiffened to what imposture of attention he could manage.

Again, he took my arm, this time steering me through the gauntlet of reporters.

"I wanted to tell you—"

"Tell me what?"

"I'm off," he said.

"Off?" I blinked at him, as stupid as if I'd just waked from Freeze.

"You remember. Hashimoto-sama invited me to Tokugawa. If I miss this ship, I don't know when I'll find another, and my trust fund isn't big enough to let me charter anything." His grin, impudent, threatened to melt the ice I was drawing about myself. "You'll have your peace and quiet back now," he said. "Jim's gone."

"Gone? How do you know?"

"We talked a time or two. He slipped away on board a freighter, at oh-six-hundred. I saw him go."

Let him go, I thought. *One less burden. We therefore commit your body to the ice, and you can rest.*

The thought was tempting.

My uniform weighed heavy on me, and the reeks of cheap dye and my own sweat, unfamiliar to me after all these years on ice, were enough to make me gag.

Take it off, Marlow, I told myself. *You won't be wearing it much longer.*

I had tugged off the overtunic before I noticed that a red light glowed on my comm unit.

The demands had started already.

I didn't have to comply. I could simply say I'd changed my mind and decided to retire. With my accumulated funds, I could even return to Earth, write my memoirs—hell, I felt sure Jones would help me sell them—and live out a long, safe, and prosperous life.

If you called that living. After all, how many veterans made it all the way back home? How many veterans had hands as clean as mine? Maybe, it was time to *do* something after twenty years on ice, to justify the honor I'd been given—and the life that had been returned to me.

Lots of people would say I was lucky. Certainly, I was luckier than Conrad. Or Jim.

I shivered, despite my quarters' heat, already anticipating a painful interview with Marshal Becker. He'd been through enough that he'd spare me what I knew was true: resigning now would be jumping ship.

I activated the comm. Just as I thought: my appointment had come through, and I was required in all haste to join Alliance Relief Vessel *Gavroche*.

One tour as its exec, and then, who knew? I might finally realize my dream of ship command after all.

Suddenly, I wasn't nearly as cold.

Shenango's World

12

The airlock's massive valves slammed with an impact Jim could feel through his work boots. He spared the valves, set into heavy steelcrete, constantly reinforced, a glance as if he gave a damn if they were corroded or not. What mattered was that, until they ground open once again, he and his casual labor squad were exiled from the relative safety of the domes to the violence of Shenango's World as surely if this were the last day when the sheep were separated from the goats. In that case, Jim and company were playing the goats for all they were worth, which wasn't much. Rote warnings and orders from the gang boss squeaked in his helm's cheap comm like karaoke filtered through helium.

Bullied at last into rough formation, the work gang squelched and shambled through the muck that constituted much of what passed for landscape on this wreck of a world. Even when Jim's feet achieved solid rock, it had a greasy, precarious feel. Shenango had never come under fire, but it was as much a casualty of the war as any planet that the Secess' had actually slagged.

The world had been settled about three generations before the war. Not much more than remotely habitable, it had the advantages of location, location, and location—as Effendi Nasser said with his dry chuckle: it was on the trade routes between the No Man's Worlds and the inner systems. And, because its settlers lived in domes, it could be industrialized fast, without the precautions that more settled worlds demanded. During the war, its shareholders had turned its industries to producing chemicals. Some of them were obviously weapons. Like most people on Shenango, Jim knew that and very truly didn't want to know any more.

Even before the war, Shenango had made up with cheap labor what it lacked in materièl. That was part of the reason its settlers had kept their domes and even expanded on them: no time or equipment for simultaneous production, terraforming, and remediation. The war had made the situation go from tricky to precarious, and Nasser's dream of making the devastated world bloom looked like another of those things the old man wasn't likely to see realized.

Like passing on his dream to a family. Or any kind of heir at all.

Jim jerked his chin against the comm. Damned mass-produced envirosuit didn't fit quite right and reeked of cheese gone bad, despite what passed for the best efforts of burned-out suit mechanics who'd never have been let anywhere near a deep-space rig.

Still whining? You ought to be over that by now.

He'd had a better suit, one he'd worked on in what free time he'd managed to scrounge, but he'd left it behind along with his credit balance when he fled Esdras Nasser's private dome.

The Patron had such hopes of you, too.

He sure picked the wrong one to pin his hopes on, didn't he?

The voices inside Jim's skull were starting up again. They'd compelled him to stand his trial at Havilland Roads. They'd forbidden him to explain, not that he could come up with anything that remotely explained himself to himself. Though the trial had stripped him of rank, of livelihood, it was the voices that made him exile himself from anyone who showed any signs of liking or accepting him.

Nasser was simply the latest casualty of Jim's crime in fleeing *Irian Jaya*. Damn shame, really. The Patron was old, polycultural, with relatives on worlds like Ararat and, unlucky for all of them, New Amman and God knows where else, scattered past reunion. He'd hoped his sons and daughters would work this land with him, making a sick world bloom, but they'd disappeared into the Fleet in those last days when they were throwing experimental ships, cubs with no flight time, anything they had against the Secess'.

It wasn't Nasser's fault that he'd replied to a letter written on Jim's behalf by one of the fools—a veritable plague of benefactors—who still thought Jim could rehabilitate himself. The Patron needed a supervisor with tech training, a likely man who needed a future, and a future far better than he deserved was what the old man had offered Jim.

He'd liked it: after a life in ships and the cheapest bunks on deteriorating stations, the old man's overheated residence dome, the bright lights, the fruit trees, the cherished rugs and brasses were luxury beyond his worth. He'd come to respect Nasser. And the old man, whose life should have taught him what happens when you care for people, had warmed to him.

They'd started to be friends the night Nasser had limped in one night after an excursion Outside he shouldn't have taken and Jim didn't have the clout to prevent. Jim had risen, offering Nasser the overstuffed chair he liked best and fetching him a cup of the coffee he favored, stronger even than Fleet brew. He'd offered to leave the Patron in peace, but Nasser had smiled at him and asked about his family. He'd mumbled something, graceless as a boy less than half his age. With a kindness that Jim hadn't expected, he had forborne to press an employee who, day by day, grew to be more like a guest. A favored nephew. Possibly an heir.

All you have to do to get along is go along. What's one

lie to an old man who wants your help? Think of the good you can do!

Damn those voices.

So how'd he repaid a Patron who'd started to become a friend? By running away. He'd lied once, with his silence. How could he expect an old man who kept hardcopies of the "we regret to inform you" transmissions framed on the white-washed walls of his study to understand why he'd turned tail when he couldn't even explain it to himself?

Even this far out in the No Man's Worlds, his story spread. And this time, there was a witness.

The least he could do was disappear. Nasser didn't need to know he'd opened his home to a coward. Wasn't a damn thing he could do, either; the old man's honor was tied up in his notions of hospitality.

Don't go giving yourself any credit for kindness, Jim. You didn't have the guts to see his face change when you told him who you really are.

Shut up, he told the voice inside his skull. *You'll get me killed Outside, and then who'll you torment?*

As Esdras Nasser had told him, you'd have to terraform this planet to clean it up. Now the only people who ventured Outside were work gangs, and their life span could be measured in months.

Jim ran another check on his enviro-suit. Shenango's World held grudges against the humans who'd wrecked it.

A crackle-snarl-garble of instruction—Jim moved his chin again, fine-tuning the comm's pitch. So, the boss was talking fast today; they were all the way through Instructions to Security.

"Next to your breathing module is a snap-on propulsion unit," the words droned on through the tinny speakers. "Alliance law requires we equip your suit with jets. But don't be in any hurry to get away. The rain"—Shenango's constant, beating, acid rain, drumming on your helm until you thought you might go crazy and think it was a relief—"won't keep the jetpacks from igniting, but an acid index over redline can produce liftoff flares, and flares near contaminated pools might set off an explosion."

If that wasn't enough to worry about, there were the lightnings that tore through Shenango's turbulent cloud cover. They could spark off an explosion too, or a whole chain of them.

This world was the backside of beyond. So why in hell did Ty Parnell, *Irian Jaya*'s backup engineer, have to turn up here?

That was an easy one, Jim told himself. The comm unit squawked, "You, suit with the yellow stripe, haul ass!" Dutifully, he picked up the pace, slogging through muck that would have burnt through his skin in seconds if it weren't for this stinking excuse for a suit. He didn't even flinch at the ID. The fluorescent yellow, like all the other suits' color marks, made for a quicker ID than numbers, though the work gang had them too. Yellow was just rotten luck. Like finding Ty Parnell.

Irian Jaya's second engineering officer had come here to hide out, lick her wounds, whatever, and while she was at it, assemble a stake that could buy her way back to a new identity.

He'd followed Nasser on a factory tour, carried along in a cloud of courtesies, offered cups of coffee, and murmurs of Patron, Shareholder, and Effendi that, unaccountably, had filtered down to include him.

And then he saw, like a Jump hallucination, the woman who'd jeered at him on *Irian Jaya*. Had joined the captain in his plans to abandon ship. Had never stood trial and might, for all he knew, still want to kill him.

Her hair was darker now, her coverall a subdued brown. And she picked up a pocket comp and made her way to him, inclining her head for all the world as if Jim were senior management.

"I want your opinion of these bids for the new mechs," she murmured. Two of Nasser's secretaries turned around, so she added a "sir" and supplied a politely apologetic smile.

Playing for time, he'd glanced over her numbers.

"Hail to the chief," she whispered. "The new heir. What's your newfound glory worth to you?"

"Not a damn, now you're here," he hissed. "Are you crazy?"

"Sane, I think. I wasn't the idiot who stood trial when I didn't have to, mind you. You're the tin soldier, not me."

"There's such a thing as doing the right thing. . . ."

"Like abandoning ship with an ion storm coming on? Let's not fool ourselves: just because you like pain doesn't give you the right to judge me."

She'd make demands he didn't dare meet, he knew that. So, once again, he'd have to jump. If he told Nasser he was ill, the Patron would probably want to send him to the best hospital on Santayana. If he said he'd gotten a message from home, Nasser would probably load him with gifts for his family. So he'd have to bail. There wasn't any choice, except telling the truth and watching the old man's face go chill with contempt.

"Getting ready to jump ship again?" Parnell asked with a quirk of her eyebrows. Snide bitch had always been too perceptive for Jim's good.

"You stood your trial like a total idiot. Now, you've got a second chance to prove you're not a complete damned fool. I think we can deal. You keep the old man happy. You keep me happy too. I bet you're real good at it."

Her smile was meant to be seductive. But he'd seen a more fetching expression on one of the corpsicles they couldn't revive.

"I'll be back in touch," she told him, then left in case he had ideas of pushing her into the nearest out-take valve.

"Yellow, you going to stand there all day? Move it!"

"By the numbers, board! So help me, if you slip, we'll leave you behind to rot."

The work gang sounded off as they splashed toward puddles filled with the greasy rainbows of rain, fuel leaks, and waste runoff. Most of this crew were older men down on their luck, one or two vets who hadn't made it back all the way, and losers who'd find even bad luck an improvement. Sure enough, someone slipped as he scrambled on board the van. The gang boss swore as he extricated the damned fool from beneath its treads. At least this time, no genius had tried to make them board while the van was moving. Behind them rose the swell of Industrial Dome 1, rising like an infected breast.

The lake was about two klicks ahead. Maps called it Lake St. Charles, but anyone who'd come anywhere close called it Holy Shit. Despite their oxygen tanks, the work gangs swore they could smell the fumes that Shenango's storm winds blew off the lake. And there was no mistaking the graveyard phosphorescence—sickly greens and deadly roses—from the chemicals the dome pumped into it.

Thunder pealed loud enough that even the supervisors, who were used to working Outside, jumped. Storms on Shenango were always damn near seismic. This one felt like about Force 7. Lightning followed, a blue-white lattice of fire lighting up the gray horizon.

An explosion shook the ground. The lightning had touched off the lake.

"Holy shit!" someone whispered through the comm.

The van stopped.

If this thing's treads sink into the muck, we're well and truly stuck. Assuming the shock wave doesn't toss it onto its side. Give me a nice, clean ion storm any day.

Jim clutched the roll bars and huddled against the others as the driver fought to keep the van on its rapidly sinking treads.

Light, like Cherenkov radiation chained on Shenango's World for its sins, writhed on the surface of the lake.

The van rocked, jolted miraculously free, and lumbered forward, picking up what actually felt like speed on the rotten surface. They had ten minutes, perhaps, to make it to the outtake valves. With luck, debris hadn't blocked them or solid waste hadn't congealed so that it would take explosives or deadly corrosives to free them, assuming they could get them free before the fires could slag the intake valves and roar into the pipes.

Let the fires leap the pipes into the production or storage vats, and the whole plant could go up, taking the whole overpriced, under-maintained installation, and maybe the dome, with it.

Compared with that, the workers weren't even a line item on the balance sheet.

Except, maybe, to Patron Nasser.

A klaxon pierced the storm. Condition Red? Someone tell the work gang something it didn't know.

They had no choice now but to send out flyers, maneuvering in as close to the lake surface as they dared to drop more chemicals into the lake, to try to put out the fire. Might be fun to fly one of those things. How long had it been since he'd flown?

Who'd trust you with a flyer?

No one with a tampered ID would be assigned that duty. If they found out who he was, they'd take him up in a flyer all right. Probably dump him into the lake.

"We need foam by the valves," a crisp voice cut over the straw boss' shout to the driver to step on it. *"Triple pay for volunteers who'll do ground cover valves! Volunteers speak up!"*

Four hours at triple pay, on top of what Jim had already saved, might buy him a cheap berth on the next freighter offworld.

"Here!" he raised his hand. "Yellow!"

At the order, he released his death-grip on the van's roll bar, jumped clear, and—"Heads-up, hero!"—caught the foam canister hurled at him so it almost hit him in the belly.

His breathing rasped in the enviro suit. The seals of his inner helm were chafing at his temples so his sweat stung. His heart had started to pound, the way he'd gotten on the hull of *Irian Jaya,* right before he'd taken that damned jump.

He could see the fire flickering on the lake now, like blue

flame on the punchbowl his family had brought from Old Earth. They'd brought it out and lit it that last Christmas on Aven before war rationing. But this fire wasn't confined to a silver bowl. It spread over a lake surface, strange as Jump space and about as friendly.

More sweat dripped. He had the damnedest urge to scratch his upper lip even if he had to tear off his mask to do it. Bad idea. Once this stuff worked itself deep into your lungs, you were done for. Or at least, very sick.

He suppressed a sneeze. Bad things happened to people who sneezed into their respirators. Worse things happened to those who retched, and that didn't even count what maintenance techs would do to you, assuming you made it back. And then there were the idiots who died of claustrophobia, either when panic stopped their hearts or, unable to bear what felt like a shroud of vacuum-proof insulation, ripped it off and danced naked in this planet's toxic air. The work crews stripped off the suits and left them there, not even bringing the bodies in to Hydroponics for decent burial. After all, how decent could you be if you contaminated the human biomass?

Sometimes, a landmover would shovel the bones into the muck. If they didn't dissolve first.

In the year Jim had been on Shenango, "It's been getting worse," Esdras had said once over coffee. He could hear the old man's voice now. "If it is written, we can hold out until it becomes our turn on the Relief list. If not—" About that time, he would usually shrug and pour himself another cup. Nasser'd been teaching Jim to make it in those little pots with the long handles, over open flame, with cardamom, the way he liked it.

He'd shown Jim the manifests. Chemicals and ground conditions alike had all but finished Shenango's heavy machinery. Now, they used people to eke out its life span; as the saying went, people were a resource you could renew with unskilled labor that actually enjoyed its work.

Only problem was, most of the people weren't doing that well either. Population was down, and Shenango'd be a candidate for bioships once the Blue Helms got here. The trick was to hold out that long.

The squawks from the comms had risen to a frenzy. Double time. He hadn't drilled like this since the Academy, when they ran recruits in weighted suits underwater before wasting fuel on a trip Upstairs into space on people who couldn't make the grade. You couldn't sprint in these suits: just lumber and hope you kept your balance.

At this rate, all the volunteers were likely to do was go up in flames along with the intake valves. One man, Jim told himself, one man could get there in time if he flew. Assuming he didn't crash and burn on liftoff, if he could fly there without being tossed into the lake by the storm winds, he could lay down a thin line of foam and hold it until the others arrived and the earth movers joined them, creating a firewall.

What're you waiting for, coward? Jump!

He triggered jets, felt the remembered pressure against his spine propel him upward. Winds buffeted him, and he fought, using the sprayer the way an acrobat would use a pole on the high wire to balance himself: not so low he'd be tossed into the burning lake; not so high that chemicals from air cover would force him down. And pray there isn't a reflux.

Some fool was cheering. A touch of his chin turned comm volume down as far as he could.

Three. Two. One. Touch *down*. Jets *off*.

Now *move*! Knees and thighs ached as he broke into an awkward run. Without the jets, he could feel every kilo the enviro-suit weighed.

Dear God, he'd rather be weightless.

He clambered onto the half-shut maw of the valve and kicked at the bright-red manual release plate. The valve clamped shut. No vibrations underfoot: for once, they'd done something intelligent and shut down the system.

"Get down, you idiot!"

He *was* up too high, a target for a lightning strike. He crouched, angled the sprayer, set it on max, and laid down a line of foam that was supposed to be so viscous that even this rain couldn't wash it away.

At least, not immediately.

The other damn fools—scratch that, volunteers—joined him, widening the foam barrier protecting the valves from fire. Cheers erupted over the comm, and a rumble that grew into a roar that made even Shenango's embattled bedrock shudder.

He felt, as much as heard, the whine of flyers overhead, the impact of their chemical bombs on the lake, snuffing the blaze. The ground shook again. They had the earthmovers outside now, lumbering toward the valves. Those were all the sounds he could identify. But over all of them, came a roar more powerful still. He could ID that, too, dammit.

His hands shook, and a thinning trail of foam missed its mark.

You're running low. Make each shot count.

Focus only on where the foam is going. Widen it—there's a break, get over there and spray! He gestured at a suit carrying green markings on both shoulders. The man obeyed. So did the red-marked suit with the bad patch job.

Jim stared into the foam. It roiled about like Jump space. He used to think you could see visions in those clouds. All he could see was foam and more foam. He could practically smell it.

He heard a gurgle, felt the sprayer jolt. Damn, it was running on empty. He shook it and was rewarded by a spotty spray. Where were those earthmovers? Damn, they'd been promised reinforcements, and he'd have sworn he could have felt them arrive.

Hands fell on his shoulders. If he hadn't been so damn tired, he'd have whirled and hit whoever'd sneaked up behind him in the gut with his sprayer. He overbalanced, then tumbled to his knees, down in the foam. So what if they had to lever him out.

Instead the same hands lifted him out.

Jim almost fell again as the klaxons blared Recall.

Hands lifted the sprayer from his shaking hands. It would go to maintenance, then be recharged, more easily repaired than he.

Jim let himself be helped back onto the van. The work gang adjusted his hands on the rollbar as if he were precious. Blue suit lay along the van's side, a frayed thermal blanket half covering a cracked helm. The gang boss pulled it down to cover the whole body.

Bad luck to travel with the dead, but if you don't see him, he's not dead, right?

"Let's get back Inside," he said and signaled the driver.

The van shuddered to a laborious start.

With luck, there'd be a crowd at the airlocks, and Jim could shuck the suit with its betraying yellow stripe and be back at his rent-a-room before his loss was noticed. Never mind the triple pay. Maybe he'd saved the dome, but he'd made himself too damned conspicuous doing it.

THE WORK GANG'S BOSS AND DRIVER PRACTICALLY HAD TO heave each worker off the van and into the airlock, which cycled, then dilated, giving them the freedom of a dome gone mad. Jim fumbled his helmet half off, blinking at the artificial light, the safe, recycled air.

Thank God for small mercies: the Patron's secretaries had managed to keep the old man from coming out to thank the work crew. The place teemed with techs and maintenance, tugging him toward decontamination. He recognized their gear.

He also recognized the coveralls and rank insignia of Relief Force. So he'd heard right out there. A Relief vessel had landed, and now the Arvies, with their blue helms, were all over the place.

"Hey, yellow!" came a repellently cheerful, too-familiar voice. "I'll take those gloves."

Ty Parnell. She wore an engineer's coverall. "We tracked you on the monitors. Quite the hero, aren't you? God knows, you've had practice jumping. Well, this time, you covered yourself with glory. Not to mention half the foam you sprayed. God, you stink."

"I'm getting out of here," he hissed. "If you had half a brain—"

"I haven't. Got a whole one. And it's worked up a deal for you."

"What's in it for you?"

"You get your second chance. And very, very rich. I . . . let's say you look after me when promotion or bonus time comes around. And I keep my mouth shut. Unless," she added, "we decide otherwise. You're not half bad looking once you're out of this gear. You could show a girl a real good time. At least, that's what that radiologist on *Jaya* seemed to think. But she's not here. I am. How long has it been, anyways, since you got . . ."

It had to be the chemicals in the air. He was going to vomit. At least he had his helm off.

"Unless you prefer the old man," Parnell added.

Jim surprised them both by slamming his filthy suit gloves into her face. She screamed as the muck that smeared the gloves burned her face.

Jim took off. As outraged shouts and yells erupted behind him, he dodged into the shadow of a storage bin, letting the pack run by. He edged further into cover and shucked off the filthy suit with its betraying, appropriate yellow stripe, wadded it, tucked it into the bin, and stood up, brushing off his coverall.

"Freeze," came a voice that teased at his memory. Female. Resolved.

You can run but you can't hide. Maybe his voices were right this time.

Jim froze.

"They're treating that engineer for chemical burns off your suit gloves. And pretty damn mad about it, too. Frankly, I don't trust what they'd do when they got their hands on you. So, I said I'd bring you in, and they're pleased enough that the Relief Service landed that they agreed to turn it over to me. Now turn around. Slowly."

Jim turned, expecting to face an armed officer. *Watch the body for reactions.* Whoever'd come after him might not be Arvy or nonviolent after all.

A gloved hand rested beside a sidearm. Fleet issue, no less, but it was part of the Arvy mission to use force only as a last resort. The officer's assumption that she herself sufficed to bring him in was almost more intimidating than the sidearm she hadn't drawn. He could probably bring her down, and take off, but then, where would he go?

What's the matter, hero? Lost your nerve?

God, he was tired.

"All right, mister, I want to know why you'd act like a hero out there, then come in and assault that woman," she asked. The voice teased at his memory. "You going to tell me?"

His gaze slid past a ship patch that said *ARV Gavroche,* and stopped at the name badge that read *Marlow, Caroline.*

With his last nerve, he raised his head.

Slowly, he lifted a hand, pulled down his coverall's hood, and met his former officer's eyes.

Marlow went as white as she'd been at Havilland Roads. She'd been only days out of resurrection and barely made it through thawing, he recalled. Stood to reason: that was why she was in Relief now, not on active duty. It was no job for a soldier, but a job only a soldier could do.

There was nothing wrong with her mind, though: she remembered him just fine.

"Why'd you hit that engineer?" she demanded. "You don't look crazy. You didn't look crazy at Havilland Roads either."

"I don't know what name she's using now, but she's Ty Parnell. Ship's officer on *Irian Jaya*. Engineering. She was in on the plot with the captain and her superior. Jumped ship with me—" he almost gagged at the words, "then ran. Just my luck to run into her here. She offered me a deal." Jim shrugged. "Blackmail, mostly, with a spot of sexual harassment thrown in."

"Never stood trial, did she?" asked Marlow. "You jumped. But she ran."

Jim nodded.

Marlow activated the microphone attached to the blue helm that gave the Relief service its name. "Give me status report on that injured engineer," she said.

"They've taken her to MedCenter? Emergency treatment?" She nodded as if satisfied by the faint squawk that was all Jim could hear.

"All right. We may need to take her offworld. Post two guards. Armed. Secure her hospital room. She's an engineer; tell them to expect she could be resourceful."

Another squawk, more protracted.

"Tell them it's for her protection. She was assaulted, remember? I'll brief you later. Just acknowledge and comply!"

At the brief and at-long-last-obedient squirt of sound, she snapped off the comm and grinned ironically at Jim. "Looks like you've done Fleet a good turn."

"Purely by accident, sir." Fleet had bounced him, and deservedly so, but Marlow was "sir" to him still.

"Question is, what am I going to do with you?" she asked, more to herself than Jim.

"Damned if I know, Commander." No, that was her old rank. "Captain."

An Arvy, not Fleet, captaincy, but she'd finally earned her own ship. "May I congratulate the captain on her promotion?" The courtesy popped out before he remembered he was the last man in the Alliance she'd want to buy a drink for.

"Shit!" Captain Marlow's oath sounded like a prayer.

"I'm going to have to bring you in," she decided. "For your own protection, if nothing else."

At the sound of voices coming up behind them, she half turned. Now, if ever was his time to make a break for it, if he could. Strike a shipsicle—or his old officer? He hadn't fallen that far.

"I've got him!" she called. She drew her sidearm as voices and footsteps grew louder. "I suggest you look like you're under arrest," she spoke in an undervoice. "You ought to be pretty good at acting by now."

Jim forced a brief nod. If he struck her and ran, they'd catch him and probably tear him apart, and that would very much be that. But Marlow had always been decent to him. If he was under her protection—God knew why she bothered—he was safe.

"Glad to see you're playing this smart. Now, we walk, nice and easy. Don't do anything stupid, or those nice people out there hunting you will probably mob both of us."

She gestured with her sidearm. "That way."

Head down, Jim walked through a double line of workers with improvised weapons and three or four security. He dared a glance at them. They had a full range of nonlethals: tanglers, slickies, and shockers. Clearly, they didn't know whether to use them to rein in the workers or turn them on him.

A deputy moved out of line and blocked his path.

"He surrendered himself to me," Marlow said. "So he's Relief Forces business, now, not your concern, and I'm taking him to my ship."

A growl went up. "You want what Relief brings you, you play by Relief rules," Marlow said, her voice calm. "This man gets a trial. You get supplies. Do I hear any objections? Didn't think so."

Another gesture with her sidearm, purely for dramatic effect.

"Now, I suggest the rest of you disperse."

ARV *Gavroche* 13

The hatch opened, and Jim followed Marlow onto *Gavroche*'s cramped lift. He managed, just barely, not to salute the Alliance insignia as the lift unsealed. The ship gleamed. Arvy or not, Marlow kept her ship to Fleet standards of order that felt like a homecoming Jim had no right to. A small, square hold, the metal of its bulkheads gleaming, opened onto a narrow corridor, its metal polished brighter than the red panels and full-spectrum overheads prescribed by remorselessly upbeat ship psychologists. The Arvy ship might not have the luxury of wide halls and fancy stencils, like a civilian ship, but it was also missing the slovenliness of the junkers he'd worked passage on.

Not bothering to guard her back or check that Jim was following her, Marlow led the way to an ordinary cabin.

"Not the brig?" he asked.

"*Gavroche* hasn't got a proper brig, and I've got plans for what cubic we do have," Marlow replied.

The cabin berthed two, but its nameplates were empty: even Arvy crew wouldn't be asked to share with the likes of him.

"Captain, I heard you board." The lift disgorged a stocky man with red hair. He carried what looked like a medical scanner, and was slightly out of breath as if he'd run for this corridor the minute he'd heard that the captain had boarded. "Any chills, shortness of breath planetside? I told you—"

"Ankeny, what part of 'you lost this fight three planets ago,' don't you copy? We're not back at Havilland Roads. You were the one who elected to transfer when I joined Relief and you finished residency so you could keep an eye on me.

An eye, mind you, not those damn wires up my . . . seriously, Tom, I really do think your last drug regime brought body temp under control."

"I'll want to see you in Sick Bay. Him too, if he's been Outside." The way the medical officer hovered over his captain suggested he'd probably transferred from Fleet and been leaned on by his then-superiors. Keep your eyes on Marlow. Wouldn't do to have Alliance's oldest shipsicle survive Freeze, then die from some off-world crud she picked up in the No Man's Worlds.

"Not now, Ankeny. I'm going to need a security team to bring in a prisoner. I'm going with it; claiming jurisdiction's not going to make us particularly popular downworld. You're coming too. Prisoner's going to need detox, grafts, possibly corrective surgery, but I'm not telling you how to do your job—"

"Of course not, Captain," the ship's medic cut in with a grin.

"—any more than you've got a say in telling me mine. When we get back to the ship, you'll only wish you were bored. Shenango's going to want the med supplies, including cryo storage as soon as we can offload, but I want your situational analysis of colony health first."

"Aye. No use enhancing population if they all die six months from now. You want the report when?"

Marlow actually laughed. "You've got a whole twelve hours. And that's only because I'm feeling kind."

She turned back to Jim and touched the lock. The door slid aside. Just as he expected: a tiny cabin, not just bare, but almost medically sterile.

"Quarantine," Marlow said. "Or house arrest, if you prefer. Whatever: it's yours for the duration. Shower, food supplies—surplus rations; not the greatest, but you can make do. Shipsuits behind the green panel: one size, fits no one. You've comp access, but restricted. I'll take your word not to hack into ship's systems."

Ankeny was eyeing Jim in a way he didn't like at all.

"See anyone you remember, Tom?" Marlow asked. She held up a hand as the medic opened his mouth. "Good. Now forget you ever recognized him. You—" she gestured at Jim. "In there. Settle in, clean up, and get some rest. I'll debrief you when I can. You won't be under guard, but I seriously wouldn't go looking for rec, if I were you."

"Captain—" Jim began. Marlow was leaving, abandoning him on board this ship where her word was all that would keep the crew *from . . . from doing what they have a perfect right to*.

"It's all right, mister," she said. "Crew's going to have all the trouble I can handle when they get the surprise package I'll be bringing back. Get a *shower,* for God's sake. Damned if I know where you've been bunking, but we've got standard sanitary facilities—and rules—on board."

He shut his mouth before blurting out "aye, sir" and shut himself into the refuge Marlow had provided. She'd bailed him out again.

The instant her footsteps faded down the corridor, the shakes caught up with him. No time to reach the head, but he managed to remember to sink onto the floor, not the spotless bunk. When he thought his knees might hold him, he forced himself up, peeled off the filthy coverall, stuffed it into the recycle chute that was just where God meant recycle chutes to be, and squeezed himself into the shower.

Planetside, Marlow had probably relaxed water rationing, but Jim was hardly what he'd call an honored guest. And if *Gavroche* expected to take on water on Shenango, she'd pay through the nose. He took a fast shower, hot as he could stand, and made every drop count.

Clean, shipsuited, a bar of Fleet surplus rations inside him, Jim finally let himself stretch out on the bunk. It was poor enough compared with his quarters in Nasser's house. That never felt like home: this did.

Marlow had *said* he wasn't a prisoner, but warned him not to push it.

Jim cut the lights and lay back. He told himself that the

tears that seeped beneath his heavy eyelids were because he was worn out, and, if there was a lump in his throat, it was probably reaction to some chemical that had smeared off his enviro-suit when he'd shed it. If he were going to have an allergic reaction, he'd probably have stopped breathing already.

Safe, for now.

He punched the thin pillow into a semblance of comfort, wadded it beneath his neck, and stared at the faint hearthfire glow marking EXIT over the door until his eyes closed.

IN THE DAYS THAT FOLLOWED—AT LEAST, JIM THOUGHT they were ship's days and ship's nights—he tried to use the announcements on *Gavroche*'s all-call frequencies to keep at least partly in the loop.

Captain on the bridge. Captain to cargo holds. Captain to cryo. Captain off-duty. Captain leaving the ship. Captain coming on board. Prisoner coming on board (and couldn't he just guess who?). Presumably, all hell breaking loose as ship's crew realized they had no proper brig and an engineer to guard: well, that was Marlow's headache, not his.

Preparations to receive Shenango officials—*don't think of Nasser, coming on board, and pray, just pray, that Marlow doesn't decide on a little surprise reconciliation party.*

Jim had his orders not to leave the cabin. By the second day, he was slept out, and the bulkheads started to press in on him. So, he instituted a daily regime: wake up, isometrics, shower, what passed for breakfast in terms of ration bars and reconstituted coffee.

Then, a session on computer. He read tech manuals, then accessed any ship's files he could reach. Games. News, however long out of date. Research Service history, protocols, theatres of influence. Job listings, which made him laugh, as if he could actually hope for some of the postings he saw, for a life that meant more than waiting to be discovered and despised, before he logged off for the day, staring at a mandala he'd programmed the computer to project. It let him get to sleep, even though his head had started aching early that morning.

Maybe he hadn't gone into anaphylactic shock from exposure to Shenango's toxic waste, but he definitely wasn't feeling all that great.

Another session of isometrics, followed by a shower and an attempt at dinner. *You're not dying; doctor's got more important things to do than coddle a jumper.*

By the third day, he was coughing hard enough to strain ribs. Damn, he *had* incubated something.

He could feel his skin go hot and clammy by fits. A fever. Probably infectious as hell. Marlow hadn't been back to see him. Probably, she was keeping his presence on board as much of a secret as she could, which wasn't much, the way word traveled on ships. Stay away, he wished her. If he gave this crud to Marlow, the crew would probably kill him. The cabin had a rudimentary medkit with broad-spectrum antibiotics.

Take two, lie down, and call me in the morning, the saying went.

He'd give it a try.

He showered again, hot as he could stand, forced soup into a system that kept it down—barely swallowed the meds, and lay down in his shipsuit for greater warmth.

And dreamed of bootplates on a ship's hull, a gauntleted fist whirling him around, swinging toward his helm, a blow he could never move fast enough to duck. His enemy's face, circled in lights, spun, morphing as it came round—male to female to a monster he couldn't see, then replaced with that heavy-gloved fist.

So this was how he'd die. His faceplate would shatter, he'd be breathing vacuum, and he'd freeze colder and deader than Marlow ever was. . . .

Impact, and he felt the jab of a thousand points of glass, of metal, pain that made him cry out, then choke as he spun off *Jaya*'s hull, flopping like some ungainly dead starfish in deep space until he felt the light, the burning of a star pulling him into its cleanly violent heart. . . .

LIGHTS BLAZED, AND JIM SCRAMBLED. HOW IN HELL HAD HE missed Red Alert?

He hurled himself off his bunk, turning up comm volume so he could hear orders loud and clear. The tiny chrono in the cabin showed ship's time, not planet's: when had they taken the ship up?

God, he'd been out of it!

Wait. Back up. He was still out of it.

This wasn't a Fleet ship at all. Or even *Irian Jaya*. He was on board ARV *Gavroche,* not quite a prisoner, but definitely not a welcome guest.

He was a little unsteady on his feet, but quite clear-headed now, except for the circular rainbows he saw clustering around the cabin's lighting strips. At some point, maybe around the time they'd taken the ship up, his fever had broken.

"Stand down, mister," came Marlow's voice, amused, but very tired.

He sank down on the tumbled bunk. If it wasn't a shipwide alert, he had some time. He wanted to reach for coffee, clear his head, but he didn't trust the effect of synthetics on what still felt like a very chancy gut indeed.

He really wasn't doing as well as he'd thought. But that had been Marlow's voice he'd heard.

"Captain, get out of here. I'm buggy as all hell."

"I just don't get him," Medic Ankeny muttered from behind her.

"Just treat him and get out, Tom. I'll tell you what I need you to know later, all right?" The last two words took the sting from her words.

"At ease, Jim," she ordered. She followed her own orders, a little faster than she seemed to want. She was pale, her eyes dark-ringed, and she wore planet-side thermals despite the stable ship's environment.

"Can I get you something hot to drink?" Jim started to ask. This was her ship, not his trial. The Board could have died of spacer's throat to a man, but still refused to drink with him.

She waved him back to his seat. Ankeny pounced on him with tests of pulmonary capacity, an inhaler that made him gag, and a spray hypo that left a lump of drug in his arm that he just knew was going to make him sicker than whatever fever he'd had.

"You'll live," Ankeny said. "If the captain will excuse me, I have a prisoner to get back to. Your victim's condition is stable now. Skin grafts. There may be some scarring, but she isn't going to lose her sight," he told Jim. As if he gave a damn.

The door slid shut.

Don't let it hit you in the ass when you leave, Jim thought. So Parnell would stand trial as a disgraced ship's officer and not a poor unfortunate, blinded by a man even guiltier than she.

Be thankful for small favors.

Marlow reached over to supplies, pulled out a cup, and activated its heating tab.

"Know a man named Nasser?" she asked.

"He's one of the Patrons, the first settlers, here. Major shareholders," Jim replied.

"Good man?"

"Real straight arrow," Jim replied before he thought. "I mean, he was good to me." He looked down, then made himself meet sober blue eyes. She had a right to be disappointed in him. She'd pulled him off Shenango, saved his not-so-precious butt, so he could damned well bear the sight of her anger. Or contempt.

Marlow nodded. "I told Effendi Nasser I was taking Engineer Parnell—she goes by Dannon—offworld for advanced treatment. I'm afraid he didn't quite believe my motives were humanitarian. We got into a staring contest, and he asked me for the real story."

Jim held out his hand, palm upward, as if Marlow would drop the truth into it. Instead, she reached into her uniform jacket, pulled out something, and handed it to him.

It was one of the copper coffee pots, enough for two cups, maybe two cups and a refill "if you're among good friends," that Nasser had taught him to use. He almost dropped it.

"Oh shit," he whispered. And closed his hand around the pot until its edges cut into his palm.

"You've got a real genius for throwing away futures, haven't you?" Marlow said. "You could've had a good life on Shenango. Could've put yourself to good use on a world that needed you. With an old man who actually cares whether you live or die. Don't suppose you've run into much of that lately."

"And every day of it would have been a lie," Jim found himself snarling. "Did you see Nasser's house? Hospitality means something to him. He moved me in there. First thing I saw once I got over how clean it was, he's got *four* 'regret to inform you's' framed on the wall of his study. His whole family, Captain. You telling me I could stick around, maybe inherit in default of *those*?"

"If he'd wanted you to, yes," Marlow said. "He showed me your record here. Corporate version of fitreps. You more than earned your keep. Wanted you to know. And, just in case you could swallow your pride and face up . . . he sent you that. Even now." She reached over and took the pot from him. "This thing looks old. Maybe all the way from Earth."

Jim nodded. "He's got a set of them. He taught me to make coffee his way."

"What do you say, Jim? Want me to call Shenango, work something out? We can say Parnell tracked you down, that she was blackmailing you—which has the advantage of being true—and that you pulled a citizen's arrest. That's almost the whole truth. You've stood your trial, man. Paid your debt to society, whatever the right words are. Now you've got a right to go on."

She leaned over him, though he waved her back.

"Come on, man, what do you say? Makework here on *Gavroche*—we can use a supercargo with your training, and then we'll drop you off on Shenango our next circuit."

Jim shook his head. "You like that pot so much, you keep it, Captain."

"Dammit!" Marlow slammed it down on a counter. Jim took the pot from her and turned it over, examining the ancient copper for dents, before he set it down with the respect it deserved. "The old man cares what happens to you. Asked me to promise you'd be well-treated. Do you at least have a word for him? You owe him that much."

"What can I say?" Jim asked.

"Thanks, maybe?" Marlow's voice cut like ice. " 'Thanks for the life I'm throwing away again'? God forbid you say, 'Sir, I'm sorry, I fucked up; can we start over?' "

Jim chuckled around the lump in his throat. "People don't use language like that around the Patron."

Marlow spread her hands out. "Whatever. Give an old man someone to take over after he does, give an idiot a future he could use. So, why am I not surprised the idiot says 'no' and cuts and runs the first opportunity—or opposition—he gets?"

"Patron Nasser meant something to me," Jim said. "I couldn't ask him to say, 'He's stood his trial, paid his debt to society.' Man's got kinfolk on New Amman, Captain. The only reason they've got a chance to go on living is because Secess', for God's sake, *Secess'* rescued the ship I abandoned. And I'm supposed to live as a guest in his house? Sorry, Captain, but I don't think so."

Marlow drank from her cup, then grimaced. Fresh-heated, synth coffee was bearable; tepid, it was good for polishing brass. She triggered the heat seal on a fresh cup, then handed him one.

"You're putting us all in one hell of a position, Jim," she said quietly. "Nasser asked me for the truth, and you're right; he's the sort of man you tell the truth to. I told him I was taking Parnell offworld to stand trial. I had to tell him about *Irian Jaya*."

"Damn!" Jim would have flung himself down on his bunk, but he was sick of it; it smelled of sweat, of sickness; and he couldn't risk antagonizing Marlow worse.

"He knows now you were involved. But I also told him," she went on, "that whatever else you'd done, you'd faced up to it. And you were responsible for bringing her to justice. Question's now: what do we do with you?"

Why not just let me sink to my own level? Jim thought.

He owed Marlow a lot, and now he owed her his life. The only time he hadn't been inundated with offers of help, of good-fellowship, had been on board *Irian Jaya*. And even there, some of the crew had befriended him. Why couldn't people leave him the hell alone?

He must have asked that out loud because Marlow's face went startled, she laughed, and answered, "Maybe you've got an honest face."

Jim stared at her over the rim of his—some sort of reconstituted soup, lots of calories, not much taste. He sipped it anyhow, perversely touched that she'd drink with him here on board her ship.

"The truth, Captain, as Patron Nasser would say."

"That's part of it, Jim. You look like everyone's idea of someone they'd like to ship out with, someone they'd trust at their backs. Even now, I suppose we think, regardless of what you did, the person we want to find in you is in there somewhere. So we keep after you, pick you up again, set you up—Fleet owes you for this one, Jim. So do the Arvies. Maybe even Astro-Pharm, though I wouldn't expect a thank-you note from Corporate any time soon.

"So you get a free shot this time. Tell me what you want, within reason, and I'll do my best to see you get it."

Jim looked down into the dregs of his soup. What did he want?

Turn back the clock. Make me innocent again.

He'd settle for a cold citrus drink. He reached for it. Marlow didn't seem to mind.

Even if Jim could go back in time, if he could turn down

the assignment that had put him on board *Jaya,* he had found the heart of darkness within himself: he was flawed at the core. He had jumped. He could fail again. And that was the truth, the whole truth, and nothing but the truth he'd have to live with.

"I want offworld," he spoke slowly.

"You've got it. We've already Jumped, even."

"I want full access to computer. The job banks. Your word on it."

"What kind of job?" Marlow brightened.

"Nothing much. Maybe out in the No Man's Worlds."

"We've got lists here. Relief and civilian postings. Anything else you want? A whole new ID? I'll tell you, I can probably get it for you when we drop Parnell off at Base."

Marlow bent over comp. Her fingers flew, keying in authorizations, pulling up job lists. Jim joined her at the terminal, sat down, and lost himself in a trance of datascan. There'd been a couple jobs he remembered, that he'd looked at before he'd gotten so sick. He pulled them up with the speed that had always gotten him good marks on his fitreps.

God, to stay on board this ship, with an officer he trusted. To be known, yet have a place that was indisputably his . . .

Until he betrayed it.

He couldn't risk it. Not with Marlow, the only person in the worlds who knew what he was and was good to him anyhow.

"This," he said and pointed at the listing.

"Why am I not surprised?" Marlow demanded of the tiny cabin. "The good news is it's Arvy operations and I can squeeze you in. The bad news: it's plague ship op."

"You're telling me they're not scouring every base in the Alliance to find people willing to put themselves on the line? Or you want scavengers to find the plague ships first and maybe spread whatever it is killed their crews before they die too?

"Look," Jim said. "I used to have a first-class spacer's license. I was an arms officer, remember? And after my stay on Shenango, I've got some experience working with HazMat and decontamination."

"And it's not like you've got all that much respect for your own life: if they needed someone to go over there—"

Jim nodded. "Right," he said. "It won't matter if I lose my nerve again. They can just shoot the plague ship into the nearest star. With me on it."

"Like the old Foreign Legion back on Earth, oh, centuries back. I wonder how many on plague ship runs actually go by their own names," Marlow reflected. "You're a romantic, Jim."

He ignored that.

"You asked me what I wanted. I want this. Do I get it, Captain?" Jim asked.

Nasser had been a trader. He'd taught Jim when to back off and when to push to make the sale. Now was the moment, and Jim pushed.

"There's a lot of trash out there in space. Let me help clean up the mess I made. It's the only thing I'm good for."

"Have it your way!" Marlow erupted. "You apply, I'll put in a rec, and we'll flag your biodata need-to-know. Good enough for you?"

A squeal erupted from the comm unit. *"Captain, I can't hold off Medic Ankeny any longer,"* the voice came through. *"He says if you don't get down to Sick Bay for your checkups, he's coming after you."*

"What were his exact words?" Marlow asked, amusement and relief lighting her eyes.

" 'You tell that captain of yours, if she doesn't get her butt down here, I'm going to certify her unfit to command and drag her in by the collar.' "

Marlow laughed. "Tell him I'm on my way, but, mind you, it's only to save him from getting a stroke. Got that?"

"Aye, Captain. And thank you."

Marlow rose and ran a hand through the blond curls Jim remembered. They were a little faded now, a little more controlled. Guess you had to expect changes after that long in

Freeze. If you didn't count the time Marlow'd spent on ice, the two of them were about the same actual age now. Maybe he was even a little older. He felt older than God, and she certainly looked it right about now.

"When you've got that application finished, put it through to my account. You've got two hours. I'll review it and send it on. Meanwhile—"

Jim let himself yawn. "Not going anywhere. Sir."

Derelict Ship *Casabianca*

14

To the end of his life, Jim thought, he would associate trouble with breath rasping his throat raw, a combination of his suit's respirator and maintenance and his own nerves.

Even as it protected him, the suit isolated him from the rest of the universe, up to and including the bodies lying curled in their last spasms on *Casabianca*'s deck or slumped at their duty stations. He could see them. He could not feel them or smell them. And there was nothing to hear.

Marlow would have helped you find a safe soft job downworld, he told himself again. *You were the one who put in for plague ship duty.*

"Jim, you there, man? Report!"

"Confirm sensor readouts, Marshal. *Casabianca*'s a dead ship," he reported.

The Federal Security marshal who commanded plague ship operations from the ship its crew called *Cinders* sounded even edgier than usual. He'd been as spit-and-polish . . . *as Marlow,* and here he was on board a ship that was the very ashes of the RV fleet, as the ship's crew joked.

As gently as he could with his gloved hands, Jim shifted the body of the man lying across his workstation down onto the deck. Rigor had come and gone, he noticed, and transmitted the information even before he sat in the dead man's chair. He stripped out ship's passwords with the lockpick code RV ships carried. He could do a core dump in his sleep, but never had. Somehow, it seemed disrespectful to the dead ship and risky to *Cinders* and her crew.

He'd signed on for plague ship duty out of . . . who knew what? Penance? A sense that he ought to continue the work of cleaning up that he'd attempted on Shenango? But *Cinders* suited him very well. Captain Nguyen and Marshal Galen probably knew his full name and, if he wanted to think of it, his full story. The rest of the crew didn't. In fact, most of them probably went by names other than their own. In general, they displayed no family holos, spoke of no lives other than their current round of duties and their once and future shore leaves. And most of them got morose and privately drunk on the ship's days arbitrarily designated as Alliance holidays.

Most of them never knew, nor cared to know, that the battered heavy cruiser *Cinders,* converted now to search, recovery, and decontamination, had once been named *Zinderneuf.* Marlow had chuckled and told him "look it up yourself" at the name. He had, and for once, he had laughed at himself, as well as his ship.

A trader had discovered *Casabianca* adrift by its Jump point. Warned off by what might have been a spot of unauthorized cargo offloading by the *Casa B*'s dead lights blazing their evil green at open airlocks, the trader had gone for a quick reward instead of a chance that whatever had killed ship's crew could breathe vacuum and maydayed Relief. *Cinders* was closest—some two Jumps away—and therefore selected as victim of choice.

In his four hours on board investigating what looked like a plague ship, Jim had found a dead crew and systems trashed by what might have been delirium. He had already restored environmental control, though he remained suited for personal safety. His breathing, the suitcomm that served as his lifeline, and the occasional *queep!* or rattle as a system came back online were all he heard. And Command and Control center lighting was still down, except for the lurid red glow of emergency track lights.

Screens at CIC's workstations glowed the ancient blue screens glowed long before humans had left Earth System. One flickered and blanked as Jim stared at it.

"Transmitting personnel records," Jim told the Federal Security Marshal. "Wait. Computer's gone down. Damn!" He pounded the workstation.

"Wait!" Jim breathed into suitcomm. He thought a faint apology at the dead man who'd spent his last moments of life guarding this station, then pounded keys with fingers that suddenly felt ungainly as sausages.

"No, accessing backups now. Ship's log, ready for transmission. Has Communications picked up any sort of buoy?"

"What about other ship's systems?"

He supposed he'd been stupid to expect Galen to transmit any such information in clear.

"Make it fast. We don't know we're alone here."

Jim had been on board *Casabianca* for four hours now. His eyes burned from his suit's environment. Turning his head sideways, he sucked a tiny sip of water from his helmet's tube. Drink too much and he'd regret it, though probably not as much as *Cinders*' long-suffering suit techs. And they'd have ways of making him pay.

"Heading down to Sick Bay now." Not that Jim expected all that much help from medical records. Whatever it was that had turned *Casabianca* into a plague ship seemed to have taken the ship's crew out too fast for medstaff to collect them all before they died.

"Keep in contact. Maintain video feed."

"Yes sir." "Aye" would have betrayed more of his past than he wanted to give. "Checking for signs of violence."

"You want backup?"

"Negative, *Cinders,* negative."

Not if Jim had time. He was going to have to do body checks on all of *Casabianca*'s crew. No point in drafting anyone else to share why plague ship detail got paid the big credits. One person less to risk needle sticks or suit tears. Just because *Casa B*'s atmosphere had been vented didn't mean whatever killed its crew was dead. Some exotics could live in vacuum by incubating or crystallizing. Plague ship detail might be First Contact, but with a death wish attached. If you weren't sure you'd gotten clean before you sent the drifter into the nearest star, you either went with it or quarantined yourself till you came down sick or starved.

But if what took out the ship was murder, the rules changed.

Jim stalked through *Casabianca,* his feet tapping out a funeral drumbeat on the dead ship's decks. A body sprawled face down by a lift. Jim knelt, turned the woman over awkwardly—careful of sharp objects that could give him a lethal stick even through the composite of his gauntlets. The face had gone flaccid, mottled with whatever it was that had killed ship's crew. The deck beneath the corpse was a mess, defrosting as life support warmed the place.

Definitely not murder, unless someone was using biotoxins.

Jim quickened his pace toward Sick Bay, then activated his suitcomm again.

"They all seem to have been killed by some viral agent or biocontaminant." Dispassionately, he recited clinical details—vomit, blood decomposition, excreta. Just as well protocols, along with common sense, ordered him to keep his helm on. Assuming he didn't spew his guts up into it. God, Maintenance would kill him quicker than plague.

"Got another problem down here, sir," Jim added. "Oxy's redline now, and I've got one refill. I'm reluctant to tap into ship's spares."

"I'll bring some over," said Galen.

"Negative!" Jim's objection was instinctive. "Just vent cylinders out the aft airlock. I can fly back and pick them up."

"Takes too long. You need backup, man. Unless you want to be a hero."

That answered one question Jim had had: if Galen knew who Jim really was, he'd never have made a comment like that. Even Marshals obeyed a ship's unwritten rules.

"I'm coming over. Two of us can offload evidence twice as fast."

"Want me to meet you at the airlock?"

"Negative. I'll find you in Sick Bay unless I hear otherwise."

Medical computers weren't just down, Jim realized. They'd been systematically stripped and destroyed.

"Not a plague, then, sir," Jim reported to Captain Nguyen.

"We're not here to speculate," she snapped. *"You and the Marshal conduct the preliminary investigation, then report."*

Nguyen was a tough one. *Cinders* mythology said she'd been Fleet, but the admirals decided she'd flown so many missions her number would probably be up next time she flew. They shifted her to a base, which permanently soured her disposition, and she'd quit right after Armistice. For all he knew, it was all true. God knew, she had the temper for it.

But Nguyen had never played Dragon Lady at him before. Must be that the captain didn't want to speculate in clear transmissions.

So.

This operation had just gone from plague ship mop-up to mass murder.

Better get as much done as he could before Galen arrived. Not only were the medical computers stripped of data that might help F&P—forensics and pathology—identify whatever bioagent had taken out the ship's crew, a search indicated that many of Sick Bay's most valuable equipment had been removed.

Just as well Galen was coming over from *Cinders*. Two could cover twice as much ground as one.

A touch on Jim's arm, and Jim tensed as if he were about

to go into Jump without a ship. Galen steadied him, and if he grinned, at least his visor was still polarized and Jim didn't have to see it and take notice for future reprisals.

"Medstaff wants tests of the bodies and the waste," he said. "I told him we'd conduct the tests, then upload them."

Jim grimaced. Even if he were sealed away in a suit, violating the bodies of long-dead crew was an unpleasant business.

"No use delaying," was what he said. He took his sampler out of his suit pouch.

Galen rewarded him with an approving grunt. "Situation's got its bright spots," the Marshal replied. "We'll only be uploading data, not sending actual samples back to the ship."

It was an article of faith on *Cinders* that Galen was a definite ship's asset: he had the nastiest, most suspicious disposition on plague-ship detail.

He hoped.

ONE EXCEEDINGLY UNPLEASANT HOUR LATER, JIM TRANSmitted the last test.

Galen turned to him. Sweat and a red flush of anger discolored Galen's skin, all the way to the top of his bald head.

Suitcomms beeped, and both men jumped.

"Gentlemen," Captain Nguyen said, *"scan shows Jumpsign. Estimated entry into normal space at 600,000 klicks. Two ships. Get back here."*

It would be the work of ten minutes, no more, to return to CIC, set course for the nearest star, then dash back to *Cinders*. And that's what they'd have done if this were no more than securing a plague ship.

"How long do we have, Captain?" asked the Marshal.

"You don't." Clearly, with something Jumping in-system, Nguyen wasn't going to leak mass/velocity projections.

"Captain's quarters," Galen said. "On the double. Sorry, Captain."

In theory, Federal Security could override a ship's captain. In practice, it rarely did. So, Galen was going to push it—

not just rid the system of a plague ship but try to find out what—if not who—had caused it.

They ran, panting in suits better adapted to zero G and absolute zero than to a ship's corridors, into officers' country. Captain's quarters were bigger than any he'd seen since *Irian Jaya*. Captain's records held significant anomalies.

"A third of the crew—just vanished. Including the captain," Galen summed it up. "Where'd they *go*?" he demanded of the inside of his helm.

Damn shame Jim couldn't rub his temples through a vacuum suit; he had a bitch of a headache started, like knives through his sinuses. "They might have been able to get the first ones to die to the airlocks."

"Would've left trails," Galen objected. "And if the others were falling ill and dying, there wouldn't have been anyone to swab the decks." He grimaced.

"I'm an arms specialist," Jim said before he thought. Was. "Not a pathologist. What's your take on this?"

Galen brought a gauntleted fist down on the absent captain's worktable. "I'd bring the doc over, but since Shoumatoff transferred, he's the only one we've got," Galen snarled. "Nguyen would space us in our underwear.

"Do the math, mister," he told Jim. "The ship left drifting, airlocks open, dead lights on. Stripped of critical installations. Weapons, too. The crew dead—messy dead, as many as we could find."

"We're meant to think this is a plain-vanilla plague ship, dump it, and leave, thank you very much," Jim said.

This was starting to stink worse than the ship. Just because the ship's crew had been murdered didn't mean that they couldn't have been killed by some exotic planetary biocontaminant rather than a known poison. Perhaps it was still alive on the ship.

Galen nodded.

"One thing doesn't add up. Say someone killed the crew and disabled the ship with every indication of coming back and getting it. Along comes *Cinders* and dumps it into the sun. What's in it for whoever poisoned the crew?"

Galen shot Jim a "don't be stupid" look.

Comm squawked again. *"Two ships,"* said *Cinders*' captain. *"ETA one point three hours."*

In a moment, Jim would have the rest of the puzzle worked out. "They removed everything they needed, but left the ship's hull integrity intact. Helm and engines still respond: I checked the instant I reached CIC. But they didn't take personnel records."

"Meaning that this ship wasn't intended to be found."

"Or," said Jim, deliberately keeping his body language, assuming Galen could read it through his suit, noncommittal, "it wasn't expected to be found by us."

Galen bent to open drawers, found them locked, and cracked the locks with a skill that Jim found highly intriguing. He launched a kick at the desk drawer he had opened, tearing it free of the desk. A scrap of plass followed, and Galen pounced on it.

Jim leaned over his shoulder to read it. Hard-copy transmission . . . planetary coordinates . . .

"Well, soldier?" demanded Galen, deliberately goading him.

He knows. Probably the only way Marlow could help me get the job. But he let the captain send me out here. Dear God, don't let me fuck up.

Jim activated the computer terminal, calling up navigational databases.

"Position is well into the No Man's Worlds." He traced the holocartographic projection that emerged. No one had tried to hack the system. "Meteor showers, a stray comet or two, gas clouds the size of several solar systems . . ."

If he'd been standing watch on one of his old ships, he'd have gone to alert status immediately. If Galen knew the worst of his background, he also knew the rest of it. "Marshal Galen, as your security, I recommend you return to ARV *Zinderneuf* immediately," he said formally.

Galen flashed him a "you've got to be joking."

"In fact, sir," Jim said, escalating the situation, "I require it."

"A moment more," Galen held up a gloved hand. "You agree we've got scavengers?"

"I think we've got hostiles braking in-system," Jim replied. "And they may be hungry. Now move!"

He saw Galen off, then set off himself at a run, heading to CIC to start *Casabianca* on her journey into the fire.

MUST BE GETTING OLD. OR LAZY. OR JUST WORN OUT FROM running ship's corridors in a suit built for zero-G with two hostiles coming in-system. Jim could smell his own sweat in the recycled suit's air as he gasped for breath and flung himself into the chair at the helmsman's duty station.

He locked in a course that would turn *Casabianca* into a comet hell-bound at nearly light-speed for this system's star. No point in making it easy for the scavengers if they had a mind to play catch with the *Casa B.* A faint hint of G-force pushed him into the helmsman's chair as the ship picked up speed. Damn shame to burn her, but better burn the ship than leave her—and *Cinders*—to scavengers.

"Marshal Galen," he spoke to the Federal Security man who, by God, had damned well better be waiting at the docking bay. "Please take off now."

"Leaving you? Remember what happened last time you played hero?"

A low blow. No time to hurt. No time to run.

"Hardly, sir. We have a duty to make sure that the ship can't be recovered. And I'm expendable."

"Gentlemen," came the warning from *Zinderneuf, "two ships insystem. V-dump completed. New vector now—they're dispersing to flank us. . . . Get your asses back home or I'll fry them myself!"*

"You heard the captain!" Jim snarled.

He sighed in relief as he saw the docking bay open and

Galen's scout streak back toward the temporary safety of *Zinderneuf.*

A shot from the welder that hung from his belt destroyed the navigation controls. *Lash the wheel; steady as she goes,* his consciousness gabbled in a blend of fear, nostalgia, and adrenaline.

"You idiot! You think I want Marlow to ask why I let her friend get his ass fried? I'm giving you a direct order, mister. Haul yourself out of there!" Nguyen's voice crackled with rage.

You took oath to obey direct orders, didn't you? All lawful orders. And you didn't break that oath. Not unless you were sure you could win by disobeying them. If you succeeded, you were a hero. If you failed and you got lucky, you were only messy dead.

He'd been worse.

Environmental system indications began creeping toward red, exterior hull temp along with it as *Casa B* streaked toward the photosphere. The radiation numbers were nothing short of terrifying. He'd done the math on how long his light scout could last at these temperatures and radiation levels. He didn't like it.

"I'll turn the ship and exit on the dark side," Jim told his captain. "If I boost to max, I should be able to escape the star's gravity well."

". . . before radiation fries you? I'll have the doc waiting for you in a lead suit." Then Nguyen laughed. *"I suppose you want me to herd those ships your way,"* she said.

"Only if they're hostiles."

"Oh, they're hostiles all right, mister. Right! Prepare to board FedSec Marshal Galen," the captain let Jim hear her order. *"All right, mister. Your colleague just boarded. Now, will you get yourself out of there or are you prepared to play boy on the burning deck all the way down?"*

"On my way," Jim said. He made the last course alteration, turning the ship to give himself a ghost of a chance, and ran for the docking bay.

* * *

PRESSURE THRUST JIM INTO THE PILOT'S SEAT OF THE SCOUT as he blasted out of *Casabianca*'s docking bay, practically before it was fully opened. He raced toward home, pushing acceleration, trying to keep the scout in *Casabianca*'s shadow as it fell, fighting to tear it free of the star's prodigious gravity.

If the scavengers took a shot at him, he was fried. He might well be already: the dosimeter was doing seriously evil things. He spared a hand from controls, reached into the med supplies packed into his seat, and injected himself. If he survived, he was headed for a long time in Sick Bay, losing hair and heaving up his guts, possibly a marrow transplant, and that would be nothing compared with what would happen when the captain got her hands on him.

Maybe he'd be smarter not to come back. Jim bit his lip, tasting the copper of his own blood. Too easy.

If he died, they'd think he was a hero. Even he didn't deserve to die with a lie that big on his account.

The scout rocked. That was what you got when you played hot pilot and redlined the engines. A glance at radiation levels showed that "hot" pilot was damned near the literal truth.

Only a couple thousand klicks till he reached home. If he reached it. Scanners showed warning shots streaking toward the scavengers.

"*Zinderneuf* . . . *Cinders* . . . come in," he hit comm. He felt a bit like an atheist praying and a bit like Judas. Nguyen didn't need to be distracted right now if she was taking the old ship against two raiders.

Damn! The engines jolted, hurling him forward against the console until he felt ribs snap. He was dead in space.

He sagged in his chair, waiting for his air supply to go. He supposed it was a quicker death than radiation poisoning.

He still had scanners, so he watched Nguyen herd one of the scavengers toward its target, firing with a vicious precision she must have learned in the same school that he had, picking off its engines so it followed *Casabianca* into the sun.

That's one! he could imagine her saying before she turned to take on the second.

Don't come too close, he wished her. *Don't get pulled in.*

Nguyen pulled the ship back, firing as she retreated. She wasn't trying to destroy it, just drive it off. Galen must have told her about the plass. Why risk the ship when you could send a fleet to take out a scavenger base?

"Yes!" He pounded his fist on an armrest as the scavenger achieved Jump. Damned sloppy. He wondered if it would emerge anyplace remotely recognizable, then wondered if he cared. He didn't. Not about that. Not about anything.

So damned tired . . .

"Zinderneuf *to scout . . . report!"*

Asking if he was alive.

"Engines are offline," he said. "I'm drifting."

"Have you got thrusters?" asked Nguyen. For once, her voice was neither cool nor angry.

"Aye, Captain." No point pretending they didn't share an Academy background. "Suggest retrieval . . . odds are unacceptably high . . ."

He fired thrusters anyhow, as dizzy from this new lease on life as he was from the anti-radiation meds.

"We're coming to get you, scout. Hang on. Help us out."

It would have been easier to drift. But he nursed the crippled scout's thrusters until *Cinders* edged up alongside. He could see the radiation levels sink as the ship's bulk maneuvered between him and the sun.

"Thanks for the shade," he managed. "Anyone got a cold beer?"

He heard the familiar babble of procedure from docking bay, roused himself to fire the thrusters—microbursts positioning the scout till *Cinders'* people could come out and fetch him home.

They were on him practically before the doors closed, in full protective gear, pulling him from the scout, peeling him from his suit, strapping him down.

Galen, wearing radiation gear, came over to his gurney,

royally pissing off the CMO. "Looks like you're going to live. You may not enjoy life much for awhile, but—" he pressed Jim's shoulder with a gauntleted hand. "Welcome back."

He knew. Knew it all. And welcomed me home.

When *Cinders* returned to base and reported, there'd be talk. Lots of it. And Galen *knew*. Nguyen probably knew too.

There'd be too damned much chatter. Sooner or later, attention would fall not on *Cinders*' mission, but on its crew. And the worlds would know what Nguyen and Galen had permitted on board. Unacceptable.

Maybe Jim could talk to the CMO and be too sick to leave his ship, but not sick enough for a transfer to station hospital. He'd have to think about that.

Later.

Bad enough *Cinders* had risked herself to bring him home. A good ship. His ship. He couldn't let her be dishonored.

System Station Raffles 15

My eyes ached from the explosive blink that meant System Station Raffles' Legal Affairs needed yet another retinal scan, and I didn't think I'd ever get my thumb clean from the stamp pad that had been delivered to *Gavroche* along with what seemed like a bin of paperwork. Stationmaster here either was obsessive-compulsive or had taken the notion of a "pre-war standard of service" to the nth power.

I had my doubts about which war Raffles meant. For that matter, I had my doubts about Raffles, but, "Ignore the public relations," read the note that accompanied my orders here, "they're the best for the kind of work we need." So, obediently I blinked, squinted, and thumbed away as sensors told me that Hull Maintenance was already out and about, reinforcing Jump shielding, and that my techs were suited and waiting at the airlocks.

Ah. The master agreement, and they wanted what? An actual signature? Didn't these punctilious fools realize how easily that could be forged?

More of this shiny new station's ridiculous pre-war amenities, I decided. They already had my retinal scan on file—multiple times, and the public health medstaff that had stomped, enviro-suited, on board just as if we were a plague ship, as soon as we could get an auxiliary lock open, had exacted enough blood and tissue samples from every one of *Gavroche*'s crew to clone the lot of us.

I signed, sealed the ostentatious document—plass disguised as heavy paper down to the fake watermark—and signaled for a messenger. Time was—and if Raffles was really serious about pre-war courtesy, station management would know it—ship's captain would hand-carry the Master Agreement. But one courtesy call was enough, and I'd already been over to the Fleet base.

I'd juggled schedules, fought with my conscience, and lost a battle with my exec GW, which was short for George Washington Parker, another Fleet veteran who'd gone from regarding himself as my baby-sitter to regarding himself as my right-hand man—and possibly thumb and forefinger on my left, and what were *you* grinning at, mister? So, thank you very much, I was actually allowing myself forty-eight hours of shore leave, long enough to see an old friend and pick up a few tapes, maybe a bottle of brandy or so. Captain's supplies, such as they were. And then, I'd relieve my exec, who'd be sitting at the Cape of Good Hope Hostel waiting for me. GW was right, even if I didn't feel like giving him credit for it. Refitting for a long, deep-space tour was going to have us working watch on watch.

First shift had won the draw from the bowl in my quarters kept sacred for the purpose to determine who got shore leave first. They'd already trooped off to wage war with the local beer surplus and sack their credit balances. The others knew their duty schedule. Comm buzzed.

"Marlow."

"Station's airheads are here, Captain," GW's deep voice came over the comm. *"As soon as you're off-ship, they can begin oxygen exchange."*

"On my way," I said. About time they changed the air onboard: even with fresheners, it had gotten a bit ripe. Having no wish to learn to breathe vacuum, I swung my carryall over my shoulder and started toward the main personnel lock.

It yawned onto the entropy of the docking bay. Transports, some painted yellow, some blinking with a spectrum of warning lights, whined, grunted, and sidled around containers bright with the holographic ideograms that, from Earth to the No Man's Worlds, meant Food Supplies.

Coils of pipe the size of one-person scouts, loaded one to a float pallet, hovered above the shiny metal decks beside cargo-sized airlocks, waiting to be shoved Outside. Personnel carriers whirred down the aisles created by storage. One eeled past pressurized cylinders of replacement oxy, and pulled to a stop outside what we might as well call my ship's front door. As station crew swung down, my own people boiled out of locks and hatches.

How long had it been since we'd seen faces other than our own? Much too long, judging by the enthusiasm with which my crew shook hands, clasped arms, then turned back to business.

"Got everything you need, Captain?" came GW's shout. He'd started in Engineering, and his eyes were flicking nonstop from the ship to the fascinating collection of equipment in docking bay.

I'd better. Once the ship was sealed to facilitate cleaning and oxygen resupply, I wouldn't be able to board again except in emergency and in full pressure gear for which, of course, Raffles Station would extract a rental charge and a penalty fee. Probably a hefty one.

"I'm last off," I agreed, signed out, and left my ship. "See you at the Cape!"

Even if I'd finally licked that little problem with regulating my body temp, docking bay was damn cold. Condensation had formed into pools of ice—small ones, unlike the ones I'd seen last port, when two of my engineers had jury-rigged skates, of all things, and conned the local techs into trying them. We'd treated one broken leg and then had to placate the stationmaster—the injured party had been a station employee—with ship-brewed whisky. Raffles' seals were better, as warranted, so we'd be spared the skating competitions this time, but docking bay would stay cold until human efforts warmed it.

I tugged down the blue helm that gave the Relief Service its nickname so it covered as much of my ears as it could, and pulled up the collar of my station-going rig. Metallic blue, with captain's insignia set in gold bands on the shiny cloth of my jacket, emblazoned with the Relief Services seal across the back: the heraldry of post-war Alliance, and easily recognizable across a crowded docking bay.

"Captain, over here!"

Ryutaro Jones, who'd been leaning against a pressure cylinder, nonchalant as you please, straightened, waved in a civilian's version of a salute, and strode across the deck as if he was completely at home amid the turmoil of coils, tubes, and working crew.

I grinned at the sight of him. When he'd befriended me—and incidentally gotten a story that had made his face as recognizable as mine across the No Man's Worlds—he'd been little more than a precocious kid. It wasn't just that he'd filled out, with what looked like solid muscle on arms and shoulders. His venture to Imperial Tokugawa in formerly Secessionist space had matured him from a boy with the glow of celebrity on him to a man even more celebrated, but less unfinished, equally at home with who he was—and who people thought he was.

My eyes blurred, but damned if I'd let him see it.

Instead, I folded my arms and studied him. Studied him again, deliberately glancing up and down so he could see me doing it.

He had started to bow with the exquisite manners I recalled from his Secess' kinsman, Hashimoto-sama, but recovered and came forward, holding out his hand. His dock jacket and trousers weren't the flashy silver that inner-systems spacer-wannabes squeezed their fat selves into when they had the credit, but a deep bronze. Being freelance, Jones didn't wear the insignia of corporation or service. Besides, his face was too well-known to need it. Instead, lightning flashes of pewter flared across chest and shoulders—meticulously picked up in the color of the gloves he wore tucked with such offhand elegance into his belt—testimony to the fact that no ship's officer would be ordering *him* to lend a hand any time fast.

"Well, will you look at you?" I drawled. "Jones, if you're dressed like that, how in hell's an honest spacer going to get you to earn your keep?" In the very earliest days of his career, trust fund balances back on Earth frozen about as solid as a shipsicle, Jones worked his passage from station to station. He'd earned his keep, too, I'd heard.

"You tell me when and where to report for duty, Captain," Jones met my grin, strode forward, shook my hand, pulled me toward him for a back-pounding hug, then guiltily released me from his young-man's strength.

"I haven't been a shipsicle now for years," I told him. "I won't crack."

"And I'm glad to hear it. Still, it's cold enough to freeze off . . . It's cold. If you're sure you don't need me to hoist coils or steer float pallets, let's get out of the docking bay and into a warm drink."

I refused his offer to sling my carryall over his own shoulder. "I've got your *Willow Bridges* in the bag, Jones," I told him. "Be glad if you could sign it." I'd worked my way through three prints of Jones' latest book—the prize-winner he'd written about his trip to Tokagawa. It had won the venerable Booker Prize back on Earth, not that people out here cared about that: what they did care about was the testimonials on its case, which praised it for helping people on both sides of the border make peace with their memories. "To bind up the systems' wounds," an official on Tokugawa had paraphrased an old Earth official, and you should hear what the Alliance psychs say. I keep ordering it and lending it, and people keep "forgetting" to give it back.

"I'd be honored," Jones said. "And then what?"

"And then?" I laughed. "Write me a scandalous dedication. Then, I'll sell it and pay my passage back home. Give you a cut of the proceeds, even."

"Cam!" Jones reproached me. He signaled for a carrier, swung aboard, and hoisted me up onto the transport, little more than a flatbed on floats, with a couple stanchions to grab hold of.

"You serious? I mean," he dropped his voice, dismayed, "are you serious about needing credit?"

As the carrier lurched into movement, I batted at him. "Joke, Jones. Damned fool."

He huffed out his breath, exaggerated relief, and grinned. The two loaders and one—looked like a comptech, judging from the trance she was off into—ignored us.

"That's a relief. Here I am, set to interview you—our brave Blue Helms, rebuilding the galaxy, and how you've come out of time warp and rebuilt your life along with the outback worlds to help Old Earth—and you're ready to pack it in and head back? Lousy news, Cam. Have a heart. I'm only as good as my last story."

We managed a laugh out of that one.

The carrier picked up speed, and we hung on to the cold rails. "I've thought about going back, haven't you?" I asked. "Don't you still have living family there?"

"Every time I think of heading Home," he said, "I find me another assignment. I get to skip the routine stuff now, focus on the new, the strange, the downright scary. You'll love this one. Kind of what they used to call a Cook's tour of stations. Earth pays me, while the stations put me up in prime quarters, so I can write about them and bring in tourists. Your shore leave's on the house, Cam."

"Damned if I want to jeopardize my amateur status just to see how the other one billionth lives, Jones." I said.

He was a good-looking boy. Any woman my age with one eye and half a brain would have seized the day and a night or two or three.

We'd never served together, Jones and I, but we knew the same people. Call it shipmates, once removed. Shipmates don't mess with other shipmates. Prejudicial to good order and discipline and all that.

"C'mon, Cam. I'll have them post guards." Was Jones actually blushing? Must be the cold.

"Only on that condition, mind you," I let myself be persuaded.

I didn't know what kind of billet Jones had in mind, but it would be good to be warm, good to bunk where cubic still mattered, but wasn't critical, and best of all to bathe in water that didn't make you remember what it had been recycled from and eat food that hadn't been freeze-dried, reconstituted, and probably worse. This past three months, we'd been on preserved rations, and I was sick of the taste of rat. Next trip would be longer. This was why we'd come this far inside Alliance, for an upgrade of the Jump engines, reinforcement of *Gavroche*'s sixty-year-old hull, and rebuilding of our cargo bays to let the ship make the longest hauls.

"What've you dug up this time?" I asked.

"You'll love it," he said. "The most fabulous fake I've run into yet. You've seen Raffles' infodumps, haven't you? The whole station's obsessed with 'returning to a pre-war standard of courtesy and service.' "

"With a rate scale to match. Too rich for my blood." If we hadn't needed refit of a kind we couldn't get in the No Man's Worlds, *Gavroche* would have stayed out-system where we belong.

"Well, this hostel I've got us rooms in isn't just pre-war,

it's a model of a pre-war ship. Old Earth, blue water. Civilian."

"Which war is it pre?" I shook my head.

"Apparently, this ship—the *Queen Mary*—was quite the thing in its day. Then, it served as some sort of troop carrier during its war—old Earth's second World War, they told me. Management's taken advantage of the planet to recreate its decor—all wood veneers, the more the merrier. The Queen of Woods, they called her. You have to see it to believe it."

I've seen systems where one of those wood panels could feed a family for a year. How the other hundred-*billionth lives*, I thought.

Still, if Jones' readers, or his editor, were paying, I'd force myself to enjoy the show.

When Jones gave me the high sign, I swung down off the carrier and trotted after him into—on board?—this overpriced replica of a Terran luxury liner. The lobby was paneled in mellow wood. It was softly carpeted, muffling the clack of metal-plated boots and making people lower their voices. And it was staffed by uniformed clerks so discreet they pretended not to recognize Jones or take notice that the woman with him wore Arvy dockside gear and was easily two decades older than he.

In good order, they relieved Jones first of ID, then of my presence. "Nineteen hundred hours," Jones called after me as I was taken in tow by a uniformed personage. "Meet me for drinks in the First Class Lounge before dinner!"

"If the lady would follow me?"

I managed not to say "aye-aye, sir" to the personage who bowed me with the ponderous decorum of an admiral through an elaborately wrought brass gate, down a flight of stairs, and into a long, narrow corridor that seemed to curve, imitating the curve of a sailing ship's keel.

"If the lady wishes a guide," I was told, "she has only to signal when she is dressed." The functionary's glance clearly indicated that my best dockside gear was completely inadequate. Relief Service had no mess dress, but I was damned if I'd let Jones down.

I looked at my jacket and gestured. *Your recommendation?*

"Your stateroom computer has a wardrobe rental facility," he added. "Or you may order direct from Piccadilly, our shopping area in First Class."

Sounded like a plan.

SHADOWS POOLED IN THE CEILING HIGH ABOVE US, BUT CANdles glowed, reflected on the white cloth enveloping the tiny, choice table we were bowed to with such grace that it didn't even seem like an affectation. White cloth napkins without a single mend in them. Menus bearing the ship's heraldry, elaborate food pornography—to my unaccustomed eyes—in at least three languages. The dining room was larger than I imagined primitive shipwrights could have built or modern shipwrights would have found useful: except on troop carriers, there was no reason to serve eight hundred diners all at once. And no troop carrier—or any starship currently under construction—would ever have been so lavish.

"Outside" glowed projections of sea and stars; within, as Jones had promised, it was all wood and luxury, cream and gold and beige. We stared up at a model of Earth's Atlantic ocean, with two tracks on which lights moved: a crystal replica of the ancient "ship" itself and its sister ship, named after another queen. Crossing all that water without proper navigation equipment or any computers at all: now, that took nerve. Give me Jump, backed-up navigation computers, and a competent helm officer any day.

"Jones," I said, "this is preposterous!" I held up my wineglass to the candlelight with the studied gesture I'd learned, before the war, when Fleet had sent us through charm school.

The sleeve of my rented gown fell away from my arm as I admired the color of the wine. Wine-dark, like old words for sea. The wine had been imported in storage balanced by gyroscope so it would travel well. Then it had to be given time and space on station to settle. Then the cost had to be tacked onto the bill.

My rental gown was blue, of course: I could count on one hand the number of times I've worn anything else since my resurrection or before it. But this blue wasn't the coarse heavy fabric of Fleet dress uniform or the industrial-strength of Arvy gear, but a filmy indigo with a starfield of silver threads shimmering through it. I'd held it up to the light when the steward delivered it: I could see my hand through it, but once I got it on, it covered me completely—a source of some comfort when your chronological age is sixty-something, never mind the fact you've only been awake some forty of it, and you're seated across from a man in his late twenties. I saw the other women and some of the men—many of them out-system tourists squandering their life savings—eyeing him and whispering, "That's Ryutaro Jones. You know, the author." Then they'd shift to me and turn speculative.

Back off. I'm his bodyguard, I thought at them.

"Here's to preposterous, then." Jones clinked his glass with mine. "Absent friends."

Last time I'd made that toast was after Jones told me my oldest friend went out the airlock at Havilland Roads. My glass halted halfway to my mouth.

"Shit, Cam, I didn't mean to—"

"Absent friends," I replied, and drained the glass, welcoming the rich, mellow burning that went all the way down. "God, Conrad would have loved this. But it's still preposterous. So. Tell me. How was the sake at Hashimoto-sama's?"

"All this is Eldest Uncle's fault, you know, Cam," Jones said. Visibly relieved we were over the Moment, he signaled for more wine. "He's retired now."

"Retired? What's he doing now he's not fighting us?"

I remembered the tall, robed officer seconded to Havilland Roads. It had been Red Alert, and he was on his way to deal with a ghost ship, but he'd made the time to insure my safety.

"He's built himself a scholar's retreat—another old Earth

tradition. He practices his calligraphy and cultivates chrysanthemums."

"Chrysanthemums?"

Jones shrugged. "Big white blossoms. Something to do with family history, I think. I told him I was thinking of going Home. He took me to see the family swords and told me I hadn't earned an honorable retirement yet. So, instead of packing it in, I hitched a ride on the next Arvy ship, wrote up my trip to Tokugawa and some other stories, sent them in, and"—he gestured with his wineglass—"here I am. Here we are. You know, our people tried to buy the original of this ship, but they wouldn't sell. At least, not to us. It finished up its days as a hotel. Beached. Hardly seems right."

"Hardly seems affordable. My God, Jones, the power consumption alone—"

"I've studied its P&L. This ship earns her keep. Besides, the veneer comes from downworld. Maintenance keeps a good thousand stationers in jobs, and it's a draw over three or four systems. Once I file my story on Terra, management's hoping for even more business."

"You make me feel so old," I complained.

"You don't look a day over thirty," Jones assured me.

That wasn't a direction I felt like going in. I was senior here; I could change the subject, and I did. Fast. "So, what's the story you're looking for, Jones? Fleet's oldest shipsicle makes good?"

"That'll pay the rent. But what I really want is to tape you for part of what I'm going to call *Tales of the No Man's Worlds.* I heard you'd been out on Shenango. I'd like to get that story from you. You wouldn't believe how interested readers are, now their asses are safe, with how the No Man's Worlds survived at all."

Dinner arrived, in a parade of fresh food, not frozen or reconstituted, enshrined in heavy chafing dishes and a flourish of at-the-table preparation. When we'd finally convinced staff we really didn't, but thank you very much, need any more pre-war hospitality, I picked up my coffee cup and gave Jones my best captainly look.

"All right, Jones. Give. For the past half hour, you've been looking down and away, and don't tell me it's my imagination."

Jones shook his head. Clearly, he wasn't ready to tell me yet what he'd brought me here to tell me.

I've got forty-eight hours. I've an exec who deserves time off and a ship to refit. On the double, mister, I thought at him. But that was war-time thinking. Let a thing go unsaid, and you—or the person you wanted to say it to—might not be in the wardroom the next ship's day to say it or hear it.

So the war was over. Sometimes a direct assault wasn't the best strategy.

Target acquired. "I saw on station's manifest that old *Cinders*—Medical Investigations Ship *Zinderneuf*—got released from Quarantine. I think I'll go over, talk to the captain."

Nguyen wasn't all I wanted to see on board *Cinders*. I hadn't heard word one from Jim for more than a year, but that isn't surprising. Jump-message costs in the No Man's Worlds are almost as high as . . . as "pre-war levels of service." But now that we were both on-station . . .

The hell with tact. I'd just scored a direct hit.

"All right," I said. "Spit it out, mister."

Jones shook his head. "It's not that easy. I've been trying so hard. Cam, how could I have known I'd get to the point where I'd go from covering news to making it?"

I waited him out.

"It's our old friend."

I drained my cup. It had cooled and gone bitter just like ordinary ship's coffee. "You've seen Jim."

I was stifling. Maybe it was this damned hothouse environment, not my body playing tricks on me. I'd already lost one career. "Let's get out of here," I muttered.

Jones rose and held my chair, mindful of the "pre-war courtesies," omission of which would have caused a stir in this mannered little enclave. They probably were in the operating manual or something.

"Care for a walk on deck?" he asked for all the world as if we were on Old Earth and on a real ship, not this overpriced theme park.

The "decks" running outside this hostel's function rooms were the closest thing to Old Earth teak that Raffles Station could get. Abruptly, I was sick of the prefabricated gaudy sunsets management was offering this shift. Ersatz South Pacific skies for a ship whose range had been the icy gray waters far to the north? This ship's memory, and her honor, deserved better.

"I'd just as soon avoid the light show," I said.

"You'll like the Observation Lounge," said Jones and steered me from the Cabin Class Dining Room on a rising tide of whispers.

CONCENTRIC HALFMOONS OF A BAR, ELABORATE WITH SHINING chrome and silver, and dark-upholstered little islands of solitude and comfortable chairs: a wave of Jones' hand brought us to a table that overlooked the forward "deck," and conjured a waiter who carried a bottle kept ostentatiously dusty and two balloon glasses almost the size of pressure helms.

Jones poured for both of us, handed me a brandy, then brought his hand down on the table with more violence than "pre-war courtesy" called for.

"All these simulations make my teeth hurt. Let's have an end to them." He gestured, and the projection of a tropical night, phosphorescence cresting on the waves, vanished, to be replaced by an honest starfield and a reassuringly normal, if unaesthetic, view of fuel and oxy cylinders in safe off-storage station. Less deliberately picturesque, of course, than Raffles' designers intended, but I liked the real view better.

Jones had a sip of his brandy. Let's be honest and call it a healthy swig, an insult to brandy of this quality. And price.

"What is it, Ryu?" If the nickname was a step wrong, I'd apologize.

"What's the play about the Old Earth tech who woke up and thought he'd been an ass?" Jones said. He tossed back another brandy.

"You'd drink that with more respect if you were paying for it. And you don't look like an ass. Not that I can see," I told Jones. "Maybe, if you could just tell me what you want me to hear just as if you weren't a worlds-famous writer who has to tie his words up in fancy ship's knots—"

"Plain words, then, Cam. I really did plan to make my name, then go home. But Hashimoto's words have a way of getting under your skin. He's right. I haven't earned the right to retire, and the idea of going home and playing celebrity makes me gag. What about you? Look at all you've been through. But can you honestly tell me you'd be comfortable going back to a place we've never seen that we all call Home anyhow?"

"Damned if I know." I laughed and had a sip of the brandy. It went down smooth and lit up like a nova.

I kept my eyes on Jones. As ship's captain and officer, I'd listened to a lot of young crew in my time and learned to watch for cues. "I've started to think about it. I don't want to leave the service and stick around in the Outback, either, telling stories that get bigger every year and looking for an easy berth or a warm place where I can lie down and get old. Do you?"

"Maybe I'll show up at *Gavroche*'s docking bay, offering to work my passage. Will you take me on?"

"My crew tells me the whole truth, Jones. Can you?"

Another direct hit. Jones flinched at it.

"Captain . . . Cam . . . I seriously fucked up, and it's not me who's going to pay for it. It's Jim."

Oh God, now what? I'd pulled Jim out of at least two situations now, and I gathered that they weren't the only ones. Gossip travels faster than ships through Jump. Given the size of the No Man's Worlds, there aren't that many of us out there who Jump from star to star, and we tend to know each other—and all the same stories.

So, when a man not all that young any more, but still fair-haired, likable, and competent—just what, ordinarily, you'd want on your roster—shows up and takes the first job offered him, it fits into a pattern, and that pattern says *Jim.* You wanted legal salvage? Refitting? Someone knowledgeable to assist ship's officers in station supply depots? He was your man. And he'd be the best damn employee anyone could have until someone mentioned *Irian Jaya,* someone recognized him, or he made himself conspicuous.

Then, he'd disappear, leaving gaps not just in the work, but in people's lives. Like Nasser on Shenango, who'd lost four children to the war, but found it in his heart to trust Jim. Nasser wasn't trusting now; and that, as a man nears the end of his life, is a terrible thing, and one I had my share of blame in.

When I'd pulled Jim off Shenango, I'd taken some care to help him choose a ship. *Zinderneuf* had a reputation everyone knew about but never mentioned: a lot of its crew, even its officers, were on their second or third identities. They were skilled, true, but they were also discreet: they protected their secrets and their shipmates' secrets. I really thought he'd reached safe harbor at last.

In which case, freezer burn really had done bad things to my brains.

Jones stood and wandered to the windows, staring at the cylinders orbiting Raffles Station as if they might blow at any time. I gave them a quick once-over: no distress lights or security; let's have more brandy. I loaded Jones' drink, got up, and brought it to him.

He drank fast, as if he'd stood on an actual ship's deck and taken a chill. Apparently, life support had manufactured quite an effective breeze.

Another boy with a guilty conscience, Marlow. Let's see you salvage this one.

"I'll tell you," Jones said, looking away. For God's sake,

did he think I was going to call Security and throw him in the brig?

"*Cinders* has been through some interesting times," he began.

I nodded.

"It had a run-in with something that looked like a plague ship, but I found out that there were enough personnel irregularities, enough systems missing from the ship that Captain Nguyen flagged the incident as probable scavengers and went on Red Alert. Didn't help that two ships Jumped in-system just as *Cinders* was ready to pull out. Jim took charge of setting the plague ship on course with the nearest star.

"Those two ships—well, he stayed on board the plague ship longer than he should, to insure that no one could secure it and whatever killed the crew, then had to pull out fast. Took a lot of radiation."

"What makes you responsible? Getting a God complex now that you're a bestseller?"

"*Cinders*' medstaff thought he needed better care than they could give. Ship got a bonus for demolition, so they headed in from the No Man's Worlds. As they exited Jump, they got another call."

"Another plague ship? They'd be within their rights to pass it along."

"Not plague," said Jones. "Survivors of a raid. They were lucky, in a way of thinking. Whoever crippled the ship didn't take ship's survivors' primary comms or life support—just Jump drive components. And a few people, mostly children. A couple women."

"Damn! This is a business for Fleet, not Medical."

"Fleet's onto it. But *Cinders* transferred ship's survivors. Some of them were in pretty bad shape. The fight had gone to hand to hand.

"Jim could scarcely get out of his bunk without blacking out, but, seeing Sick Bay was packed, he made them discharge him. More to the point, he insisted on light duty. Light! I don't call walking with walking wounded light,"

Jones added. "Medstaff said he had a real knack for dealing with survivor guilt. Other people's, that is."

"How do you come into it?" I asked before Jones got side-tracked any further.

"Fleet ordered Nguyen to bypass the outer stations and debrief here. The fact that station's got first-rate medical facilities probably played a part in the decision. As luck would have it, I'd just arrived here myself to check this out"—he patted the table—"I was hanging around the docks, you know . . ."

"Yes," I made myself smile, hoping Jones would lighten up. No joy. Quite literally. "It's a very bad habit you have."

"And so I heard when *Zinderneuf* hooked up with station. As soon as the ship cleared Quarantine, I went over to the hospital. It was under security lockdown, but hell, Cam, the day I can't get around first-degree lockdown, I *will* pack up and go back to Earth."

"So you got in, and you found Jim. Will he recover?"

"No residual damage, and his hair's already growing back. That wasn't the problem. Next time I saw him, he told me he was planning to leave the ship. Nguyen had actually offered him the chance to rejoin once he was released from hospital, pay his passage from ship's funds, even."

"Name of God, why *this* time?" I interrupted. Jones' face fell further.

"Because I'd *talked* to him. More than once. That attracted attention. What was Ryutaro Jones doing spending time with a crewman who'd just gotten done heaving his guts out? Then the newswires got wise of it. There were stories, a time or two, and the old one surfaced. I tried to kill it, but they'd already released his image."

"Nguyen knew," I muttered. "For that matter, so did the Marshal on board, Galen. It had been a condition of taking Jim on. He had to come clean. We didn't tell him, but he'd have to have figured out that his chain of command was already in on his worst secrets. For God's sake, he could have found asylum there!" I almost slammed my brandy glass down on the rail, then remembered how frail it was. Why waste brandy? I drank it instead.

"That's what I said, Cam. But he said he had shipmates to consider. They had secrets of their own. Now he'd attracted so much attention, even if it did die down, he was a liability. Guess he liked them, liked them a lot.

"So he left to protect his ship."

Jones slumped. Shadows drifted over his fancy stationgoing rig, making him look drab and tired. "Told you I'd fucked up, Captain."

"Once it all blew up, what did you do?" I sighed.

Jones shrugged. "What else could I do? Offer him money? He wouldn't take it. I made a few calls, then made myself scarce. A couple days later, I went back to the hospital. Jim had checked out, then dropped from sight. Captain Nguyen—when I went to see her, she ripped me another—'Leave it alone, you've done enough damage for one best-seller' was about the mildest thing she said." He had another mouthful of the brandy. "I suppose I deserved it."

So Jim had gotten to Cynthia Nguyen, too. Maybe I wouldn't be so fast to pay a courtesy call. *Cam, you coward.*

Jones put his head in both hands, massaging his temples with long, supple fingers. If he thought it was bad now, just wait till he woke up.

A moment more, and he'd be weeping. I took the snifter out of his hand. "Come on, Jones. Let's call it a night. I'll get you back to your room. Stick your finger down your throat, drink as much water as you can, and take an alcodote or five, will you?"

I expected to have to wedge his shoulder under mine—*look at the two drunks in evening clothes; she's old enough to be his mother*—Jones didn't need that kind of buzz. But he managed to stand, then navigate till we transited the brass gates leading to guest quarters. Then, he collapsed against me. I got him in a come-along-with-me hold and half dragged, half led him to his stateroom, propped him against the bulkhead, inlaid with more fancy wood, surprise, surprise, and fumbled for his hand.

Jones gave a muzzy brandy laugh, and tried to nuzzle my neck. I pushed him away. "Idiot! Damned if I'd jump you. Just put your hand against the lockplate, will you?"

I got him into his room, pushed him down on the wide bed, already turned down for the night, and tugged off his boots. I ordered alcodote from the dispensary—another item on the bill—and wrestled two down his throat. He gagged, which reminded me. Stateroom, dammit, only had an anachronistic flash disposer, not a wastecan, but I set an ice bucket by his head to take care of the inevitable.

"It's not fair, Cam," Jones was muttering. He reached out to grab my arm, and I sidestepped, with no intentions of getting into a wrestling match with what was going to be a very sick drunk thirty years my junior. Especially not in a rented dress.

"I get my life," Jones lamented. "I even get another good story that I get paid for, my image on all the news services, Jones on the spot. But Jim loses his latest future. Not damn fair."

"Life's not fair, mister," I responded, the immemorial bleak comfort of senior officers. Then I plopped a wet cloth over his head, filled a pitcher of water, and left. If he didn't materialize by eight hundred, I'd send the hostel's medstaff after him. Otherwise, I'd see him at breakfast and probably be heartlessly cheerful.

You went on. You just damned well went on, unless you were like Conrad Ragozinski, who'd spaced himself because he was too fastidious to outlive Jim's scandal.

I went back to my stateroom and changed my borrowed glory for honest Arvy gear. It was late, I'd been drinking, and I wished I could leave this show-off parody of an honorable ship for a spacer's hostel, but I still had work to do.

Not wanting to alert anyone who might still be nosing about station records, I uplinked with *Gavroche*, had them patch me through to *Zinderneuf,* and prepared to take my medicine.

Cinders' watch officer said Captain was offshift. Never mind that: captains talk to captains, and Nguyen finally picked up. She was wearing a slate robe and a chip on her shoulder. Even shorter than I, she was sallow with fatigue, her dark hair almost buzz-cut to accommodate a pilot's headset and eyes that looked like they'd stared into Jump space for too long.

Now what did I want, she demanded, seeing as she had a 0500 launch window and a crewman, damned decent spacer till he'd gone Jumpy, who'd insisted on quitting before his contract was up. He'd forfeit all pay for the voyage, including hazard pay and bonuses, but, no, he wasn't broke. She'd thrown some station scrip at him, that should keep him going long enough to find work, and if it didn't . . . he'd made himself not-her-problem anymore.

Furthermore, Captain Nguyen asked in a low voice that made me glad I wasn't Jones, was it reasonable, was it truly reasonable, Captain, to vouch for a man who promptly disappeared the instant he'd begun to be worth his keep, then wake a captain who had an early launch, and for what purpose? Would I be satisfied if she sent out a search party? Or would I expect her to delay launch and maybe lose her launch window on a damn station where the port charges were enough to break her?

Jim had jumped again, was all. She should have known better. He was a grown man with every right to leave her ship if he wanted, and she had other crew who weren't happy at all about the proximity to reporters, let alone Ryutaro Jones. One loss was more than she'd wanted to take.

Besides, she said, he'd dropped out of sight as thoroughly as if he'd disappeared into Jump.

"Do you think he's left Station?" I asked, because I had to say something else after the apology she was owed. I was heating up myself, and not at her.

"You're welcome to try to find him," she said and broke contact.

16

I had six hours max before I was due, wide-awake and cheerful in the Grand Salon of this gilt-edged barge to improve Jones' hangover and sing for my breakfast. I was too worked up to sleep.

A quick check of my vital signs told me it wasn't my system breaking down. Medstaff would have my head or other parts of my anatomy if I worked round the clock. Medstaff could take its collective head and shove—

That tack wasn't getting me anywhere.

If I were a loser, where would I hide?

Nguyen implied Jim had gone off-station. That may have been disinformation: regardless of what else she said about his not being her problem any more, she could have been protecting him.

But she hadn't known him as long, or as well, as I did. Or spent as much time with medstaff. By now, Jim was probably wobbly on his feet, assuming he wasn't falling down a lot out of sheer exhaustion. He might still be heaving from the after-effect of the meds pumped into him to stop him from glowing in the dark or developing a bumper crop of cancers ten years from now.

Jones had said his hair was growing back. So he probably was doing a great imitation of a refugee from a detention camp trying to convince a new employer he was fit to work.

Raffles Station was the kind of place where they bowed to you onto its upper levels if you wore Fleet uniform or flashy metallics or if you had enough credit to buy your way in. Jim had—what? No station account or ship's papers now, nor way of getting either. Just a handful of scrip Cynthia Nguyen had thrown at him.

She'd probably rather have thrown something heavy. And hit him hard.

Thing was, unless you had enough credit to navigate Raffles' "pre-war standards of hospitality," you dropped like the proverbial stone, sinking down and down, as much in lockstep with the rest of the losers as if you'd been tied to them and told to jump.

On Shenango, after he'd left Nasser's house, he'd headed for the Casual Labor center where his strength and skills had found him work.

He'd look for casual work again, I was sure of it.

But he was newly out of hospital, next thing to walking wounded. That made him weaker, vulnerable. The rule holds for any port—ancient Tyre or Shanghai, or Raffles Station: once the vulnerable hit bottom, they're prey.

What's it to you? I asked myself. Any sensible person would let water seek its own level. When had Jim become my problem?

I filed that one away for further processing and called GW at the Cape of Good Hope. The hostel's name was starting to make me nervous.

"How's shore leave among the rich and famous, Captain?" he greeted me. One advantage of being black, he'd once told me, was that the circles under your eyes don't show much when you worry. Well, he wouldn't have that advantage much longer.

"Meet me dockside," I ordered and broke contact.

I tucked my usual shoregoing kit—comm, sidearm, tracer, and some other convenient tech—in about my person and beat the exec there by long enough to steal a glance or three at whatever I could see of my ship's refit—at this point, mostly storage and pipe scaffolds that blocked the main lock. On top of everything else my exec had to do, he'd have to monitor me. I could see reproach coming as I explained. His shoulders went stubborn, and his lower lip began to jut out with a protest I knew I deserved. There's no way that going off alone into a risky district for a worthless old shipmate is anything but a stupid captain trick.

At least GW wasn't wearing the "Is this a symptom of freezer burn?" look he'd gotten when I first came on board.

"And make sure I've got a room at the Cape," I told him over my shoulder. "Please. Life on board the *Queen*'s enough to make me turn to regicide."

At least I left him laughing, a deep rumble that warmed me all over.

Raffles was stuffed with enough credit that some of it would filter down to the lowest levels of the station. It would lure not just petty thieves out to scrounge a stray storage cylinder, a system component, or maintenance supplies, but the real scavengers whose operations were profitable enough to let them pay for cover stories. They didn't stop at lifting storage tanks or cargo bins: they hunted live bodies.

THE PACK OF SCRIP I'D DRAWN BOUGHT ME A FEW CONSTRUCtive leads that took me down, always down, into Raffles Station's lower levels.

By the time I hit the lowest level, down where the deckplates' metal shivers from orbital microcorrections by station thrusters, I'd gotten hotter than Nguyen. Shipsicle or not, if I found Jim, he wasn't going to have to worry about scavengers: I personally was going to beat the shit out of him. Run off like that after I'd vouched for him, would he? We were going to have a little talk, I decided, and I was going to do most of the talking.

The fourth makeshift bar I spotted, tucked in around massive structural elements near the lift tubes, had pretensions to being law-abiding. Glowing plates clearly indicated exits and emergency gear—though I'd have hated betting my life on how well it had been tested or even how long ago. The bar was dark, though, hunkering down in kind of an ambient red light from space heaters that overpowered ancient halogen ceiling strips. Despite the constant hum of ventilators, the bar stank of sweat, fear, oily food, spilled drinks, and industrial chemicals.

I put my hand on my sidearm, prepared to fire through a pocket, if need be, peered in and actually saw a flash of thinning fair hair, broad shoulders, slumped now. Was that exhaustion, sickness, or disappointment?

Contact!

I dodged behind a battered metal beam, pulled off my jacket, and threw it back on, but inside out now so the flash, the Blue Helm insignia, and captain's sleeve braid were out of sight. I ran fingers through my hair till it stood up in unruly curls, reminded myself to slouch, and peered back into the bar. I felt the warmed metal of my locator, tucked in against my skin, and hoped my crew wouldn't have to track me. Stupid captain tricks, indeed. God, I was going to kill Jim.

A rough and ready interview, clearly, was ending. Jim held out his hand, palm up, as if helpless to argue further. The man with him pushed himself back from the scarred box they were using as a table, shrugged, and walked away, without a look back. Jim half-rose, moved his mug an inch back and forth, as if that itself could change things, then slumped back down. He waved away the barbot and rubbed his temples. Maybe he was drunk on top of everything else. Say he'd had a drink in each place he'd stopped: if he entered one of these places, he'd have to drink.

The timer on the makeshift table dinged, and a red light went off. Order or move on.

Jim stood, supporting himself against the table, and started to walk out. He wasn't real steady on his feet. God, did I know what that felt like. You were dizzy, your breath rasped in what felt like totally inadequate lungs. Your eyes watered, and objects acquired rainbow coronas. My guess was Jim was hungry, but didn't want to waste scrip by buying food he couldn't keep down. Assuming he had any money left.

"Need some help, shipmate?"

Two men moved in, one on either side. I edged closer, tagging my tracer to record. My palm, wrapped about my service-issue gun, twitched. It's always open season on scavengers, and these were small-scale scum. If I took these two out, Fleet probably wouldn't even slap me on the wrist, and if it did, Jones would make a stink if I asked him.

Now, there was always the possibility that the two men plying Jim with a steaming mug of day-old coffee, another one that looked like some sort of spicy soup, and a chunk of bread were simply good citizens helping a spacer down on his luck. I've seen some surprising acts of kindness; hell, wasn't I down here looking after a shipmate?

But there was also the greater possibility—on old Earth, they'd say a man got Shanghai'd. They'd stolen the word from one of Earth's oldest ports, taken out by Tokugawa early on in the war. It doesn't glow any more, they say, but of course I've never seen it.

You found a man, gave him a drink, drugged the drink, and carried him off. Alternatively, you got him drunk, then steered him away to sleep it off. Either way, the man was never heard from again.

Jim, damn him, knew those stories as well as I. Better, considering the company he kept. But the idiot looked up and smiled at the newcomers. He wasn't precisely trusting, but he'd always found friends.

I had sensible thoughts of signaling GW for backup, then giving him a direct order not to come down here himself. But it would take time to get security down here. Besides, if I went public on this, it would call attention down on Jim's head and possibly on Cynthia Nguyen's. I owed her one.

Sidearm drawn so they could see the nice bright glow at its muzzle of a full charge, I stepped out of the shadows.

"Friend, don't even think about eating that soup. Drop it now. You two. Leave your scrip on the table. All of it. You've got sixty seconds to clear out."

I got my back against a comfortable beam and raised my weapon.

The barkeep, a big man long since run to fat I didn't want to get close to just in case some of it was muscle—or armor—

started toward me with "Now just a damn minute . . ." These station rats probably paid him off.

I shot out a ceiling light. Those halogen things can set a nasty fire. A patron not quite as drunk as the others attacked it with foam from the emergency gear. The barkeep kept on coming. I fired at the tarnished, rackety bar, sawed out from some ship's hull-plating. Bottles crashed, and the reek of mixed drinks made the place a serious garden spot.

Jim stood, uncertain. Did he even recognize my voice? Dammit, had the drug been in the coffee, not the soup, with its concealing spices? Or was he just worn out from radiation sickness, treatment, shame, and a night's drinking? He was as wobbly as I'd been after resurrection. Damn, if he collapsed, I'd have to call for help and hold off these gentlemen till it arrived.

The lights were coming back on inside his head now. He knew he was in trouble. His eyes met mine, and I nodded.

"Got a nice little business here, don't you," I asked the stack rats. "You may as well profit from damn fools slumming or spacers down on their luck. Hold the fools for ransom, but what do you do with the spacers? Sell them to deep space operators?" I asked. "How much did you expect to get for this one?"

"C'mon, ma'am," whined one of the would-be kidnappers, a too-thin man with bad teeth, "we were just trying to help out a sick man. He a shipmate of yours? We'll hand him over to you. . . ."

He and his partner were trying to flank me, get two for the price of one. I fired off a warning shot.

"How much?" I demanded again. The charge glowed reassuringly on my sidearm.

I edged around and gestured with it. "Put your scrip on the table. Doesn't matter if it's not all from Raffles. We're none of us particular." Bad Teeth tossed crumpled notes onto the table.

"Now," I nodded at Jim, "you pick it up. Half. Other half's for the barkeep. Damages. Pay off your debts, mister, and get out of bed with the stack rats, or so help me, I'll send in more than Pest Control."

"Cam, I don't need their scrip," Jim said. "Or you to rescue me. You've already done—"

"Shut the fuck up," I told him.

The barkeep grabbed the notes Jim had left on the table. As Bad Teeth's partner, a nondescript marked only by an attempt to repair a scar on his forehead, started toward him, the barkeep punched him out. Bad Teeth bolted and fled.

"This is a law-abiding business," said the barkeep.

Right. And we never fought Secess'.

"What are you going to tell their keepers?" I asked, just-curious-like.

He shrugged, counting the scrip. "Who cares? If they go back, they'll be dumped out the nearest airlock. This ain't enough to cover damages, lady—" he started toward me, and I waved him off with my gun.

"What do you think you are—that *Queen* operation up on First Level?" I told him.

"You!" I jerked my chin at Jim. "Move it. That way." I backed out of the place till it was safe to turn and run for the lifts.

As the doors slid shut, Jim collapsed against a battered panel. The lift began to lurch and whine upward. Probably, you could cut it off at controls, but I figured the barkeep didn't have those kinds of contacts. He'd cut his losses instead and, after awhile, think he'd come to that decision all by his law-abiding self.

Jim doubled, and I braced myself, expecting him to collapse vomiting onto the deck. But he held himself up, breathing deeply, trying to control his gag reflex. The fight he put up almost made me want to forgive him.

"Nguyen told me I was welcome to try salvaging you," I said. "Scavengers would carve you up for lungs, liver, and God knows what else. If they didn't work you to death."

"Captain, I can't begin—"

"Then don't start!" I told him. "I'm not doing this for you.

I'm doing it for Jones. He's got this theory he cost you a future. He didn't know you didn't want one. He's trusting that way."

Abruptly, I holstered my sidearm. I was starting to like waving the thing around entirely too much. In fact, now I was out of the range of fire and Jim wasn't going to spew up everything he'd eaten for a week, I was starting to like this whole situation too damn much.

Now what?

Bringing Jim to the *Queen* was almost as much of a stupid captain trick as going after Jim solo. I sighed and handed Jim a card.

"*Gavroche*'s crew's staying there during refit," I said.

The lift shuddered to a halt. Third level. Dressed as he was, Jim could about pass muster here. "You can probably get a bath, a meal, and decent work clothes here. Find them. I'll see you at twelve hundred hours."

GW would be fit to be tied. I couldn't wait to see his face, but there was another face I needed to see first.

Jim stared at me.

"That scrip should cover it," I said. "I'd spend it before someone else tracks you down."

He jerked his chin up. Shit. I didn't have time to argue him out of this latest attack of false pride.

"If you don't show up before we lift, you'll be stranded here," I reminded him. "In that case, you might as well cut your own throat. And if you didn't do that at Havilland Roads or Shenango, I'm betting you won't do it now. Twelve hundred hours, mind."

He wavered, threw out an arm to steady himself. That wasn't just stress.

"Jim," I asked. "Are you sick? Did you take the meds they gave you when you discharged yourself?"

"Sold them," he said.

That did it for my temper.

"I gave you an order, mister," I snapped. "Eat, bathe, dress, report twelve hundred hours. Now, hop to it!"

He managed to slip out just before the lift doors sealed.

I didn't know if I'd see him again.

I didn't know why I was grinning like a fool. I'd been resurrected too long for it to be freezer burn.

My chrono showed it was long past oh five hundred. Nguyen, that lucky woman, had taken *Zinderneuf* off-station. By now, Jones would be waking up and wishing he'd died.

Damn good thing I'd never had children. They might have been sons. Laughter threatened, but I damped it, reported in, and ordered my long-suffering exec to get a room for Jim and some sleep in that order. GW managed not to wince, laugh in my face, or look relieved in a way I'd have had to take offense at.

I hadn't felt this alive in years.

Time to get back to the *Queen* and see how Jones was doing.

My other charge sat huddled in the Cabin Class Dining Room, where we'd eaten the night before. The artificial ship's morning that management had laid on—just another dazzling day at sea, and we're all just so damn happy we could puke (assuming we hadn't already)—was obviously far too bright for him. His eyes were bleary slits, and he was tossing down water the way he'd gulped last night's brandy.

"Morning, Jones!" I called out cheerfully. Slapping him on the back would be overkill, I decided.

I let the waiter seat me and pour coffee. Jones' nose twitched at its scent. At this sign of intelligent life, I pushed my cup across the table at him. The waiter produced a scandalized eyebrow—and another cup.

"Better?"

"God." He stuck his nose into the cup as if it contained the water of eternal life.

"You wanted a story for your new book," I said the instant we'd shooed away the pre-war hospitalities and I'd ordered a breakfast that made Jones' face shift from white to sallow green. "Wait till you hear what I did last night."

17

"Got a delivery for you, Captain," GW's voice came over my personal comm rather than the Cape of Good Hope's intercom. I'd disabled that the instant I'd entered the room GW'd gotten me; hostel intercom had a bad habit of piping in not just music but storm sounds. We're rounding the Cape of Good Hope; the water's choppy, yeah. Good thing they didn't mount the whole place on hydraulics so they could make us all as seasick as Jones.

"The roster says you'd signed out for leave at eleven-thirty hours," I said.

"Delivery arrived as I was leaving. If it merits your personal attention, it merits mine." Always cautious, my exec sounded skeptical to the point of rebellion.

"Bring him up, GW," I said.

I began to shut down my systems, clear away the stacks of ship's business that had greeted me the minute I'd walked in, matters Jim didn't have a need, or a right, to know. This berth was little bigger than my quarters aboard *Gavroche,* and almost hospital-neat (revolting thought): sparkling metal, polished brown and cream panels simulating honest bulkheads, and heavy furniture with padded cushions, not molded plastic seats. One bulkhead featured a photorepro of blue-water ships rounding the Cape of Good Hope back on Earth. The others had false portholes that I'd blanked, rather than have to look out on broadcasts of gray skies, rain, and heaving seas.

Despite the geographic fakery, the room was perfectly comfortable, even if it didn't come close to the opulence of the stateroom I hadn't slept in the night before. And at these rack rates, we'd be lucky if some bean-counter didn't question my expense report.

I turned back to my spreadsheets. Time to stop adventuring and put in an honest morning's work, Marlow.

Deskcomp shrilled. High-priority message incoming. Probably orders. It better be. I opened handcomp and prepared to transfer and decrypt. A half hour later, I called down for coffee and leaned back.

So. We'd have to lean on Raffles to finish refit forty-eight hours faster than estimate. We weren't headed back out to the No Man's Worlds, at least not right away. A couple supply runs—mostly medicals, biologicals, and critical personnel—and then we were ordered to report in at Aviva, no later than . . .

Once we hit Aviva, I decided, I had every intention of dumping Jim onto Becker's watch and his dubious mercy. Assuming Jim didn't jump ship before then.

THE LIFT TEN METERS DOWN THE CORRIDOR RATTLED AND whined, bringing me back to alertness. Just in case, I made sure my sidearm was where I could reach it if I had a mind, and waited for bootsteps, followed by the door chime. The berth's spy-eye showed me GW. He wasn't even trying not to glower. Behind him was Jim, so recently bathed that his hair—and the collar of his worksuit—were still damp.

"Come in." I released the locks. The door slid aside.

"Captain, may I speak to you?" GW asked, stepping in ahead of Jim.

"Always." I waved Jim inside.

"Privately."

"I'll be with you shortly," I told Jim. "Have a seat."

I stepped out into the hall with GW.

"Captain, I recognize this man," he began.

"Can't fault your memory, GW. We took him on board at Shenango, remember? When we took that renegade engineer into custody. What's your problem? Wasn't as if he gave us any trouble. He even earned his keep."

"He's trouble just by being who he is!" The anger simmering in my exec's dark eyes reached boiling.

I nodded. "That's one thing you two have in common. He thinks he's trouble, too. Had to pull scavengers off him last night. They'd come hunting spare parts."

GW snorted. "Anyone who'd buy that one's heart needs his head examined and his money back. Captain, I know Arvies don't play by Fleet rules, and it's captain's discretion about taking on supercargoes, but if you're thinking of—"

"That's what I'm thinking of, GW."

"Then I protest, Captain. I protest most strongly."

"GW," I drew the syllables out, "you and I both know Fleet doesn't officially believe in jinxes. All crew officially has to know is that he's transferred to us from *Cinders*. Captain there was completely satisfied with his performance."

Zinderneuf might have a reputation of her own, but, God knows, it was better than Jim's.

"Crew's not going to buy that, Captain," GW said. "Crew picks things up on dock—"

"A working crew damn near inhales rumors out of Jump space, and we both know it," I said. "The man's paid his price. Deserves a second chance. And," I held up a hand, "it isn't as if I'm planning to use him for any jobs outside the ship. Or as if this is a permanent berth. As soon as we can, we'll drop him off someplace. Happier?"

"I don't like it, Captain. Crew won't either."

"Crew will go along if you lead."

"Under protest, Captain."

"You can log it, GW. If you don't, I will."

My exec glowered at me. I glowered back. I was within my rights to take on a supercargo. Out of my mind, maybe, but within my rights, and he knew it. I won the battle of the scowls, but just barely.

"Now," I shifted topic fast, "about that shore leave of yours. Will you *get* before I have to take disciplinary action by doubling it?" I shooed him away. "I'm the last person in the worlds that man in there would jump. Now, out of here!"

At least, GW left grinning. You don't want to be at odds with your exec at any time, especially if he's as good as GW.

This morning's work had shown me: I could justify taking Jim on by referring to crew roster. Three had left the ship here. Kobalevsky had left to take a stationside job, Maelen had transhipped to her homeworld—no surprise there, and Singh had been approved for transfer to an inner-systems run as purser. Soft berth, but my money was Singh would get bored within six months and spend half his savings trying to rejoin an honest ship. No one had jumped: I'd have been surprised and hurt if anyone had tried.

So we had cubic enough to fit in more crew. Which we needed.

At a pinch, Jim could push a broom, load, or tote coffee. Waste of a good mind, all of that. I knew from before my Freeze that his math was good enough to take over some of Singh's duties. I'd gotten first-rate work out of him on the Shenango run. He'd earn his keep. If he stayed.

I turned back into my room.

Jim straightened to attention. Damn the man. After last night, he had no right to look as if he hadn't been sick, drugged, and damned near kidnapped. His hair was as shiny in the light from the ceiling panels and as carefully arranged as the men whom I'd seen last night on board the *Queen*. He wore a neat gray coverall, one step down from a shipsuit, with a heavy jacket one step removed from Fleet blue, over it. Nothing flashy, just solid quality that he must have found secondhand. He looked like a free spacer who'd left one job and was heading for the next with a tidy credit balance and a clean work history.

"Thought I'd told you to have a seat," I remarked. "Coffee?"

"Thank you no, I prefer to stand, Cam. Captain." He reached into the jacket pocket, and I forced myself not to tense. *If you prove GW right, Jim, I swear I'll come back and haunt you.*

"I'll accept 'captain' from you," I agreed.

What he pulled out instead was neatly folded station scrip. "Change," he said. "From the money you gave me last night."

Damn the man, was he worrying GW thought I'd bought and paid for him? I wasn't that old yet.

"Keep it. Consider it walking-around money. You may want a drink or personal items you can't get in ship's stores. You're coming with."

"Your exec hates my guts."

"Doesn't mean he wants them sold to scavengers. I'm taking you with us this run. Light work. You can stay in your cabin most of the time. We can drop you off at Aviva, some place reasonable. This living-on-the-edge act has gotten really old. If Alliance had wanted you dead, it would have executed you itself."

I paused and took a deep breath. I was too old to go prowling downstation all night, then put in a full day's work, I truly was.

"Want something to eat?" I asked. Maybe he'd be a little more reasonable over a meal.

"I've got money," Jim said, meaning the scrip I'd given him. "The First Officer—"

"Mr. Parker—"

"He looked at me as if I—"

"First Officer Parker isn't using his imagination. I'd say you were a little old for a boytoy," I said. Couldn't a woman, a senior officer, take an interest in a younger man's life without . . . I decided to ignore the whole issue by gesturing to computer. "Order us what you like, will you?"

For a miracle, he obeyed, then set out the food like a well-trained steward. It was a civil meal: ship's courtesy, talk of small matters, news of his former ship. When we got down to coffee so strong it could almost be Fleet issue, Jim looked over the rim of his cup at me.

"Why didn't you let them have me? Finish things for once and for all."

I slammed my own cup down. "Haven't you been listening to me? There's a reason, you know, why you get all these jobs you walk away from, why Captain Nguyen damned near ripped my head off when I called her. Regardless of the one mistake you made—and oh, I'll agree, when you fuck up, you do it big time—there's too much good in you, too much use to be had out of you that I'm willing to see it wasted. We've come through the war. But we've come through on our knees, just like the Se—like our former enemies—and wasting potential's no way of getting back on our feet."

Jim was staring at the picture of the ship rounding the Cape, far, far from the rest of humanity. I brought his attention back to me by slamming my hand on the desk. "Listen up, mister! What gives you the right to deprive the worlds of your skills? God knows, it cost enough to teach you."

"All my life, I wanted to do great things, and then, the first time I got any real responsibility—"

"You jumped." There was no point in easing the bandage away from the wound. I watched him flinch, then steady. "You wanted to be a hero. Failing that, you want to be nothing. Well, I'll tell you, mister. The ship—the last ship you ran out on—was named after an outpost full of gentlemen rankers who wanted to find someplace on the edge of their world to retreat to: march or die, they liked to say. But we don't live back then. We're more civilized now, and we have to clean up the mess we make."

I watched him watch me: there seemed to be a spark of attention there, a spark that, maybe, I could fan into hope.

"We've got to try," I added. End of pep talk. I met Jim's eyes. What was I looking for? Applause? A God-bloody conversion experience?

He didn't even try to win the staring contest. "How can I try, Captain?" he asked, his words hushed and strained as if saying anything cut at his heart. "I can't trust myself."

"Who can you trust, then?" I asked.

"You," he said.

I only hoped I was up to it.

18

The rest of our time on Raffles, Jim kept to his berth. I'd seen his discharge records; as soon as *Gavroche* powered up, I'd have him in Sick Bay, and he knew it. Meanwhile, he insisted he couldn't just lie there, subsidized by a ship and a service he didn't have a right to. Either give him something to do or . . .

You don't threaten me, mister, was on the tip of my tongue. But I did need replacement crew. It was a fair trade: food, shipsuits, meds, bunk, and privacy got processed into competent work.

By rights, I should have had his expenses deducted from his credit balance. Assuming he had one. When I checked, I wasn't particularly surprised to find out Nguyen had lied. *Cinders*' captain probably figured I'd take him on; she knew as well as I did the stink Arvy Central was likely to raise if I let someone—let alone Jim—deadhead. I made a mental note that I owed her a very expensive dinner next time we hit the same port.

I had GW post guards in case any scavengers had reprisals in mind, then tipped off Raffles Station. Too bad for that barkeep.

Station news reported that Jones had shipped out. He sent a note and a bottle, but hadn't called, probably embarrassed or trying not to cost Jim anything more.

SOMEONE ONCE DESCRIBED SPACE TRAVEL AS BOREDOM PUNCTuated by a series of emergencies. And Jump. No way around that particular problem unless we want to go back to traveling below C level and taking centuries to get from Raffles to the No Man's Worlds. Frankly, I thought it might take centuries just to pry Jim out of his cabin, the same high-security berth he'd had on the Shenango run.

"Don't even try," Medic Ankeny caught me on the way to his cabin and treated me to a private, one-on-one Red Alert. "You've got a sick, scared animal. You put food and water within reach. And you wait for him to come out."

So we'd waited during loading and unloading, during the tension leading up to Jump and the long sine curves of monotony that follow. It was like Raffles. Resources went in; work came out.

So, gradually, did Jim. Ship's gossip reported sightings of a newcomer—always a source of interest—venturing into the galley at off-hours, pacing the unsecured decks down by Engineering, or staring out at Jump space. He even started to nod at working crew, but rarely spoke. And when traffic built up as the watch changed, he retreated.

Then, someone passed him the word we were delivering biosupplies to a low-population word, and the Jim sightings ended. He retreated altogether to his cabin. It wasn't quite bleak enough to trigger sensory deprivation, but it was getting there. And the flow of work ceased.

"You think I've got time to make housecalls?" Medic Ankeny snarled. Still, he made the time rather than run the risk, as he so elegantly put it, of finding Jim hanging from the shower. I could have told him better, but I had my hands full.

About that time, crew shut down their pool about how long Jim would last before he jumped ship. Tell you the truth, I don't know how many knew—or cared. *Gavroche* didn't have as high a proportion of vets as *Cinders* in her crew: the ones we had kept their own counsel. The newbies, well, one taciturn vet is very much like another. We made our zygote run and headed out into the Dark.

Gradually, the workflow picked up, and Jim ventured out again, looking pale and brittle.

Still, I wish he could have chosen another time to venture

into the CIC. I could have ordered him out, but I wasn't concentrating on anything but the upcoming Jump. We'd reached the hard-to-breathe moments once Helm has checked and rechecked, the last few course corrections are being prayed over, Captain's convinced the ship will make the leap, and waits only for Helm to announce we're in position.

Given the ambient gas clouds, this Jump was tricky. The clouds were nothing too big, maybe a couple light years or so, but they were dense enough to look pretty on screen and play hell with sensors. Nerves were combat-taut, and Jim picks that minute to venture into CIC to observe. I hadn't thought to say, as I'd say to any normal passenger, yes, by all means, pay a social call, but not during Jump transition. Before the war, Jim had stood watch with me on *Hardcastle*.

It wasn't the same thing at all. As soon as Jim ventured in, you could see he felt that he'd made a mistake, but couldn't admit it by backing down.

Jim's hand twitched, cutting off a salute. He saw what he'd interrupted and backed up, dropping into an observer's seat beside Sensors, probably trying not to compound his intrusion. He clenched his hands: don't touch anything. His eyes flicked from screen to screen. I saw him tense at a course correction, hiss as scanners took a second too long to compensate and the scroll of arcane blue and green symbols flowing across the bottom of the screen slowed minutely.

I leaned over my own screens where the dataflow was building and building. *Ten . . . nine . . .*

"What's that?" Jim snapped.

GW whirled on him. "Get out!"

"That shadow!" Communications had hands on Jim's shoulders . . . was propelling him out. . . . *eight . . .*

"We've got incoming!" Jim shouted over his shoulder.

God, suppose it was aliens. Since we'd left Earth, we'd seen them, and they'd seen us, and we'd given each other as much room as we could. But what if they'd been watching and were—

Seven . . .

I slaved sensors to my command station. Shadow? We'd blocked out the false reflections. I brought up magnification. Matched against computer's records of alien sightings. Not alien, then. But incoming.

Incoming was as bad as shadows. Crash into it, make a tiny star, and end the use of this Jump point for all time. Shut the local systems out from space, maybe for centuries.

Six . . . five . . .

Computer ran the shadow against ship patterns, found a match, confirmed in a flashing circle of red light. Second confirmation on not-aliens. Another ship. Not exiting Jump, but being cast out of it like trash.

"We've got a ghost! Abort Jump!" I ordered, and felt my guts twist from de-accel and attitude and vector twists as Helm's instincts kicked in to save us.

"Red Alert. Acquire target!" I yelled. My voice sawed up and down registers, slowed, sped up, and distorted as the leading edge of the ghost's Jump wave caught us and tried to suck us in.

Sirens started to whoop up and down every scale at once, shaking us in our seats—those of us who hadn't been tossed against the bulkheads as course changed.

"Reverse!" I was boiling, freezing at once. My shout vibrated in my skull, a red and orange urgency with a bad smell.

I slammed my hand down on my console and saw distorted bones shine through the skin. So close to Jump. Too close.

You could be sucked into Jump or be trapped there what felt like forever while your ship deteriorated slower than your sanity.

GW shouted hull-pressure numbers. *Gavroche* lurched again in every direction at once, staggered, then hung, dead in space. Sensors flatlined, exploded into a chaos of alerts, then fought to stabilize as the ship's apparent motion started up again. Eyes blurred; CIC seemed to stretch, then compress, smaller than before. Ship's integrity teetered now on the red line between safety and abandon ship. Jim and Comm toppled and rolled, tangled, across a deck that had seemed to billow and go soft only incalculable instants earlier.

My hands moved as if they belonged to some automaton sending out its remotes through emptiness. I couldn't take my eyes from the screen where normal space and Jump roiled and warped and reached out for us. I saw clouds—not honest gas clouds like the ones that hid our Jump point, but the billowing mists of Jump in colors normal eyes were never meant to see. Nausea threatened, but I had no body, only cognition for as long as my mind could endure.

Oh God, I was sinking through my chair, it was evaporating out from under me. A minute longer and ship's integrity would fail. We'd all fall through the plates into vacuum and keep on falling. . . .

"More speed!" I shouted. "Back us off from that thing!"

The engines screamed and took hold, shaking us to bones we could feel again, the right strength, the right shape.

Gavroche and normal space solidified beneath us—and the ghost fully emerged.

Someone was being thoroughly sick—blessedly human, mundane reaction. Blessedly human mess.

"Clean that up!" I snapped.

Communications extricated herself from the tangle of arms and legs, and hurled herself at her duty station.

"Getting ship's ID, Captain," she told me and wiped a bloody nose with one hand. "Ship's ID over a Mayday. Wait . . . now, she's hailing us. . . ."

My God, there were people on board, still sane enough to call to us.

"Pipe it through," I ordered.

Shrill words tumbled over each other as if the speaker reached a precipice of hysteria and poised there, somehow not falling, *"For God's sake, Captain, stand down! This is Corporate Vessel* Glasgow, *Aven registry! Scavengers boarded us at . . . "* crackle of static *". . . stripped ship's systems, offloaded . . . oh God . . . thank God you're here . . . off-*

loaded civilian passengers . . . sent us into Jump on timed release . . ."

The youngest in CIC, Communications Officer Pat Morias would have been pretty in a wholesome, outdoors way if she ever got any sun and wasn't white with horror. She was the only one of my officers with no military background, but she was holding up. "*Glasgow,* do you require assistance?"

"Keep arms locked on target," I ordered and demanded ship's ID. We'd render aid only after we were sure to five decimals—at least—that that ship wasn't about to go critical or fire on us. "What do we know about *Glasgow*?" I let my voice carry so Pat's station could pick it up.

"Alliance heavy-cargo vessel Glasgow, *Captain. Owned by Galeries-Midland-Spencer plc. For God's sake, stand down!"*

I glanced down as a dataflow from the ship reached my console. Entered Jump at . . . the coordinates flashed across my screen in red. My vision blurred for a shocked instant.

Jump entry had been six *months* ago. Yet *Glasgow* had survived. Ship must be sturdy as a damn *planet.* But prolonged Jump's a test to destruction. What gives first? Life support? Engines? Clearly, they'd collapsed, ejecting the ship from Jump at the nearest point. It was a wonder anyone survived, let alone survived sane.

"Tom," I signaled Sick Bay. "That turbulence was a ghost. Live crew. Get your triage teams on deck. And listen in."

"Marlow of *Gavroche* here, *Glasgow,*" I answered the ghost ship's hail. "What's your status?"

I paused, then asked the question that would determine whether I fired now, in the next instant, or never.

"Have you got plague on board?"

"Negative, Captain, negative." Weary patience in that voice now. *"Scavengers tracked us and locked on . . ."* static broke transmission *". . . Forced us down, out of Jump and . . . stripped ship's primaries . . ."*

Like something out of a bad dream—a Scavenger fleet sophisticated enough to lock onto a ship, track it through Jump, and force it to disengage before boarding and stripping the ship of whatever systems and personnel it had a mind to.

But not blow it up, oh no . . .

"Who'm I speaking to?" I asked. "Can you give me visual?"

"Hamish, Peter, Junior Helm, sir!" Ship's crew, not transplants from corporate headquarters. Static jittered and danced onscreen, resolving into a thin, tired face, spacer-pale. Helm Officer Hamish brought up a shaking hand, not to salute, but to push back limp hair as fair as Jim's.

No bruises that I could see; if scavengers had released them months ago to drift in Jump, the injuries that could heal probably had, leaving survivors staring into the swirls of Jump wondering whether engines would give out before supplies.

"You're senior? How many casualties?"

"None, Captain. Not anymore. They took our medic." The man's voice cracked as if he were even younger than he sounded. *"We've forty survivors, forty-three if you count the catatonics, we lost one yesterday. Yesterday? How long've we been in Jump, Captain?"*

"Don't tell him, Captain. Not yet. We need him functional," warned my medic.

Hamish laughed, a horrible sound that screeched up the scale and ended in a sob. *"We had eighty, but scavengers killed fifteen when they boarded, and we've been losing them since they cut us loose on Jump timer. Said what—and who—they stole earned the rest of us our lives back."*

Someone growled behind me.

"Belay that," I whispered, off-mike so Hamish couldn't hear.

"It could be a trap," GW reminded me, also off-mike.

We'd be wise to disable the ship, assuming we couldn't—or shouldn't—blow it out of space.

Jim leaned over Sensors.

"Captain," he put in, ignoring my exec's glare. "No weapon signatures. We'd get trace radiation if they'd been on-line in the last month. Those emplacements are *stripped."*

Glasgow carried Aven registry, and Aven was Jim's homeworld. Would he lie to protect a ship he'd never seen?

GW shot me a look. *You going to trust* that*?*

He'd been a damn fine arms officer once.

"Nothing wrong with his *eyes,*" I told GW. "I'll want confirmation on weapons signatures and full personnel scan. Tom, you still there?"

"Sick Bay's prepped, Captain," the medic reported. *"Glassware's all cleaned up. Next time you feel like dancing, invite me to the party."*

"I want one of your teams suited up. Full environmental gear." I paused. "They're going over. Tell them to make sure that ship isn't just clean, but clean enough to eat off her deckplates. They'll draw sidearms. Lethal setting.

"Mr. Hamish," I said. "We're sending over a rescue party. Please identify a secure docking port. We will be armed. Do not resist."

"No resistance, ma'am. Not that we could." Not old enough to have served through the war.

"Captain—" Jim's voice again.

"Sick Bay for you," I said.

"Aye," said Jim as he disappeared. At a run. Combat nerves.

I accessed all-call. If all went well—assuming you could call a ghost ship and forty survivors "well"—we'd have Sick Bay packed, and Ankeny would have his hands full. His and anyone else's he could find to help him.

I felt myself starting to shake with combat nerves of my own. Probably the rest of my crew felt it worse.

GW looked at me, then, ostentatiously, at his chrono. Shook it.

I know the watch has changed, mister.

"I'll ride this one out," I said. "If *Glasgow* checks out, I'll meet Mr. Hamish and his people *and* any corporate reps down in Sick Bay.

"Mr. Hamish?" I called over to the disabled ship. "Tell your people: as soon as our team checks you out, prepare for evacuation."

"My ship—"

Rather than leave *Glasgow* for the next pack of scavengers, we should destroy her. But you didn't just blow up a valuable ship if you could get it moving under independent power or take it in tow. "GW," I said offline, "tell Engineering to start working on a tether. In case."

If Hamish had lied to me, I'd blow his ship myself. If he wasn't, he'd might wish he were only facing Jump, not the blizzard of forms that was about to engulf him. "Are any of *Glasgow*'s corporate crew alive? Otherwise, as senior ship's crew, you'll present ship's certificates of registry along with your own certificates and ship's personnel folders when you come aboard. Corporate crew can start assembling a cargo manifest so I can notify Aven as well as Fleet and Relief Legal Affairs."

Prosaic duties. Routine. Soul-saving. Hamish's back seemed to straighten—at last, a task he understood and could do now that mind, body, and ship had stopped turning inside out.

"Signal Central," I told Pat. "Transmit through Jump. Ask if they want us to divert or continue on course."

Central would scream at the cost of trans-Jump communication, but, with any luck, Legal would assess Galeries-Midland for T&A—transmission and administrative—costs.

I settled back in my chair, drank enough coffee practically to send me through Jump *sans* ship, and let my teams report in. GW and Ankeny had drafted aux crew: between preparing to take *Glasgow* in tow and dealing with forty trauma cases, no one was going to do much sleeping. Just as well. No way Sick Bay was large enough to deal with the emergency. They'd be setting up wards all over my ship and lining the bulkheads with gurneys.

It would have been easier just to blow them out of space.

WE WERE ALL STAGGERING AND ON STIMS BY THE TIME CENTRAL came through with new orders: max speed to Aviva in the Inner Ring. Trauma facilities had already been alerted.

Glasgow's crew wore on the nerves worse than isolation or Jump. It wasn't just the crowding in the corridors or standing watch on watch. Or the strain on Engineering's nerves or Helm's from the technical obscenity of taking a tethered ship with us into Jump. We were operating outside the regs because, to be perfectly fair, no one had ever been crazy enough to think up a situation like the one we were in, let alone come up with rules to cover it.

"You think we'll ever get a full night's sleep again?" asked GW. He, three of my other officers, and I had retreated to my cabin. Given the near-certainty that Sick Bay or Engineering could pull us out of anything we were doing, we'd all solemnly decided it was too hard on the system to be waked up for another extra duty shift. Better to stay awake, we decided.

Ordinarily, the chief medic would have put a stop to that, but the chief medic was on stims. Besides, if we slept, what we'd seen in the *Glasgow*'s crew's eyes might come back to haunt us.

It was safer to huddle together and talk.

"How much is a ghost worth?" GW fumbled for a topic that wouldn't set the group brooding again.

Tired faces lit with speculation. I didn't have to be a space lawyer to know salvage laws dated all the way back to Earth's blue-water admiralty law.

"We've taken her in tow in free space. Legal will have to decide if she's ours outright," GW argued.

"Galeries-Midland might offer a settlement," Pat Morias said. She brightened, but couldn't maintain the energy level. "Likelier, they'll try to fob us off with a token reward."

Faces turned to me, my very own little hydroponics garden of sudden greed.

"Stand down, people. Relief Service doesn't accept rewards," I said. But salvage, now that was different.

If *Glasgow* had already been written off as a loss, it was probably ours, worth untold billions, less the cost of refit, and even a considerable sum if she had to be sold as scrap.

Arvy ships weren't like corporate ship hire-ons: we didn't have shares and points and bonuses. We were quasi-military, and if admiralty law held, so did salvage and prize law. For even the newest sign-on, funds from *Glasgow* could make the difference between comfortable retirement and makework, with public assistance at the very end. I muffled a completely inappropriate grin with a rat bar. Did even the clouds of Jump space carry silver linings? Ghoulish of us to think so, and if we weren't all so damn tired, we'd all be properly ashamed.

Time to check Sick Bay, I told myself and forced myself back onto swollen feet.

By the time I threaded through the crowd of cots, gurneys, and drafted crew that turned the corridor outside Sick Bay into a small mob, the screaming had subsided.

"Sorry, Captain," Celia Hankins greeted me. Tall, too thin, with a reputation for imperturbability that looked a little frayed around the edges now, our backup medic rubbed a bruise on her cheek. "We just had a seizure, and the commotion set off a panic attack. Someone got a little violent. No," she said, "two panic attacks."

She looked away from me at a handcomp. "Trank intake's up twenty percent today. Damn."

"Next time, duck faster," I said. Knew better than to tell her to get some rest.

I peered over Celia's shoulder where the creased lab coat showed bloody finger prints. A *little* violent? Behind her I could see my crew—others of my crew—seated by *Glasgow* bunks, holding *Glasgow* hands, reassuring them as they'd done every minute since they'd come on board that they were safe, *Gavroche* was a good ship, Captain wouldn't let anyone take them, and we were heading into the Ring to an honest-to-God planet.

"Where's Medic Ankeny?" I asked.

"Mopping up," she said. "He'll be out of surgery in—"

"Jim, Rob here . . . he's breaking loose!" I heard restraints, fastened with kindness more than good sense, snap. A man pulled free, moaning. He rolled off his bunk, crouched, and tensed. Cubic foot for cubic foot, Sick Bay was probably one of the places where you could improvise a seriously deadly weapon fastest. I tensed too.

"You're safe, Rob," came a new voice I identified as Jim's.

I raised an eyebrow at Celia.

"He's been spending most of his waking hours here," she said. She shrugged. *Isn't like he's got much else to do.*

He walked over to the crewman, who brought his hands up, fingers flexing in a way that looked like a stranglehold waiting to happen.

"You're not going to do that," Jim told the man. "No scavengers. Just friends. I'm your friend. Come on. We'll get you some water, and you can lie—"

Rob dropped to the floor, wrapping his arms about himself. His knees came up to his chest. Retreat to the womb, was it?

"Steady," Jim said. "You're too big to be carried, but we'll see what we can do. Captain?"

I knew when I needed to lend a hand. And a voice, reassuring him that This Was The Captain, and we had Everything Under Control.

Right.

Together, we got the man back into his bunk. Jim snapped the restraints more snugly. "I'm sorry," he told his fugitive. "I don't like this either, but it won't be for long. Think of it like an anchor, making you safe. No more Jump."

I watched his hands as he pulled a thermal blanket up and smoothed it. They were gentle, and before he saw me watching him and his face blanked, it showed a terrible, tender caring.

Did Jim see in each maddened, injured, or mindless *Glasgow* the image of the people he'd fled on *Jaya*?

Did one balance the other? Hadn't a clue. I did know I was going to log one hell of a commendation for him and not tell him that. Or the RUMINT about salvage.

Maybe this disaster would win him the second chance we always hoped he'd take: a decent, useful, dignified life. Never mind salvage: he'd seen the ghost first; that might even get him a bonus. Each time his hands had been filled, he'd empty them. It was perverse, a kind of violence against the hopes of those who'd helped him. I didn't know if I could bounce back from it again.

Why do you bother? I asked myself, not even for the hundredth time.

Might as well ask how much a ghost is worth. Or a second chance.

ARV *Gavroche* 19

"Captain, I'm getting—"

"Another towing service, Pat?" I interrupted my communications officer.

"Contractor, sir," she replied. "Insists he will not be underbid."

"Transmit the usual thanks, but no thanks."

Since we'd come in-system, Pat Morias had been fielding calls from everything from shipbuilding companies to personal financial advisors (they must have smelled profit the minute we emerged from Jump with *Glasgow* tethered) to baroque elaborations of cosmetic surgery. I'd gotten a backache from leaning over her station, helping filter legitimate traffic from all the predatory chaff.

Galeries-Midland's legal department had started burning up the relays the instant we came in range, and I threatened to put Relief's First Contact specialists on them for translation if they didn't start talking to us in plain speech. Given the current ratio of static to useful signal, if our legitimate superiors wanted to contact us, they wouldn't be able to get through.

"This call's a shipbuilder," said long-suffering Pat. "Sensors show we've got a tethered ship, and the woman I'm online with wants to make sure we know we're going to burn out the engines if we don't sign on right now with her employers."

"Everybody's an entrepreneur," I sighed. "*Gavroche* is going into refit. Tell her to submit her bid like everyone else."

"Don't you love being popular?" GW glanced up from his readouts. "Ever been popular before, Captain?"

"I'm getting flashbacks to resurrection. Refitters and contractors are offering us the suns, the moons, and the stars, from here out to the No Man's Worlds if only we sign with them, talk to them, whatever. My personal favorite's Deep Space Systems' offer of what amounts to three years' operating expenses for a testimonial. Longer and stronger tethers," I said. "Speaking of which, Pat's at the end of hers. Pat?"

"Captain?" Morias was too professional to let her voice reflect the *now, what is it?* she had to be feeling from the current barrage.

If I felt barraged, she had to be damn near overwhelmed. Commendation time for Pat.

Three days after we'd taken *Glasgow* in tow, *Gavroche* had picked up some engine vibrations. I distrusted them, and my chief engineer liked the feel of them even less. As a result, I'd requested priority repair authorization even before we got in-system. From a contractor approved by Relief, thank you so much, not one of these high-pressure operators who'd been making my comm officer's life livelier than she needed.

"I don't want you wasting your time with these 'thanks but no thanks' to small businesses," I decided. "From now on, put 'em on tape. I'll review them and get back to them at my convenience."

Which might very well be never. Or while my crew was on leave.

"On course for Aviva Orbital," GW informed me. "Making final course corrections now."

My readouts showed the familiar colored waterfalls of data,

the shifting geometries as *Gavroche* slowed and altered course.

"Tugs within range, Captain," GW added after a moment.

CIC's primary screens showed the weird conformation of the incredibly sturdy repair vessels that had arrived to release *Glasgow* from her tether and tow her over to shipbuilding. If, as the woman burning up the relays to my comm officer hinted, we were straining our engines, the tugs could probably tow us too.

"Hail them," I ordered. "Engineering? Tugs in range. Prepare to cast off."

"Inertial damping initiated, Captain."

The instant the tethers were released, I could feel the difference in *Glasgow*'s engines, thrumming through the deck plates.

"We're being hailed from Aviva's surface," Pat Morias rasped.

For the hundredth time this watch. Big surprise.

"Captain told you to tape the sales calls," said GW.

I held up a hand, forestalling the rest of GW's "I am the First Officer" reminder. If Pat reported a new hail now, I needed to know about it.

"Captain, it's Marshal Becker."

I straightened to not-quite-attention in my seat. So he'd gotten through my report already? He must have bumped it to the head of the queue.

"Put him through." *Gavroche* had been downloading, ship to Relief Central installations, since we entered the Aviva system. I'd transmitted my preliminary report—and the request for refit—as soon as I could organize my material. But I hadn't expected it to jump this high up the chain of command.

At least, not this fast.

"Captain Marlow?" My imagination reproduced the craggy old face even before the image solidified on-screen. He hadn't aged that much since Havilland Roads. God, the first time I'd ever laid eyes on him, when he'd spoken right

before the war, when I'd been commissioned, I'd thought he was as old as the Big Bang.

"Sir." Stand up, Marlow. At attention. But the old man was smiling at me.

"Cam, well done! The minute you're out of quarantine, I want you to report to Central. Meanwhile, we're following your exchanges with Galeries' Legal and Corporate guerrillas. Legal is standing by to assist."

"Thank you, sir!" It would take a legion of judge advocates to get us out from under a multi-planetary corporation determined to assign blame, collect damages, and repossess a ship it had abandoned, and I'd be glad to let Becker's team handle the job.

"Pat, your autosignal needs to say salvage questions should be directed to Central." That would take care of the officious types who tried to insist on talking only to the captain, preferably this very instant, and preferably by bullying my comm officer.

Now that those talking egos had a choice between a mere Captain Marlow and the head of Relief—Becker had just drawn their fire, and he knew it. Which left us with genuine transmissions about planetfall.

"Captain, we're being hailed by Port Quarantine," came Pat's voice.

"My compliments to the Quarantine officers, and we are prepared to welcome them aboard at their convenience," I said. "Their earliest possible convenience."

I wanted to get downworld and report to Becker in person. Just as much, I wanted to get *Glasgow*'s wounded off my decks and into a secure medical facility.

"They were only awaiting your word, Captain, to launch."

So, an hour later, we had envirosuits with scanners infesting our corridors, and we were all trying to protect backsides, arms, and various vascular systems from drive-by medical tests.

And of course, one of the envirosuits would have to turn out to be a reporter disguised as a medic. Naturally, in strict performance of our duty, we had to catch, strip, and have the bastard medically tested—since, after all, he'd boarded a ship that hadn't passed Quarantine—before we tossed him into the brig-or-equivalent-thereof (note to self once again: see about construction of a proper brig while *Gavroche* is in refit). I positively was looking forward to pressing charges.

I actually found myself missing Ryutaro Jones. Granted, if he'd been within half a lightyear, he'd have tried to get on board and get the story. But, unlike the man now sulking in custody, if—when—Jones had been exposed, he'd have grinned and shrugged in a way that damn near could make co-conspirators of us—as if we could hardly blame him for carrying out *his* self-appointed duty—then volunteered to lend a hand. And he'd have known how.

GW passed me the word that crew had started pools about who was going to lose his temper first and start swinging. I had GW shut down the pools on the grounds that I was out and out likely to be the winner and I hated to see them lose their money.

After twenty-four hours of inquisition that turned up a still and three cases of 150-proof vodka, a contraband cat, and some improbable reading material we classified as applied anatomy—but no plague—the envirosuits withdrew.

We suffered through a brief orgy of speculation by Aviva system media: what-if-they-really-do-have-plague, the life stories of everyone unfortunate enough to have their images on file, a special on me (I should have let crew run that pool and put money in it, then won my own bet and collected), and another wave of entrepreneurs whose messages Pat duly taped and forwarded to me, whereupon I erased the lot of them.

All the all-clear meant was that we could get back to work. Delicate work this time, loading our traumatized *Glasgow*s onto the shuttle Aviva Technical University Hospital sent up. Medics swarmed out of it, walking, one on one, alongside the gurneys holding the crewmembers who were either zoned out in deep trank or wearing restraints.

We paired each of the walking wounded with *Gavroche* crew, in many cases, the same man or woman who'd spent the most time with this particular *Glasgow*.

That gave me double duty: reporting in *and* minding Hamish. I could hardly begrudge the time. Hamish had done one hell of a job keeping bodies, souls, and ship's systems together until *Glasgow* dropped out of Jump.

I'd noted that in my report. I'd even broken my own rule about communications silence and talked to one Corporate type for the sole purpose of saying so. Maybe it would add up to a pension on disability for Hamish. God knows, he'd earned it. And to top things off, he was making a complete recovery.

After sleeping around the clock, Hamish had insisted on reducing his trank intake, then weaning himself off it while my CMO hovered. He'd stopped spooking at every sound or flicker in the lights.

I wished the rest of his crew were doing as well. With any luck, the flight down wouldn't be too turbulent. They didn't need trauma from a rough drop into a gravity well.

From the corner of my eye, a glimpse of Jim escorting a crewmember on board made me call my first officer.

"GW?"

"Aye, Captain?"

"Along with everything else, keep an eye on Jim, will you? I'm damned if I want to lose him to a stray reporter after all the work we've put in on him."

"Aye, Captain." Long-suffering, our GW. He probably thought it was a waste of time. Let him jump, and good riddance. But GW took my orders. Even if he didn't much care for Jim—and he didn't—GW had made thwarting news media his latest hobby. He'd have a tail on Jim longer than the one on that cat the medics had turned up (and who was living off the fat of the land now in the purser's office). If Jim tried to clear out, GW would restrain him *and* give me, as captain, plausible deniability. If Jim appealed it as wrongful arrest, we were screwed. But if he did that, he'd be courting precisely

the kind of publicity he always ran from. So I figured we could hold him long enough for me to talk reason into him yet again.

As the medical shuttle entered atmosphere, naturally, it just had to hit turbulence that turned Hamish white around the eyes. He recovered fast, though, threw off his safety harness before it was quite safe, and was out and about, soothing his crew while life support laid on air fresheners to cover the reek of fear and a couple cases of old-fashioned air sickness.

When we'd gotten everyone settled back and cleaned up, and the shuttle was nosing down toward West Continent, I actually found a minute or two to stare out the nearest port. Aviva was bisected, not just by the terminator between day and night, but by the red and black rock of the Marcus Archipelago and the East Continent, with a few volcanic peaks actually touched by snow, and the green of West Continent.

During the war, Aviva's settlers had retreated into the domes set up after first landing. The planet had taken a few hits, but the domes had held, and the Avivans had been among the first in this sector to venture out from their shields and begin terraforming once again.

Now, an honest-to-God planetary spaceport at Gan Salem showed no evidence that Aviva had ever been part of a war zone. Maybe the port was civilian territory, but Security sure enough met us at the docking bay and led us through a mobile hall, past a variety of checkpoints—some of them medical rather than military—set up for the occasion, and into a cavern of a room that damned near induced agoraphobia in anyone used to cramped shipboard quarters.

After our bout with the fake medic, Gan Salem Security promised us they'd close the port till we got our people out, and I believed them. The facility might be secure, but the number of workers, engineers, security, and officials still imposed too many unfamiliar faces upon *Glasgow*'s crew, and I couldn't say I was crazy about it either.

Remembering the terror of my first excursion after I'd been

thawed, I drew Hamish's arm through my own. I could feel his shakes.

"Not long now," I promised him. Then I had to spoil a perfectly good reassurance by stopping dead in my tracks.

I couldn't rightly say I was totally surprised to see Ryutaro Jones. Little bastard, looking like he'd never skipped a meal or a night's sleep, was leaning against a pale green marble pillar that arched up into vaults of white and blue, sculpted to resemble lotus flowers.

He came upright and strolled toward me until a chest-high security barrier. As he set his hand on it, grinning as he prepared to vault over, three helmeted security ops came up behind him. They grabbed him so eagerly I could tell he'd already made a world-class pest of himself.

"This time we're throwing you out!" they told him.

"This is Gan Salem municipal property," Jones began. He spread out his hands. *Can't blame a man for trying*. "Captain!" As the guards started to march him away, he shouted over his shoulder at me. "Is it true Marshal Emeritus Becker's called you in to brief you on a classified mission?"

Several people in civvies, who should have been going about their business, assuming they had any business there at all, paused. I gestured to the guards to wait.

"Jones, dammit!" It was a more civil greeting than he deserved. "Even if that was true, why would I tell you?"

"Because we're friends, Captain," he grinned at me. "You need a hand?"

"I'll give you a hand," I offered, showing him my fist before I walked over and shook his hand. Might save him a well-deserved roughing-up by the guards, and then again, it might not: I really didn't care.

He tried to grab my arm and hang on. I pulled free.

"Sober up, why don't you?" I asked. I owed him something embarrassing. "Throw the damn pills away. All they do is give you delusions."

The onlookers turned back: so the noise was just a drunk, bothering a visiting officer? Security could handle that. One of them snickered. Jones flushed bronze along his nice high cheekbones, unbruised so far.

I jerked my thumb *out!* at the guards, who began to hustle Jones along.

He actually laughed. "Nice going, Captain! See you later!"

That was what I was afraid of. I checked my sleeve in case Jones had a friend who was into spy circuitry. Not even a snag.

"Talk to you when you're off-duty!" he called cheerfully and didn't even make the guards drag him away.

"Who's that?" asked Hamish.

"Media puke named Jones," I said. "Despite what you just saw, he takes 'no' for an answer."

Some of the time.

If that didn't reassure Hamish, the sight of all that security had to have eased his mind that his surviving crew didn't face attack-by-media.

Younger, stronger, and taller than I, he let me steer him toward a ground carrier as if he were a sick child. I gave him a light push, urging him into a seat, and belted him in. He tried to turn, watching as his crew was loaded.

"Let it go, man. They're in good hands. It's your turn to rest, now," I told him.

The carrier whooshed up on its air cushions, forcing a yell out of one *Glasgow* whose face ticced constantly. A woman under deep trank moaned. Hamish fumbled with his safety restraints, but a medic batted away his hands and attended to the trank case herself.

I gestured to the driver to speed up.

We drove past the spaceport's landing fields, past meticulously ordered stands of trees, their leaves stirred by winds I longed to feel on my hair. Signals flickered, red, blue, and green, while the mellow light of late afternoon seemed to promise peace, even if it was peace somewhere for someone else. Even the clouds looked like something off Old Earth.

The carrier angled into a sharp turn. I flung an arm out in case Hamish's balance failed.

"Not long now," I assured him. "We're taking you and your people to hospital."

He nodded. Aviva Memorial was the jewel in the crown of this planet's Technical University. During the war, it had served as a medical facility for half this sector. The Avivans had given it the luxury of a parklike setting in the center of what had been their first domed settlement. We sped past lush ground cover toward the building—actually a series of buildings joined by skywalks and ramps.

I heard the driver reporting in to hospital staff as the groundcar purred up a ramp to a low entryway.

A crowd had stationed itself outside. Someone pointed, and the whole pack headed toward us, recorders flashing and flickering. Baying on our trail. I didn't see Jones and didn't expect to. Media mobs were beneath his dignity.

Hamish touched my arm.

"Don't suppose we could run them down, Captain?" he asked.

"We'd never survive the paperwork," I said.

The carrier whirred about a hundred meters past the media pack whose stampede after us was being blocked by security to a secured entrance. Doors slid open, reflecting lights from the mirror-bright doors that closed off access to the rest of the hospital.

Hamish unsnapped his safety belts. For a miracle, his hands had stopped shaking. "Come on," he told his crew. "Don't forget to thank Captain Marlow." One or two of them tried to cheer.

He reached for my hand and shook it, then turned to help release his crew. Tom Ankeny gestured thumbs-up at me as a swarm of personnel eased *Glasgow*'s crew toward the sanctuary we'd promised them.

I REASSURED HAMISH THAT GALERIES-MIDLAND WAS FOOTING the bill. Whether they liked it or not, there was no way in hell *Glasgow*'s crew was going to be charged for their care, and there was no reason why Relief Services should foot the bill when we had a nice, fat multi-planetary to absorb the charges. Just as I was promising I'd see him later, my comm went off.

"Cam Marlow?" It was Marshal Becker again.

"We've just settled *Glasgow*'s crew."

"Tell their CO I'll stop by tomorrow, please." Now that Hamish had seen his people safe, he'd permitted himself to be sedated and it was hitting hard. He let his hand drop at his side and managed a weak grin.

"He heard you, sir. Says thanks. Personnel transfer's complete, with only a minor infestation of media," I added.

"I trust your discretion, Captain," said Becker. *"I'm sending a car around to the North Portico for you. We need to talk."*

We need to talk. If ever there's a phrase calculated to cause mess, inconvenience, and high anxiety, that's the one.

Find Jim and sit on him, I could have told GW, but he already thought I'd taken too many risks on a loser I wasn't, for God's sake, even sleeping with. As for Jones, Jones wouldn't bother with GW, not if he knew Becker was downworld.

"You have permission to sleep out of your ship tonight," Becker added. So this wasn't just a matter of talking to the Marshal Emeritus, it was debriefing, and it was going to be formal. Just what I needed.

Still, there's only one possible response to "we have to talk" from the top of your chain of command, and I gave it. "Aye-aye, sir."

BECKER'S CALL GAVE ME OFFICIAL SANCTION TO MAKE MY escape from a place where the buzz of medical electronics, the reek of drugs and antiseptics, and the suppressed whispers of fear and tension, masked by deliberate calm, reminded me forcibly of my resurrection at Havilland Roads.

GW walked me down a long corridor to the medcenter's North Portico. The corridor was paneled with a translucent stone that picked up the last embers of Aviva's sunset and retained them. Colors pooled in glinting crystals and glinted off veins of metal, and seeped into the stone. A door with clear panels slid aside, letting me stand in the open air for the first time in . . . I didn't have time to do the math because, right then, I felt the wind. Natural, planet-weather wind tugging at my hair beneath my helmet.

The hospital smells faded out of immediate recall, replaced by the spicy scent of the trees, backlit as if they were statues, that lined the Portico, alternating with low hedges of some prickly shrub so dark it seemed black in the twilight. My eyes filled, and I blinked away shimmer. My sinuses twinged, giving me an instant of vertigo, the way you get when you shut the jets off your suit in space. Then, the tension in my shoulders melted away. God, I was tired. I wanted to go out into that lawn, lie down on it, and let the planet's energy have its way with me, unscientific as I knew that sounded.

Ahead lay the unmarked car Becker had sent. It was powered down, showing only station-keeping lights that acquired rainbow shimmers as my eyes filled.

How long had it been since I'd spent any time at all downworld? I'd forgotten how comforting planets could be: humanity's first and greatest fortresses—even a planet in the process of learning to sustain human life.

I muttered something in response to GW's farewell and headed toward the car, blinking to clear my eyes so I wouldn't trip and go sprawling like some newbie in zero G. A door opened in what had been a seamless silver panel, and I slid inside. A computer screen glowed by one of the seats. Absentee briefing? I had several thousand questions I needed to ask.

I just wished, seeing I was going to be formally debriefed without time to return to my ship, I'd thought to pack a clean uniform.

"Good evening, Captain," came a familiar voice.

Damn all, what was *Jim* doing here?

Aviva, Downworld

20

Jim saw the *Glasgow* crewman who'd been his particular charge safely into the hospital and deeply asleep before he turned to leave.

I'm just a spacer, an old friend of the captain's, he'd reassured the physicians at Aviva Memorial. All right, so he was presuming a little on the "friend" part of the "old-friend" equation, but he and Marlow went back decades, if you counted her time in Freeze.

Time to clear out now, Jim told himself. He didn't want medical types poking and prying at him, thanks, and he'd seen that damnable Jones in Gan Salem spaceport, even seen Marlow take him by the hand before security'd managed to throw the spoiled little pest out. Jones had cost him one future already.

Well, Jim had known the mission would be successful. Too successful for him to dare remain.

So, it was time for Jim to disappear again. The question was how. If he presumed to beg a shuttle ride back "Upstairs" to the ship, now docked at Aviva's orbital facility, the exec would look at him as if he weren't just trash, but a damned nuisance. Maybe one of those companies that had so plagued Marlow during the trip insystem would welcome a spacer with no papers, but good skills, if he could be hired cheap enough.

Marlow didn't need him hanging around. One day, she'd stick her hand in the fire for him once too often and pull out, not another miracle, but a charred stump. She might miss him. Crew wouldn't, especially the Fleet survivors. Only loyalty to their captain had kept the vets' mouths shut and fists unclenched this long.

"You're part of *Gavroche*'s crew, sir?" asked an orderly. She was small, olive-skinned, and she smiled helpfully up at him, innocent of how she was cutting the plans out from under his feet. "We've arranged accommodations."

So he had no choice but to smile back and follow her to the shelter where he could find ground transport. She wrote down the name of the hostel, which she handed him, and, as he waited, he evaded her questions about his name, his work, and his plans for leave.

At the mid-priced hostel, ID made out in Jim's last alias, which claimed status as a civilian contract employee, sufficed to check him into a cube about the size of his berth on board, but so determinedly upbeat in its green and yellow furnishings that he fought down claustrophobia.

But at least, this cube had a door—even if it was enameled green—that he could lock, its own tiny bath facilities, a computer he could access, and a miniserver from which he had enough credit to buy overpriced beer or synth coffee. It also had a comm that buzzed at the least convenient time, which was, frankly speaking, any time at all.

He spilled the coffee on the green fake-lacquered desk unit, swore, and mopped it, ignoring the demand that he communicate. It buzzed again.

He slapped active the red "do not disturb" light.

His door slid aside. A man in Relief Service uniform filled the doorway. He was tall, stocky. Almost as dark as Marlow's first officer. MURAD, H., read his nameplate, beside which an ID holo twinkled. But Jim didn't need name or ID to identify the man: warrant officer, one of the old breed that didn't just know where the bones were buried, but had probably stuffed more than a few of them in the ground himself.

And he greeted Jim by what he thought of as his "old" name. All of it.

Sweat broke out on Jim's forehead. He could feel a treacherous flush on his face and a chill in his belly. He reached to block Murad's entry, but the man lunged in and knocked his arm aside. He didn't even have to try hard.

Jim came back, swinging, but Murad blocked him. No sweat marred his bald head or the glossy synthetic flesh of his right arm.

"I can hardly say it is a pleasure meeting you," said Murad, releasing Jim. Electronics—probably an esophageal implant—resonated in that voice, a sign that at some point, the man had either taken heavy fire or smoke damage. So Murad, H., was another Fleet vet, seconded, like Marlow, to Relief by grace and favor.

Could they find no better use for a hero than to fetch the likes of him?

Warrant Officer Murad opened a sealed pocket and handed Jim not a tape, but an old-style written message.

"Instructions," he said. Orders were for honest officers.

Jim tore open the message and put up his eyebrows at the signature. Marshal Becker himself, requesting his presence. Jim didn't fool himself thinking he was moving up in the worlds.

Meeting Becker, who'd seen him thrown out of Fleet, was a pleasure he could do without. Well, he was civilian now; he could refuse.

But not with Warrant Officer Murad looming over him. If he tried to break and run, that would be fine thanks to Cam for pulling him out of a riot, a slaver's trap, and the rest of the downward spiral toward losing his soul.

"You will please accompany me, sir," said Murad.

"You know damned well I'm not 'sir,' " he said, the last snarl of an animal who had been most civilly cornered.

"You will please follow me."

I stood my trial. I paid my debt, Jim wanted to protest. It sounded too much like begging.

He grabbed up a jacket—gray to match his shipsuit; not honest spacers' blue—and followed Murad to a sleek silver groundcar.

Aviva's day was cooling toward evening. Sunset glowed

on the horizon like somebody else's hearth. A cool wind played across his face, but failed to cool the shame in his eyes.

As the burden of his guilt held him paralyzed, Murad's prosthetic arm reached out for a come-along-with-me grip.

Probably, Murad could catch him without breaking a sweat. *Who's that you've got, Warrant Officer? No one,* he could imagine Murad answering, say, the pretty young orderly who'd wanted to know his dinner plans. *Remember the officer who abandoned* Irian Jaya? *Wouldn't call him "anyone," would you?*

Jim shuddered, breaking the spell.

Murad gestured *get in,* and shut the door with a decisive *snick* before heading up front. No doubt he was glad not to have to sit with Jim. *"Yes, sir. I'll fetch the deserter. Does the Marshal require I sit with him too?"*

The groundcar started, purring down one of the curved roads that meant it had been carved out of the rock when Aviva's settlers were still confined to the domes of Gan Salem's First Settlement. Within a dome, all roads were ring roads: you quite literally ran in circles. There was a joke there, if Jim felt like laughing.

If only he could get the door open, he could hurl himself out and roll free before the car reached an elevated road. He tried the lock: the door held. Damn.

"Make yourself comfortable, sir," came Murad's voice, without even a twinge of irony.

Nothing to be done: Jim sat and waited as the groundcar whispered to a halt before the portico of the hospital he had left only hours ago. Through clearsteel tinted the same silver as the car, he could see a figure in Arvy blue turn from his—no, her—companion and hurry down the steps.

Marlow.

Murad released the door. Jim was stronger, younger than Marlow; it would be the work of seconds to push past her and vanish into the evening. Hell, even if Cam broke a bone or two—he'd heard enough to know that years in Freeze could leave you brittle—she was in front of the finest hospital in the Sector.

And Murad would kill him. Well, that was one way out, even if he couldn't take it.

If he laughed, he would probably bleed to death from the wound it made.

"Good evening, Captain," Jim said. He drew back, offering her as much space as possible in the groundcar's cushioned, official interior. Plush gray upholstery. A water dispenser. Computer access. All the comforts of . . . headquarters.

Marlow slipped inside, nodding at him like old times, and here he was: a stainless officer again, waiting on his captain.

She drew water and sipped. A lift of her eyebrow offered him a glass. He refused with a curt headshake. At least, he could show respect by not making her drink with him.

Marlow darkened the car's interior lights and set the computer he hadn't dared touch on a lightning scroll. Politely, Jim kept his eyes away from the screen.

Maybe the information she was absorbing would tell her, among all the no-doubt-far-more-important information she was absorbing, why, when she reported for debriefing, she found a disgraced officer riding with her in a groundcar more luxurious than Relief Service had a right to even dream of. Maybe once Marlow knew why he was along for the ride, she'd tell him. She'd always been generous.

The backlit screen glowed on her hair, not quite as gold as he remembered it. The blue and green lights of the board revealed the faint lines and puffiness that showed her age, including the years she'd lost.

Marlow's not young anymore, Jim realized with a twinge of sudden fear.

She didn't need more trouble, but she'd protected him. A woman like Marlow—she ought to be sitting back on Earth, celebrated by the likes of that young Jones, damn glossy kid who never put a foot wrong in all his life or let what little he'd scrabbled together fall from his hands because he deserved less than nothing.

The light shimmering on her hair hurt to watch.

They passed a checkpoint between some older fields not quite rich with crops and new plantations of terraformed land. Jim could damned well bet Murad was reporting in, but what? *Sir, I am bringing in the captain and her pet coward?*

Now, they were the only car on the road. No point in trying to throw himself out and pick up another ride.

Marlow glanced up at the checkpoint, then turned her attention back to the computer screen, leaving Jim to the discomfort of his own thoughts and the time the chronometer doled out in slower and slower increments.

"Look at that!" Marlow broke the silence. Jim peered out into the night. More plantings, softening massive walls that soared up in the middle of a flat plain. The luminescent trees revealed outbuildings leading to a central court, higher than the structures that surrounded it. An impressive, columned entrance, like an Old Earth villa, loomed up, lights glowing between the pillars.

"Built like a fortress," Marlow remarked. Her hand, by reflex, brushed her hip. No sidearm. Jim straightened his jacket. "Probably rebuilt after the war. I think I remember hearing Aviva took three strikes outside the dome. Suicide missions."

Jim raised an eyebrow at her just as if he were still her junior officer.

"No," she answered his silent question. "This isn't headquarters. And we're not dressed for a dinner party. Becker must want me—us—to meet someone."

Murad brought the groundcar to a predictably silent halt in front of the entrance, then cracked the door by hand for them and stood at attention. Marlow climbed out, squared her shoulders, nodded Official Thanks at Murad, and damned near marched toward a double doorway at least four meters high to the dark figure waiting for them. Jim kept to her shadow, forcing himself to keep his head up, his step untroubled. He was sure Murad had his eyes on him.

And probably a sidearm to boot.

21

"Captain Marlow," Marshal Becker greeted me, coming out from between two columns in the high-arched entryway. "Cam." *Well done* resonated in his voice, and he took my hand and pressed it for a moment.

Lamplight glowing high overhead deepened each wrinkle on his face. On station, the light would have seemed like exposure of old wounds. Here, the lines and shadows on Becker's face didn't look as much like scars as the woodgrain, rich with use, on ancient carvings I'd seen before the war.

Jim braced to attention, or tried to after the years of exile, the burden of anger and guilt that had slumped his shoulders. Becker nodded to him.

"The young man who has done so much and thrown so much away. You will excuse the manner of my summoning you." Not a question. Not a request.

Jim responded in the only way he could, by straightening further and saying "Sir."

"Come inside," said Becker. "Captain Marlow knows by now that this is no Relief Service facility, but a private home. And it is rude to keep one's host waiting."

He led us through the impressive entryway. Heavy doors, reinforced with the same dark metal out of which the overhead light fixtures had been made—"forged" seemed like a suitable word for their somber weight—closed behind us with the added *snick* of hermetic seals.

We entered what appeared to be a reception room. The walls were thick, not softened by the translucent stone panels I'd seen at Aviva Memorial, but plastered, a deliberate reminder of a long-ago past. Running along the ceiling and the flagged stone floor were dark wood moldings that seemed to cast shadows of their own. Light glowed in the perforations of the central chandelier, wrought of the same dark metal as the fixtures outside.

Scrap. Recycled from a ship, but how many years ago?

The wall to my left was filled with what looked like a hand-painted map of Aviva. Its brushstrokes and images were almost deliberately primitive. On the opposite wall was an elaborate tree, its branches adorned with faces and symbols that were strange to me. I could see a regular pattern in the stone floor, only partly concealed by the heavy table in the center of the hall: whoever had built this place had included an escape hatch.

Becker went over to the table, as heavy as everything else in the place. The only thing on it was a ceramic tray that held a pitcher and glasses. He poured water into three glasses, handing one to Jim despite his shocked attempt to draw back.

"I knew you made your own rotten luck," Becker told him. "I didn't know you had become such a snob. Your host takes hospitality seriously. Go ahead and drink."

I hid an exceedingly nasty smile behind my own glass. Becker had confounded Jim worse with a single kindness than I'd been able to in all the years I'd known him.

The wall across from the door held double doors, surrounded on each side by dark wood shelves that held artifacts I only wished I had a chance to examine. I wouldn't find here the weapons and citations of retired military, that was certain. Or the statues I'd seen displayed on Raffles as trophies. I did see one figure with long, extended wings, a candelabrum with many branches, what looked like crude attempts at handicraft, and a piece of equipment, half slagged, that I couldn't identify. There was even an archaic ship's bell, its brass brilliantly polished.

"Come," said Becker. "Your host is waiting."

He opened the double doors onto a central courtyard. It lay open now to the night winds and stars, but a certain thickness in the walls suggested to me that it could be covered, either by a dome field or the same sort of clearsteel we used on board. In the center of the . . . the *atrium*—I had the old term right, I was sure of it—surrounded by large ceramic squares in the same pattern as the pitcher in the hall, was a pool from which water bubbled, constantly refreshed from some natural source deep underground.

I wanted nothing so much as to sink onto one of the deliberately rough-hewn wooden chairs beside the pool and listen to the play of water as the wind overhead whispered me to sleep. Behind me, I heard Jim's answering sigh.

His footsteps echoed on the stone behind me as we crossed the courtyard. The lights mounted on the walls caught us, sending out long shadows across the stone, moving as we did.

Then the "host" Becker had said awaited us came out from his study to meet us, his hand outstretched. We paused, and so did our shadows. I heard Jim draw in a breath of astonished respect.

"Commissioner Neave," Jim whispered.

Becker moved in at Jim's elbow, making sure that this time, at least, Jim wasn't going to run.

The man who faced us didn't seem to merit it. He was a taut brown man, weathered, despite what had to be many years spent in space. He didn't look as old as my computer briefing had told me he was—not much more than my actual age.

At his level on the chain of command, you had to start wondering if someone was slipping anti-agathics into the rest of his meds. They had them on Santayana, I knew, and I'd long suspected Becker was taking them.

Unlike Becker, this man didn't look old. But his true age lay in his eyes, alert and piercing, with a scholar's relentless attention, as if the fire you could see in them fueled him rather than consumed his strength.

I could hardly share Jim's awe: I was in Freeze and drifting through space when the war, right before the Terra blockade, had pried then-Professor Amory Eliot Neave away from his comfortable Old Earth university chair, forcing him away from the study of military history and toward helping to make it.

Neave had worked with Becker during Operation Seedcorn. After the war, he'd sat on the bench during various war crimes trials on trivial matters like genetic tampering and planetary slagging. And he'd traveled circuit with Marshal, then Sector Governor, Becker, as he tried to harvest the colony worlds his Operation Seedcorn had established in such desperate haste.

He might even be worth Jim's awe.

"Captain Marlow," said Commissioner Neave. He waved away my salute, taking my hand instead. And, unlike Becker, he held it and actually almost bowed. "Amory Neave, at your service," he said.

"Begging the commissioner's pardon," I asked, "but isn't it the other way around?"

"That remains to be seen," Neave replied and led us into a study furnished with the art and equipment of at least ten planets that I recognized. The room was a harmonious double cube, twice as long as it was wide. Here were no somber archaisms of recycled metal, plaster, hand-painted murals, and rough-hewn wood. The walls were paneled in the translucent stone of modern Avivan architecture, and the light fixtures were inset—including the two-meter rotating hologram projected onto the pale wood conference table that showed Aviva and its progress in terraforming its land.

Darker wood held what looked like very old paper books bound in supple leather, flaking a little at the edges. More books, mingling with tapes, hard copy, and shimmering disks, threatened to tumble off a desk that also held two computer screens, one of which was built in. The only anachronistic touch was a heavy wool rug in dark red and blue geometries, roughly finished with the coarse white fringe I heard you got when rugs were hand-loomed and tied off by hand.

Was this a home or a museum?

"Isn't this a lot of space for one man?" I asked. I'd been out of it when Neave was establishing the reputation that had

Jim speechless. Damned if I was going to be as impressed as the briefing led me to believe I should be.

He laughed. "Since Armistice, I mostly lived in a ship's cabin and my databases. Before that, after my family sold its last farm, I stayed in university apartments: spacious, but nothing like this, not after my second marriage . . . my children moved out too. When I moved to Aviva to assist Abram with Operation Salvage, I acquired this . . . house, I suppose you'd call it. It was a central meeting place, one of the first buildings put up when they ventured out beyond the domes. In what I like to call my spare time, I'm restoring the place."

"My briefing covered Operation Seedcorn. I think I may even have heard RUMINT about it before I went into . . ." I made an "out the airlock" gesture with my free hand and looked at Neave's hand, holding mine. He released it.

"Operation Salvage, though? First time I heard about it was on the ride over. Congratulations on the new appointment, sir," I added to Becker.

"Seedcorn and Salvage aren't precisely congruent, you'd say, Captain?" asked Neave. "I argued for calling this new operation Project Harvest, but Marshal Becker insisted it have a name that began with S, like Seedcorn."

Neave gestured me to a seat, a low wide chair cushioned in natural leather so soft it made me want to curl my legs up under me and relax for a couple of hours, and waved Jim and Marshal Becker to a long couch before choosing a chair much like my own. A low table faced him. Becker set his glass down on it, allowing the rest of us to follow suit. A coffee service occupied most of the table, displacing more books. Near Neave's reach lay a judge's gavel, its wood well-rubbed as if its owner often picked it up as he worked out some ethical or logistical problem.

"I've arranged for a light meal to be served in a little while," Neave said. "Unless, Captain, you require food sooner? I gather some medical challenges remain. . . ."

"Nothing that interferes with—" I hadn't had a single episode of freezer burn since I left Havilland Roads, at least, nothing that Medical could use to invalid me out of Relief Services too.

"Cam, no one's even hinting you're unfit for service," Becker put in.

Even Jim, seated across from me, looked ready to bristle in my defense. Maybe I needed to get over myself.

"Captain, my apologies. I've spent enough time shipboard to have realized how that must have sounded to you. Coffee, anyone?" asked Neave. He bent to pour, a host's custom.

Becker flicked a glance at Jim. By the rules Becker knew, it was obviously the duty of the junior-most officer present to pour the coffee and hand it round.

Jim straightened, shocked.

Becker held his eyes.

Jim sighed. "Allow me, sir," he said. His hand shook as he reached out to take the pot from Neave, but he poured without incident and handed the cups around like the well-trained ensign I remembered. He even acknowledged Neave's thanks with a smile that reminded me of the boy for whom Fleet had held such hopes.

Sipping the coffee gave me a chance to glance about Neave's study. Now that my eyes had adjusted to the room, I could see its walls were lined with pictures and holos, images of the men and women, Alliance and Republic both, who had held the line during the war, then found themselves struggling, after it, to rub out the boundaries that so much blood and suffering had drawn.

The man to whom this place belonged—to whom it had been given as an incentive for settling here—valued civilization. He had set himself, for whatever reason, to put us at our ease with what I was damned sure was the skill of long practice. But they hadn't given him that direct commission for his social skills. In his civilian, civilized way, Neave was as relentless a fighter as those of us who'd been on the front lines.

Becker was in charge. But for the first time, I understood in my gut what the phrase "gray eminence" meant: this urbane, quiet presence. Who wanted something and would no doubt tell us in his own time.

Neave set down his cup.

Apparently, that time was right now.

"I will be frank with you," he said. "In the culture in which I was brought up, straight dealing was valued. A man's word—or a lady's—was his bond. At the same time, we placed considerable reliance on long preliminary discussions. Amenities must be maintained, you know: besides, they're a way of getting to know who you're up against. Now, though, at my age, with so much left to be done, I have become impatient with long preliminaries, except as an art form that, frankly, we—and the No Man's Worlds and beyond—have no time for. I ask your pardon for that, Captain."

I inclined my head the way I'd seen an admiral do once. This Commissioner Neave had the grand manner. So, I'd have to act like a great lady, wouldn't I? Assuming I could. The very idea made me smile, but I was surprised when he smiled back.

"So: when Abram told me that *Gavroche* was inbound, Captain, I asked him to bring you to see me. Candidly, I was curious."

I let him have it with both eyebrows. Neave chuckled and glanced over at his desk. He'd probably faced down fleets of captains.

An unwelcome thought occurred to me. "I ran into Ryutaro Jones at Gan Salem spaceport. Before Security ejected him, he asked if Marshal Becker was planning to brief me for a secret assignment."

The Marshal brought his fist down silently on the table.

"Young Jones again," said Neave. "He has attempted to approach me a number of times. He is quite—"

" 'Persistent' is the word he prefers," I said.

Jim choked on his coffee, and Neave chuckled.

A sudden, horrible thought struck me. "I don't suppose he's going to join our little house party, is he?"

"Not by my invitation," Neave said. "Young Mr. Jones *says* he wants to help write my memoirs."

"Probably, he does," Becker observed.

"But I am quite capable of writing them myself, when the time comes," Neave replied. "Last time he contacted me, he compared me to those ancient governors from Earth's Age of Exploration. I confess myself intrigued by the idea. And mildly flattered, which I suppose is Mr. Jones' intent."

Becker coughed, and Neave nodded.

"Back to the subject at hand. After the genocide trials on Cynthia—"

My briefing had included a summary of that trial. A junior officer had had to assume command of one of Becker's Seedcorn colonies. Tasked with protecting the refugees settled on Cynthia, she'd tried to wipe out a life-form that turned out to be sapient—one of the few alien races that could thrive on the same real estate as humans. After the war, when Becker and Neave himself came back to Cynthia, she'd charged herself with genocide and insisted on standing trial for what was, of course, a capital offense.

"I burned out. Questioned everything. I needed a safe place," Neave went on as if I'd been rude enough to question him. "Clean air, decent people, hard, honorable work. I had heard of Aviva from one of the Cynthian colonists. He was a native of Ararat, and a very worthwhile fellow. But Ararat and its traditions were too close to . . . to what had occurred on Cynthia. Let's call it a wound I had no role in inflicting, but that I was privileged to try to heal. Almost as soon as we lifted off, I took myself off duty and told Abram I was thinking of going back to Earth."

He exchanged a glance with the old man. "Abram disapproved. Somewhat vehemently. As I recall, he called it a—"

Failure of nerve? Dereliction of duty? I'd experienced Becker's verbal firepower. Odd to think of a civ on Neave's level saying "yes sir" and sucking it in.

"Abram suggested I join him to work on Operation Salvage."

"Commissioner," I said, hating myself, "if you've reviewed my files, you know that there are certain types of missions I just wouldn't be fit for either."

He turned, reaching for the coffee pot.

"Please allow me, sir," said Jim.

The pot was empty. Neave raised an eyebrow and touched a panel on the arm of his chair.

"I wanted to meet you, Captain. But it is your associate for whom I have immediate use. A job, Mister . . . ?" he let the question of Jim's name hang discreetly in the shadowy air. "Perhaps you would be more comfortable thinking of it that way. Can we assume you wish a new position?"

Jim's coffee spilled as he set it down, the cup clattering as it almost fell from his shaking hand. He rose. Fast. I half expected to see Warrant Officer Murad appear to restrain him.

"Relax," said Amory Eliot Neave again. "The suggestion is honestly meant. One thing my time on Cynthia gave me was experience in dealing with people who insist on regarding themselves as outcasts. But I really must observe that casting oneself as a tragic figure may carry a certain romantic grandeur, but it really is not very useful."

I stifled what would have been an extraordinarily unkind laugh. After the years Jim had spent playing the No Man's Worlds equivalent of the Flying Dutchman, to adapt a phrase that Neave probably was no stranger to, Jim was so used to regarding himself as something outcast and accursed that Neave's matter-of-fact handling of his situation didn't just bring him up short. It brought him up flat against the prison wall of his own building.

After what you've put me through, it serves you right, I thought, and shot Jim a look. Since we were among gentlemen, no one laughed.

The door whispered aside. Instantly and predictably, Murad's looming height filled it. The warrant officer had one hand free. With the other, he was clutching Ryutaro Jones, his prosthetic hand bunching up the too-expensive fabric of his jacket in a way that made it impossible for Jones to free himself and practically impossible for him to breathe.

Both my problem children. I wanted to beat my head—or theirs—against the wall.

"This individual was spying," Murad told his superiors. "When I arrested him, he claimed to know Captain Marlow."

"Jones, when you clutched my arm, you couldn't have left a tracer!" I interrupted the warrant officer. I looked down at my hand. Unmarked. Unstained.

Jones tried to hold up his own hand. "Pheromones," he explained. "Cynthian technology, Commissioner. Cam, when I shook your hand—"

"On Cynthia, they used that technology to attempt to wipe out an intelligent species. And now you see fit to use it for surveillance. One might suggest your choice of tactics is in deplorable taste," Neave observed.

Jones bowed a deep apology in a way I assumed he'd learned on Tokugawa. "How else could I have gotten your attention?"

"You have it now, sir. You may not enjoy it, however." Amory Neave turned toward Warrant Officer Murad. "Hamid," he said, "would you please tell the kitchen that Mr. Jones will be joining us for dinner?"

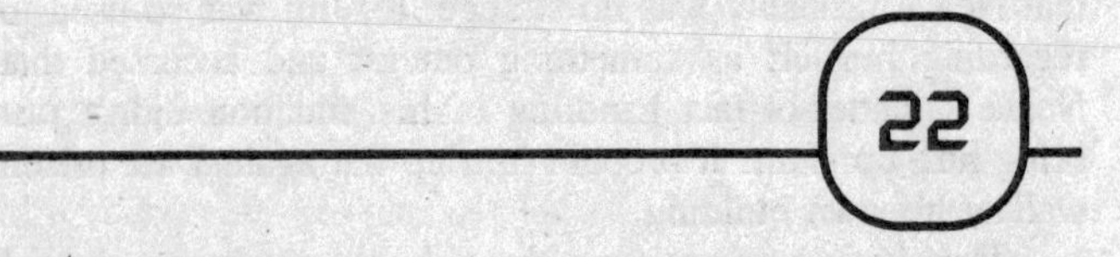

22

Jim held his wine glass up to the light in the dining room.

He was drowning in golden light the same color as the wine. He could see in this mirror the illusion he'd have traded his soul for, assuming he still had one: five people dining surrounded by the trappings of high culture, Fleet training stiffening the spines of two of the four, sheer audacity keeping the newsman from the type of shame that Jim himself felt in the presence of the others.

He sipped the vintage that Commissioner Neave had pronounced "complex" and set down his glass before he could burst into an ironic laugh that would have shattered the illusion of peace, acceptance, homecoming that this dinner represented to him. Blameless officers could spend their entire Fleet careers without dining in circles as elevated as this. All you had to do, it seemed, was get yourself disgraced.

Commissioner Neave sat at the head of the polished square table, Marshal Becker at his right hand, Jones beside him, and Jim at his left. Neave had made quite the ceremony about seating Marlow, the only woman and the only one of them in uniform, at the table's foot. His eyes rested on her often, and he smiled at her in what Jim recognized, despite their ages, as an extraordinarily decorous invitation to the dance between man and woman.

Jones had noticed too. He'd flicked Jim a cheerfully cynical grin, to which he'd responded by glowering. God, he'd have liked to invite him outside, only Murad would probably be there and grab each by the scruff till they stopped.

He was sick of Jones, with his good humor and his stories and his meddling in Jim's life. And now, his offhand assumption that Neave was entitled to smile at *his* Marlow.

Marlow's a grown woman, Jones' grin reproved him. *And you're being a jealous asshole.*

Jim had heard rumors about Marlow and Conrad Ragozinski back on Havilland Roads, whispered by guards too bored to remember they weren't talking to him or even supposed to be speaking in his presence. They'd trained together before the war, Jim knew. Ragonzinski had been present at Marlow's resurrection. Jim closed his eyes on an unwelcome mental image of the iron man who'd pronounced his damnation actually unbending, leaning over the waking woman and taking her hand, her first human contact in her new life.

Marlow would have had no reason to see the inflexible, stick-up-the-butt side of the man. And even if Jim still wished

Ragozinski had taken his header out that airlock before his trial, what Marlow saw was Marlow's business.

Neave smiled again at Cam, drawing her out with skilled questions about Hamish of the *Glasgow,* another one who'd succeeded where Jim had failed. He took a desperate gulp of the golden wine to dull the edge of his resentment. Never mind the "complex bouquet" on which Jones complimented his suddenly acquired host, Ryutaro damn-the-man Jones who could turn trespass into an invitation to a dinner party grander than anything Jim had ever known.

The wine was better anesthesia than trank. It took the edge off his senses without sending him to sleep. It even let him, when the thread of the conversation passed to him in courteous turn, to express admiration of the survivors and the way *Gavroche*'s official crew—not counting him—had taken them to their hearts.

"To the example you set, Captain?" asked Neave, raising his glass to Marlow. She turned her face—and the compliment—aside. "Every crewman rose to the occasion," she said. "Everyone on board."

Jim almost choked on his next gulp of wine, but Neave was rising now, making the cultivated offer of Terran brandy in his study. He gestured for Marlow to lead the way. As Jim rose to follow, he found Becker's eyes on him, glinting with ancient malice.

It's your turn in the barrel.

Neave gathered them with practiced skill about his bookshelves, holding the library he had had extravagantly shipped out from Earth. "You may appreciate these, Mr. Jones," he remarked. "Assuming your letter to me was not blatant flattery." He pointed at the books. Histories of those governors and plantation owners who built their tiny empires, waiting for the day when they'd be finally able to return home, and finally, finally realizing that their homes were here, where they'd made their lives.

"So, you indeed feel a kinship to them, sir?" Jones asked, seizing the moment.

Neave chuckled and passed him a fragile balloon glass

glowing with old brandy. Jones nodded absently, his attention riveted on the ancient books.

"So Aviva has become home to you?" Marlow asked. She ran her finger down the spine of one of the books, picking out the details of its deep green binding. "I congratulate you."

"If I were to return to Earth now, I suspect I would feel a stranger. I might even," Neave added with a glint of surprising mischief, "find it a trifle dull. And I am certain, by now, the younger men and women in my university would treat me with the courtesy one reserves for relics of a vanished age." Again, a knowing smile at Marlow.

"Years ago, I was active in Franklin-party politics, but I confess, politics don't interest me the way they used to. Besides," he added, "I notice that neither you nor Abram have made the long trip back yourselves."

Marlow laughed. "Ask Jones here to tell you how he planned to return, and one of his Secess'—Republic, I mean—cousins from Tokugawa scolded him, saying he hadn't earned the right. Man named Hashimoto-sama. Ever come across him?" Marlow asked.

Jones had whirled around, was trying to silence her, but Marlow smiled vengeance at him. He lifted his glass and drank to her.

Neave threw back his head and laughed, the cords of his throat in sharp relief above his conservative gray tunic. "You know," he told Jones, "you're another one. Some years from now—ten, twelve—I suspect you'll finally realize that the only part of you that'll ever return to Earth is your stories."

"They are the best part of me, Mr. Commissioner."

"Are they?" Neave asked. "Consider tonight. If Warrant Officer Murad takes you back into Gan Salem, I am certain you'll be prowling about my house again come morning, in which case I would not want to answer for Murad's disposition, if I were you. You have eaten at my table: I am reluctant to lock you up. So, I will take the risk of offering you a choice: what you are about to hear would make a remarkable story. You may tell it—possibly risking everyone in this room, not to mention the fate of an entire world. Or you can play a part, albeit a minor one, in it."

Jones bowed again in the Tokugawan fashion. "Hashimoto-sama would cast me out of the family if I betrayed a host's confidence, sir."

Jones might have broken every rule of etiquette in three systems. But as far as Jim knew, *he* had never broken his pledged word.

Becker gestured at Neave's library, at the wealth of possessions, new and old. "Mr. Jones, I am now what you may become: only my writing will return to Earth. My other legacies remain here. After all, I am a good Franklin, and this is a matter of utility. On Earth, my collections would mean nothing, except a matter of my university's trying to pry funds to store them out of my executors. Here, who knows? I may become to Aviva Technical what John Harvard was on Earth before there were even nations in North America. I confess, the idea is one that flatters the vanity I have not been able to stamp out."

"Your children wouldn't want your personal effects?" Jim ventured to ask. His father had—for all he knew, the old man was still alive—treasured a library of fiches, disks, and some, not many, costly paper reprints, paltry next to even the little he'd seen of Neave's collection, but much cherished. Father had spent one winter cold because he'd spent credit he needed for a new coat on an authentic bound book.

"What my children needed—or wanted—of me, they've had," Neave replied. "These books belong here."

"So you're not calling yourself an exile anymore?" Becker asked.

"Is that what you think?" said Neave. "Have you forgotten our old debates?"

He ran his hand along a shelf, pulled out a slim volume, its leather binding curling over from age and use, and read: " 'I think it is the lonely, without a fireside or an affection they may call their own, those who return not to a dwelling but to the land itself, to meet its disembodied, eternal, and unchangeable spirit—it is those who understand best its severity, its saving power, the grace of its secular right to our fidelity, to our obedience.' "

Jones was watching Neave as if transfixed. Marlow, though . . .

"Yes," said Marlow. "That's true." She sounded as if she were waking up with a key to every dream she'd ever had.

Jim turned a gaze on her as sharp as Neave's. Marlow had always been the one surrounded by friends, by colleagues, the captain of a ship, his rescuer.

But she had spent the better part of her adult life unconscious, drifting apart from humankind while the lives of everyone she knew ticked past and the worlds changed. Any hearth she had was her ship; any loyalty beyond her crew was to the Alliance.

"I first read those words when I was scarcely out of boyhood. But I think Captain Yeager of Cynthia Colony first taught me their meaning, though, God knows, she had people, family, she'd traded her soul for," Neave said. He carried the book with him as he led the way back to their earlier seats.

"Did you ever know Pauli Yeager, Captain Marlow—Cam, if I may? A fighter pilot, and from what I heard from those better able than I to judge, a talented one. Abram here assigned her to Operation Seedcorn because her reflexes and fighting skills were traits he didn't want to see snuffed out by the next Fighting Star. He gave her a chance for life—"

"I don't think she ever forgave me for stranding her on Cynthia," Becker put in.

"Can you blame her, Abram?" asked Neave. "First you took away her wings. Then, if you listened to her, practically her first act after her commanding officer was killed was to systematically wipe out an intelligent species with whom her own husband had established First Contact. If you hadn't grounded her, she wouldn't have had to do that. Of course, if you hadn't grounded her; she might have died the next time she fought. And Cynthia Colony would almost certainly have perished."

"I never knew her," Marlow said.

"I heard something about this," Jim surprised himself by venturing. "Wardroom gossip. One of these 'slit your throat after hearing' stories. I'd be glad to know more."

Jones flipped up a thumb, in a gesture that meant thanks. *I didn't do it for you,* Jim thought at him.

"I regret I cannot share the full story with you, sir," said Neave. "But I would be fascinated by *your* reaction to the captain's tale."

A moment longer, and Neave would lure Jim out of hiding the way a serpent lures a small bird. Neave would coax the secrets, the shame, out of him and into the light here in this civilized room.

He made himself meet Neave's glance, though he feared his own eyes begged for a mercy he hadn't earned.

Marlow coughed, as if the brandy were too strong for her.

Reprieve of a sort: when Neave turned to her, she shook her head so the light glowed on her fair hair.

A moment longer, Neave suspended Jim between concealment and confession. Then, he continued. "At least," he said, "Yeager and her colony brought their children up clean. Captain Yeager did not offer that in extenuation, but she did say it was her only reason for living. Personally, although it was not my place to have personal reactions, I think she was exaggerating. She spoke as if she was at the end of her life: I doubt she was even fifty yet, my own age at the time.

"But isn't that the way of it?" he mused, turning to Becker. "Your old men dream dreams, your young ones see visions, and they're both pretty damned ruthless about other people's burdens. Like yours," he shot at Jim.

"Other people have survived worse and gone on to make decent lives for themselves," Neave said. "If Captain Yeager damned herself, it was to give life to a generation, a colony. For what have you sold your soul?"

The question hit Jim before he could guard himself. "You know what I am."

"I know what you did. What you were convicted of, yes,"

Neave said. "Make no mistake: I don't minimize it. Your action was reprehensible. But it was, let us say, a lapse in judgment. Panic, if you will, although, yes, I know you had no right to panic. Captain Yeager's actions took planning. But your actions afterward remind me of hers. She could have killed herself. So could you. But I have to take into account her record on Cynthia and yours after Havilland Roads. What I, as a civilian, would call conspicuous valor on Shenango. Your work with plague ships. Even on board *Gavroche*: one or two of *Glasgow*'s crew may well owe their chance at sanity to you."

Neave threw back his head and laughed. "My dear man, don't look so outraged. Everything in your files, not just your trial, is a matter of public record for those who know how to ask."

"You're good, sir," said Jones. "You'd make a great investigative writer."

"Praise from Mr. Jones!" Neave held up his glass. "Don't sound so surprised, young man. When I left Earth, I was already a scholar, and I was made—thanks to Abram here—an investigator and judge."

"Was that why you had me brought here?" Jim asked. "To judge me again?" The resentment in his tone surprised him. So did the fact that no one reprimanded him.

"Oh no," said Becker. "We brought you here so you wouldn't run away again, this time not from punishment, but from praise or reward."

Jim brought his fist down on the table, making the brandy bottle jump. Becker bent forward to rescue it.

"If you know my record, then you know I have done nothing to deserve praise or reward."

"Ah," said Neave, "the tragic pose. You wish to expiate, but how can you when you have so clearly demonstrated that you believe yourself the only one with the right to judge when you have served your time? You're a prideful son, aren't you?"

Neave turned to Marlow. "I had hoped it was only romanticism. I wish it had been. But we have no banners, no armor except pressure suits, in this day and age. We cannot afford it. Jones' kinsman has retired to his gardens and calligraphy, to fight no more forever. So what we have here in your young friend is the penitential model—"

"Dammit," Jim shocked himself by exploding. "Don't talk in fancy circles over my head. Talk *to* me, if you've got to talk."

Neave tapped his book again. "What I am saying is that there is nothing new under the sun. Or suns. Not even your crime, your sin, if we may call it that." The book fell open to a well-thumbed passage. " 'The fact remains that you must touch your reward with clean hands, lest it turn to dead leaves, to thorns, in your grasp.' You feel your hands are not clean, so you turn away from what you've earned."

"Oh God!" It was the truth, the unbearable thing. Jim knuckled his aching eyes, hoping to blot out this newest shame or the sight of Neave's too-perceptive eyes.

And in front of Jones, who was lapping up his humiliation along with the best brandy Jim had ever tasted.

Silence . . .

"I didn't hear a question?" Neave prompted.

"Why're you wasting your time on me when there are so many people, so many worlds whose needs are so much greater?"

"I don't suppose you'd accept the idea that you—and your friends, and yes, you do have some—deserve concern? In all your training, didn't anyone ever teach you the 'needs of the one' paradox? Good God," he exclaimed in a completely different tone, "are we raising cultural illiterates out here?"

That forced a laugh out of Becker.

"Calm down, Professor," said Marlow. She poured Neave more of his brandy, then topped off Jones' glass.

The paradox had begun life as a cliché out of Old Earth's legends and passed into the core curriculum at the service academies, where cadets cursed its name. Now, Jim wanted nothing more than to go away and sit, maybe in that peaceful atrium with the night wind cooling his eyes, and think about it for a year or two.

But Neave was pressing on.

"Which is more important? The needs of the one, or the needs of the many? In my youth, I'd have answered 'the needs of the many,' of course. But what if we can combine the two?" Neave demanded. "Your need and the needs of the worlds. Thesis. Antithesis. Synthesis. What would we have then?"

"Suppose you tell me, Professor. If I'd learned my lessons at the Academy, I wouldn't be in the mess I'm in now," Jim said. Too damn bad if he sounded sullen, even if he was speaking to an elder statesman who was his host. He had more to worry about than social crimes.

"Fair enough. If you are looking for blame, I will indeed fault you, but for depriving humanity of what you could have given it if you'd served to the best of your ability. You might even consider the irony of these past few years. Do you realize that you've actually done better service as an outcast than you did as an officer, where what you could accomplish was circumscribed by your chain of command? There's a paradox for you to resolve. But not in the classroom. In the rest of your life."

In that moment, Jim hated everyone in the room, watching him the way you'd watch a ship you were about to fire on. *Stay on target . . . stay on target . . .*

"Well, what's it to be?" Neave demanded. "Are you holding out for *ego te absolvo, fili mei,* or will you settle for being worked to death?"

"I don't want a damned thing from anyone!"

"Ah, so it is your standards for which you punish yourself, not the people you've disappointed?" Neave smiled at Marlow, as if he'd known her, and prized her, for years. "If it were I, I would try to forgive myself. And even if I could not, like Captain Yeager, I would condemn myself to endure.

For the sake of the"—here Neave's irony bit deep—"greater needs of the many.

"You say there's blood on your hand? Then scrub it off with dirt and hard work. You need a job? I'm offering you one."

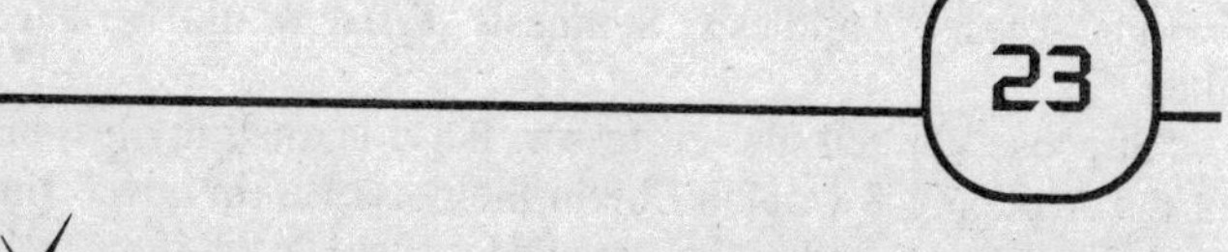

"You're talking about the scavenger build-up, aren't you?" Jones' lighter voice sliced across Neave's measured presentation. "I've been watching this. And Captain Marlow's last few missions—there's always scavengers somewhere in the distance. But in this case, we're talking prewar, aren't we? Something out of your own past, Commissioner."

"Go on," said Neave.

"Planet's called Exquemelin, out beyond the No Man's Worlds. A real bitch to get to, with gas clouds hiding the Jump points. But you've been there. You and Marshal Becker here. Way before the war. You were still in training, Commissioner, and you had to be pulled out."

"Jones!" Marlow's voice was a warn-off beacon, but Jones went on.

"That wasn't just a matter of war coming on, either. Someone really screwed up there—you, maybe? And you've waited all these years to set things straight?"

Becker stood, rested a hand on Neave's shoulder. "Abram, if we haven't come to terms with it after all these years, we're no better off than our guest here," Neave said, gesturing at Jim. "Captain, thank you for your defense, but you can stand down now: Mr. Jones' words, believe me, are milder than those I've used myself. Mr. Jones, I commend you on an excellent job of investigative reporting. If not, precisely, on your party manners."

Damn privileged-character Jones. If Jim had been the one to ask such questions, and in such an accusing tone, they'd have had Murad in here straightaway.

Jones naturally, took the praise as permission to pry further. Well, if Jones was the one to ask, he'd listen. Maybe Jim could learn something that would do him some good.

"If you're going back there, chances are you failed," Jones said.

You're pushing it, Jim thought. *Keep pushing, and they'll get Murad in here for you. Good. I'll watch.*

"Not totally," said Neave. "Let's say I—Abram and I, back when we were students—left a great deal unfinished."

"So, what kind of judgment sends the likes of *him* to do what you couldn't?"

"Jones!" Marlow snapped out.

"Come *on,* Cam. They want something, don't you see? And they want to use Jim here to do it. If you're lost, they'll be asked questions. But if they send *him* . . . I know his record after the *Irian Jaya* as well as the next man. He's damn good. But if he's lost, no one's going to care."

Jim swallowed his temper along with the last sip of brandy and set down his glass. "Commissioner, several hours ago, you said something about plain speech."

"I should think Jones just gave you a bellyful of it," Neave remarked.

"I'm still waiting."

He had been baited enough.

Neave laughed. "Here. Have more brandy. We'll all have more brandy. We'll do this in what they used to call the high Persian fashion: decide while we're drunk, then wake and discuss it again tomorrow, sober."

"Well enough," said Becker. "I take it, Amory, you think our friend here's the one for the job?"

"You won't find a better," said Marlow.

"We don't want a better man, Captain," said Neave. "As

Mr. Jones pointed out, if a better man goes missing, there'd be questions asked. Whenever Mister . . ." he spoke Jim's full name deliberately, knowing that the others in the room flinched for his sake, "is known for who and what he is, his effectiveness comes to an end. Where we have a mind to send him, he will not be known. So he is good enough to be used. Assuming he allows himself to waver from his usual pose that he is good for nothing."

"We do have a task in mind," Becker cut in smoothly. "Jones is right. Even before the war, we'd known scavengers were stepping up operations. The war diverted our attention and gave the scavengers other things to think about. And other prey. Now, I still receive intelligence on the planets that comprised Operation Seedcorn, and where I can deploy resources to protect them, I do. But there are other worlds too, worlds that . . . have eluded official perceptions, let us say. Eluded them for years. This has enabled them to escape interference, true: but now—"

"Like the one you visited before the war? If you don't officially know about them, the only way you can help them is covert ops?" Marlow said. "This explains your interest in my ship."

Becker nodded. "Amory, let's show them."

Neave rose and walked over to his work table. The holomodel of Aviva, with its green fields encroaching on the native rock, rotated and glowed, reflected on the polished wood. Pulling out a keyboard stowed beneath the table, he replaced the globe with a projection of a sector of space Jim had never seen. Lights flickered and gleamed, with denser projections that he knew represented gas clouds hundreds of light-years in length, explosions of protostars, creation and destruction in action, tamed to fit on a table. A movement of Neave's hand, and a serpentine streak of white light edged in and around the gas clouds.

"The Straits of Aquila," said Neave. "Your records said you were a good pilot once," he told Jim. "For the purposes of this exercise, I'm defining 'good pilot' as one without undue reverence for his own skin."

Jim whistled under his breath as he studied the white light that represented the optimum course through the Straits. He pointed to opacities in the holomodel. "Can scanners even get through some parts of that? It looks awfully dense. To get through that . . . No telling where scavengers might be massing, assuming they haven't found themselves a planetary base. I'd want to either be heavily armed in case of ambush, or damned fast: no telling where scavengers may have set up operations."

"I've always worried that they'd organize," Marlow said. "I've been listening for years."

Jim met her eyes. "That time on Raffles Station you pulled me out of that bar—"

Marlow nodded. "I think they were looking for live bodies for something. Not just spare parts."

"So that's where you were," Jones said. "Why didn't you tell me what you'd been looking for?"

Myths had haunted the No Man's Worlds, just as, long ago, they'd haunted the seas of Earth, of pirate bases and pirate fleets, attacking cities. Pirates, said the "they" who lounged in cheap bars on shabby stations, had found worlds all their own. Pirates planned to exploit asteroid swarms, using the smaller rocks to bombard planets, or threatening entire systems with engines mounted on larger ones, warping them out of orbit, hurling them into stars. Their impact would be less than minuscule, but there was always the chance, given a livelier-than-usual star, of destabilizing the photosphere, of bigger-than-usual radiation storms or prominences. The stories went beyond far-fetched into lurid fantasy, but they still weren't something any planet-bound culture—or even one able to evacuate its people—wanted to risk.

"You didn't have a need to know," Marlow said. "Now, you've dealt yourself into the game."

"Let us," said Neave, "rule out the livelier aspects of the stories we've all heard. If scavengers actually operate on a planetary scale, it's not to destroy the planets. If I were a scavenger . . . Mr. Jones," he gestured at the reporter as if calling on some inadequately prepared cadet.

But Jones was more resilient than that. "If I were a scavenger—instead of what you'd call a news-puke," he flashed a grin at the others. "If I had the resources in terms of people and ships, I'd want to use a planet as my own private supply depot. Agriculture. Natural resources. Mining, probably, and industry. If the planet were remote enough, I wouldn't even have to hide operations much. I'd try for a buy-in from the locals, especially if they were low-tech."

Jim took a deep breath. Maybe he could blame what he was about to say on the brandy. "They may be stepping up operations. Before the ion storm, I'd set up watches on the *Irian Jaya*—" the ship's name tasted vile in his mouth, like the moment you know you're going to vomit everything you've eaten and drunk all night. "We'd taken fire once, and frankly, I expected them to try again."

A bioship like *Irian Jaya* would have been a greater treasure than all the galleons of Old Earth. He put his hands over his head, pressing hard, as if he could eradicate his memories.

"What are you suggesting, sir?" He turned to Becker.

"This isn't a handout," Becker said. "There's every chance you could be killed in a ship malfunction, caught by scavengers—I gather you've had a lucky escape or two already—or even murdered by the population of the world we want you to go to. It's far from unified. We'll start briefing you tonight. In fact, you can count on staying here while Captain Marlow's ship is refitted."

"What about me?" Jones demanded. "If you're planning to have that two-ton warrant officer of yours detain me for the 'good of the many,' I warn you, people will come looking for me."

"Another melodramatic young man," said Becker. "I'm afraid, Mr. Jones, that you're about to jeopardize your professional standing. You wanted information. You're going to get it. In return, you're going to be our eyes and ears inside the Alliance and all around the No Man's Worlds, if you can handle it. But this is one news story you'll report only to Captain Marlow."

Jim opened his mouth on a protest, saw Jones ready to blurt out something that probably would be even stupider, and forced himself to silence.

"Cam, your report did say you felt yourself fit for action, didn't it?" Becker asked.

Marlow nodded, then muttered something under her breath.

"Don't look so worried, Captain!" Neave laughed. "Honestly, you look like a mother who's sent her last-born off to school for the first time. Both of them."

Jim shrugged. The byplay between his captain and Amory Eliot Neave was suddenly of no importance to him. The snake hadn't just lured in the bird; it had been caught in glittering, tempting coils.

If he failed, well, he owed the universe a death.

"Don't you want to know what's in it for you?" asked Neave. Still testing, goading.

"What's it matter?" asked Jim. "If I do this—mind, you, *if* I do it—it'll be because it's worth doing, not because I expect a damn thing out of it."

Neave had found the reward that would buy him: he wanted to be able to face his life again with clean hands.

I sat and watched Amory Neave's study erupt into frenzy. Briefing, it seemed, would begin immediately. Before Becker took Jim off with him to give him the first of many tapes and models—and probably to keep him from indulging his usual disastrous tendency to jump ship—he had called in Warrant Officer Murad, ordering him to return to Gan Salem and collect Jim's gear. When he saw how Murad eyed Jones, Becker took Jones with him too.

Brandy and tension left their smells in the air. Neave rose, opening doors and windows rather than adjusting climate control, before he settled opposite me in a deep-cushioned chair.

"And so Ryutaro Jones gets all the information his greedy little heart could desire," I said, trying to lighten the mood of the room.

"Virtue is its own reward," Neave said. "Persistence is certainly a virtue."

"I should apologize," I said. I wrapped my arms around me. The light was paling toward dawn, and I was starting to feel the chill. I glanced over at Neave. Despite the crowd, despite the brandy, despite the charges Jones had made, he was holding up well. "I should have asked the Warrant Officer to run me back to the city."

"You are welcome as a guest here."

"I can hardly supervise *Gavroche*'s refit from your country home, Commissioner," I protested.

"You're entitled to some leave, aren't you, Captain? Take a couple of days here, why don't you?"

I opened my mouth on the ritual "don't want to be an imposition" and shut it again as Neave went smoothly on with, "You could be of great help preventing your friend from indulging in his usual vice of running off. Or teaching Mr. Jones manners with his fists."

"I'm likelier to help Jim with that," I muttered. "I never thought Ryu was such a loose cannon."

"Tactless," said Neave. "Not inaccurate." He gathered up brandy glasses, putting away books he—and Jones—had taken down, tidying the study in a kind of way that allowed him, so very casually, to keep his back toward me.

He went over to a narrow metal table behind one of the couches. Resting on it was a chest so old its wood was almost black. Hinges and strips of a metal that bore a patina much like aged copper covered much of the chest's surface, the metal twisting into sharp flanges and crooked angles. Neave ran his hands over the metal, then opened the massive lock with a metal key, rather than the touch of a palm or the flash of a retinal scan. Odd. If the chest contained things too valuable to be kept unlocked, why not retrofit it with serious security? Probably because the chest itself was a valuable antique.

Civilian thinking. "Valuable antiques" were for transit, for other people, not for living with.

He set a ring, a sidearm that I recognized as being forty years out of date, and a notebook, bound in burgundy leather, on the table. "I'll need these for my part of Jim's briefing," Neave said, his voice remote.

Raising an eyebrow to ask permission, I opened the notebook. Handwritten notes, not a transcription, on durable, acid-free pages that would probably outlast the binding and the chest that safeguarded them.

"The handwriting is a little cramped. I didn't know how long I'd have to make the notebook last."

Suddenly, the curves and spikes of Neave's writing came into focus, and I deciphered four words. "My wife the princess died. . . ."

Quickly, apologetically, I set the book down, beginning to stammer out words like "unconscionable interference . . . so sorry." Neave smiled with the same kindness he had shown me since I had entered his home that evening. "It's been a long time since I was the dreamer who wrote those words. Felt that way. But I'm not ashamed."

"Commissioner—" I began.

"Amory, if you please," he said. "While I would be pleased if you knew of me what that book contains, for now, however, it's part of what our young friend needs to prepare himself. And you . . . you look like you could use a night's sleep or"—he glanced out the window—"what's left of it."

Common sense and social embarrassment warred with annoyance that this man, who was probably around Becker's age, even if he didn't look it, could think I was fading fast.

"I suppose if I don't rest, you'll report me to my CMO?"

"I would hardly consider blackmail appropriate behavior for a host, would you?"

Outflanked, outmaneuvered, and read far too accurately for my preferences, I turned a yawn into a smile.

"We've all had far too much brandy," said Amory Neave. "Abram will be a bear in the morning, and we can all take turns glaring at each other. You may try to plead your resurrection as an excuse for a hangover, but personally, I consider that dubious theology."

"Do you always talk in circles?" To my surprise, I found myself laughing at him, scarcely sleepy at all.

"Only after too much brandy," he admitted. "I really should join Abram and help him brief Jim. But first, your host will show you to your rooms." With one hand, he sketched a gesture so elaborate—but stopping short of offering me his arm—that I laughed again.

He led me down the corridor across the courtyard I had seen earlier that evening, and into a hallway that looked enough to be guest quarters. The walls were plastered like the entryway and, like it, painted in primitive murals that, when combined with the glowing panels of the ceiling, seemed utterly sophisticated. He touched a panel on a door made of the same dark wood as the furniture in his study and showed me into a sparsely furnished large room, divided by an intricately carved set of shelves and worktable into a sleeping area and study.

A vase—hand-thrown pottery rich with subtle patterns of iridescent metallic swirls—stood on the worktable, holding a spray of the dark native foliage that shifted and rustled outside the clearsteel panel that formed one wall. He walked over to it, touched a fastening, and heavy woven cloth of a deep, satisfying copper fell down to the wide planks of the floor, making the room feel as if it were still night outside.

"It is quiet here," said Neave. "Private. And you would honor Marshal Becker—and myself, of course—by considering this your home any time you are on Aviva."

He bowed as he had done when we were introduced, and left me, standing in the door before I could thank him. I walked into the sleeping area and palmed on the light built over the bed, noticing that my hand had begun to shake, the way it did when I pushed myself too far for too long. I had meds to control the tremor, but when they wore off . . .

This wasn't a time or place I needed to use them, I reprimanded myself. I was among friends, or at least colleagues.

Someone on Amory Neave's staff had left me a robe and quite acceptable substitutes for my usual personal kit, I discovered. The soaps and cleansers had a light, natural scent, a scent of spring, of flowers, not the more pungent chemical fragrances you bought on stations at appalling prices. I poured water and gulped it down, then wet a cloth and held it against my eyes, as if I had come to the end of a long bout of weeping.

The room was quiet, the bed, if plain, more comfortable than many I had slept in for years.

I should get up and check the lock, I scolded myself. I managed to turn over so my nose was buried in a pillow that smelled of herbs and sunlight, and shut my aching eyes.

I WAS NOT GOING TO ENJOY THIS, I REALIZED AS I POURED myself out of bed. I pulled back the treacherous, merciful curtains that shielded me from Aviva's sun—now so high in that pale-blue sky that it said seriously bad things about my time sense and my discipline—and managed not to flinch at the light.

Thank God for small mercies: neither head nor stomach ached as much as they deserved, and my suite had its own water supply.

I dressed and retraced my path of last night, hunting breakfast.

The window panels along the corridor leading to the dining room had been opened, and a wind blew across the hall, stirring my hair.

In the dining room, all the curtains had been tied back, and

I saw doors opening onto a garden that stretched down a long slope into a thicket of dark brush. Sun sparkled on the table, on the sideboards, and reflected off flatware and pitchers and off faceted glasses. I flinched from the intensity of the light—and, I admit it, the sight of Jones heaping his plate from the (equally too shiny) dishes on the sideboard, then eating with a young man's genial ferocity.

Becker simply leaned his head onto one hand. Neave, seeing me, began to rise. I waved him back to his seat, served myself lightly, set my plate down, and began to think better of it. I could smell fried food, heavy oils, and something peppery, rising from Jim's plate, making me think of the useful things an unprincipled officer could do to take revenge on savages who gorged themselves when she could barely look at food.

Jones' eyes met mine over a cup of coffee that smelled like something I would sell my soul for, assuming last night's brandy hadn't killed it. They glinted maliciously—revenge for my cheerfulness in the face of his dire hangover some months back on Raffles Station. Then, because Jones was a humanitarian and a merciful man—and because I'd otherwise have had to kill him—he didn't just push the coffee pot over to me; he poured me a cup. Bless the lad.

Coffee. Water that sparkled in a faceted glass, hurting my eyes. Juice pulpy enough to be fresh, not reconstituted.

I thought I might live.

Jim bounded into the room, his face flushed, his eyes glowing like a resurrection that had nothing to do with thawing a shipsicle from years of Freeze. His mouth stretched into a grin that made every muscle on my scalp ache.

"Captain!"

Softly, Jim. Softly. Your voice is making the dishes shake. And you're about to shatter my sinuses.

Jim pulled a chair with a squeak of wood along wood that made me shudder. The scent and enthusiasm of tired, brandy-sodden, exuberant male threatened to destroy my equilibrium: my digestion was already shot. "Look what Commissioner

Neave gave me! His own diary from the time he was on Exquemelin. I'll have to return the notebook after I've read it. Read it? I'm going to memorize it!

"My God, Captain, do you know where that man has been, and what he's done? Granted, Marshal Becker is a remarkable man, but I've known of him for years. Commissioner Neave, though. I finally understand what my father"—in all the years I had known Jim he had never once spoken of the man—"meant by 'a real gentleman and a scholar.' I've never met anyone like him."

"You will make me conceited, sir," said Neave. He glanced at me and lowered his voice. "Allow me, Captain." He passed me a dish that held tiny white pills: alcodote tablets, which metabolized ethanol byproducts. I washed two down with water from a stemmed glass whose sparkling facets no longer hurt my eyes.

"I won't let you down, Commissioner," Jim said. "But I have a few questions. I'm sorry, so sorry, about your wife. Can you explain again what her relationship is to Magnate Oulian?"

"Aliset was his half sister," Neave said. "My friend Oulian—we were very young when we met. I was doing fieldwork on Exquemelin, and he took an interest in me, then a liking. Hadn't expected to like an offworlder, especially one who believed that technology wants to be free, not confined to a single caste. We'd argue about it, drinking late into the night. Your tolerance for brandy's a decided asset on this mission, Jim. God knows, you'll need it. Just give Oulian the ring. Show him the sidearm. A safe-conduct or visa would have served even better, but been so much less romantic."

Abram Becker looked up and nodded. Apparently, he'd already had his alcodote and was methodically overloading his system with the sort of breakfast—high-carb, high-fat, high-spice—that made lesser mortals—like me—profoundly queasy. "But didn't Oulian marry a second cousin?"

Neave downed half a glass of water, then sighed with contentment. "Oulian married my dear Aliset's sister, Vasinat. I gather they have a grown son now. More coffee, Captain?"

He gestured at Jim to pass the pot back to me. "It's empty. Shall I ring for more, sir?"

As he spoke to Neave, he looked and sounded like a boy, infatuated with the stars and the men and women who traveled among them.

A little old for hero-worship, aren't you? I thought.

Coffee seemed to arrive at a gesture from Neave, and I set about rectifying my poor circulatory system's blood-caffeine imbalance. One day, I promised myself, I was going to win that argument with my CMO that caffeine was an essential blood factor, not an addiction.

Meanwhile, Jim simultaneously tucked away a breakfast even larger and more disgusting than Becker's and explained what he, Neave, and Becker had apparently stayed up all night discussing.

"He's extraordinary, Captain!" Jim exclaimed. "What he's been through! Did you know that Commissioner Neave fought off a scavenger attack on Exquemelin with only two ships?"

"The dominant culture isn't retro-evolved, Captain," Amory Neave told me when Jim paused for breath and, incidentally, fought Jones for possession of a bowl of fragrant purple berries awash in cream. "Exquemelin was settled, not in the regular way, but by a lost ship. What starflight capacity it has is pretty much the monopoly of what I can only call its ruling caste, which is descended from the ship's command crew. My old friend Oulian is—I forget how many 'grands' ago he told me the ship's captain was to him."

"The commissioner mobilized them." Apparently, Jim had negotiated a truce over the berries. "They adopted him, and he showed them how to—"

"Much too flattering a portrayal," Neave put in. "I was young, on leave from my teaching post. Did I say I was doing field work? An exaggeration: I'd about decided I wasn't going back. Apocalyptic thoughts, you know, Captain: the war's coming; I shall find myself a retreat well away from the battle, and think deep thoughts; perhaps become a gentleman farmer like your Uncle Hashimoto-sama," he shot at Jones, who looked up with a sharp grin.

"Hashimoto-sama waited until after the war," Jones objected.

"Precisely," Neave replied. "I learned you don't run away from battle without encountering another, and harder, one. By the time I'd learned my lesson, I had lost . . ."

He turned away to get more eggs. By the time he turned back, his face was under control. "We sustained heavy losses defending ourselves. It wasn't just scavengers, of course. They had allies on the ground, Oulian's old enemy, Melinkor. I wasn't fool enough to think we could counterattack on two fronts, so we went to ground. There was illness. My wife Aliset, our child . . ."

"I am so sorry," I said, hating myself for the blandness of the words.

"More of us would have died if Abram hadn't insisted on looping back—"

"Amory, how many times have you lost this argument?" Becker interrupted, deliberately cheerful. "It was a routine patrol. Exquemelin had already been mapped, so I simply looped back—"

"I'm no pilot, but even I know transiting the Straits is never routine."

"Not at all. I wanted to keep my eyes on Exquemelin for Operation Seedcorn. I set up a sort of quasi-consulate there, but I have not been satisfied with—"

Neave bent forward and interrupted his friend. "The woman's dead, Abram. It's time you replaced Vortimer with a better man."

Becker sighed. "He deserved his chance. Now, it is the turn of our friend here."

I could feel the alcodote scouring the poisons from last night's brandy out of my frontal lobes. The food began to smell more like food than sewage.

Jim pushed his plate—his second plate—away. "Once I regain my license . . ."

"It will be limited," Becker said.

"I won't let you down," Jim promised quickly. "I'm sure I'll be able—"

"There'll be a ship," Becker said. "I'm not promising that it'll be fresh out of the dockyards, but it'll be Jump capable. Who knows? It may even hold atmosphere long enough for you to get downworld."

"This is the biggest thing that's ever happened to me," Jim declared, his face flushed, his eyes shining. "Look!" He held up a ring, made of metal that shimmered like a rainbow. "Oulian gave it to Commissioner Neave as a sign they were brothers. It's from metal off the hull of Exquemelin's First Ship. Like something in a story, isn't it, Captain?"

He tossed it glittering into the air, so bright it hurt his eyes as well as mine. He almost dropped it as it fell. "Damn. I can't risk losing this. It's how I'm to identify myself to Magnate Oulian!" he exclaimed.

He reached into his shirt and pulled out a chain like the ones many of us in Fleet use to hang identification on. Again, he flushed like a boy. "I took the tags off," he told me. "But I never had the heart to get rid of the chain. If I'd pawned it, it wouldn't have brought me that much." Carefully, he unfastened the chain and hung Oulian's ring from it, then tucked it carefully away.

"The Commissioner said last night scavengers have been spotted near the Jump points leading to the Straits. Vortimer"—Jim's lip twisted in a sneer—"hasn't been much use keeping them away or putting the fear of God into Melinkor. So, if scavengers landed on Exquemelin again, without Neave, they could take it, make it into the kind of planetary base they've been wanting."

"That's where you come in?" I asked because, clearly, Jim desperately wanted me to.

"Yes!" he said. He seemed delighted by it, the adventure

and the danger, even the failure of Vortimer, whom he was to replace.

Assuming scavengers could agree long enough to conquer a planet, I thought. I widened my eyes and flared my nostrils—a courteous way of not-yawning and not showing it. Jim had risen. Now he was striding up and down the dining room, gesturing, as he explained how one of Becker's Operation Salvage vessels had picked up an encrypted transmission and opened such contact as was possible.

I picked at some fruit in a light syrup and fought a furious irritation that had nothing to do with the alcodote. Jim was too old for knight-errantry, too old by far. But maybe this would be the making of him. Finally. I'd watched him stripped of rank and decency at his trial, and, God only knows why, pulled him out of riots and plague spots and scavenger dens that would have turned him into a lobotomized slave or spare body parts. And now, in one night, he was transformed, carried back by the second chance Neave and Becker had given him, to the golden ensign I had smiled over long ago.

"I can't begin to tell you, sir, how—" Jim's voice went husky.

"Then don't," Neave said gently. "Please sit down and finish eating." His eyes met mine, and he shook his head, a little ruefully.

I ought to be relieved he and Becker were taking Jim off my hands. Damn, was I the only one at breakfast who was immune to alcodote?

I was damn tired of pulling him or, for that matter, the rest of suffering humanity out of trouble, and fed up with the Relief Service and its shabby excuse for an operating budget. And above all, I'd had a bellyful of tiptoeing around medics, who could certify me unfit to fly and would do so in a minute if they suspected I was showing even the smallest sign of Freeze trauma.

I'd outlived my friends, my family, all except . . . *Conrad*—the memory suddenly ached like a thawing hand . . . except for Jim, the coward, the jumper, the intolerable pompous bore who was striding up and down this sunny dining room babbling about his new mission with the zeal of a first-year cadet.

Maybe I should have died with *Hardcastle*. Maybe I should hole up for good in some retirement village and bore the hell out of all the civs who'd sat out the war, bought their sons and daughters out of service, and never once ventured offworld. Or maybe I was ready for a visit to Earth, though the idea felt alien. Jones owed me; he could help with introductions. A speaking tour—oh God, so *I* could be the pompous, lecturing bore.

Neave leaned over and poured me a glass of water.

"Sooner or later, it'll all catch up with him and he'll drop where he stands," he whispered. Then, more loudly, "Captain, there are messages from Gan Salem's refit facilities. They need your signoff before proceeding. I told them you were on leave, and I didn't want to interrupt your rest, but now that you're awake . . ."

Like Jim, I was in love with my rescuer. I left the table—and an exultant Jim—and went to rescue my ship from the torments of bureaucracy.

Behind me, I could hear Becker chuckle. "When you finish," he called, "come back, Cam, and I'll explain the role *Gavroche* will play in all of this."

I bit off a curse that would have melted the chain of command, then turned on the threshold to explain to my lawful superior that it would be a cold day in the coronosphere of a white dwarf before he could inveigle me and mine into serving as Jim's personal ferryboat. But Becker had already turned his attention back to Jim.

Jones, of course, was eavesdropping for all he was worth—and finishing off the last of the berries.

Neave had risen to his feet when I left the table and hadn't yet reseated himself. When I turned back, though, he caught my eye, smiled, cocked his head, and mimed a quick salute.

An unfamiliar rush of warmth intimated that it was in my interests to listen to any suggestions Becker might have, especially if they brought me within range of a stopover on

Aviva. I was no longer in any hurry to retire to Earth. Why should I creep back to a home world I'd never seen when there was so much to do out here—and all the people I cared about?

RV *Gavroche*, the Straits of Aquila

25

At a Jump point by a fifth-magnitude star, RV *Gavroche* emerged into real space. A ship was waiting, despite micrometeorite and radiation levels that made Marlow frown at her workstation. *Gavroche* might loom over the smaller ship, but it answered her hail with the ease of old acquaintance with Relief Vessels and the assurance of a ship that knew this space all too well.

"Specialists," said Marlow. "You can transfer now." She nodded at her first officer to take her station, then walked out of the Command Center with Jim. The bargain had been made before they Jumped. His passage was part of it.

"You shall hear of me," he promised Marlow.

He'd had to fight back tears of hope he hadn't felt since long before he was commissioned. He felt young, new, undamned.

"Do you suppose you'll ever come back?" she asked.

By the way Marlow's face stiffened into an officer-mask, he knew his face had frozen.

Damn you, man, she's been mother, sister, rescuer, and you freeze her out.

Marlow forgave him this rejection, too. She rose, embraced him, then pushed free, punching his shoulder in mock anger.

She was bound back to Aviva, he knew. He bit his lip before he told her to save her hugs for Neave. He'd seen how the man looked at her. If nursemaiding Jim had helped distract her from making a life of her own, he should have disappeared into the No Man's Worlds years ago.

Here, at the end of their voyage together, he should not have chilled her, thrust her out of his emotional range. He wanted to run after her, tell her how much he owed her, thank her for his life ten times over, to be sure; but most of all for this second chance to prove himself.

Adrenaline spiked in his blood, more potent than any shore-leave drunkenness, and he whirled and waved, startling the flight crew.

"I'll make you proud!" he shouted, his voice arching up like a boy's before it breaks, echoing off the bulkheads.

Jim's transfer vessel *Blue Ridge* was a battered old trader, but Marlow had guaranteed it, so it must be safe. Or as safe as things got out in the No Man's Worlds.

None of Jim's new ship's crew spoke to him. There weren't many of them, and they all had duties more pressing than coddling a passenger wished on them by the bigger, richer (the term was relative) ship that loomed over them, offloading the precious medical supplies that bought Jim a passage, if not a welcome.

On board his shabby trader, Jump warnings and safety drills were taped, looped, and distorted on deteriorating speakers that echoed off dull gray bulkheads. Crew scuttled by as he emerged for drill, intent on their duty stations.

They resembled each other: thin gray womanless men, stunted by their years in space on board a ship whose protection against radiation, especially where they fared, appeared defective. Their pallid faces and hands were blotched by keloids or the deadly bloom of a tumor not yet excised. They barely spoke among themselves, as if years of enforced companionship had taught them to understand each other and their tasks without words.

As a boy, Jim had spent one summer studying an anthill, watching workers emerge, working with an obsessive determination, building day by day, oblivious to the inevitable boot or backhoe. The last week he was home, another boy ploughed into the anthill and asked Jim why he couldn't take a joke. Jim had ploughed into him and entered the Academy with a bruised lip.

Blue Ridge was another anthill, good enough for use, not good enough to be brought back and sheltered in the mainstream. Like Jim himself.

When a squawk of the defective communications tape signified an end to the drill, Jim followed the lightstrips to his cabin and did not venture out again.

His quarters were even more cramped than *Gavroche*'s improvised brig, their bulkheads clean but unadorned, even by scratchmarked initials of prior occupants. It was fitted with a sleeping pad that reeked of antiseptic and it boasted a minimal—rudimentary, in fact—head so he need never emerge. As if he were being interrogated, or observed, the lights shone constantly. And the damned things hummed.

As Jump followed Jump and the bleak walls pressed in, Jim thought he'd be glad to trade his isolation for oblivion in an emergency pod.

To think that way was to flirt with death. Maybe Marlow had been retrieved, but it had taken twenty years, and her ship had blown along what, before the war, had been a regular trade route. The Straits of Aquila were isolated even by the standards of deep space travelers: a magnificent desolation of vast gas promontories tens of thousands of light-years long. Here in the Straits, stars were giving birth in conflagrations that made each passage in and out of Jump the risk it had been in the earliest days of Jump travel when the engines faltered and Jump points were less securely mapped. Even in Jump, Jim could feel the titanic energies of workaday genesis tugging at the ship, attempting to seize its tiny energy too.

One grace *Blue Ridge* granted him, which would have been an incalculable luxury anywhere else: his cabin boasted its own viewscreen. In Jump, its backlit glow was as comforting as a fire in a waste prowled by wild beasts. He especially liked watching one immense gaseous cloud. Each time the ship emerged from Jump, it looked different: a horse's head;

a camel's back; a serpent; and finally the eagle that gave this sector its name, crowned with yellow, white, blue, and red stars, some flickering, some spinning on unimaginable axes. Aquila shimmered with green-tinged "feathers" of gaseous haze that coalesced into "wings" that mantled out over ten thousand light-years.

The ship Jumped and Jumped again, groaning uneasy transits. During ship's nights, Jim would emerge from shallow sleep, filled with unremembered dreams, and lie awake, fearing to feel the attraction of incalculable energies upon this mote of a trader, snatching it from the safety of Jump into Aquila's pinions or its insatiable beak.

Once, he woke in a cold sweat, crying out in despicable panic. He made a panicked grab for the Fleet-issue blaster Marlow had pressed into his hands before he'd requested permission-to-leave-the-ship-sir.

Damn. He'd forgotten to take its charges.

Unless he could wangle a weapon from the silent, anxious crew, he would land unarmed on Exquemelin.

Probably, it was for the best.

When the runner dropped out of Jump again, even before Jim's bones and sinews shifted back into place after the transit, the comm in his cabin crackled to uneasy life: *"Passenger to the docking port."*

An actual voice this time. Probably, they got so few passengers there was no point in making a tape. But even now, they didn't even use his name.

"LADY TOLD US, 'LEAVE'M HERE, LET'M FLY H'MSELF IN.' S'that truth?" A metallic whisper from a man whose slate coverall bore marks that designated him petty officer. Probably, he had an implanted larynx. A cheap one.

Jim started, unused after the long silence to voices other than his own. Half-abashed, he calmed himself.

He shrugged. "If she says."

Now, he had a chance to look over the one-man ship. Neave and Becker had spent enough time and effort on him that Jim thought they at least would give him a fighting chance to make planetfall in one piece.

Rickety, the word came to him. Its hull was shiny with age. Not pitted, which would have been fatal, but worn.

Jim shifted his bag of personal effects—including Oulian's sidearm, the useless blaster, and a book or two—onto his left shoulder to receive the command rod that would unlock ship's systems to him. The ring Neave had given him hung around his neck, not just ID but his talisman.

"Orders," he said.

"Scout'll hop, not Jump. She'll get y'there, if y'don't . . ."

Jim nodded. *God, don't let me fuck up.*

After that shared moment of silent prayer, he turned away. Already, he had more interest in this new ship than in a man who knew and cared as little about him as he did about any crewman on this ship.

"Captain says: tell'm, course laid in. Don't meddle with comp, sir, that's best. Keep to the comm schedule laid in . . . We'll circle . . . make pick ups, drop offs, not regular like but unless we blow up, we'll be there. Y'got that?"

Amazing: he'd gotten a "sir" out of this . . . this ant of a petty officer.

"Please thank him," Jim said, meaning it, and turned to go.

"G'd luck, sir." The crew knew the passage through the Straits. If they wished him luck, he'd need it.

EAGLET, JIM NAMED THE MINIATURE VESSEL THAT, AS THE petty officer had told him, didn't so much Jump as hop, tiny steps in Aquila's nest, each step some light-years closer to Exquemelin.

It was a sickly *Eaglet.* It lurched at the touch of micrometeorites, careening from ion gust to ion gust. It seemed to waver, which gave Jim grave doubts about the diamond coating of its navigation chips, but he dared not open the installation to check. He tried not even to think about the engines, beyond standard diagnostics.

Eaglet had its own communications buoy, just like a real

ship, Jim thought. *Sorry,* he told it a minute later, silent apology. Then he laughed. Getting spooked, was he? Talking to a ship. Well, it was all he could talk to.

Eaglet's comms were functional, although the Straits of Aquila's colossal radiation would overpower its puny signal.

If all else failed, the ship would be Jim's hibernaculum. Or his coffin.

No use calculating the odds of pickup. Some million years from now, some newborn star might incorporate a frozen speck that had once been a man and a ship that failed.

Just when Jim finally drew close enough to Exquemelin to believe he would actually get there, *Eaglet*'s wings faltered.

The ship had groaned and rattled as it exited Jump for what navcomp told Jim was the last time. Its primary boards had held stable. But on the secondaries, red lights had flared. Prayer, diagnostics, and percussive maintenance had doused those lights.

Second star to the right, Jim muttered to himself, and straight on to Exquemelin.

A failsafe whooped: the ramscoops were overloading. The interstellar medium was so thick that any intake at all gave them more matter than they could use. Much more, and they'd explode.

He powered down, letting inertia drive *Eaglet* on. He promised himself he would muster the courage to try a microsecond's burn in what he'd called his next watch.

Watch on watch, he nursed the ship along, peering at his flight path on computer as if he prayed for salvation. Life support held; there were plenty of rations; and, of course, there was always Freeze, suicide with a hope of resurrection.

But Neave would think I ran away. And Marlow.

Freeze was not an option.

Computer pinged, putting forward viewscreens on auto.

A world, mostly gold and deep green and blue, glowed before him, haloed by its atmosphere, frosted with cloud cover. Exquemelin. He laid his palm over its image, haloed now by more than clouds. *"Dear Earth, I do salute thee with my hand."* The line from one of his father's oldest books made his eyes blur.

For a moment, the world shimmered, full of terrifying hopes.

The warmth of Oulian's ring around his neck was comfort: Neave had passed the token on to him. Neave was worthy and had passed it on, so therefore, he, too . . .

Autosystems hurled him into a bulkhead. The viewscreens went to black, but not before a burst of light struck his eyes, and he cried out. The ship shuddered and yawed, buffeted by the explosion of—

Missile, computer told him. Small, archaic, but quite deadly enough to have ended his hopes right then.

If *Eaglet*'s autosystems had been less nimble, he'd have been dead. Now, heaviness in the ship's "feel" told him he was in trouble before his eyes stopped streaming and he saw deadly red lights bloom even on the primary boards. The secondaries were already crashed.

Get *Eaglet* down, he told himself.

He struggled back to controls, locked himself in with the safeties (one of which looked ready to snap), and began descent. The engines whined, then whined louder as he veered hard over. A lethal flower blossomed—too close.

Eaglet went skidding into the exosphere, and he fought to control entry. Too fast, too acute, and *Eaglet* would overheat and burn. He'd land, all right, but in cinders, the steadfast tin soldier, true unto death.

This time.

At least, let me see my enemy! Half a prayer, half a curse. He brought the ship around, correcting attitude, whispering imprecations at hull temperature.

Incoming, computer told him. There it was.

Eaglet was only light-armed. His weapons training was worse than nothing against a stronger ship. It gave him just enough hope to stand and fight, which could be fatal.

Still, he accessed armscomp, called up firepower . . .

Damned if I'll run again.

And went tumbling again, to correct course the way an overmatched fighter staggers up from the mat and faces his opponent, nose streaming, head down. The engines missed, whined again, raggedly, missing beats. He wouldn't be able to evade the next attack, much less counter it.

Down. Get down.

Armscomp showed him his enemy was powering up for the kill.

A ship half again *Eaglet*'s size darted by, firing with a skill that might not owe thing one to Fleet training, but was damned effective. Natural genius out there had just saved his ass.

Eaglet was falling through the cloud cover now, coming down, coming down fast, too damn fast, into a drunken patchwork of water, hills, and fields, spinning, spinning . . . his restraints snapped, tossing him to his knees, but he kept his hands on the controls, forced *Eaglet*'s beak up until the angle of descent became something more akin to landing than a crash.

Eaglet wasn't going to make it out of this in any shape that would ever fly again, he told himself, unless this planet boasted a damned good dockyard. Still, a good landing was anything you could walk away from.

Ship's computer lit a flickering screen, showing him landing vectors, even offering him—valiant in death, his *Eaglet*—a choice of landing sites. One was not five kilometers from where Neave said he should be.

It was a bloody miracle.

In that instant, the miracle died, along with ship's engines. Computer survived, showing him his optimal flight plan, suggesting he match course if he could coast.

He flew blind. He flew by wire.

He flew his *Eaglet* into the ground.

Exquemelin, in the Straits of Aquila

26

Jim struggled up from black clouds shot with red and yellow fire. The tiny cockpit was thick with smoke. Life support crackled and wheezed, attempting to clear the air with the last gasps of its own strength.

Fire on board? Terror cleared the last mists from his head. He coughed and gagged and grabbed for the extinguisher beneath his chair. He wasn't in his chair. He remembered now, the restraints had snapped, and here he was lying on the deck, flung against a console. Lucky his neck hadn't snapped too.

Jim levered himself up and staggered across—you couldn't call two steps a corridor, could you?—to the padded shelf he'd bunked on. His kit lay below. He grabbed his kit, then lurched along the remnants of the emergency lights to the escape hatch.

He popped its explosive bolts with a blow of his fist. The hatch flew forward, and Jim all but tumbled out of the wrecked craft in a billow of acrid smoke. He managed eight or ten blind steps before he stumbled to his knees, heaving with coughs, until he lay face down, tears streaming down his face, arms wrapped about his ribs. When he could bear the light, he found himself near the edge of a field. Small fires smoldered around *Eaglet,* set by its impact, sending up dark plumes of smoke into a brazen sky. What looked like molten metal glinted nearby: a lake bordering Jim's improvised landing area, reflecting the sunlight.

He ducked his head, hiding from the too-bright sky and water and fire. Now, he crawled through wet ground cover. There was no way he could put enough distance between himself and *Eaglet,* if it blew. But he had to try to get under cover. He could feel shadow now on his aching neck and back.

Now, he dared look up. He had made it into the leading edge of what looked like a considerable forest, slender boles of white that supported lattices of branches crowned with leaves like golden coins. Deeper in were sturdier trees: substantial trunks of bronze and gray soaring up into a canopy of fronds so wide that they created a kind of twilight. He gazed into it, seeing a network of high-arched roots, half-covered by fallen leaves, that offered him some hope of concealment.

Behind him came the unmistakable sounds of a ship, hovering, observing. He crawled faster, attaining the shelter of those roots just as his enemy touched down.

If they came hunting him, damned if he wanted to be found ass end up, saluting the sky. He turned around, facing outward, pulling dry fronds over him for cover. Suicidal move, if that fire spread. But the ground cover here was springy with moisture; the soil into which the roots fed was damp, darkening his smoke-stained shipsuit.

He heard a landing ramp drop, boots ringing as two, no, three people left their ship, and listened for clues, voices.

"You'll be able to make yourself understood," Becker had assured him.

"The language has mutated since First Landing," Neave had explained. *"I have some tapes, the beginnings of a dictionary—"*

"Amory—" Becker had cut off what bid fair to become yet another of Neave's scholarly lectures, this one on linguistics. Marlow had laughed, and Neave's face had gentled.

These men were laughing too, but there was no kindness in their amusement.

"Damn that Stal Viat . . . a week's work patching . . ." The deep voice with an angry edge belonged to a largish man, whose body showed early signs of sagging. But there was still plenty of muscle underneath that gut.

If you'd charged that blaster, you'd probably be fool

enough to use it, he told himself. *Shoot these three, and who knows how many more like them they've got at home?*

"Don't know where the little bastard gets his skill. Isn't as if he's ever been off this dirtball, no damn proper training . . ." Jim matched the voice to a smaller, almost ratlike man whose skin was peeling as if he was having a hard time adapting to the sun. *Spacer,* he thought.

"One of these days, that grudge match you've got going with Oulian's son's going to wreck your judgment. If it hasn't already. Thing is, we brought down this ship; we've got it; and he hasn't. Now, get those extinguishers and put out those fires. Not likely, but they just might hit something and blow us all into the Straits." Another spacer, this one in a neat shipsuit that bore no insignia. He was slight but taut, a thin brown man much like Neave, until you saw the livid scar across his face that rippled as he spoke.

"Not in this humidity, Chief—" The angry man, this time.

"No? You want to test that and report back to Melinkor, let alone the Commodore?" said the one identified as Chief. "This isn't a committee. Do it. While you're at it, check for lifesigns. If the pilot's from outside, chances are he's got sense to crawl away. We'll send the locals to hunt him. In case he's armed, no use risking one of us. But we might be lucky and find him cold."

Jim let the fronds fall. Not Fleet, surprise, surprise. Fleet would have scanned for survivors, put out fires, and not planned to use civilians to do what ought to be their job.

He was getting the beginnings of one godawful headache. Concussion, maybe. He felt himself yawn, then freeze. It wouldn't do to hole up and sleep. He should get up, keep moving.

After they go, he promised himself.

You wanted to be a hero. You failed. Now, you've got a chance again, like something in a story. Stay awake until they go, then move.

He listened for the asthmatic wheeze of fire extinguishers, the tramp of boots through the ground cover, the grunts and mutters of men about "No one's inside, Chief!"

"There's blood on the deck; that ship's pilot must have hit hard . . . can't find ship's registry or log . . ."

"Leave it," ordered Chief.

"What about using it as a decoy?" asked Angry Man.

"Set up a charge primed to blow if someone—say, Stal Viat—attempts to go over it?" Chief jeered. "If he and his father were fools enough to fall for that, we'd already control this whole damn backwater. Now, move it. We've got a report to make Upstairs."

Jim heard the whine of hydraulics as the ramp lifted, followed by takeoff.

Relief.

Oh God, his head hurt.

He retched, forced himself to stand, and staggered on. Head for the water. There would be people by the water, he was sure of it. And besides, he was so thirsty. He'd had immunizations back on *Gavroche*, his arms had ached for a week. If he hadn't had a histamine reaction by now, he probably wasn't going to.

The fronds ruffled and shifted overhead, murmuring to him. *Sleep, sleep.*

Not yet, he told himself. With the fires out, he could smell the water. Not much further. A drink, he promised himself. A wait, then a longer drink. And then he could wash off the smoke, the blood, tend the cuts on face and hands that would leave one hell of a trail for anyone with a nose, or scanner, to track him. Then, he'd see about shelter.

He fumbled open the collar of his shipsuit. Ring was still there, though his neck was chafed where the chain had cut in when he'd gone flying on impact—he meant "landing." His spine ached as if someone had tried to play a loud tune with mallets on each vertebra.

He made it to the water, knelt, drank, and tried to get up. Instead, he felt himself sprawling face down.

He hadn't come all this way to drown, he told himself.

Then, he blacked out again.

* * *

How long have I been out? was Jim's first thought as he wavered back to consciousness. His face was wet. He lay on a cool flat surface, quivering with constant motion, and punctuated at intervals by what felt like hoops that pressed into his back. On both sides of him came the brush/splash of paddles, the ripple of water.

But it was dark, too dark. He couldn't have been out that long.

There was a wet cloth on his head and a blanket or coat flung over him. He needed a bath, needed one badly, under the light weight of the blanket, but at least the copper reek of his own blood was gone. Someone had patched up his cuts.

His headache was gone, and he felt no nausea from the movement of the small boat through the water. So he hadn't had a concussion after all, for which small mercy, thank you someone.

He wanted to push the compress back from his forehead, to see who'd taken him up and ask where he was being taken. Better not, he warned himself. His rescuers might not be rescuers after all, but the men who'd followed him down. Or perhaps they belonged, if not to those men's commodore or whatever, to the one they had called Melinkor, who had to be some sort of ally.

Given that they'd done their damnedest to shoot him out of the sky, he wanted no part of them. They had an enemy, apparently, someone named Stal Viat. Blearily, Jim remembered another ship, drawing the first ship's fire from *Eaglet*. The enemy of my enemy is my friend, and he'd heard the wreckers call Stal Viat son of the Oulian he'd come all this way to meet.

"He sleeps too long," came a voice, huskier than the wreckers', from over his head. Concern in that voice, but reluctant.

"Perhaps he will find healing in his dreams," a second voice answered. "He will need it when we bring him to Melinkor. And the sooner—"

"Yes." They paddled more rapidly, hurrying to deliver him

to Melinkor, or whomever, who was not a patient man. The name teased at Jim's memory. Neave had mentioned a Melinkor, hadn't he?

Probably, every stroke of those paddles took him closer to trouble. Briefly, he considered rolling out of the boat and taking his chances. Lacking his kit, lacking everything but his battered shipsuit and the ring still comfortingly hung round his neck, his chances wouldn't be good. Scratch that idea. If Neave had mentioned Melinkor, Jim at least ought to see the man.

Besides, this time, Jim would be damned if he let panic force him into another jump.

Think, man, he told himself, as well as he could with a head injury. He could use that as a defense, at least long enough to get his bearing. Head-injury cases sometimes forgot things. Lots of things. Neave had told him that Oulian's people on Exquemelin prized their dreams, studied them. And this man of Melinkor's had just borne that out.

What was it one of his rescuers, kidnappers, or whatever had said? He seeks healing in dreams? Sounded like the best idea anyone had had all day.

He made his breathing regular, deeper, welcoming the darkness of sleep.

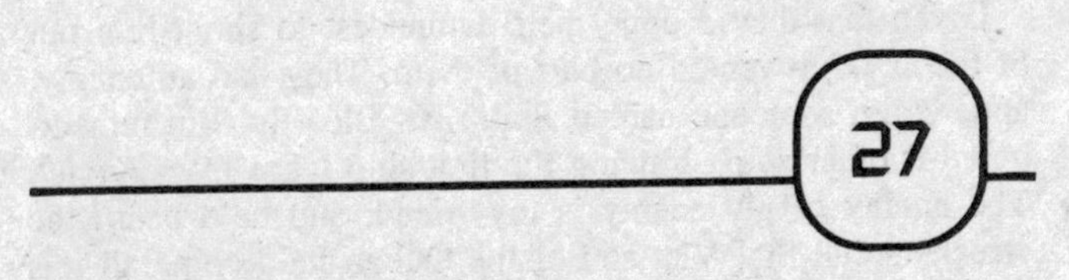

27

Jim woke with a cry. He was finally lying on a flat surface, and he was blind and nearly stifled. God damn, he wasn't dead: why'd they bury him?

He thrust himself upright on a wobbly hand. With the other, he pulled a wet cloth off his face. He saw his shelter blurred and doubled through a headache that mated lancing pain and dizzying rainbows at the edges of his field of vision.

"Rest," came a whisper. Hard, given the ringing in his ears, to separate it from the rain trickling down on what he had been able to see: a low ceiling of wood, rough-hewn and gray from exposure to the elements. The light had been unbearable. Now he saw it came only from a window slit across from him.

One thing had gone right. His captors hadn't taken him offworld yet. But this . . . this holding pen of Melinkor's could hardly be best guest accommodations. "Can't say I think much of the hospit—" he began.

But "Rest," said the voice again. A hand pressed him down onto the blessedly unmoving floor, wood, only lightly padded. He tried to look at the person tending him, but the cloth came down on his face before he could focus his eyes. He felt a cup's hard rim press against his lips. *You don't know what's in it!* warred with thirst.

Whatever was in the cup made him yawn. It made the dizziness, and then the room, and the whole world go away into cool gray oblivion.

When he woke again, the rain had ended, and the cloth on his brow had dried. He rose, a little too rapidly for caution, but the spasm of dizziness and the ache in his gut were hunger, not concussion. A wooden cup lay beside him, dry as the compress he flung aside.

"Is anyone here?" he called. If they'd bothered to bring him here, you'd think, at the least, they could have left him something to eat. Wait. A tube lay beside him, the markings on it half worn off. Compressed rations, the sort you found in evacuation pods: low-fiber, high moisture. Rumor had it that the things could about outlast the heat death of the universe; this one looked as if it had.

Well, he'd be damned if he'd recover from concussion only to fall prey to food poisoning.

"Is anyone there?" he called a little louder. "I need food, water . . ."

He needed something else. His kitbag—at least they'd left

him that!—lay opened, its contents scattered about. Frantic searches told him that Oulian's ring still hung on the chain around his check and his sidearm lay safely hidden in a concealed compartment of the bag.

But Marlow's blaster was gone. And his comm. Unless he could escape and get to Oulian and any communications system he'd managed to preserve, *Blue Ridge* would think he was dead.

"Hey!" he called.

Two people, both men, entered his—room? cell?—and almost met his eyes. Alike enough to be brothers, or at least close cousins, the newcomers were almost a head shorter than he, dark-haired, dark-eyed and with their olive skin carrying that peculiarly grayish tinge that darker-skinned people got in a climate colder than they were meant for. They wore neither uniforms nor shipsuits, but clothing designed for heavy use in drab colors broken only by the unexpected garishness of synthetic scarves at their necks, worn like badges of office.

"You should have slept while you could," said one of them. "Melinkor gave orders that he wanted to see you the instant you woke."

Mustn't keep Melinkor waiting, now, must we? Jim thought. He was clearly still a power on Exquemelin, one that Neave hadn't spoken of with that good a will. And hungry, unshaven, disheveled, and needing with increasing urgency to find a head, step outside, or whatever, wasn't precisely how Jim wanted to meet a local magnate.

"I need to wash," Jim said. "And something to eat. I can't eat *that*." He gestured at the ancient ration tube.

His guards' eyes met in shock. "Of course, we can bring you food, water," the younger of the pair blurted. "But it is poor stuff, locally grown. We thought to honor a guest. Regardless—"

His elder elbowed him in the ribs, and he scurried off. Jim rubbed his grimy hand along an unshaven chin and tried not to shift from leg to leg. The guard's face relaxed: *yes, very funny when you don't need to relieve yourself and someone else does,* Jim thought in vexation. *I hope it happens to you. In vacuum.*

The man pointed, and Jim followed.

When he returned, the ration tube had been replaced with a bowl that held what looked like one step above fish soup and a mug of some dark liquid whose herbal fragrance teased away the vestiges of his headache. One bowl. One cup.

"You won't join me?" he asked.

"Melinkor wants to see you," was all the eldest said.

Better eat fast, Jim told himself. He dropped onto the padding on the floor that could only be called a bedroll by the greatest of courteous exaggerations and began to scoop up dinner, supper, whatever with the piece of flatbread he found between cup and bowl.

"Good!" he told the guards through hot, spicy mouthfuls. And it was, the best food he'd eaten since his stay in Neave's house and, before that? He couldn't remember.

Laying aside a well-cleaned bowl, an empty mug, he reached for his kitbag. If it hadn't been stolen along with the blaster, he had a spare shipsuit.

"Come now."

Jim shook his head, then tugged his battered clothing into what order he might. "Very well, then. Bring me to this Melinkor of yours," he said, attempting formality.

His guards hustled him across an open square that held what must have started life as a pool, but was now a puddle, dirty and matted with brown vegetation. The square was too crowded with people, hungry ones who looked up with too-quickly-doused hope as he passed, to be a courtyard like the one leading to Neave's living quarters. Or anything but a downcheck on Melinkor's leadership abilities.

Clearly, the man meant it as a waiting area for the less-than-favored. Jim's guards gestured him forward through a door wider than any he had ever seen.

The room he entered was large, high-ceilinged, built of the same wood he had seen earlier. But where the boards of his quarters had been roughly hewn and nailed together, the woodwork here was wasn't gray from exposure, but silver from careful carpentry and polish. False columns ran up the walls to the great overhead beams, as wide as a man's waist, that formed the rafters upholding a roof high overhead. Rafters and ceiling were elaborately carved and painted. But along the walls . . .

Jim wanted to laugh. Here he was, brought by guards into a native ruler's—what would you call it? his throne room?—all carved woods and handicrafts like something out of one of Neave's books, and the place was a junkyard for remnants of technology as old as the ration tube he had rejected. Neave had never explained what lost-generation ship or cold-sleep carrier or *prototype to a bioship,* he thought with a familiar pang, had gone off-course, survived to pass the Straits of Aquila; and disgorged its passengers here on Exquemelin.

But one thing was certain: since that ship had made planetfall, every bit of tech it possessed had clearly been hoarded, state treasure for a petty dictator.

And as much as possible of what was now outdated and rusting junk was crammed into this room, which otherwise would have been beautiful. No wonder Jim's guards had spoken of the concentrate tube as a way of honoring their guest and been baffled and a little afraid when he had demanded better. To their way of thinking, there was nothing better or more honorable.

"Move," came a whisper from the elder guard. Why, the man was terrified. He gestured, his hand dropping to his waist. Was he armed? He was afraid enough that Jim didn't want him at his back with a loaded weapon. He started forward, his eyes darting from the old tech that cluttered the floor, a menace to navigating the room, looking for—yes, that was clearly a later importation, and so was that monitor.

At the other end of the room stood a large chair, separated from him, from the rest of the people wearing drab coveralls and those garish scarves, by intricate twisted mats. In it sat a man with a blaster—Jim's blaster—on his lap.

Melinkor, Jim thought, and strode forward, his head high.

He knew the drill, if not from his father's stories, then from the "charm school" he'd been sent through when he was young and had hopes of a bright future. March down the center, brace, incline your head, and intone "Sir," keeping your jaw square. Play-act for all you were worth, and never, never, never crack a smile.

He took it slow, making time to study the man, who looked to be in late middle-age. Originally, his hair had been almost blue-black. It was disagreeably mottled now with yellowing white, and receding from a forehead that narrowed almost as much as his chin. Alone of the men in the room, Melinkor wore facial hair, mustaches following the lines of his face, drooping into an expression of perpetual discontent.

Melinkor's attention was focused, not on him but on a man leaning over his chair, somewhat taller, thinner, and older than the others and, unlike them, wearing an orange jacket that Jim could identify as being part of a flightsuit some fifty years old.

"You tell the Commodore he dreams mad dreams," Melinkor demanded, as if he, not the man beside him, were the petitioner. "I have told him, I can do nothing, nothing, as long as Oulian's thieves raid my treasury! Unless, of course, he and his were to help me, instead of demanding our strongest backs and our finest tech.

"Now, you!" he turned toward Jim, as if brushing aside a complaint he could not answer. "Do you come with news? Does your Alliance return to us? Your Vortimer is useless, worse than useless, a thief, in league with . . ."

His voice trailed away into a whine, then into a cough, and he reached for the cup resting on the broad arm of his chair, stained darker from what were probably years of spills.

Jim thought to say that he'd been sent to replace Vortimer, but reverted to "Sir." He let his eyes rest on his blaster, glad once more that it was uncharged.

"You will communicate with your ship," Melinkor said. "Tell them we need supplies, modern equipment, weapons, if I am to protect my people against thieves!"

No wonder Neave hadn't liked Melinkor, Jim decided. "Your Excellency is mistaken," he said formally. "I have no ship. Your men saw the ruins of my lander."

"Do you think I'm a fool, a savage?" Melinkor demanded. "You didn't get here in that . . . that lander. The ship that brought you through the Straits, where we cannot go—"

Jim shook his head. "They have no more use for me than . . ." He shrugged. "I came here because I thought there'd be profit in it. I'm hardly the only one, am I? There was some talk I'd replace Vortimer—"

"Good!"

"But if there's no profit . . ." Jim extended his hands, spreading them out on either side of him as he'd seen a grifter do on Raffles, way downbelow, "I may as well go back to the lander and see if I can salvage its transponder, signal for pickup."

He didn't like this man, Jim told himself. Not at all.

Melinkor laughed, then waved his hands. "Why are you waiting? Where is tea, tea for me and my guest!"

Two women scurried forward, neither wearing any distinguishing scarves or jackets of what was clearly high-status synthetic from offworld. One carried a low table of dark wood, carved in a complex pattern that drew the eye in along it and soothed mind and heart, incongruous in this junkyard of a throne room. The other carried a tray, holding cups and pot in a celadon so delicate that Jim could imagine Neave touching it with an admiring finger.

Melinkor, however, snatched up his cup even before the tray touched the table.

If Jim were to drink with him, he would have to bend and pick up the cup, presenting the back of the room with a picturesque view of his backside. Sorry, mister. That wasn't part of the charm-school course.

He moved closer to Melinkor's throne until he was actually standing on the mat that divided it from the rest of the room, then folded his arms.

"A chair for my guest!" Jim stood, the hair prickling on

the back of his neck, until scraping noises behind him told him a chair—a plain thing, but complete with armrests and back—had been brought. He dared to glance over his shoulder, saw the chair in place, allowed himself a stiff nod, and sat. His tea was handed to him, a warmth welcome to his hand in the dank air. He nodded thanks, which seemed to be a surprising novelty to the woman who served him.

"This," Melinkor said, waving the blaster at Jim. "We are out of the trade routes here, but this is an official weapon. What is your connection with the people called the Fleet?"

Jim shrugged. "Haven't got one. As for the blaster, it's stolen goods."

"You're lying," said Melinkor. "I know you came here on a ship. Yes, on an Alliance ship."

"I came here on a private trader. I never knew its name. They never gave me a break," he added, making his voice into the grifter's whine again. From his times as an outcast, he knew exactly what to say. A man with an unblemished past wouldn't have.

"I didn't owe them a thing. It's their own damn fault I stole the lander, disabled their security, and took off on my own."

"You lie. You say you came to replace Vortimer, and Vortimer claims to be from the Alliance—"

"I don't care what lies that lazy incompetent tells," Jim said. "I came here to replace him. If not officially, then . . ." he let his lips twist in what one of the 'leggers had used as a smile, the nastiest he knew.

"Then you have associates?" Melinkor asked. His face went from petulant to angry to sly—or what passed for it—in an instant. Volatile, weak, and dangerous, Jim thought. "The Commodore"—he grimaced—"swore you would bring here a great ship, heavy with freight, but that you would give it to our enemies."

Jim blinked at that, then forced a laugh.

"If I had a 'great ship,' why would I come here?" he asked.

Melinkor gestured again. Another man, younger, healthier, and wearing garments that looked even more like a shipsuit than the others, came forward holding yet another piece of high-status scrap.

"Do you recognize this?"

It was *Eaglet*'s transponder, reeking of a remembered, acrid smoke that made Jim fight not to cough. One panel was fused, another bent at an acute angle.

Wasn't as if you actually expected to use it, Jim consoled himself.

"Fix it," ordered Melinkor. "Fix it, and bring us friends, supplies, the ship the Commodore says you own, and we will talk again." Contact with *Blue Ridge* and its protectors, if he could fix it. If he dared fix it and give it into Melinkor's hands.

He signaled, and the transponder was dumped into Jim's lap.

Abruptly, Melinkor rose. Jim rose, too, although more slowly, and made himself stand at attention while the man exited by a door, curtained by a rust and brown tapestry, to one side of his throne. His advisors, preening in their shabby offworld trappings, followed him. Everyone else rushed from the room. One serving woman darted back and snatched the celadon cup from his hand before she fled.

There being nothing else to do, Jim deliberately sauntered out into the courtyard, such as it was, and retraced his steps to the room he'd waked in. Not much to his surprise, his spare shipsuit had gone missing. He sighed, packed *Eaglet*'s transponder into the bag, and headed for the courtyard.

Neave wasn't paying him to sulk in his quarters.

Come to think of it, Neave wasn't paying him at all.

IT TOOK JIM TWO MORE DAYS TO REALIZE NOT JUST THAT HE needed more equipment to repair the transponder than Melinkor was going to allow him, but that he was in even more trouble than he'd expected.

He'd been moving rather slowly: food, like tea, had to be bellowed for and, unless you were Melinkor, rations were kind of scarce on the ground.

If this is how he treats the help, why do they stay? Jim asked himself, trying to bend a circuit board back without snapping it in half. *Why not run away to this Oulian?*

Three people, all wearing locally produced, shoddy garments, edged by him, as if they expected him to hurl the transponder at their heads or perhaps shout an order they didn't dare obey.

He had already learned that anyone he looked at straight tended to disappear. He'd gotten rather good at studying people out of the corner of his eye, with his head down. Now, pretending to be intent on his repairs, he glanced around.

Good God, that man—long-legged and fast-moving—whom he glimpsed in the side corridor leading to Melinkor's audience room was wearing his shipsuit! Grubby as the one he had on was, it at least served to minimize his offworld status. No one as dirty as he could possibly have the kind of power Melinkor wanted.

He wanted another look at that man, and he got it. Not quite as tall as Jim, but considerably broader. Not his shipsuit, then, but one as much like it as if it had emerged from the same production batch. So, where had this man . . .

He strode out into the courtyard. Jim watched people look away from him and imitated them, drawing into a recess to hide his too-great height, his pale hair. The man stamped across the courtyard, water splashing onto the legs of his suit, and out the main—indeed the only—door.

But not before Jim had seen the badge on breast and arm of the newcomer's suit. He'd seen replicas of that badge scrawled on pipes in faraway stations and knew, when he saw it, to draw a weapon, if he couldn't retreat.

Scavenger mark. If only he'd been able to learn them better, he could even know now who his enemy really was.

"Upstairs." Jim recalled his trackers saying the day he crashed here. The Commodore. The Chief. The Angry Man.

Scavengers, all of them. Who'd probably be glad to acquire the likes of Jim: for information if possible; for a strong back, if need be. They probably thought Exquemelin was open for the taking. And, he realized, if it weren't for Neave's old friend, it probably would be.

And Melinkor damned well knew it. Knew it and whined at Jim to call for help because, crooked as he was, the off-worlders he knew were more crooked than he.

Offworlders: all they had to do was interrogate Jim under drugs, and he'd probably spill everything he knew, unless he could summon the moral courage to kill himself.

Moral courage. Him? Not likely.

He would have to escape. Escape, get to Oulian, and set about Neave's mission.

Leaning back against the wall, Jim studied the courtyard that had become his prison. It had one entrance, through which, presumably, he'd been brought in and out of which he'd gone, precisely once, yesterday, when Melinkor was feeling brave enough to make noises like a host. Beyond this building lay an open yard, and past it a stockade, actually built of local wood, rather than the force shields Jim was more used to. It was high enough, certainly, but it had been hastily built and was in bad repair from the shoddy construction and the rains that fell every afternoon.

No wonder Melinkor whined for more tech. He had to know how fragile a wooden stockade was against an advanced culture's weapons. Matched against ship's arms, it wouldn't even make a tidy little bonfire.

Still, when viewed from the ground, the stockade's walls were high, topped in some places with jagged pieces of masonry and rusted coils of what looked like antique concertina wire. During his morning walkabout with Melinkor, Jim had watched two workers struggle to wedge a pole into place. The thing had kept bending, and they had sworn until someone in a flight jacket had come, tongue-lashed them into silence, and ordered them to replace it with something less flexible.

Supple things, those poles.

Supple enough?

Thunder in the sky . . . Did it herald the daily rainsquall, or was it a ship, coming in for a landing?

Judging from how people tensed and scuttled as if their chores assumed the importance of battle stations, Jim bet it was a ship.

And he wouldn't bet on the chance that it wasn't coming for him, or that, in the wrong hands, he'd be as useful to scavengers dead as alive.

Another rumble of thunder, this time, the real thing. Jim looked up at the sky and prayed the rain would come on time.

For once, his prayer was answered.

He'd need a diversion. He delved into his kitbag and pulled out the transponder. Too bad he couldn't repair it, but just because it would never transmit again didn't mean its power source couldn't be jiggered into a small, but satisfyingly noisy grenade. He stepped back into shelter, drying his wet hand on his battered shipsuit so he wouldn't shock himself, and set to work. Circuits twisted; boards shifted; lights flashed in a new pattern. He could hear the whine start, counting down. Three minutes to detonation.

He drew three deep breaths, flooding his system with oxygen, almost hyperventilating. The adrenaline flooded through him, hitting his system hard.

Not yet.

Slinging his kitbag about his neck, balancing the transponder, he walked out the door, as if following his leader to the ship. No one stopped him.

Poles were still lying about by the main gate.

He picked one up and hefted it. No knots. No visible flaws.

Taking the pole, he backed up. Behind him, he could hear clamor that meant that Melinkor was on the move again, presumably to his audience hall, presumably to receive today's cargo of scavenger.

Jim was out of time.

As the rains came down, Jim backed up a couple of steps more for good measure, hurled the transponder, and heard and felt it go off, followed by screams and a crash as if walls had fallen in.

Light and shockwave from the grenade pushing him forward, he splashed at a run through the immense puddle that filled between the hall and the stockade, planted his pole, and jumped for his life, high over the wall, flying over it, far above the wire, to come down, his legs in a stream, his face slamming into its muddy bank.

In other circumstances, it could have been funny.

Instead, he coughed till he gagged, spat out the mud and water he'd swallowed, and struggled free of the muck, which made sucking sounds as if reluctant to release him, and ran for his life.

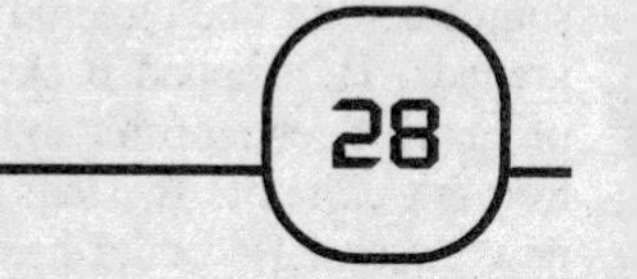

Jim ran till breathlessness doubled him over and he almost retched from coughing. At least the mud would camouflage him, he thought. But as it dried, it would flake off. Hell of a note if they could track him by following a trail of mud clots.

And then there were always the possibilities that Melinkor's tech junkpile had some sort of scanner that could track his body readings or that the scavengers "Upstairs" would come through with state-of-the-art scanners.

The ground roughened, angling up so suddenly he almost fell. Neave had said Oulian's people lived on high ground he'd compared to an Old Earth mesa.

Jim brushed off the worst of the caked mud—wouldn't do to leave traces now—and started up, trying to divide his attention between hand- and footholds and available cover.

A handhold gave way, and he saved himself from sprawling by a corkscrew twist that damn near took him into a pit. Ten meters further up, as he cowered in a tempting bit of cover, he looked down just in time to avoid stepping on a root—no, that wasn't just a root, that was a lever that would have released a rockslide that would probably have hurled what was left of him right into the arms of any search party Melinkor may have wanted to send after him.

So, he couldn't count on hugging each bit of cover, could he? Exposure made the vulnerable spot between his shoulder blades prickle. At least his stained shipsuit made him the same color—more or less—as the ground. He'd just have to move fast and hope that "Upstairs" didn't have a flyer to waste on the likes of Melinkor and his petty spites.

It was clear that Oulian, unlike Melinkor, didn't just hoard old tech or beg new toys out of scavengers; he—or his people—used every inch of ground to advantage, and they had minds he'd cheerfully praise for their ingenuity and sheer bloody-mindedness, assuming he survived the ascent.

Wind whipped about him as he climbed, drying the sweat that scalded his ribs, then chilling him. He extended the hood from his shipsuit's collar and tugged it up over his head. Given competing risks of hypothermia and the target offered by the unstained hood, he'd take being a target: low efficiency rating for Melinkor, he thought.

He paused again to catch his breath and look for pursuers. Melinkor's compound lay far below, encircled by the scar that marked not just its rough stockade, so futile against energy weapons or an airborne attack, but the assault made on the forests that marched down to silvery lakes. The trees were tall and straight, crowned by gold and bronze foliage.

Beyond one of the lakes was slagged earth, where *Eaglet* had come down. It had stopped smoking. Just as well: he didn't like the idea that his landing here might have caused a fire. He liked even less the idea that scavengers "Upstairs" could turn this whole planet into slag.

He didn't think he was high enough for the air to start thinning: he must be tiring. After all, he'd had that head injury, and he'd been shorted on food and sleep for the past couple of days. He coughed again, and again bent double, spitting until his empty gut stopped heaving. When he resumed climbing, he went almost on all fours.

Got to get back in shape, he told himself. Except for the occasional bout of manual labor, he'd spent the past decade shut up in ships, knowing himself an outcast, shut out of places like gyms and recreation decks.

Watch it, he warned himself. *You're almost at the top. They'll have surprises. . . .*

Only his handgrips stopped him from skidding on a carefully placed pile of loose rocks that would have sent him toppling downslope onto—yes, there was a pit there, and he'd be willing to bet a month's pay, assuming he still drew pay, that there were punji stakes at the bottom of it.

Oulian's people made their land fight for them.

He had to rest, at least for a couple of minutes. He smeared tears and mud off his face and crouched behind a rock, panting and looking about.

The world below him was surprisingly unspoiled, given Melinkor's lust for tech and the scavengers who teased it along. Below were the forests with their crowns of gold and amber leaves, broken up by lakes. Up this high, he could see that Melinkor's compound wasn't the only settlement: he saw another built on platforms jutting out into a lake, and yet another, an ordered pile of rocks like the prow of a ship atop another mesa. It looked like something from the stories he had poisoned his youth by reading, and now he was a hero in one of them.

You thought you were the hero before, and look what happened to you. Get a move on, man, he told himself.

He leaned out further, then froze: there was motion there, broken by the occasional rockfall triggered by a climber not as watchful as he had been. He looked more closely at the tiny faces: staring eyes, mouths open on curses he couldn't hear for the rushing of the wind and the water . . . yes, that was water he had been hearing, and the air had turned damp.

A water source! The very thought was reassuring, not just for this mesa's ability to withstand attack, but for his own immediate needs. Where there was water, there would be people, people who, unless Neave were a liar on a scale Jim couldn't begin to comprehend, would welcome him.

Time to get up now, son.

His father's voice? He was in worse shape than he'd thought. Good thing he was so near the top. Risking it on rubbery legs, he staggered out from the protecting boulder and found smoother ground.

Smoothed ground, that was. Someone had taken pains with this particular stretch of ground, building a secure path that led . . . the blood was hammering in his temples, his ears were ringing, his skull buzzing, and he heard a kind of rushing sound . . . He could feel water on his face now. . . .

No, he wasn't hallucinating or blacking out. The rocks grew damp, slippery, and he fell headlong once, scraping the skin from his palms and shredding the right knee of his shipsuit.

For a moment, he stared idiotically at the water that gushed from a basin of worked stone over the lip of the mesa. There would be people here, perhaps, guards. Help for him . . . oh God, if the scavengers sent backups for Melinkor, he'd have brought danger with him. . . .

Briefly restored by the spray on his face, Jim forced himself up the last few meters, falling up the last part of the incline rather than stepping up onto what was, at long last, a reliably flat surface.

He raised his bleeding palms in case guards watched him. His sight was blearing again, going double; he'd never quite recovered from that landing, and he wove and staggered like a burnout from downbelow levels toward a cluster of buildings—that grayish wood and pale stone that looked like it had been hewn from the side of a cliff.

People were shouting, running back and forth. Someone challenged him, but he rasped, "Melinkor's guards, they're after me!" then gestured, with blood dripping down his wrists and onto the ground, and stumbled toward the settlement he saw. There would be fire there and clean water and maybe people who would treat him gently. He was conscious of how, inside his shipsuit, Oulian's ring rested near his heart.

Low walls, a barricade with a gate, lay before him. The gate was open, but as he approached, two slender figures—boys and a girl in their late teens—began to push it closed, staring at him. He put on a burst of speed, weaving like a drunk, and got through before it closed. He staggered into the village. Children tripped, screaming with outrage as adults pulled them out of range. The adolescents from the gate ran out to him.

Then, he heard running footsteps, rapid, purposeful, more than one pair of feet.

Guards. Finally, guards.

What the *hell* had they been waiting for? His rage at them was completely incongruous. Lucky for him that they had. *They could have shot you. They still could.* He wanted to laugh, but they'd probably shoot him for sure.

A red haze was blinding him, but he didn't need eyes to reach for the chain around his neck, pull it out, and show the ring Neave had given him.

"I've been sent here for Oulian!" he cried. "His brother Neave . . . he sent me!"

The chain broke under Jim's desperate grip, and he lashed it back and forth until his hand fell open. He staggered, he was falling, and then two men—a young man his height, but as dark as he was fair, and a stocky man in early middle age—ran forward. They had sidearms at their belts, they moved as if they knew what they were doing, but they caught him, held him as gently as a brother, and brought him in where, at long last, there was light, warmth, fire, water, and an end to running.

"I have to speak to Oulian!" he gasped. "Oulian! Take me to him."

God, he was wheezing, drooling with exhaustion. His stomach heaved again, and pains stabbed down his limbs. The crash, the fear, the run, the climb after long inaction had taken their toll . . . *electrolytes shot to hell,* he thought before muscle and stomach spasms blotted all thought from his consciousness.

A woman with hair the gray brown of the weathered wood caught him and pushed him down onto a soft surface, then just let him heave. She wiped his mouth, held a cup for him, pulled it away when he would have gulped at it like a fool—*you don't want to be sick again!* Gently, she forced his hands down, then numbed them with something that felt cold. She snapped orders to people Jim couldn't see, then turned back to him.

"This is Oulian's house," she said. "I am his wife. You are our guest."

"Melinkor . . ." Jim gasped. "They're coming. . . ."

"And if they are? We are well guarded by the land, and my son patrols by air. He will keep you safe," said the woman. "As he did once before."

"The pilot," Jim whispered. "Flew across my flight path when I was coming in—"

"I tell Stal Viat he is too reckless," the woman said.

She held the cup to Jim's lips again, then finished the work of bandaging his hands, torn by so many falls.

"Now," she said. "Sleep. Dream of healing. When you wake, there will be time to speak."

Jim closed his eyes. One night aboard *Gavroche,* after too many long watches and one night off watch with wine, Marlow had told him how practically her last memory before resurrection had been the order, "Shut your eyes before the ice forms, or you'll thaw damaged."

But in that sleep of cryotherapy, what dreams had come to Marlow? Jim had always wondered. Marlow had never said. And no dreams had ever come that he could interpret.

He woke to firelit darkness, the scents of fire and ash and something savory he hoped he'd get a share of. And voices whispering.

"Setelin went back. Alone, which is foolish. I wish she would stay with us," complained the old woman's voice. "And I wish you would take better care."

"She doesn't like to leave Vortimer alone with the trading post's tech. If he didn't wreck it trying to download secrets he could sell. Not now, with the Commodore trying to rouse Melinkor to fight us. He claims the people in his fort have built the ship, so now the fleet will have to come and bring him treasure."

Spectacularly bad sense, Jim thought.

This new voice, young, furry with laughter, went on speaking. A good voice, Jim decided.

"You might as well try to make me stay home as if I were still a boy dreaming that I could pilot a ship," the voice said. "Setelin and I have agreed. She will keep watch and report back to us."

"I do not like this. You at least, when you play hero, you are armed. She has only her wits. . . ."

"As long as she is the only one who understands the traders' tech, she is safe. She needs to keep it safe."

"She could bring it here!"

"She thinks that moving the outpost's tech here would cause Melinkor and the offworlders to ally against us," came a deep rumble of a voice. "It is her mother's legacy to her, and her right."

"I offered to help," said the young man's voice. "She told me it would be impious to leave her mother's grave to Vortimer to tend."

"That one! When the poor woman was alive, he never left her alone. And now he'd dig up her bones to see what tech she took down into the grave." The old woman muttered something else that ended in an angry hiss, then subsided.

Not wanting to be thought an eavesdropper, Jim raised a hand. Someone had put Oulian's ring on it. The hand looked clean and pale, disconnected from him, curiously languid. He let it fall upon his chest.

"Our guest's waking up!" said the young man's voice. With deft, tanned hands, he raised Jim and eased him against his shoulder as if sensing that the first need he decently could confess was to see.

He blinked out, saw bright eyes, people sitting on cushions in a dimmed room. Mostly women, he realized, under the command of the aged, thin, active woman who had taken him in. Now that his eyes were tracking, he saw her long skeins of graying hair were bound up and clasped with metal studded with . . . those were ancient microchips, worn like gems. Other chips clasped the glittering synthetic of the long coat she wore.

Seated across from Jim, like an image carved from stone or paralyzed, was an immense man whose massive shoulders glinted as if he had been cast in gold and bronze—or wore a cloak intricately patterned from the foil blankets of long-ago emergencies. A thick, muscular neck emerged from this robe of honor, supporting a muscular neck and a squarish head, tied up in a kerchief of the same fabric as his cloak. The corners of his mouth drooped, etched by thin mustaches. His eyes seemed to peer out from a heavy ledge of brow, but did not move. Nothing about him moved, except the hand he lifted, as remote and pitiless as an idol floating through space. His fingers were almost as thick as a child's wrist: no wonder Oulian had left the ring for Jim. There was no way he would ever wear it again.

Another gesture, and the thin-faced woman, Oulian's wife, laughed, nodded, and fetched a bowl. To Jim's shame, she began to feed Jim until Oulian gestured once more, and the young man set him down without a murmur.

"When you are well," he said, "I wish you would tell me of your trip. I saw you land—"

"Crash, more like it," Jim murmured. The soup seemed to warm him all the way down. "I'd have bored a hole in one of your forests if . . . wait . . . that ship . . ." He tried to prop himself on his elbows and gave it up as a bad idea. "Neave said you . . . was that . . ."

Then this was Stal Viat, Oulian's son, doing duty as a nursemaid. Jim stared up at the young man, as open-faced as a newly commissioned ensign: dark large eyes beneath arched brows, a swathe of dark hair below a red cap made of some sort of brocaded synthasilk, surmounted with a button made from a computer chip. *Court clothing,* Jim deduced. *To welcome me?*

He was surrounded by one of the ruling families of Exquemelin. He lay in their care, and care they seemed to, instantly and warmly. The thought brought tears to his eyes.

Stal Viat chuckled. "I haven't had this Fleet training of yours. Will you teach me?" Real hunger underlay his voice.

"You fought well enough to save my life!" Jim said and put out his hand to grasp the other man's.

"You would have landed safely by yourself," said Stal Viat, shaking his head. "I saw it in my dream the night before." He smiled, the smile of a boy right out of the Academy, unstained, his whole life stretching before him like a scroll of honor.

Jim rolled his eyes. *These people valued dreams,* Neave had said.

Probably from their time in Freeze, Marlow had added, and she wouldn't joke about a thing like that.

They cherished shadows as much as the bits of tech they hoarded. And this was what he had to work with! But the old man had accepted him. The old woman had taken him in. And this vibrant young man had saved his life.

Stal Viat was smiling again. "After you sleep, we will talk. You will tell me your plans."

He was a guest in these people's home. Mannerly guests brought gifts. He had no notion of what gift would please them best. An immense yawn almost cracked his jaws and made his eyes water. But it let in some sense.

"What if we steal Melinkor's tech?" he asked. "Then, it won't matter what this Commodore of his wants."

And in case he wants a world full of slaves, we'll have the tech to protect ourselves.

He took Stal Viat's delighted laughter down with him into contented darkness.

* * *

CHILDREN WERE GIGGLING OUTSIDE. THE INCONGRUITY OF children on board a ship brought Jim rapidly awake, and he remembered: not a ship. Not captivity, either. He had made it to Oulian's stronghold, and he was safe, at least for now. He had not heard children laugh like that since before the war.

The laughter became shrill and drew nearer until a reproachful hiss silenced it. Footsteps scuffled away, and Jim heard a bump against the door.

"Let me help you." Jim grinned as he recognized Stal Viat's voice.

"Melinkor probably never bothered to feed him!" grumbled his mother.

"I knew you'd say that. But there's enough on that tray—it's much too heavy for you to carry—for a small army."

The door swung open. Oulian's son edged past his mother with an immense tray.

"Did you dream well?" he asked in this world's version of "good morning."

"Very well, thank you," Jim replied. It would have been more polite, more friendly, to speak of his dreams, but he had slept too deeply to remember them. "Enough food for a small army?" he added. "I'd say it would feed an entire ship's crew."

Dew clung to Stal Viat's hair. "I see you've been out already. Then you must be hungry. Please, join me."

From the younger man's grin, Jim knew his invitation wasn't just right, but welcome. Hoped for, even.

"Mother, I'll see to our guest," Stal Viat said. "I think he will want to dress. Perhaps his clothes have dried by now."

Jim had wanted to rise, to greet Oulian's wife politely and thank her for her care, but he wasn't wearing enough to make that anything but an ordeal for all concerned. He contented himself with as cordial a smile as he could muster.

The woman laughed. "As if women did not change you, bathe you, dress all you men when you were little!"

Stal Viat chuckled, set the tray down, and closed the door behind her.

He handed Jim a steaming mug: the same savory tea he had tasted in Melinkor's stronghold, but far, far better. "Thank you," he said.

"I've been up seeing to our perimeter defenses," Stal Viat told him. "If you could make it up the side of the mountain, others could too. Mother must have thought your dreams made you hungry!" he exclaimed, investigating the contents of the tray. Enough to feed several hungry young men, Jim saw. Abruptly, he felt not just hungry, but as young as Stal Viat, who curled his legs beneath him on a low chair beside the bed, took a well-filled plate on his knees, and tucked in while talking at a great rate.

"My mother thinks you should not get up today," Stal Viat said. "But I think your muscles are sore. You must work out the strain. So, you will eat, then dress, and walk about the plateau with me. When you are tired, there is a hot spring nearby, and we can soak in it before dinner. My father has asked that you sit by him, but he knows how far you've come and will release you to your dreams as soon as the tables are cleared." He tilted his head on one side.

Jim bent over his own plate. The fumes of some spicy sauce were clearing his head. Now that he was awake, now that he wasn't so hungry, memory of the impetuous promise he had made to steal Melinkor's cherished hoard of high-tech material the day before came uncomfortably to mind. It had seemed like a fine boast at the time. Now, Stal Viat was watching him as if he could simply snap his fingers—one of them wearing the ring his father had given an offworld friend before either Jim or Stal Viat were born—and make it all happen.

This innocent seemed to think Jim could do anything, be anything at all provided it was brave.

"I'd like to take you around to oversee the defenses," Stal Viat was saying. "I'm sure you know some strategies that Father and I don't, and we'd be grateful for—"

He drained his mug and set it aside decisively. *A moment longer, and he'll insist on fetching my clothes so I can get up and start creating this future they think I've brought them.*

God, don't let me fuck up.

Seeing him sitting there, silent, Stal Viat paused. "But perhaps you are still tired, still sick," he ventured. "My mother said I was not to trouble you before you felt well enough to move."

I will make myself believe this will work. I can. I will.

"I believe you mentioned something about some clean clothes and a tour of your defenses," Jim said.

Stal Viat's face lit with a grin that made Jim feel clean to his bones.

BY DAY, HE STRODE ABOUT THE PLATEAU WITH STAL VIAT, climbing down to inspect some installation or other, viewing this strategic point or that.

At times they sparred, trading local combat tricks with the hand-to-hand techniques Jim had learned in the Academy and in the lowest reaches of a dozen star bases, before they eased aching muscles in the hot springs, which lay below a formation of planes upon planes of a red rock studded with crystals in black and gray. Water cascaded over the rock, falling from level to level, forming pools of different temperatures, cooling as it fell. Jim would lounge in it, his new friend and his people attentive nearby, and watch the sun set above the forests far below, where golden leaves were turning bronze.

After all, he had lost his conditioning in the long transit of the Straits of Aquila, he told himself to rationalize the waste of time. It was only sensible to regain his strength. He felt as if he were also regaining his youth, as it seemed, unstained and as full of promise as it had been before he'd boarded *Irian Jaya*.

When the evening wind began to make the contrast between the steaming water and the cool air a little too crisp for comfort, he and Stal Viat would lead the way, sometimes talking, sometimes singing, back to Oulian's house. Bright lights were always set out to welcome them—sometimes torches, sometimes flares from old emergency gear. Oulian was always quick to seize his hand and speak of his dreams, either those of the night before or the ones Stal Viat was teaching him to cherish for the future.

Jim remembered being the son of older parents. Obviously, Oulian and his wife worshipped their son, who kindled them into renewed energy and effort. They might have been content to keep what they had held: Stal Viat wanted more, wanted better, than small-scale political maneuvers punctuated by the occasional raid. He wanted peace, stability; and if he had to make himself the major power on this continent to get them, then he would take on Melinkor, the Commodore, and anything else he had to.

Clearly, he saw Jim not as a ticket offworld, but as a source of information, of training: an agent of progress.

Damned fool.

LONG BEFORE STAL VIAT HAD TALKED HIMSELF OUT ABOUT his hopes for the future, long before Oulian's clever-handed wife, or Oulian himself considered Jim in any way recovered, he decided to move to the outpost that Neave had established long ago, managed—mismanaged was more like it—by a man named Vortimer.

His decision was the subject of three nightly debates, followed by three morning analyses of everyone's dreams, and an eruption by Stal Viat and his mother about a person named Setelin. Jim had heard that name his first night on Oulian's plateau and that he connected somehow with jeopardy, with whispers and rushed visits and muttered wishes that she could stay someplace safe.

Jim thought Neave had said something about a daughter. About someone's daughter, if not Vortimer's, a woman who traded in information and refused to be moved.

Even Oulian conceded that Setelin's position was dangerously exposed.

Well, if this Setelin were in danger, Jim promised Stal Viat, he would do his best to help her out. And if the situation proved untenable, he'd be back for help. Ultimately, that lame promise was what convinced Oulian to let him win the argument.

Stal Viat grinned and patted him on the shoulder, grin and gesture telling him how unlikely he thought it that Jim would need his help. When the dreams next morning turned out to be favorable omens, Jim seized the day.

29

Moving to Vortimer's meant leaving Oulian's fortified plateau for a short climb downslope, to a smaller plain watered by a mountain-fed stream.

It was not, he saw instantly, a change for the better. The neat prefabricated buildings Neave had put up decades ago had fallen into disrepair: Vortimer lived in what looked like little more than a lean-to built against the side of a cliff.

He had been, apparently, expected. Melinkor had sent up his gear the day before, and he found it stacked outside the dilapidated lean-to, and Vortimer was going through it, apparently not for the first time.

"Hey you, stop that!" Jim said. Not the best of greetings for a new associate.

Vortimer turned, startled, but not in the least bit embarrassed at being caught in the act. He was a ratty little man who reminded Jim of a pawnbroker in Raffles' Downbelow, the sort of dishonest trader who alerted scavengers when a mark defaulted on a loan. Bathe him, dress him in the finest clothes from Upstairs, put him in company with a man like Neave, a woman like Marlow, and he would still seem to need not just a bath, but decontamination.

Vortimer hadn't gone native. He'd gone rotten.

He was as full of apologies as he was of greetings, assailing Jim's ears with an obsequious babble of speech from which he could extract no hint that Vortimer was aware that Jim had come to replace him. Jim was Neave's observer, Vortimer's honored guest, potentially the most wonderful event to afflict Exquemelin since Planetfall, if not the Big Bang, until Jim flinched from the menacing insincerity of it all and began to turn away. Having won the point, Vortimer practically arm-wrestled Jim for the dubious privilege of carrying his gear. And he gestured him elaborately on ahead.

With more common sense than Jim would have expected, Vortimer had built his paltry house against a natural cliff that stretched back some way into the living rock. A line of stalagmites bisected a sort of central hall, making it look remarkably like a ship's brig. Assuming a ship's brig possessed both crudely strung cold lights and torches made of some oil-soaked wood that spat and flamed, coating the roughly smoothed roof of the corridor with streaks of soot and sending out a dance of light and shadow.

Jim half-turned, as if ascertaining that the square of daylight behind him was still there. "I assure you, sir, it is perfectly safe, although I daresay you are more used to vacuum than trillions of tons of rock overhead. Exquemelin's initial seismic assay reported no significant tremors. I keep telling the girl she should do another, but she is sullen, useless. . . ."

To say don't worry about earthquakes or cave-ins simply brought them to mind, and with them, the fear of them. He longed for a pressure suit, an airlock, and the comforting emptiness of space, and didn't Vortimer just know it? The little rat was showing all his jagged stained teeth in a triumphant smile.

Good that Stal Viat wasn't here to see Vortimer place Jim at such a disadvantage.

Thinking of his friend gave Jim the moral courage to press on. He turned into a small chamber, also equipped with columns, festoons of fiber cable, flickering lights, and, just for safety, a torch or two and an ancient tube of what looked like oxygen. No quakes? Not damn likely.

"I'll just take this room," he said.

He turned to toss his gear into the nearest of the rooms, not giving a good goddamn if he displaced Vortimer or not, and brought up short against a woman who was trying to leave it.

She gasped, enormous dark eyes widening with surprise. Like almost everyone on this world Jim had met, except Oulian, she was short, barely shoulder-high on him. Even in the torchlight, he could see that her skin was warmly tanned, her long hair was black, flowing down over proud, delicate shoulders, and the hand she raised to her mouth to conceal a gasp of surprise—at least, he hoped it was surprise; he hadn't bumped into her that hard—was small and graceful. In her other hand, she held a spray of golden leaves that covered her body like a sash of honor.

"My daughter, Setelin," said Vortimer. "Child, this man comes to us from offworld!"

"My mother was the consul's wife," Setelin spoke directly to Jim, dismissing Vortimer's words.

"I gave her a home after he died and I replaced him. Gave a home to a woman who knew the systems here, but never, never taught me, and to her ingrate daughter. It would not kill you to call me father, girl. With respect, for I am a respectable man."

Setelin let her eyes play over Vortimer's stooped figure. She was not taller than he but carried herself so well she seemed that way.

"I have not earned your contempt!" Vortimer snapped. "She taught you, that bitch who kept her legs together and—"

Setelin raised her hands to her ears, leafy branch and all. Pushing past Jim, she ran out of the cave into the light.

Jim stepped into the room and retrieved his gear. His eyes adapted to the gloom, and he saw leaves set among water-smoothed rocks in a shallow dish, a sheer scarf, hanging over a simple chair. He glanced away from a bed draped with colored shawls. Setelin's quarters, clearly: he had intruded. Vortimer would either be offended or find it funny. Probably the latter. He backed out fast.

"I've had enough surprises for one day," he told Vortimer. "Do you have a room in this warren that's vacant, or do I take up quarters outside?"

"Stay there, for all the good it'll do you," said Vortimer. "Like mother, like daughter."

Jim's instinctive dislike of Vortimer crystallized into full-blown contempt.

"You know," said Jim, "if you want her to treat you with respect, you might try not insulting her mother like that." He turned his back on the man and strode out toward the clean air.

Hell of a bunking arrangement. Vortimer claimed to be this Setelin's father, yet vilified her mother, and Setelin—the voice was familiar—was Oulian's ally, Stal Viat's friend, and who knew what else to him. Well, he'd hardly be justifying Neave's trust in him if he went back to Oulian and admitted he'd made a major mistake. He'd just have to tough it out.

He strode away from the cliff-face, hoping to walk off the doubts and the anger that were clouding his judgment. The wind tugged at his hair, and he turned toward a promontory, jutting from the ledge, overlooking the forest. The ground was cleared, a segment of it about the length of a man—no, a woman—marked off by black rocks. A grave, Jim thought. And in the next moment, as he watched Setelin tenderly set down her spray of leaves, he knew whose.

He walked toward her, deliberately scuffing up small rocks so his footsteps would announce him. Setelin was kneeling inside the black rocks. With loving care, she brushed the dust and soil that had accumulated away from the crystals of the immense geode that marked her mother's grave. Sunlight flicked over the cleansed stone, and the crystals glowed a rich amethyst.

Along the geode's rim were letters, too worn to read at this distance. But to come any closer without permission struck Jim as an intrusion.

"When we were young," Setelin said softly, "Stal Viat and I spent weeks hunting for rocks we thought held crystals and smashing them open with hammers. I pretended they were Vortimer. Every single one of them. Stal Viat said that it was better to smash rocks than Vortimer's skull, even if they were not so hard."

Her voice choked, and she gestured.

"We found this geode and brought it here to her. We borrowed Oulian's blaster, oh, I suppose he knew, but he couldn't come, so we had to. We took turns trying to etch her name on the rock with a blaster. I don't know why we didn't lose any fingers, but—"

"Maybe she was looking out for you," Jim ventured. His father would have approved of the sentiment.

She shrugged, skepticism and resignation combined. "We worked hard to make a proper memorial." She bent her head and the long black hair, under a scarlet cap, fell forward in soft wings to hide her face. "This is all I have left of her. I don't remember my father, but Mother told me . . . told me he was very smart, and very brave. Unlucky, too, or he would not have finished up his life here. But after he met her, she said, he spoke no more of bad luck."

"I'm here now," Jim said. It seemed a tiny thing to offer. "Will you come back in?"

He held out his hand. "Come on. I won't let him talk to you like that."

She sighed and rose, ready to accompany him. "Another one to fear for," she murmured.

He raised fingers to his brow before he left the grave, either in a half-salute to a long-dead woman's grave or a courtesy to her daughter. It won a tiny smile.

DINNER WAS SPARSE, SOME PRESERVED MEAT WITH SOME RESEMBLANCE to fowl, an imperfectly washed bowl of dried-out tubers, and flatbread, washed down with a watered-down version of the tea Jim had begun to get used to.

"She's sulking," said Vortimer of Setelin, who had murmured that she wasn't hungry and retreated to the cave-room that was hers. Jim had heard a decisive thud that told him that she had slid the rock panel across the doorway, sequestering herself. "Not that she's much use around here at the best of times."

With little incentive to linger, either over food or conversation, Jim retired early, securing his own door, enough to listen if Vortimer had a mind to go prowling in the night. At one point, early in the night watch (according to Jim's timepiece, restored by edict of Melinkor), he heard the man race out into the night, shouting oaths and hurling rocks until, muttering to himself, he returned to his own quarters and Jim persuaded himself that it was safe—if he were to maintain any sort of vigilance in daylight—to let himself doze.

Setelin emerged from her solitude at what only flattery could call breakfast. The tea, thanks to her, was improved, and served in mugs the cleanliness of which would not challenge Jim's immunizations. But they had only the remnants of the flatbread from the night before, and it was not a food that improved with age.

"You're giving the new consul no good idea of our hospitality, girl," Vortimer replied to her inquiry whether he and Jim had dreamt well.

"It was not I who rose shouting in the night," Setelin retorted. "It used to be that Stal Viat's mother would send us meat every time there was a hunt. When my mother was alive . . ." she broke off, sighing. "I told her my garden is more than adequate. And then Vortimer decided that her messengers were spies or thieves and took to throwing rocks at them.

"It may be," she added, "that Vortimer intended to frighten them into dropping whatever they carried."

"Enough of that!" Vortimer snapped. "You know Melinkor tried to kill me, at least twice last year, and once, when the rains fell, and there was that mudslide, I was nearly—"

Setelin nodded. "Perhaps, this time, the messengers left us something," she said. She rose from the table, and Jim heard the door leading from the caves sliding away.

"Can she handle that?" he asked Vortimer, who shrugged, staring into his tea as if his night's dreams were reflected there.

"Yes, she finally got strong enough. I suppose now, I have to watch out for my life from her too. When she was younger, I knew she wouldn't murder me as I slept because she'd be walled up in here with my body."

Jim rose and went outside. It had rained during the night, and the wind that swept across the high plains was fresh and sweet with moisture.

Setelin stooped over a parcel that had been left right within the lean-to so that the fibers that wrapped it were only somewhat dampened.

"Cantu has been here," she said. "One of Stal Viat's associates. He's older than we. When we were children, playing at explorers, he always watched out for us though he thought we didn't know."

"Let me," said Jim, and heaved the parcel up onto his shoulder. He could smell the food within and took care not to drop it. Likely, it would be the only fresh food they'd get until Vortimer took it into his head to charge out into the night at another messenger.

But he was wrong. Now that Jim had arrived, presumably to put an end to the rock-throwing, a number of Oulian's people took it into their heads to call with such eagerness that Jim realized that Oulian's wife and son weren't the only ones to worry about Setelin or, as they said, to greet Vortimer's associate.

The word "associate" was probably all that protected them from eruptions of curses and rock-throwing.

As the days passed, Jim decided, those outbursts were preferable to Vortimer's self-pity, which chiefly manifested itself in laments that he was unfortunate, that Neave had refused to trust him or send him the resources he needed, that he deserved. It was never, it seemed, Vortimer's fault. Responsibility for mistakes, for failures, for inadequacies fell firmly on anyone else's head, the nearer or safer, the better. Safest of all was the dead, and it was these muttered diatribes of coldness and faithlessness that erupted into foul complaints about Setelin's mother that frequently drove the daughter out-of-doors.

Whatever mistakes the woman had made—and she must have made some extraordinary ones, to wind up here—she had not passed them on to her daughter. Setelin did not remember her father, only a silent woman, almost a ghost of what she must have been, who attempted to keep the outpost in some semblance of working order, raise her daughter, and, after a time, teach her what she knew from her husband of the outpost's store of tech, information, and arms.

Obviously, she had not taught Vortimer: the alliance of what should have been a docile, downworld wife with a daughter who, day by day, grew in wit, strength, bloom, and a quiet firm contempt for him galled him to this day.

He had repaid contempt with abuse. And the woman had died weeping.

Like Neave and her mother before her, Setelin did not trust Vortimer. She had moved the post's computer, by Jim's calculations some forty years behind the times, into the least wrecked of the outbuildings, the only one that boasted a lock, the codes for which never left her person.

Jim was kneeling by the corner of a shed furthest from the cave, patching its foundation, when a whisper, scarcely louder than the wind, floated from the cover of the ground scrub on the slope.

He turned, his hand darting for the sidearm he had resumed wearing: scarcely enough to defend himself against anything but Vortimer in a foul mode, but reassuring for all that.

"Cantu, sir," the whisper came again. "I am Stal Viat's man. Did she not tell you?"

Jim pretended to ease a rock into place. "That you looked

out for both of them, yes. And that sometimes, you bring food."

"This time, I bring word. Do not trust that man," Cantu hissed.

Jim remembered Cantu now, a man shorter than he but stockier, with a dark square face, jaw and brow of equal width beneath a receding hairline. He turned around and saw a quick grin flash.

"You bring old news." Jim returned the smile.

"You are as rash as Stal Viat! And if I tell you you will be killed?"

"I have not dreamed of my own death," Jim said. "And if I die, I will not die alone."

He would have thought that death would be release of a sort, provided he died for a purpose, Neave's purpose or Oulian's, and didn't waste his life falling off a cliff, crushed by boulders, or murdered one night by Vortimer, who would protest till his own execution that it hadn't been his fault. But his death would break his promise to look after Setelin, would leave her without—not protection; the woman had made her spirit into a fortress stronger even than Marlow—but without company, moral support any nearer than Oulian's village. He was at least of use to her in that.

"He is a spiteful fool," Cantu hissed. "He dreams of forcing Setelin to call for a ship, call down aid—"

"You mean the Commodore?" Jim asked bluntly.

"Hush! Do you hear him coming? You are as rash as my children," Cantu scolded, and disappeared back up the slope. Jim heard a scattering of pebbles and prepared to lie about them to Vortimer.

Cantu returned the next day, with gourds and a smoked haunch of meat; the village's stores were crowded, he told him, and Oulian's wife requested that Jim honor them by receiving these paltry gifts.

"You lay in Melinkor's hands," Cantu hissed at Jim. "What you do not know is that the Commodore commands no men on this world whom he does not steal. He robs Melinkor of people and keeps them in a kind of outpost that makes Melinkor's stockade look like a child's model of our village."

"If the Commodore's fort is so strong, why would he bother with the likes of Vortimer?"

Cantu jerked his chin at the shed where Setelin guarded the base computer with codes and stunners. "Be on your guard," he said.

30

In the days that followed, others from the village made the climb down the rocks to the outpost. Two or three times, Jim heard laughter bubbling from the garden and saw Setelin working with other women of her age. She smiled, and years fell from her face, making her a girl again.

Once or twice, a crew of men aided him in prying up a ruined wall and building it to prevent the soil from running off the ledge in the autumn rains. They had been singing some song Jim did not know as they levered up the rocks, each one bellowed in a different key, with all of them chiming in for the chorus and Jim trying to follow along, when a streak of light darted across the sky.

The song broke off.

Moments later, Vortimer came into view, an expression of such hatred on his face that no one had heart for music anymore or to do more than warn Jim, as everyone did. "That man hates you. Take care," they would whisper.

Jim spent the next day in Oulian's compound, studying the Survey maps that he had painstakingly preserved and comparing them with more recent drawings that showed the sites of the Commodore's fortifications, the landing field he used, and Melinkor's compound. Last of all, and too risky to commit to maps, Oulian directed Stal Viat in tracing out on the ground the siegeworks they had built on the mountainside, the locations of their weapons caches, even the caves under constant guard where their own few aged ships were hidden. And after Jim swore he could draw those maps in his sleep, Stal Viat rubbed out the drawing.

By then it was sunset. Torches were being brought in to supplement dying cold lights, whose flickering cast shadows over the faces of Oulian and his son, and a savory odor teased at Jim's senses. Vortimer had been out late the past couple of nights, and supplies had been even shorter than usual.

He could stay for dinner, stay the night, stay forever, but what, he asked, would Setelin eat; Setelin who guarded the tech hoard that had belonged to her mother and before that, her father the consul?

Cantu accompanied him back downslope, bearing a torch and a pack stuffed with food. Another, even heavier, weighted Jim down. They were followed by the men who had helped Jim raise the retaining wall, songs and all. "Just let Vortimer try to drive them away!" Cantu shouted. "Our singing will scare him off!"

Jim laughed, warm from Oulian's hall and this unexpected gift, not of food, but of protection. Just let Vortimer try something. He was in no mood now to tolerate the little rat.

But, when Jim and his escort finally made the last slide down into a post that seemed all the more dismal in comparison to the home he had left, Vortimer was nowhere in sight. The men refused an offer to stay and eat the food they had brought. Setelin emerged, very quiet, and helped Jim unload the packs. They shared out part of the spoils, and then, because there seemed nothing to say, Jim stretched elaborately and retired.

Setelin remained by the fire, scraping away at what looked like a fused panel. Anywhere else, it would have been discarded without a thought.

* * *

RED ALERT WHOOPED ABOVE JIM'S HEAD, LIGHT FLASHING on and off, screaming at him to rise, to rush to battle stations and await the order to fire. Only he could not fire, he could not move: except for the flares of the alarm, the lights were gone, the drive was gone, scanners were dark, and life support would go next. He was trapped in the dark, bound by his own fear again despite the order to wake, to wake now and fight!

He wanted to escape into sleep; Marlow had slept for twenty years and missed the war, but, "Get up! Get up! Get up!" came the cry, and he shook all over.

Oh God, the ground was shaking. Terror of being trapped inside the cave as the air failed woke him in truth.

He was not alone in the dark. What seemed like an avenging angel in white loomed over him, brandishing fire. He flinched from it until his eyes, when he squeezed them open, could bear the light. It was Setelin, bending so close to him that heat from the torch she held was almost a physical pain. She shook him again, her face more drawn and anxious than he had seen her, even when Vortimer's insults were at their vilest.

Jim leapt to his feet. He had slept clothed. Instantly, Setelin put a weapon into his hand: not a cautionary stunner but the blaster Marlow had given him. How had she gotten it from Melinkor? One of the spies and informants—the friends—that she seemed to have must have smuggled it out. A light on its grip glowed red: she had found a means of charging it.

He swallowed and blinked gummy eyes. "How can I help you?" he asked.

"Can you face four men with this?"

He had been an Alliance arms officer. Her question almost made him laugh. "Oh, more than that," he said. Damn. He was exhausted, his mind was filled to bursting with Oulian's defenses, Neave's words, and now Setelin broke in on his rest with a blaster she had never bothered to tell him she was able to charge.

She drew him out of the cave into the patch of rough

ground that separated the dilapidated prefabs from Vortimer's lean-to. Jim glanced in and found it empty.

She led him toward the shed she had made her own bastion, where she stored her father's gear. "You were to be killed while you slept," she told him.

"Shit!" he hissed. He had thought it was some need of Setelin's that had driven him out, some insult to her or to her mother's grave, but it was only the usual mumbo jumbo about a threat to his life. Who had dreamed a new threat this time?

He felt a jaw-cracking yawn coming on. *Yes, yes,* he thought, *let's get on with it so I can either die or get back to sleep.*

"They are behind the wall," Setelin breathed, almost standing on tiptoe to reach his ear. That damned retaining wall he'd built! He almost laughed. For certain, no good deed went unpunished. "They wait for the signal."

Fire from the torch streamed out, shaking and snapping like a thin sheet of metal in the night wind that brought the scent of golden leaves and fresh water from the valley below. It would be hard to see enemies in the darkness beyond the torchlight. They were a target, yet he felt no fear.

"Who's to set them off?" he asked.

Setelin shook her head, exasperated.

Who do you think, idiot?

"You slept so restlessly that he grew fearful. I watched, too."

"You?" Jim asked. The wind seemed to scour his eyes, and the night was very clear, very beautiful. He had rushed into the night barefoot, and strength seemed to rise from each clump of dirt, each cool rock, up along the nerves of his spine to make his head spin and his eyes dazzle. Overhead, the stars seemed to erupt, reforming into the spangled pattern of eagle's wings, mantling across the light-years, that had won this reach of space its name.

"I watched," she said. "Do you think this was the only night I watched?" He could see indignation and exhaustion in her eyes.

He could hear the ground scrub crunch some meters away.

"Vortimer!" he called. "You son of a—"

"Run!" Setelin told him, her voice breaking.

His throat went dry and he lost the power of speech. No, they hadn't trained a stunner on him—not yet, or he'd have been flat on the ground, not simply wavering.

He looked at the woman gesturing along the path that led to her mother's grave.

"You must run, run to Oulian. They are frightened now: our voices, the light"—she brandished it at the wall—"the charge on your weapon. They know you're alert now, that you're brave, bigger than they, with training they can't match."

"Then why should I run?" Jim asked. If this was the test, he was master of it.

"Tonight, you won. But what of tomorrow, or the night after, or after that? I cannot always guard you." She was shivering as they ran, thinner than he remembered. How many nights had she stayed awake, watching over him? He had had no idea.

"Go to Oulian, you must go to Oulian," she insisted as though she tried to hypnotize him. Indeed, Jim seemed to follow her, half in a trance, past the circle of black rocks that marked her mother's grave, onto the path that would lead upslope to Oulian's village.

"If I run now, I will never stop running," he told her. "Let's take them." He bent lower. "The rocks at the far right," he whispered. "They piled them up. We were going to mortar them the next dry day. One shot from this at the base . . ."

A well-aimed blast would topple the rocks, possibly send the men cowering behind them down the mountainside into the valley. Easy enough for a man with Fleet training.

"Run ahead," he told her. "Let them see you're free and clear. They won't hurt you."

Not as long as they needed the gear Setelin hoarded. If they did not . . . Jim found himself following her as if an unseen cord bound the two of them together.

She ran, as light as if she wore a-gravs, past the wall. The instant she cleared it, Jim fired.

The rocks toppled downslope, but he heard no cries, no falling bodies. With a leap, he cleared the wall and found nothing but a pile of ground scrub, heaped up in a pathetic attempt at cover.

Gradually, he realized he was not only staring at the ground scrub, but it was staring back. The red light of a full blaster charge was light enough to see bright eyes in a face smudged to hide it from the light, an arm, then a shoulder and chest wearing a shipsuit dappled in a crude attempt at camouflage.

"Come out!" he shouted.

Dammit, all this terror for one assassin! Whether he belonged to Melinkor or this mysterious Commodore, or whether Vortimer had bribed him with a promise of who knew what, Jim was furious. For a moment, he longed to jump this imbecile and beat him raw with his fists.

But the man rose to his knees. Steadying a blaster at arm's length, he drew a bead on Jim.

The face was avid, terrified past hatred and fear into a kind of rapture.

Mister, you are one dead son-of-a-bitch, Jim thought to himself. Almost tenderly, he fired and watched the man go incandescent in the moment of rushing him. He was gone before he could hit the ground. Jim saw his blaster fall and scooped it up, without taking his eyes off the wall.

"Who else wants to die?" he demanded. He saw a squat man holding only a stunner and jerked the blaster at him. He didn't have a prayer if Jim fired, and he knew it.

"Not me," he said and dropped his weapon.

"How many more?" Jim demanded. The fire drew closer. Setelin bent to collect Jim's captive's stunner, then stood at his back, keeping the torchlight from blinding him.

"Two, sir," said the man. He coughed from the stench of ozone and vaporized flesh and could not stop staring, like a bird before a venomous snake, into the blaster's tiny lethal muzzle.

"Out of there!" Jim snapped. Two more men climbed up from beneath the lip of the plateau, dropping their weapons, their empty hands stretched up in entreaty to the stars.

JIM GESTURED WITH THE BARREL OF HIS BLASTER FOR THE three to walk ahead of him. Another gesture, and they had formed up into an absolutely silent row. Light from the torch played over their faces, which were drawn with fear. The torch burnt clearly, and Setelin's hand did not shake.

"Link arms!" he ordered.

They obeyed. He jerked the blaster toward them.

"The first one of you who pulls free or turns is a dead man," he said. "Now move it!"

Setelin at his side, Jim herded his prisoners toward the edge of the plateau. The mountain's slope was gentle here. If a man fell and slid, he stood a good chance of surviving. Too good a chance. Setelin had seen him kill once already tonight. That had been in a direct confrontation. This would have been an execution. There was a difference.

Air and adrenaline were intoxicating him. He felt he stood taller than he had ever been.

The three men, their arms linked, stood at the lip of the plateau. They had to be unsure of whether Jim would kill them now or . . .

"Take my greetings to Melinkor—or the Commodore, it doesn't matter which, until I come myself," Jim said.

Obedient to him—or, more likely, to his blaster—they didn't turn a hair. "Jump!" he shouted.

When they hesitated, he fired at the ground behind them, which crumbled, and sent them toppling down. He could hear shouts of pain, fear, and shock, punctuated by rockfalls.

Then Jim turned back to Setelin. The night's fear caught up with him in that moment, and he thought his heart would explode as he gazed at her.

She hurled the torch out into the night, a tiny comet arcing after the three would-be assassins. It hit the ground with a clatter and went out.

Then, she turned toward him. In the starlight, he could see the tiny pulse hammering in her throat.

"I can handle Vortimer myself," she said, calmly tucking the weapons she had collected into her belt. Tiny as she was, her long hair flowing down over her white robe, she looked absurdly dashing and piratical . . . and completely enchanting. "You had better go now."

He fought to breathe, then struggled to win back the power of speech. "You want me to go?" he asked. "You really want me to leave you?"

"It is only a matter of time until you do," she replied. "Like my father: men come and go. Mostly, they die. I have always known this, but until tonight, I have never feared knowing. So go. Go now, before you do more harm than you already have."

Even on that damnable *Irian Jaya,* there had been women who wished there had been time, who looked at him the way Neave had started to watch Marlow. Their eyes were not as bright as Setelin's. Or as sad, made larger and more luminous by unshed tears.

"I won't ever leave you," he forced the words out. "You. A pearl of great price. A jewel. Mine."

He heard Setelin draw in her breath sharply. Greatly daring, he put out his hand and touched her face. She had always been so fearless, but now she dropped her eyes. He drew her into his arms. She trembled, but did not move away. She had stayed awake, guarding him; how weary she must be, how frightened, not for herself, but for him and her whole world. How cold. Well, he would warm her.

Jim bent and kissed her hair, then rested his chin against its sleekness, ruffled by the night wind. She was warm now, pliant, as she decided to believe him and relaxed into his arms. Her hands, stroking down his back, were the best thing he had ever felt.

He tilted her chin up. So brave, meeting his eyes with her fears, her doubt, and her desire, the match for his. She was brave and he had been a fool, not to have seen before. This was the best thing, better than Marlow's friendship, better than Neave's trust, better than Oulian's welcome. . . .

"How long?" he began to ask, like an utter fool. She shivered and rose on tiptoe, so they were almost eye to eye: he could see himself haloed with starlight in her eyes. She brushed his lips with hers, and he felt his knees go weak, and drew her closer to assuage his own trembling with her warmth.

"It's cold," he whispered. "We should go in."

When he took her hand and started back, she matched his pace, so close to him that her very breaths and heartbeats were timed with his own.

Aviva, Orbital and Downworld

31

If Aviva's refit facilities hadn't been the best in the sector, you'd have had to tie me down to make me go there, which is what Chief Medical Officer Tom Ankeny damn near did.

"Come on, Cam," *Gavroche*'s resident sadist coaxed. "You know GW will nurse *Gavroche* through refit. Get yourself checked out too."

What was it Tom thought the specialists at Aviva Memorial could do for me that he couldn't? Resurrection had already cost me one career.

Tom steered me, hand ready at my elbow In Case, to the umbilical mating *Gavroche* to Aviva's orbital station. I'd have preferred to take my gig, but, after the late unpleasantness off Shushan, we'd had to cannibalize it for parts.

It wasn't that I didn't trust GW to steer my ship through refit. I'd trust GW with my life and had, a number of times, not least Shushan. It was the damn downworld medics on

Aviva Memorial I didn't trust further than I could spit, assuming they didn't take that reaction as further evidence I was unfit to command.

Pat Morias was offwatch, leaning beside the tube's iris. Usually, you had to chase Pat away from Communications even when she was off duty. Moral support, no doubt.

"Take care, Captain," she told me. "Write if you get work."

Very damn funny.

I paused, which meant Tom had to stop too. Just to annoy him, I bent to inspect a discolored patch on a power conduit. I straightened back up, slowly, adjusting my face so no one saw me wince. Three broken ribs, a punctured lung, and a lacerated spleen aren't things you simply bounce back from.

"I'll write if she doesn't," said Ryutaro Jones, standing beside Pat, duffle at his feet. If Pat picked up the lounging-and-sarcasm habit from him, it was high time I got the spoiled bastard off my ship. He turned for a final smug inspection of the white enamel patchwork beside the umbilical. His work, that patch. Not only had he reported to me during the Shushan raid—Becker had turned him into a thoroughly useful operative—but once we'd tossed the pirates off our decks into the brig we'd finally improvised and not a moment too soon, he'd volunteered to be hands and feet for the crew. After as brief an interval of hazing as could be considered honorable, they'd taken him at his word and started him where all good crew starts, doing scutwork.

Actually, Shushan was more aggravating than it was dramatic: some pirates took a cutter-pod and boarded *Gavroche*. Things got hand to hand fast. The boarding party and my crew had been too mixed up for me to risk gas on deck or simply vent atmosphere. Someone jumped me from behind. I remember the weight on my back, a crack, the sickening breathlessness of the pain before adrenaline took over and saved my life. I managed to fall free, then whirl and kick the man who'd sneaked up behind me where it counted.

Then, quite literally frothing at the mouth, I rallied my able-bodieds—including Jones, who could never obey orders like "stay in your cabin till the fight's over" worth a damn—to drive them back with hoses venting liquid oxygen. And then, finally, I had time to pass out.

By the time I fought my way out of the painkillers Tom had me on, I had to turn cruel, deaf ears to suggestions that the crew space them or work them over with hammers. Ankeny, serve him right for knocking me out, got stuck thawing the bastards out as best he could. As soon as the survivors were processed, they'd be shipped to Aviva Memorial's secure wards. Never saw so many cases of freezer burn in my life. Scared the hell out of me.

"We can trust Jones to get the captain downworld, can't we, Jones?" Pat asked, grinning. Apparently, spraying pirates with LOX is a bonding experience. And seeing their natural enemy in the form of a spruce young journalist crouched on his haunches polishing the deck the good old-fashioned way has a remarkable effect on morale.

They'd even visited him in Sick Bay—a little matter of some lost skin from the LOX—and told him stories to take his mind off the grafts. Probably, he'd recorded them, but they didn't care. He was ours. One of us.

"Assuming Jones can stick his nose into Gan Salem Station without Security throwing his ass out." Now Ankeny contributed to the hazing. The only patient who'd ever matched Jones for sheer crankiness, he'd said, had been me.

"Stop worrying!" Jones said. "I was the first person to interview the captain when she woke up. You think I'm dumb enough to risk my prize subject?"

His eyes met mine. Jones was the best ally I could have in case some medic at Aviva Memorial, some damn civ hotshot surgeon decided to test me, call me into his office, sit me down, and force me through a learning experience that added up to one thing: you're grounded, Captain. Pack your gear; thumbprint goes in this square; blink for the nice retinal scan; and go collect your pension.

The trick was to stay away from medics, except for Tom, whom I knew I could trust to massage my fitness reports.

Jones draped the strap of my bag over his shoulder, picked up his own gear, and tenderly took my arm—for all the worlds as if I were some crippled great-great aunt. I jerked myself free and led the way, nose in the air, to the civilian shuttle and another unpleasant bit of solicitude. Overprivileged damn Ryu'd conspired with Tom to book us into First Class.

"Ship can't afford this," I said, starting to dig in my heels. "Where's the purser?"

"Take it up with my editor," Jones said. "I expensed the ride."

Sticking the newsfeeds with the tab for the ride downworld had a certain larcenous charm, I'll grant, even if my private guess was Jones had paid for it himself. He's never been able to lie to me worth a damn.

"I don't suppose you'd say I gave you the slip once we land," I suggested.

"I gave the first officer my word," Jones said. "It's as much as my life is worth to go back on it." He waved away the steward, checked my buckles (neatly trapping me), and strapped in.

So much for my idea of going to ground in some hostel somewhere and just getting some rest. Jones wouldn't let me. The crew wouldn't just kill him, they'd withdraw their trust.

Jones shepherded me past the lotus pillars and security checks of Gan Salem station. If he was a terminal pain in the ass about making sure I didn't give him the slip, he was clearly alpha newsman in this sector, which kept the other pests away.

But intrepid Jones got a surprise—and a good comeuppance—once we got outside.

Warrant Officer Murad, H for Hamid, stood at rest beside a silver groundcar I remembered only too well. Coming to ponderous attention, he saluted me crisply with his prosthetic arm while glaring at Jones. So Murad still had a mad on because Jones had slipped through his security?

"Officer Murad!" Jones said, turning up the cordiality and

bringing out the needle. "Good to see you. I promise, I haven't got any pheromone tracers on me this time."

"You're tempting fate," I muttered out of one side of my mouth.

"It's a dirty job, but someone's got to do it, Captain."

Ponderously, Murad ignored this by-play. "Captain Marlow," he said, the words rumbling through his esophageal implant, "with the captain's permission, the Commissioner has sent me to bring you to the Residence." Jones grinned at the formally twisted syntax. Murad ignored that too. Lucky for Jones. Never saw a man for living on borrowed time like that, except for one.

I didn't want to see Amory Eliot Neave now, not when I was injured, not when I might be grounded for good. Neave had a weakness for me, I knew. The past two trips I'd made here . . . without Jones . . . I thought the feeling might be mutual . . . but no future at all is better than a soft future grounded in pity.

"I am supposed to report to Aviva Memorial for treatment," I said. Hell of a note when a hospital looks like a better option than a friend's home. I flashed Jones an "all right, who squealed?" look.

"Treatment has been arranged at the Residence," Murad replied, standing at attention. His eyes didn't so much look at us as through us. He touched a stud on his belt and the groundcar's door opened. "If the captain will kindly board . . . and . . . Mr. Jones."

I gestured for Jones to get in first: not just protocol, but precaution in case Murad had a justifiable desire to slam the door on his ass. Murad settled me with as much care as Jones had on board the shuttle. "Welcome back, Captain," he said.

Three whole extra words? The worlds were coming to an end. Jones gave me a look, which I ignored.

A decanter of pure water glittered, cold and pure, in the groundcar's bar. As the car started, Jones poured, just like a good little ensign.

"Official welcome, Cam? If Neave's taken an *interest*"—I

glared at him—"guess you don't have to worry about staying grounded."

I eased an incipient case of spacer's throat with the water. "Jones, if you can't talk better sense, I'm going to sleep."

I eased myself into a position that didn't mash my ribs against the strappings Tom had put on me with the care of some ancient Egyptian embalmer. Murad hadn't dimmed the windows, and I blinked sleepily at the sun, which gleamed off Aviva's trees and hedges. Sun and leaves formed a soothing, intricate pattern, and I fell into a light doze. Privilege of age.

By the time I woke, we were out beyond Gan Salem's shield rings and into the fields. More of them were green now: Aviva's terraforming efforts were really taking hold.

I sipped more water as the car drew up before the Residence. It eased the cough; I didn't want Amory to see me wheezing and hacking.

He was waiting for me beneath the lanterns welded from old ship parts that I remembered from my past trips here. Even before Murad could leave the car, Neave had leapt forward to open the door and hand me out with the archaic care I recalled. He took my bag himself and nodded dismissal at Murad.

I *think* Jones managed to grab his duffle before Murad drove off.

"I'm relieved to see you looking so well, Caroline," Neave said. "When I heard you were injured, I confess I was expecting—"

I shook my head. "Much ado about nothing." He grinned: my last trips here I'd had time to poke through his library.

"I thought my residence could afford you a few more amenities than Aviva Memorial, efficient as its facilities are. There should be no trouble about speeding your return to your ship."

I glanced away, to hide my relief.

"We need you," he added. *I need you* was what I didn't know if I wished him to say. "And, of course, Mr. Jones. I have completed another chapter since your last visit, Mr. Jones, and I shall welcome your critique. I've taken the liberty of placing some books you will like to see in your room, the same accommodations as last time. And, of course, feel free to use my library."

Jones bowed Tokugawan-style and won a chuckle.

"Thank you, Commissioner." I decided it was high time I said something, anything.

"You know better than that, Caroline," he said.

He knew better than that too. I hadn't been Caroline since my too-short childhood.

"It's Amory, just as it's always been."

Neave escorted us through the main hall, then through the atrium with its fountain, splashing welcome at us, lotuses floating near its rim, and into the windowed corridor toward the guest quarters. These corridors felt almost as familiar as my ship, and I felt myself relax into their welcome.

Made me damned nervous.

Jones angled cheerfully off to his usual room, leaving me alone with Amory, who led me to the suite that had been my home downworld. The raku vase I liked, with its iridescent bronzes and greens, had been replaced by a flat ceramic dish filled with water and rounded pebbles. One lotus blossom, blue, with a tinge of lilac, floated within.

"Genetically engineered," he said. "Aviva's latest export."

Beyond the carved room divider, the plain low bed that had given me such rest had been replaced with top-of-the-line hospital standard, complete with bioscreens. "All the comforts of home, I see."

Amory didn't quite flush. "Aviva Memorial set conditions for your coming here."

Oh, I was going to *space* Tom Ankeny. On second thought, that would be too quick. Maybe I'd turn the LOX hose on him and take bids on where I should aim it.

"Let me reassure you about your medical treatment, Cam. A team of medics will report to you tomorrow. For now, I am sure you will wish to rest until dinner. We will meet at sundown. If you are hungry before then . . ." He gestured at the comm light, now glowing the same blue as the lotus.

The door slid closed. Neave's footsteps receded down the hall. I bent somewhat painfully to retrieve my duffle and unpack. I was breathing more easily now than I had since the attack. Probably the benefits of a lush, planetary atmosphere. I would bathe in water that had not been recycled. I would eat food that had not been reconstituted. And Neave had just lifted my fear of being told I was no longer fit, no longer useful.

Now, if only my eyes would stop blurring.

THE OTHER TIMES I HAD DINED WITH AMORY, HE HAD INsisted on a level of "proper service" I hadn't endured since Raffles Station. After awhile, though, the unobtrusive formality of the staff and Neave's attentive courtesy had become almost endearing.

This dinner had been set out buffet-style. "People may be coming and going," Neave explained the extra place settings. But the fruits and vegetables glowed with ripeness, easily as beautiful as the flowers on the table, which looked pretty edible, too. He himself had caught the broiled fish that day, he told me, and preened a bit.

Dismissing staff, Neave poured the golden wine I had learned to like into generous glasses that caught the light of sunset slanting in from the floor-to-ceiling windows. He had even had music piped in. Its archaic, intricate formality was almost as refreshing as the wine.

Jones, of course, wasn't at a loss. "Thank you for the flute music in my room," he said, bowing.

Neave inclined his head. "I find Handel more suitable for meals," he said. "Or perhaps Vivaldi. God's in his heavens; all's right with the worlds; and here comes the final, triumphant resolution on a C-major chord. Tokugawan music requires more disciplined listening, at least for me."

I didn't understand a word they said. But I smiled anyway.

Footsteps at a window brought me sharply aware. Neave

rose and let in a dark-haired man about my height and Jones' age, who gave a hasty tug on his wrinkled formal tunic as if he'd just scrambled into it.

"Dr. Marx," Neave nodded.

Jones rose in courtesy.

"My patients told me to go on ahead and eat. They will join us briefly for after dinner if they feel up to it."

"Patients?" The word came out too shrill. I reached for my water glass, though I'd have been happier with the wine. What this adversary in the form of a doctor didn't see me drink wouldn't hurt me.

"Two crew from *Blue Ridge*," Neave said. "You know the ship."

I set down the glass.

"The ship's navigator and chief petty officer are on medical leave."

A run or two through the Straits won't kill you, but it's different for specialists. I hadn't liked the look of its people last time I hooked up with them. If Neave had brought them here for treatment, I was inclined to forgive him for conspiring with my CMO.

"You are an oncologist, sir?" I nodded at this Dr. Marx. If I'd tested positive for cancer, surely, Tom would have started treatment already.

"They've already had their bout with the specialists." The man's light tenor voice was so pleasant it should have been registered as a deadly weapon. I could just imagine the jokes about his bedside manner. "I'm strictly general practice. As soon as my patients recovered from treatment, Commissioner Neave had them brought out here for rehab." He had his back to me as he helped himself hastily to fish and salad. "If you know anything about the straits-runners—"

"Somewhat," I murmured, carefully not looking at Neave *or* Jones.

"Then, you know their crews keep to themselves. The wards at Aviva Memorial practically made these two agoraphobic, so we thought they'd do better here. Commissioner

Neave was kind enough to let us set up the guest house as a sort of infirmary."

Marx set down a well-filled plate and began to eat, as if fearing he'd be called away. He waved aside Neave's offer of wine. "I'm still on duty," he said.

I managed not to glare at him. Amory had promised I had nothing to fear, but I feared this cheerful doctor shoveling in the food at Neave's table.

"*Blue Ridge* is too isolated," I remarked. "But all the ships in the No Man's Worlds are a little strange. Two hundred years from now, we probably won't recognize a tenth of their customs. Two thousand years, assuming a high rate of mutation, the straits-runners may not be—"

"Remotely human?" Dr. Marx finished my sentence doctor-fashion through a mouthful of fish. "You'd be a better ship-master than a geneticist, Captain, or God help the Alliance. Still, the possibility is something we—the staff here—want to guard against. Inbreeding. The fragmentation of the species into space-faring and planet-bound."

"You think that could be the cause of the next—"

"War?" Marx cut into Jones' thought, as if the word were an obscenity. "We're not going to let it get so far. Never again. The Secessionist war taught us the folly of letting ethnic and racial identification inherited from Earth divide us. The culture we're rebuilding now is so precarious that we must hang together . . ."

"Or we will assuredly hang separately." Neave laughed and pushed a filled wineglass toward Dr. Marx again. "Aaron, I haven't heard my old political slogans turned on me at my own table that neatly in years!" He saluted the physician with his own glass.

Marx nodded, then turned to Amory, raising his eyebrows in question. "I was letting you catch up with my other guests," Neave said. "I don't think you've had an uninterrupted meal since you moved out here. Captain, may I present Dr. Aaron Marx? Doctor, Captain Caroline Marlow of the Relief Vessel

Gavroche. And Ryutaro Jones, whose work you've surely read."

"Honored," Marx said, efficiently consuming his dinner and looking for more. He rose to serve himself and passed behind my chair, more closely than I would have liked. He paused.

"I am supposed to examine you tomorrow," he announced. "Your chief medical officer sent us your records. Forgive me for talking business at the table, but suppose you tell me what you think is wrong with you."

Jones opened his mouth to begin diversionary tactics.

"I took some damage in a boarding action," I said candidly. "Pirates."

Usually, the word diverts civilians about as well as a red alert, but Marx wasn't fooled. Reluctantly, I continued.

"Broken ribs, a punctured lung, some damage to my spleen, my CMO said. What he's really worried about is how well I'm holding up. I took some freezer burn during my resurrection some years back."

"Cryogenic trauma," Marx corrected me. "Yes, you're *that* Marlow. The baseline restoration case. We're using your medical history to help treat the people you brought in. But let me tell you, Captain, if you were going to have problems beyond the usual senile deterioration, they'd have showed up already. Of course, if you're planning to expose yourself to any heavy radiation—"

"Perhaps this topic might be pursued more appropriately after you and the captain have conferred?" Neave suggested. His voice was polite, but firm: a host making command decisions about dinner-table conversation like the senior officer in a wardroom.

Jones leapt into the breach with an astonishingly tactful—for Jones—political question. Marx rose eagerly to the bait. Their young men's voices rose, refighting the last generation's battles with an earnestness that made me smile. Years ago, I had been able to summon that kind of passion—and to eat in mid-argument without choking on my food. Now, I preferred to sit back, fingering the stem of my wine glass as I watched Amory watching the doctor and the reporter as if they were promising students.

Finally, Jones sat back and closed his mouth. Even Dr. Marx seemed to have had enough to eat. "I believe we are ready for dessert," Neave said. "Shall I call your patients, or will you bring them here?"

"I'll call them," Marx said. "They're used to me."

He disappeared through the long windows, an uncomfortable interval during which Jones, Neave, and I surveyed each other.

Finally, irrepressibly, Jones broke the silence. "Commissioner, isn't this your cue to say, 'I suppose you're all wondering why I called this meeting'?"

"No," said Neave, rising. "This is my cue to greet my other guests."

"Here we are!" Marx stepped briskly through what I now recollected from some long-ago scrap of reading were called French doors.

Two men followed him more hesitantly. "May I present *Blue Ridge*'s navigator, Vanya Ostrogorsky, and Crew Chief Yang Cho Lee?"

I'd only worked with *Blue Ridge*'s purser and her master. It wasn't prejudice to say all the straits-runners looked alike, regardless of their racial or ethnic background: anyone who'd ever dealt with one of them would instantly identify their caution, pallor, and constrained posture, all occupational hazards from spending your life in cramped ships subjected to high radiation. Not to mention the cancers for which Neave had brought them here.

Marx be damned: a couple centuries from now, given inbreeding and spontaneous mutations, they'd be well on their way to becoming a separate species. Assuming any of them survived with their fertility more or less unimpaired. RUMINT had it that the women in the straits-running culture lived on carefully shielded stations, earning their way by managing refits and finances for the entire clan.

Blue Ridge's two runners stood straighter than the ones I remembered, as if they had finally decided to trust planetary gravity and not constantly keep one hand for the ship and their knees bent in case they fell. If the overhead lights were any indication, they weren't quite as gray and lacked the facial lesions that had worried me on the captain and purser. If Marx had gotten agoraphobics outside, I was probably safe in his hands.

For straits-runners, these two might be miracles of social adjustment, but they were still very shy, standing in Dr. Marx's shadow, looking away from the rest of us.

"I'm glad to see men off *Blue Ridge,*" I made my voice quiet, as if I spoke to frightened animals. "She's a fine ship."

They turned to each other, and nodded.

"Captain Marlow," Nav Officer Ostrogorsky said softly, not meeting my eyes. "My captain speaks well of you, and your friend does you credit."

Friend? Neave, although I couldn't see *Blue Ridge*s speaking of him with such familiarity. A moment later, I made the connection. They meant Jim.

Dammit, this was starting to bear astonishing resemblance to one of Neave's better set-ups. All we needed was Abram Becker just happening to drop in for coffee to complete the innocent family party.

"I hope he's well," I said politely. "And I'm glad to see you're getting the care you deserve."

"Your friend is very well," Ostrogorsky replied. "He was an . . . a quiet shipmate."

My plan had called for him to leave *Blue Ridge* on the smallest ship that could handle the last leg of the Aquila run.

Secrets. Surprises. At some point, Amory Eliot Neave owed me one hell of a long explanation. But Ostrogorsky was whispering on, "We wait only for our discharge to return to our ship before the next two can come here. The Commissioner intends for all of us to be treated. We have established a rotation schedule that will allow us to fulfill our contracts while our shipmates are healed."

He and Yang nodded at Neave—salutes were for officers, and bows weren't in their repertory.

Jones was leaning forward, his eyes shining, his mouth open at the prospects of what he called "the story of a lifetime" each time he found one.

"What may I offer you? I understand Dr. Marx is overseeing your diet," Neave said.

Marx walked to the sideboard and uncovered a dish of fruits and a tray of pastries. "These will do you no harm," he said. "And I want you to drink as much of the water as you can."

Jones pulled two chairs away from the table invitingly. When the *Blue Ridge*s didn't move, Marx picked up a plate and began to fill it. "Come," he said, lowering his voice.

To my surprise, the crewmen looked at me. My eyes stung: no doubt some pollens in the air. "Downworld food always looks strange after a long cruise, doesn't it?" I said. "You keep thinking it belongs in an exhibit, not on your plate. But it's not doing any good out there on the sideboard, and if you don't eat, it'll only go to waste. Unless, of course, Dr. Marx is still hungry."

I thought I almost saw smiles. Maybe they didn't know what to do. Then it was for a commanding officer to lead them. Poor bastards, so scared and shy away from their home ship.

"Let's see what they've got for us," I said, joining Marx in filling up a plate. "These look good"—I pointed to a bowl of strawberries that never saw a hydroponics tank—"assuming you're not allergic. Are they, Doctor? And the last time I had these little iced cakes, they were sweet, but not heavy enough to keep you from sleeping." I talked them through the entire tempting array. Ostrogorsky even ventured to choose *two* raspberry tarts. Real butter in those crusts.

With the gentleness Jones had shown me at Havilland Roads, he helped Dr. Marx coax the two crewmembers into their chairs. No wine for them, but they drank glass after glass of the sparkling water as Marx and Jones kept up a soothing patter of conversation. The crew chief, who seemed content to let Ostrogorsky, as senior officer, talk for both of them, even smiled once.

Finally, after even Dr. Marx had eaten enough, Neave rose.

"It has been a long day for you," he told the *Blue Ridges*.

That was dismissal. They rose and nodded again, this time at all of us.

"At some point," Jones said, "I'd be glad of a word with you. Several words. There are people—more people like the Commissioner—who need to know about the job you do, where you've been, what you've seen. What you—and the other ships like yours—need."

"Why not now?" asked Neave. "You and Dr. Marx can walk them back to the guest house—it's across the gardens—and continue your conversation there."

Jones' escort seemed a drastic suggestion to the *Blue Ridges* but at a nod from Dr. Marx, they fell in with the idea.

Jones awarded Neave and me both glares and followed.

"He'll probably get another book out of it," Neave said, laughing.

"And he'd rather be here, learning what you have planned. Because you do have something planned, don't you, Amory?"

32

Neave sat motionless at the head of his shining table. The emptied plates and the last of the wine seemed somehow forlorn. The music he had ordered piped in tinkled on in its exquisite, oblivious geometries. It no longer reassured me.

He pressed a button beneath the table, and the music subsided in mid-phrase.

"Come sit by the fountain, Cam," he said. "We'll have coffee there, and Aviva produces a more-than-tolerable ice wine I want you to try."

I allowed him to pull my chair back and guide me to the atrium. Lights glowed in the water, the shadows they cast dancing with the strands of white lights that twisted along the potted blossoming plants that filled each corner. From a small table, Neave gave me coffee and a glass, like breath caught in crystal, filled with a potent, almost syrupy wine whose flavor enticed and relaxed me.

At his gesture, I seated myself on the broad rim of the fountain. I was glad, at least, for Fleet discipline, or this world of Neave's—unobtrusive staff, archaic music, and talk of "tolerable" wines that were delicious beyond anything I had ever drunk—would have made me as edgy as the crew of *Blue Ridge*.

I held up the glass. "It's wonderful," I said. Even if I lacked the proper words for wine, I could at least say what I liked. "Another of Aviva's exports? You'll make this a rich world yet."

Amory Neave glanced up into the night sky. The night wind riffled his thinning hair. "If you've ever seen a slagged world, you know Aviva already is rich past price," he said. "Look!"

A tiny fire, then another and another, streaked across the dark sky. "I was told there would be a meteor shower tonight. I'm glad it's clear." He sighed.

"Then we're in luck."

"Are we? I would miss this if I left," he said.

I decided the wine had a bitter aftertaste and set my glass aside with a click.

"Do you plan to return to Earth?" I asked in a hoarse voice that didn't sound like mine.

"Several times this past year, I thought of it," Neave admitted. "Once, I even went as far as to check ship schedules. Then, information reached me that made me realize that the time for me to leave had been years ago."

"Is there ever a right time?" I asked. I decided to give the wine another chance. Still too sweet, but it took the chill off the ice that had formed in my belly. Foolish of me to care.

"For what? For escaping one's duty or a place one is bound to? Never. For returning home?" he shrugged, his expression wry. "Frankly, if I even have a home anymore, this is it."

"You do very well here," I observed.

Neave set his glass down so hard I expected it to shatter, as if the music that had played throughout dinner suddenly broke into jangling discords.

"Look in the water, Caroline. On Earth, there is a long-legged insect that scurries across still ponds. It is very light, superficial, and it keeps in constant motion so it doesn't sink. I feel like a waterbug: accepting this house, filling it with the collections of a lifetime, dabbling in agriculture and exports, while all the time—"

"Amory, what's wrong?"

I stood, glad for the first time that evening that I was wearing fatigues, not the blue dinner dress I remembered from Raffles Station and a night when Jones wept into his brandy. I still had that dress, packed away somewhere. Blue dresses might be a part of Neave's world. They'd never been part of mine.

"Let me refill your glass, Cam," Neave said. "This is a long story, and not one I'm particularly proud of. Do you think I liked feeling relief when I heard you'd been injured at Shushan? I despised myself. Still, I knew it meant you'd be back here and—"

My face and throat and hands went hot, then cold, then hot again. "Amory, there is no need for this. I am always glad to see you." I looked up into his face, which twisted in the shadows. I even managed to laugh. "I don't think you're telling me . . . just . . . that you want me," I went on, turning my face away so he wouldn't see the memories of Ragozinski the night before he killed himself, frozen in my eyes. "And I don't know what I'd say if you did."

He put out a hand to me, a friend's hand, a comrade's hand,

nothing more, I told myself. "But for me to say anything at all, you must tell me what you want me to know."

Neave's bark of laughter made me flinch. "Cam, I'd like nothing better than to tell you . . . just to let it be." He shook his head and settled back down on the fountain's rim, his posture alert, an officer explaining a plan of action, not a civilized man spending the evening with a woman whom he cared for. "Please let me say this much. I've thought of it. God knows, I have. But I'd be acting like those water-bugs again to ask you to stay, to keep you here, pretend to build a life here—"

"You're expecting trouble." My coffee was cold, as sour in my mouth as the too-rich wine.

"I've been in touch with our friend Jim," he said. "He's thriving. Once or twice, some of his people—oh yes, he's got quite the following—have taken one of Oulian's craft off-world and rendezvoused with the *Blue Ridge*. Jim helped them refit the ships and reconfigure their communications gear. *Blue Ridge* picked up a man named Stal Viat, Oulian's son—I suppose he's some sort of nephew to me—and a man named Cantu, who's become Jim's right hand and maybe a finger or two on the left."

"Jim's all right?" I asked it in a breath.

"Like a hero in a book."

I felt like an idiot in a book as I brought both hands together, applauding Jim. For once, I could say "absent friends" and not have to weep.

"Don't I wish I could simply say 'this time we pulled it off, this is one man we've saved'?" Neave demanded. "I've got transcripts of his messages. You'll like reading them, but you'll want to do it by daylight or you'll be so excited you won't sleep, and I'll hear about it from young Dr. Marx.

"Jim's set himself up in a place he calls The Fort. Used to belong to one of the local warlords. The man was a realist and tried to kill him, but Jim forced him out."

"Is he keeping an eye on the man?" I couldn't help asking.

"He's moved to a place called Silver River. Pretty site, Jim says. Not particularly defensible. And word gets round. Jim's got his ear to the ground. Meanwhile, he's been trying to act as a military advisor to Oulian, but Oulian and his people were having none of it. It is Jim who must lead, and no other. He doesn't want to—you'll have to read the letters—but ultimately, he took over this Fort place and consolidated the old warlord's hoard of technology from the First Ship's landing."

"That was how he could get Exquemelin's ships offworld at all," I mused. "They might have done, after a fashion, for suborbital fights, but Jim . . . he was a good scrounger I remember."

"They didn't know what they had, but he did," Neave agreed. "So now, they're prospering. A couple more years, and Exquemelin may start to trade, thanks to ships like *Blue Ridge*. Provided we're able to keep on helping them."

I began to pace around the fountain. "If the news is good," I said, "dammit, Amory, why'd you go and scare me?"

He rose and blocked my path, standing so close to me that the warmth of his body sheltered me from the night wind.

"Cam, did you see the shield generators when you drove out?"

"I took a nap. What did I miss?"

"They're back on-line," Neave said. He checked his wrist. "In fact, just about now—"

I only thought I felt the pavement shudder. But I couldn't have imagined how light fanned out from each shield generator, up into the night sky like water flowing over glass until they coalesced into a dome that covered all of Gan Salem.

"The council's running the numbers right now," Neave said, raising his voice to be heard over the wind that rushed in to displace the air destroyed by the passage of the shields. "They're applying for matching funds from the Alliance to build additional generators to protect later installations."

Thunder rumbled overhead, and a bolt of lightning that reminded me unpleasantly of energy weapons, crackled into a field near the Residence. It hit close by. I could smell the ozone. A siren went off. The *Blue Ridge*s would treat it like Red Alert, and Marx would be lucky if he didn't need to sedate them.

"We're going to have one hell of a storm," I remarked. It had been at least ten years since I'd been downworld in an electrical storm. I had to admit I wasn't looking forward to it. A fat drop of rain spattered on my cheek, to be followed by another, and another. . . .

Neave and I grabbed up bottles, cups, and glasses, then dashed across the atrium into the hall. To my surprise, I was actually laughing. The air was deliciously cool, chilly, even, as the rain dried on my skin and clothes. I found myself grinning at Neave, who grinned back, then set down the bottle and glasses he carried.

"I'd better check on my other guests!" Neave said.

"Let Jones help," I suggested. "Seriously. He was useful after Shushan."

"I'll just look in," promised Neave. "Why don't you take the ice wine to the library, and we can finish up the bottle?"

And he was off, splashing again through the atrium. "Don't fall into the fountain!" I shouted, just for the joy of it.

The library was even cooler than the hall, and I was glad to pick up a square of soft fabric interwoven with some glittery thread from an outsize chair and wrap it around my shoulders. I hit climate control for a little more warmth, and sank into the cushions of a large couch.

Footsteps in the doorway brought me around in time to see Neave take off his jacket and shake it, sending a spatter of drops onto the spotless floor. "That Jones! He had them so busy telling him stories of the Straits they barely even noticed the storm. So I came back. Dr. Marx says not to keep you awake too long."

"I promise not to sleep at all unless you tell me what you've been hinting at all evening," I told him. And laughed again, like the woman in the blue dress whom I wasn't and never would be.

Neave accepted a filled glass from me and tossed half of the ice wine down as if he needed its warmth. "Dr. Marx can execute me tomorrow. Dammit, Cam, it's good to have you here."

I met his eyes. At that moment, I wanted to be that woman in the blue dress, the serene, happy creature who could hear "It's good to have you here" and believe it. Who could hold out her hand, touch her friend's face . . .

"The generators," I prompted him then. "They've brought them back on-line and are planning to build more."

"Becker and I are lobbying for the next Fleet sector base to be built here. Mind you, we'll have to lease the East Continent to Fleet. The idea is to apply the lease payments to the shield generators. Even if we wind up having to pay for them, we're still going to come out the winner, when you consider what a Base's presence will do to the assessed valuation of the rest of Aviva's land."

Neave might focus on the economics of his plan, but I saw something else. "You're setting this world up to be one hell of a target before that Base goes live," I warned him. "Assuming you get it."

"There's always a critical interval between when a frontier world becomes too prosperous and when the rest of the system catches up. Aviva's already in pretty good shape. Even though the nearest base is three Jumps away, Ararat's nearby, and our planetary militias signed a mutual defense alliance last year.

"Frankly, I'm not worried about Aviva. It's got all the advantages that Exquemelin—Jim's world—lacks." His voice trailed off

I shivered and pulled the soft wrap more tightly around my shoulders. The gilt threads twinkled in the track lights that picked out maps, portraits, the occasional artifact. I saw a copper coffee pot I remembered.

"Jim," I said. "You think he's in danger?"

"Not right now," Neave reassured me. "Jim told me—here, I'll get you those transcripts—someone called the Commodore was shipping people offworld. Jim put a stop to that. For now."

I rose and walked over to Neave as he rifled through stacks and stacks of transcripts on the organized chaos that passed as his workstation. He turned quickly, standing so close to me I could feel his breath, and took me by the forearms.

A noise at the door spun us both around.

"The *Blue Ridge*s are asleep!" Jones announced triumphantly. "But they invited me to breakfast tomor—oh, I didn't mean to interrupt anything."

Even in the half-light, I could see color darken Jones' cheekbones. I was blushing too. Tomorrow, I could report to Dr. Marx that there was definitely nothing wrong with my circulation.

"You interrupted a briefing," I said, trying to rescue the situation before Jones bolted.

I met Neave's eyes, drained my glass in a silent "absent friends," then set it down. "Will you let Jones in on this, Amory, or do we send him to bed with those Tokugawan squalls as a lullaby?" I asked.

"Since you're here, you may as well listen," Amory told the younger man, who dropped into a chair the length of the room away. "No, come in closer. You don't want to have to commute to the wine, do you?

"Jones has been bringing me some of the pieces I've put together. So here's as much of the story as I know. Abram Becker and I've got enough information now to believe that Exquemelin has been targeted by wreckers. Abram calls it the Iago Syndrome."

Jones, damn him, was nodding.

"Can we at least have this in plain speech?" I asked.

To my surprise, Neave colored unbecomingly. "I'll try not to lecture," he said.

"Thank you, Professor." Jones won a laugh from both of us.

"It's a case of history repeating itself, or being about to unless we try our damnedest to stop it. If you look first at

Earth history and then the history of our expansion into space, for every colony that rebuilt itself and prepared to sign the compacts that would give it membership either in a planetary commonwealth or in a—let's call it a meta-government—such as the Alliance, there are people who see power and profit in disunity. As a result, their goal is to stop the consolidations of these governments and, in the ensuing chaos, to step into the breach and claim such a place as their own personal empire."

"You promised you wouldn't lecture," Jones commented, refilling Neave's glass. "It's damn thirsty work."

"I'll keep it brief. Or try. On Earth, we had periods of warlords. Subsequently, when we made it out into space, when a group of planetary governments thought that the Alliance was becoming too powerful, they seceded, and we're still paying the price. We've fought back to some sort of equilibrium, but now we face new enemies."

"Like the pirates in the Shushan System?" I asked. Nasty characters. Peopled from genetic stock scavenged off stolen ships and protected by contraband weapons systems, the pirates who'd moved into Shushan System had meant to move in there for good.

"There's worse," Neave said. "That's why Abram refers to the Iago Syndrome, from a line in an ancient play. The line, spoken by one of the protagonists, a noncom named Iago—you'd call him the villain—runs something like, 'He hath a daily beauty in his life that makes me ugly.' "

"Sociopath," I said.

"Precisely," Jones agreed. Wouldn't you know he understood Neave's references? "Iago became Othello's executive officer; he had trust, he'd have had wealth, honor, and yet he threw it all away to destroy his general."

"Like the wreckers," said Neave, his cultured voice chill with disgust. "Some of them didn't come back all the way from the war. And they lured in others, people who fight not to gain anything but simply because they enjoy destruction."

"Wreckers make pirates look good," Jones said.

"Jones!" I protested.

"Seriously, Captain," said Jones. "It's like this: lusting for power, property, women, whatever—those are natural appetites, even if they're savage and criminal. But the desire simply to spoil what's being built is a desire only for entropy. And there's enough of that loose in the universe already."

It was dubious cosmology, I thought, something to be argued over in comfortable rooms like Neave's library on safe worlds—assuming Aviva *was* safe.

"That's why you want a Fleet base here," I told Neave.

"Not wholly. Aviva's too well-protected to be easy pickings anymore. Still, we may as well enforce the message. Hence the shield generators and tonight's test. A base here will expand Fleet's range toward the Straits. A world like Exquemelin will lure wreckers like a homing beacon. If it hasn't already."

Probably, I had had too much wine and too many shocks at that point. And I was tired and decidedly not looking forward to a session with Dr. Marx tomorrow, plus whatever treatments he'd decide to inflict. So I just blurted it out. "*Gavroche* is a good ship, but we can't stop wreckers all by ourselves."

"This isn't really your fight, Cam," said Neave. "It's Jim's."

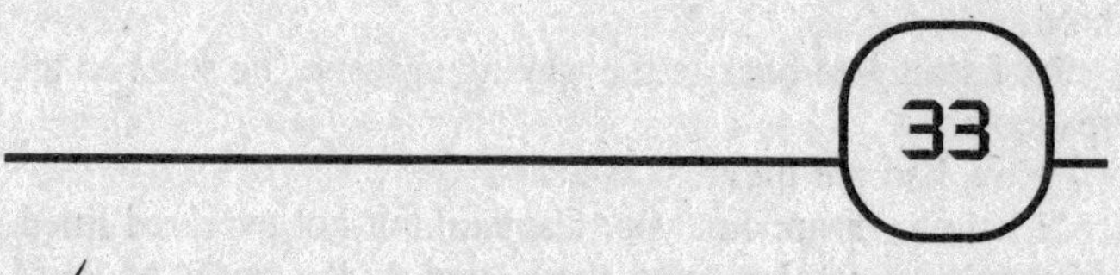

33

I slept badly that night, and dreamed enough to exhaust not just myself but the most exacting dream interpreters on Exquemelin. I couldn't remember most of what I'd dreamt—beyond a sight of Jim, about to lose his nerve or his judgment just as he'd done before. He'd been my shipmate, under my command; I owed him help; I was trying to get to him just as I'd do for any other one of us, but I was paralyzed, helpless . . .

I woke tangled in the bedsheets, dehydrated from all that damned ice wine, and with door chimes, monitors, and God knows what going off until I almost wished all I had to worry about was a Red Alert. Here it was, weird o'clock in the morning, and that damned Dr. Marx was leaning on the door signal.

Dammit, could I have done anything more self-destructive than drink too much the night before medical examinations started? Did I want *to be ruled unfit?*

It was a way out. But it would be as much of a break with my duty as Jim's leap had been with his.

I rose, rinsed out my mouth, and let Marx in. He took one look at me and downloaded the night's readings from the bed's biomonitors. "You look like you've had one hell of a night," he said.

Defiantly, I dialed the autoserve for coffee. At this point, anything I did was going to be medically self-incriminating. "I keep telling my CMO that there's a blood-caffeine factor," I commented. "Want a cup?"

If I were going to go down in flames, I might as well do it in style.

To my surprise, Marx accepted coffee, even if he did remind me to flush my system with as much water as I could hold.

As I struggled back to the waking universe, he scanned the readouts.

"How bad are they?" I asked.

"I hate to disappoint you, Captain, but not even red-lined. A couple spikes here and there, tied to the onset of REM sleep. Hmmm . . ." he approached me with translucent disks. "Roll up your sleeve, if you would."

I felt a faint prickle from his bloodsuckers.

"You haven't eaten. Don't look if it makes you queasy," Marx instructed me as the things filled and darkened.

"You've probably eaten enough breakfast for three. And taken a brisk morning stroll—"

"I ran the perimeter of Neave's land," Marx said. "I've got to side with your CMO, Captain. No such thing as a blood-caffeine factor. You're borderline anemic, though. Why not rest today?"

"I'd rather get this over with," I told him. *Prisoner, rise and hear the judgment of this court.*

"I'm sure you would." Too damn many teeth in Marx's grin. "How about this? If I give an assignment, will you do it?"

"Depends." I sat back, silently daring him. God, I hated being bargained with like a child.

He attached more of those damnable sucker-things. Then, to my surprise, he reached out and examined me carefully, with hands even more gentle than Tom's. How long had it been since anyone had touched me any way except medically or trying to kill me? Amory had tried last night.

I had raised my glass to him, in a silent toast to what wasn't going to be. Our relationship had always been business and should damned well never be anything but business. If I went to the library, I thought I could pick from all the rest of Neave's collections the ancient book from which Amory had read, the night years ago when Jim, Jones, Becker, Neave, and I had all sat there and hammered out a second chance for Jim. That book of Amory's had said it: You had to seize your reward only with clean hands.

We could take nothing for ourselves.

"So?" I challenged the physician.

"So? If I put you on a treadmill right now, or ran you through the usual stress tests, you and I both know your reactions would be down. Maybe so far down I'd have to do something we both don't want. How long since you've taken any kind of leave?"

I swallowed coffee fast. It burnt, and I glared at Marx.

"Thought so. If you hadn't been ordered to report to Aviva for treatment, where'd you be right now?"

"Supervising my ship's refit," I said. I cast a greedy eye on the comm over on the workstation. I'd waked last night with at least three diagnostics I wanted to remind GW to run. "Which reminds me, Doctor—"

"Absolutely not, Captain," he said. "Once you start talking to Refit, I'd probably have to have you removed from the next shuttle Upstairs. And I'd do it, too."

I showed him my teeth. It always got results portside. This time, it failed miserably.

"You're going to rest today," Marx went on. Slave driver. "Your breakfast will be brought you. You can get up for lunch and take a walk around with the *Blue Ridge*s. I saw you play 'I am the captain' with them last night, and it worked really well. If I like your blood pressure, I may let your first officer report to you before dinner. It depends.

"I'm not in your chain of command, Captain," Marx said. "But I do control access to your ship and your crew."

And to whether I ever could rejoin them, damn his eyes. I bared my teeth at him in a snarl. To my horror, it turned into a yawn. Damned civilian *doctor.*

"Would it be so bad to cooperate with me?" Marx asked. He took the coffee cup out of my hand. "When was the last time you slept in?"

"Tom Ankeny—that's our CMO—offered to restrain me, when I was in Sick Bay after Shushan. I suppose you'll say that doesn't count." Marx had his arm under mine, was urging me up, out of my chair, and back into that damnably high, damnably comfortable bed.

"You're going to rest, Captain. You're going to eat real food. You're going to exercise on a planet's surface. A couple weeks of that and we'll see what kind of bioreadings I can get off you before you go back to that ship of yours or any other damn place the Commissioner wants you to go to and undo all my hard work."

ANY MORE OF HIS GENTLE TREATMENT JUST MIGHT KILL ME. And the hardest part was wondering when Dr. Marx would *stop* easing up on me.

Marx-mandated amounts of sleep, food, and exercise drew not just approval, but the ability to communicate with my first officer and my ship. I tested, of course. After one all-night session in the library with coffee, the next morning I attempted to contact GW and found Marx had revoked my comm access.

The man was *conditioning* me, I told Neave in outrage that won an even more infuriating chuckle.

I had to do something to bleed off the pressure: about the only thing that offered itself that I dared accept was physical therapy with the *Blue Ridge*s. It tired me out so much that I returned to my suite and took a nap before dinner. Comm access had been restored by the time I came back. Marx must have thought I'd learned my lesson; it stayed live long enough for me to return GW's calls.

I went back to work with the *Blue Ridge*s day after day. Just as well, seeing as they'd join *Gavroche* until we could hook up with *Blue Ridge* in the Straits. Gradually, they began to speak with me without waiting for me—the captain and outsider—to open the conversation. "A valuable bridge," Dr. Marx pronounced it.

It wasn't a bridge, at least, not yet. More like a plank across a very small puddle.

In rest periods, they shared their supply manifests with me. Neave had been shipping trade goods and equipment to Exquemelin for years, it seemed. He'd stepped up shipments after Jim arrived. Let's hear it for peace and prosperity. The *Blue Ridge*s didn't know why I'd laughed.

Sometimes, I walked with them, but they'd only stray so far away from the Residence. Open fields brought on their agoraphobia—odd for people who spent their lives in space. Maybe, it was what felt like the vast open horizon of a planet, as opposed to a ship's cabins and corridors. I took longer walks with Amory Neave, sometimes with Jones in chattering attendance, sometimes alone.

The days passed rapidly. Dr. Marx dwindled into a convenience and a convenient plot with Tom Ankeny that I was going to punish the instant I returned to my ship—which I was convinced now I'd be able to do. The *Blue Ridges* went from timid strangers to prospective shipmates. And Neave?

There wasn't much he didn't know not just about this sector of space but about the Straits. Like what seemed like half the people in this sector, *Blue Ridge* crew gathered information for him. For example, its crew had seen ships destroyed and, being small, had been able to hide or elude wreckers by fleeing in the leading edge of an ion storm. Neave kept files on wreckers known to have been active in the quadrant—Amaranth, Waerloga, Hinksey Brown—and briefed me extensively on what was known of their crews, their resources, and tactics. Neave and his threat assessments might serve Jim better than any weapons.

A wary Murad brought GW out to the residence to brief me on the progress of *Gavroche*'s refit and, once Marx got a look at him, to rest for a day or so himself. My suggestion that I return to Gan Salem as my exec's stand-in lost me comm privileges for forty-eight hours.

"Am I a prisoner?" I appealed to higher authority by asking Neave.

"I'd rather you stayed," he said and touched my hand when Jones couldn't see.

"And how does that sort with my being your intermediary with the straits-runners?"

"You're the one I trust. Who they trust. And who knows Jim best." He shrugged. By now, we had reached an accommodation with which we both pronounced ourselves satisfied. I would return to duty. There would be a new voyage. There would always be other voyages. And I'd be back when I could.

Even this charmed interlude between voyages was more than we'd ever thought we'd have. We spent afternoons walking, talking idly, like friends who'd been lovers long ago and remained friends, all passion spent. We were very sensible. Didn't even touch hands.

More to the point, I finally got to see my ship.

Gavroche was in better shape than at any time since she was christened. Marx and Ankeny trapped me in her reconditioned Sick Bay and solemnly pronounced me to be in the best shape I'd been in since before my resurrection. About the time Ankeny got down to the specifics of my case, I beat a fast retreat to my cabin, almost unrecognizable with its freshly glazed bulkheads, to find, hidden behind every uniform I owned, the blue dress I'd hired on Raffles Station and then, on a whim, decided to buy. Neave was giving a farewell dinner. For once, I promised myself, I'd look the part of a dinner guest.

NEAVE HAD PLACED ME AT THE TABLE NOT AT HIS RIGHT hand, but down its entire length opposite him, as if I were his hostess. I could feel his eyes on me during the long, elaborate meal during which even Jones and Marx got enough to eat and the *Blue Ridge*s drank to the health of every person present. I heard wave upon wave of conversation, counterpoint to the music in the dining room. I even heard myself answer. No one burst into howls of laughter at my replies, so I assume I performed adequately. But always, the time would come when I felt Neave's eyes on me, and I'd fall silent.

Some silver cord, invisible to anyone else, linked the two of us. I could see that cord—I could feel it—drawing out thinner and thinner until it would snap, leaving an invisible wound. I flinched in anticipation of the pain, then looked around. No one had noticed, except for Jones, who'd spent all dinner carefully not-noticing. As long as he didn't decide to write my biography. Or Amory's.

The last toast was given, applauded, and drained. The last chair scraped back from a nearly empty table. Footsteps disappeared toward the guest house, the atrium, and the library. I rose—hard to believe I was the last person left in the room—and headed toward my quarters. I felt, more than heard, Neave's quiet footsteps, coming from the atrium, catching up with me.

Silently, he walked beside me to the suite I thought of now

as home. Outside my door, he paused. I knew he would not ask to come in. Nor would I invite him. The idea of it . . . of a senior officer and an Alliance commissioner, both of mature years, coupling on a hospital bed like soldiers on their last night of leave was ludicrous, grotesque. He was too civilized a man, and I—tomorrow I was out-bound to the Straits of Aquila to help Amory—to help Jim—keep the wrecker at bay.

There had never been a right time.

Neave lifted my hand and pressed it. "The time's passed quickly," he said, his voice low in the silent hallway. "I wish now . . . I wish there had been some other way of contacting Oulian than giving Jim that ring." He brought my hand to his lips, a light pressure that made me shiver.

If he moved just one step closer . . . but he did not. "I will leave as soon as it's light tomorrow." My voice almost broke. "You don't have to get up."

"You know me well enough to know I always see my guests off," he said. He bent and kissed me on the forehead. "Good night, my dear Caroline."

He turned and disappeared into the shadows.

Blue Ridge 34

When *Blue Ridge*'s crew rejoined their ship, I transferred with them for passage through the Straits of Aquila. Jim had asked for heavy arms. He wouldn't like the substitutes I brought, but I had some medical supplies that I hoped would compensate. And my eyes and ears: he was shrewd enough to know that if Neave liked my report, more supplies would follow. Pleading the need to unpack and, incidentally, to take the meds that my attendant sadists Ankeny and Marx had thrust on me with the threat I'd wish I had only radiation to worry about if I didn't take them, I missed the ship's subdued rejoicing at the two men's return along with the apprehension of the next two who boarded *Gavroche* for Aviva and healing.

When I figured my presence would not be an intrusion, I ventured into the ship's corridors, so much narrower and barer than *Gavroche,* plain as she is, and made my way to the ship's control center for a courtesy call. The captain had *Gavroche,* fresh from refit, on the main screens. My ship hovered there, blotting out the astonishingly lovely, lethal starfield. It resembled nothing so much as that large, predatory Terran fish Amory tells me travels accompanied by tiny guides, which it protects.

Shortly afterward, the ships parted, and *Blue Ridge* entered the Straits. Ankeny warned me that the body writes deeply in the mind: the radiation, he said, like the constant barrage of infinitesimal motes, might give me strange dreams. He was right. I felt bathed in light, not just radiation or even the gratitude of this ship's crew, but a kind of benevolence they'd gladly have given Neave, but transferred to me. Interesting variation on the halo effect, I wrote in my log.

I spent most of my time in my tiny cabin, my viewscreen active, marveling at the clouds, the promontories, the rainbows of uncharted stars. *Blue Ridge*s had already told me all they wished about Jim. He had been a quiet shipmate; they remembered him with respect; he was doing well in his exile on Exquemelin. My presence on board, they said, gave their female administrators increased hopes of trade, as well as concern for my health: the crew was ordered to take every care.

I slept more than I'd been able to since waking at Havilland Roads. So, when the summons came from *Blue Ridge*'s captain to report to him—only the second time I'd been summoned—I moved so eagerly that even the captain looked surprised.

"Sir, you sent for me?"

The captain rose, inclined his head in mild discomfort at hearing me speak deferentially and touched his console. A ship even smaller and older than *Blue Ridge* appeared in the viewscreen on maximum magnification.

"From Exquemelin," the captain said, barely above a whisper from chronic spacer's throat. One of his crew filled his covered mug. The water smelled of chemicals, and I wondered how often it had been recycled.

I cleared my own throat. I didn't think Jim would be on board, but I could hope. I was surprised at how intensely I could hope.

"They will join us in two days," the captain said.

THE CAPTAIN AND I WATCHED THE TINY SHIP—THE FLAGSHIP of what might be the two or three ships Jim had helped put back into space—approach the *Blue Ridge*'s docking bay. The captain was unmoved, but I found myself tensing: it came in fast on a steep vector that would never have been tolerated in the Fleet. And yet, I could see in the flash and sweep of its trajectory the signature of whomever piloted it: uncertified, self-trained, perhaps, but a natural.

The ship slipped gracefully into the docking bay and onto the landing pad. The airlock cycled; the ship turned on the pad; and as lights flashed, signifying that atmosphere had been pumped back into the bay, the captain himself signaled for the hatch to be opened.

I wiped my palms surreptitiously against a crisp uniform I'd saved for the occasion. In a moment, I would meet Jim's new associates, and even though he owed everything he had to . . . to Neave, I reminded myself, I thought I might be forgiven for wishing them to think well of me.

A moment later, I had to suppress a start as the captain signaled and the crew of the tiny ship were piped on board with full, archaic honors. Crew Chief Yang Cho Lee grinned. He and navigator Ostrogorsky had spoken well of the people from Jim's world whom they had met. If a ship that small could compel this type of respect, what they had said had been understatements.

I wasn't expecting banners or trumpets, but the two men striding down the ramp—a total of perhaps four long steps—walked as if they were familiar with ceremony. Both wore sturdy shipsuits. The man who went first, a stocky man who glanced right and left as if guarding his companion, also wore a jacket intricately patterned in dark blues and reddish brown. This had to be Cantu.

Cantu reached the bottom of the ramp and turned sharply aside, coming to attention, as the younger, taller man strode past him toward *Blue Ridge*'s captain and me. So this was Stal Viat. Oulian's son. The man who had become Jim's friend and brother.

He carried himself like the young officer I had such frustrating memories of: head up, shoulders back, eyes roving his unfamiliar surroundings, seeking out the people he had been told to expect. There, the resemblance to a Fleet officer ended. The jacket Stal Viat wore over his shipsuit was of some silky, quilted red fabric, a match to the cap he had pushed back on his glossy black hair. I could see light winking off some ornament at its crown: a more careful look revealed it to be a computer chip old enough to be left over from First Landing.

Even under the ghastly lights of *Blue Ridge*'s docking bay, Stal Viat's skin, young and smooth, glowed healthy and deep bronze, in stark contrast with the pallor of the ship's crew. But what impressed me most about Stal Viat were his eyes. They were dark and fearless, and as they met mine, he smiled.

He nodded respect to the captain, then came over and knelt at my feet, taking my hands and pressing them to his forehead in a gesture of respect as extravagant as it was touching.

"You are Captain Marlow," he said. "You are my brother's benefactor, and so I am forever in your debt."

So this was the native—the young man—who had saved Jim's life only to claim it forever as a friend and brother. There was something forthright about him, something charming: Jim's own damnable ability again to attract friendship and loyalty.

Impossible not to smile at him or to acknowledge Cantu, whose sturdy integrity reminded me, incongruously enough, of Neave's man Murad.

"I have seen you in my dreams," Stal Viat went on. "But then, you are no stranger to dreaming."

Well, given what Neave had told me of the locals' reverence for dreams, Jim had chosen as good a way as any to describe my twenty years in Freeze and, incidentally, boost not only my prestige but his. *Nice work, Jim,* I thought.

I examined Stal Viat's ship, a minnow beside *Blue Ridge*'s shark, itself a minnow in comparison with *Gavroche*.

The captain met my eye sardonically. *It's not too late to back out,* his glance seemed to imply. But I'd never shirked my duty before.

"I know the ship is not what you're used to," Stal Viat said, his voice hesitant. "But it is our finest, nothing but our finest for my brother's friend." He smiled at me so naturally that I could see how Jim, isolated for so long from the friendships natural to his age, had been won.

"I am looking forward to seeing your brother," I told Stal Viat almost defiantly. "When can you be ready to leave?"

STAL VIAT FLEW WITH DASH, ENTHUSIASM, AND WHAT FELT like a complete disregard for the laws of physics. In Fleet training, a pilot as rash as he would have washed out instantly; in actual combat, though, he probably wouldn't just survive, but win battles and medals. His tiny ship darted in and out of Jump, at one point dodging a ship whose conformation made me long for *Gavroche*'s computers to identify it and her weapons to blast it out of space. Stal Viat, powering down every system except life support (and skimping on that), looked longingly at the bogey, studied his arsenal for about the fifth time, then subsided with a regretful sigh.

Someone had taught him common sense.

By the time he swooped down in final approach toward

Exquemelin, my hands were wet, sweat was trickling down my sides. I assured myself that the only thing that made my stomach flutter was fluctuations in the ship's artificial gravity.

Lights in the cockpit gleamed on Stal Viat's grin as he landed with exquisite precision on a high bluff just beyond what looked like a village.

I drew a deep breath, taking pains to keep it silent, then unstrapped and pushed myself up on unsteady legs.

"Captain?" Evidently, Stal Viat had seen my discomfort out of the corner of his eye, probably about the time he dodged the spysat in low Exquemelin orbit. One good blast, and it would be one less thing to worry about—except that whoever put it there would know it was gone.

Cantu was at my elbow, ready to help the sick old woman down the ramp.

I twisted away from his capable, protective hand.

"Lead on," I told them both, relieved that neither my voice nor my legs shook as I started down the narrow ramp onto Exquemelin's soil.

The ground cover was lush, and the fronds swaying from long branches were silvery, although the slanting rays of Exquemelin's star—on Aviva, we'd have said it was late afternoon, shading into evening—painted them with a ruddy glow. Beyond the bluff, I could see more such trees, a veritable forest, water running through it, and mist rising up, level with the bluff.

Moisture on the ground and the trees glinted in the sun. As the wind blew through the cloud cover, one stray beam lanced down and touched Jim's fair hair, crowning him like a prince in those stories that tended to begin "once upon a time." For that moment, he was the young man I remembered, all his future before him. In the next, I saw the gray in his hair and the lines starting in his forehead.

Not ten meters away from the end of the ramp, he stood waiting for me. As Stal Viat came down the ramp, Jim raised his hand. An absurd fanfare of horns cobbled together from polished wood and old, even shinier tubing throbbed in the air. Stal Viat's head went up, and even Cantu puffed out his chest as they marched the brief distance between their ship and their leader.

There were tears on Jim's his face as he caught sight of me and straightened to attention.

I nodded, smiled, and stepped forward with my hand outstretched for his. Half a loaf—but he grinned just as he had the night Neave explained his mission here.

He started forward, accompanied not just by those hangers-on, but by an intense young woman whose long black hair streamed down her back. Her eyes darted from me to Jim, and she stood close to him, protective, and a head and shoulders smaller.

"Marlow," Jim said, his voice unashamedly husky, as he clasped my hand and wrung it. "You can't know what a welcome sight you are! Isn't she, Setelin?" he asked the girl at his side.

He was looking at me. I saw her face. She was lithe and beautiful and fierce, and if Jim belonged to anyone it was to her. She bowed her head to me and agreed with every word of welcome Jim spoke. But her eyes, bright and challenging and possessive, reserved judgment.

"I HOPE YOU DON'T MIND WALKING BACK TO THE FORT," JIM asked me some days later. "I need to see and be seen."

"As long as we don't keel over on our way home," I said. "What was that stuff you thought your friend Melinkor put in that tea?"

Giving me more credit for a strong stomach than I gave myself, Jim had brought me to formal audience with Melinkor, who'd apparently imprisoned him when he'd first arrived. Audience had turned into archaic formal tea drinking. The stuff had tasted worse than a prescription. My immunizations were current, but broad-spectrum boosters and immunostimulants aren't antidotes, and if I ever saw a man with the face of a cut-rate assassin, it was Melinkor.

"I have always found Melinkor's tea safe," Jim said calmly. "He wouldn't dare to poison me."

"But I'm another matter entirely," I replied.

"Possibly," Jim said. "I judged otherwise."

He judged. *He* played dice with my life? I could have shouted with anger. But at that moment, Jim nodded gravely at two men repairing a boat, waved at a woman holding a child and trying to keep her young daughter in check. The girl broke free and ran over to us, taking Jim's hand and carrying it to her forehead. He stroked her hair—long and black and glossy, like Setelin's, then gave her a gentle nudge back to her mother.

"You see how they watch," he explained in an undertone. "Regardless of what Cantu says, I don't need guards among them."

I spat, wishing for a drink that would cleanse my mouth of Melinkor's foul tea. The walk back to The Fort turned almost into a royal progress, as, from every part of the riverbank or forest, people emerged to check on the well-being of the stranger who had become their heart.

"They care about me," Jim said. His voice faltered. "They . . . they trust me, Cam. And I won't let them down." His voice gained strength. "I've grown here. God, how I've grown. And I know I'll never let them down."

I remembered Jim's enthusiasm. The assurance in his voice belonged to a man I had never met before, but whom I found it in me to like. But trust?

"You see, Captain. If you were to ask any of them, who is wise, who is brave, who is faithful, they would say me. Me and Stal Viat. They even ask me to interpret their dreams." He turned the crack in his voice into a laugh.

It was most chillingly the truth. People here hung on Jim's every word. He was the authority. He was the governor, the father figure, the judge: in some ways, he was as much the heir as Stal Viat.

I saw a flash of red up ahead, but Jim had seen it first. He brightened. "And here is Setelin, come to welcome us. Hello, girl!" he challenged her, laughing.

"Hello, boy!" His very accent. His very laugh. And, as they linked arms and walked the rest of the way back to The Fort that had become their home, even their footsteps matched. Another episode in the storybook: the man from far off and the native girl.

A very stupid story: Setelin was no more one of those guileless, vulnerable butterflies, born to be abandoned, than I myself.

Setelin had pounced on the supplies Neave had sent, thanking me with more warmth than I had seen from her before or since. Jim told me that it had been Setelin, no one else, who maintained the outpost's ancient computers, who studied their files. The upgrades and the information on modern medical care were treasure to her. She was even part of Jim's council, along with Oulian, Stal Viat, and a number of the elders.

Setelin leaned her head against her man's shoulder and swung their joined hands. Light glinted off the ring she wore—Oulian's ring that, if Neave hadn't passed along to Jim as a token, I might have worn. Her hands were tiny and competent and quick. And Jim's? Here on Exquemelin, his hands had never been soiled. His reputation wasn't unblemished; it glowed.

The Fort's gates shut behind us. They wouldn't be proof against an attack from the air or any one of a number of weapons I could think of. But they were a mighty bulwark against downworld assault.

I walked in with Jim and his sweetheart, the skeleton at their feast. I watched them laugh and lean toward each other at dinner. Somehow, I must have laughed and smiled and eaten at the right intervals and in the right amounts. But when we parted later that night, I knew that night and the ones that followed would be sleepless.

JIM HAD ASSIGNED ME A GUEST HOUSE WITHIN THE FORT. I knew I could stay there as long as I wished—my whole life, if I wanted.

I knew he was happy. The night before, I had heard him and Setelin walking about the compound, his low voice, and her soft one, singing to him songs he had taught her that came all the way from Aven. When I glanced out, he had his arm around her, holding her like something infinitely fragile and precious, her head against his shoulder.

It was all too close, too intimate. Tonight, the air within The Fort seemed too thick, somehow, laden with the sounds and thoughts of people, huddled together in their little illusion that Jim kept them safe. Knowledge ate at me: this place would lure wreckers sooner rather than later. If it hadn't already done so.

I needed to breathe, to walk apart, and think. On *Gavroche,* I'd have paced the decks. Here, as Jim's offworld patron, I had no trouble, though, persuading the guards to open a side gate and let me out. I was armed; I was assumed to be able to take care of myself, to share in their own protector's peace, and probably to back it up.

My sidearm's charge light provided a tiny bright spotlight that eased my way among the tangled lattices of trees and ground cover. The air was rich with the smells of river and soil and plant life. Overhead, some white nightflier whose name I didn't know stooped with a hunting cry upon prey that had time for half a terrified squeak. The dampness of the air soothed my eyes: I could feel my skin—and more than my skin—relaxing in this luxury of a planetary environment.

However embattled it might prove to be.

A crackle of ground scrub brought me around in a half crouch, both hands steadying my weapon.

"Captain?" Setelin's voice, but Jim's accent. "May I walk with you?"

She remained in cover. When I gestured her out, she moved so quietly I realized she had allowed herself to be heard.

"You come out here alone?" I demanded.

"I have always come and gone as I pleased. Vortimer could never stop me, nor could Melinkor," she said. Not a boast, but a statement of fact. "And I have better weapons now than I did then."

No, Vortimer could never stop her. The one time he'd actually managed to speak to me alone, complaining that the Commissioner had sent a boy to replace him, who'd always respected Neave and served him faithfully, he struck me as a whiny incompetent, much like the men who'd fled with Jim on *Irian Jaya*. Even before Jim came, Setelin had withstood Vortimer's bluster and threats. Now, secure in Jim's love and knowing that he would never countenance casual murder, she ignored him.

The sidearm I'd given Jim before he came here rested in her hand. Its size and shapeliness were deceptive: the way she held the weapon would have satisfied a Fleet arms officer—and had, I told myself.

I nodded. "Walk with me," I invited.

She looked as if she knew what she was doing. But Jim would hardly thank me if his lover were killed or captured because she'd followed me outside.

Was this a contest of nerve? Then I'd let her set the rules, and I'd award her full marks for courage. I'd been expecting some sort of confrontation.

An older woman who befriends a younger man faces a dilemma when, in the normal course of things, that younger man finds a mate. If he chooses a weakling, the older woman may find herself with two children, not friends. And if he chooses a really weak woman, a woman fool enough to envy the older woman, it will cost the older woman her protégé and gain her an enemy whose corrosive spite carries a long, long half-life.

But if the young woman turns out to be both brave and wise, the older woman gains an adult daughter as well as a son—assuming that she, in her turn, is wise enough to take the younger woman to her heart. Which was why I wanted so to gain Setelin's trust, even though Jim had always cost me more than he was worth.

"You don't have to protect me," said Setelin, who seemed

to read my thoughts with the same skill she probably applied to Jim's dreams. "Don't bother, please, trying to be maternal. I had a mother. She died weeping. I have dreamed. . . ."

She shook her head, the long dark hair flying about her face and throat. The tiny, capable hand with its deadly burden trembled.

"You do not wish to die weeping, too," I said.

"No. And I . . . I . . ." Setelin stopped short and drew herself up the way Jim had stood years ago on Havilland Roads.

"Have you come to take him back?" Her words came out controlled, hollow.

"How can you even ask that?" I demanded. "You know you own his heart."

"I am not a little girl, Captain. Yes, I know he loves me. But I have dreamed, and I have waked in the night and watched him dream. His dreams are haunted by . . . what lies out there."

She gestured at the austere high starfield at the worlds, unknown to her, that lay beyond.

"My mother forgave my father. But if he leaves me, I will never forgive him. Never!"

"He will not leave you," I repeated. "You give him something he has found nowhere else. Isn't that enough?"

"Captain, I must know what troubles his dreams. One day, it will call him, and unless I am prepared, he will go, and I will die weeping. What is it, Captain?"

I looked away. "He will not leave you," I repeated. "He cannot go back there. Not after what he has found . . . what he has made here. He is needed here. It may be"—dammit, I was having trouble with this language's gentle formality—"that more people will come like those who brought forbidden tech to Melinkor. Jim must guard against them."

"And you say that a man who cannot do that will not be valued by his own people, that they will not need him and call him home?"

Her voice thrilled in sudden, admirable defense of Jim. Perhaps, I thought, if she were disillusioned . . . but it would take a stronger woman than I to tell her the whole story. If Jim could bear for her to know, he would have told her.

"You are more his own people than those others," I told her. "I can promise you: no one out there will ever want him. He is not good enough."

Setelin drew breath in a hiss. "And you are an officer of his? You call yourself his friend? Captain, you are a liar and a fool."

She turned on her heel and walked away. Furious as she was, her passage through the ground scrub was silent. With luck, Setelin would try to console Jim for what she saw as my betrayal, binding him to her even more closely.

And I'd won half my battle, even if Setelin definitely didn't show signs of becoming a sort of daughter to me. But it was no matter: Setelin, protective in her fear, would conceal our conversation, not wanting to deprive him of anything else he cared for. Not wanting to risk all she had. And she would be even kinder, more loving to Jim to make up for what, clearly, she thought was the outside world's—or at least Captain Marlow's—catastrophically bad judgment.

Never let it be said I don't look after my friends.

Exquemelin

35

Stal Viat had ordered an honor guard for Jim's captain. They peeled off smartly, lining up as if in review around the tiny field on which the best of Oulian's few space-capable craft waited. Now, one of them stood as ready as it would ever get, prepared to return Cam Marlow to the worlds Jim was quite aware he would never see again.

These days, the thought barely hurt. He had a life here,

respect, a future. But he'd miss the captain who'd done so much for him.

He walked with her, determined to get in these last minutes together. Setelin hovered at his other side, a tender, fierce guard. Tactfully, Stal Viat had already dropped back. Supervising, he explained. Cantu, serving as pilot for this mission, waited for Marlow on board.

This close to Cam's departure, Jim had almost nothing to say beyond commonplaces: the sunlight, the water, regards to *Blue Ridge*'s crew. And a tape for Neave.

"I want to thank you again for coming," Jim said. "You can't know what it means, that you would come here to see me, see this place. . . ."

Marlow turned and smiled at him. Her face softened out of the leader-mask he'd felt on his own often enough. Some of the stiffness might also have been due to apprehension; Jim had made the passage through the Straits, and it wasn't an easy one, especially for someone used to her own ship. "You know, if you want Stal Viat to take you back to the rendezvous point with *Blue Ridge,* I'm sure he'd be happy to."

"And shame Cantu, who'd think that I—that you—didn't believe he was good enough?" Marlow asked. She shook her head, the still-fair curls catching the late afternoon sunlight, making her look younger than she was. "You can't do that to him, Jim."

"Cantu told me that he has dreamed he will return the captain safely," Setelin put in, vigilant at Jim's side. "I know she has been studying the ship's . . . specs, they're called, I think. Cantu won't have a copilot but a teacher," she added.

Once or twice, Jim had thought he heard an edge in Setelin's voice when she spoke of Marlow. He was just as glad not to hear it today.

Setelin had been unusually warm and loving, he thought, his body relaxed, at peace with itself and its memories of the night before. She had just been shy of Marlow at first, then determined to show her that Jim hadn't chosen a fool. As if he could ever think of Setelin that way: she hadn't just given him herself; in some ways, as much as Marlow, she'd given him back his own soul.

Now, she moved away from Jim's side—the vacancy there gave him a pang—and turned to face Marlow. "Captain, please believe me when I say that you always have a home here."

Marlow put out a hand, almost touched Setelin's shoulder, then let it drop.

"Thank you," she said. Her voice didn't quite break. "I know I leave my friend in the best possible hands."

Setelin stepped close to Marlow, took her hands, and pressed them to her forehead. "I hope you will guide my dreams," she said formally.

The captain blinked, blanked on the proper formula, and, to everyone's surprise, pulled Setelin into a half-hug. "Look after him. He loves you so," Jim heard her whisper and felt the blood rush up his neck and face.

Setelin stepped back, leaving Jim to escort the captain the rest of the way.

"I'll tell Neave you've justified his faith in you," Marlow said as they walked the final meters to the waiting ship.

She had one foot on the access ramp when the words erupted from him. His vision was blurring, and he blinked furiously, wanting to remember her. "Captain—Cam, do you think we'll ever see each other again?"

"God knows," Marlow said. "If I don't go Home, quite probably in a couple years. That is, if you keep proper watch. Neave and I aren't dreaming when we tell you that there are wreckers active in the Straits. Why the hell else do you think we sent you those perimeter defenses and upgraded your ships?"

"Because, God only knows why, you have always had my best interests at heart," Jim said. "You, you and Neave and Becker, you gave me my second chance. I promise you, this time I won't fail."

Marlow gestured at the guards circling the landing, at Setelin, waiting a polite distance away. "Just look at them, Jim. You know your duty. See . . ." her voice choked off. A hasty step down the ramp, and she had her arms around him in a vigorous hug, thumping his back as if she were much taller and stronger than he. "Seeing you like this—it's one of the best things I've ever done," she muttered against his shoulder. "So don't—"

That old pilots' prayer again.

He held her off by the shoulders, staring at the familiar face, older now, even kinder, to record it forever in his memory. "I promise, Captain. Now," he looked up at the sky, "you'd better take off before the rains start."

He rose to attention but, knowing his place in the scheme of things, didn't salute.

Marlow stiffened to attention too, bringing up her arm up in an uncharacteristic flourish that made it seem as if she saluted the entire compound. Jim flushed, shivered, and kept his chin high. He had not expected this last generosity.

Marlow strode up the ramp without looking back. The hatch slid closed. The undercarriage lights kindled, and he gestured everyone back to a safe distance. His eyes blurred, but he knew his footing. Setelin clasped her hands around his arm and watched with him as Cantu took the tiny ship—and Jim's oldest friend—away from Exquemelin until it was just one tiny light among many.

"Make a wish," Setelin whispered. Her breath was as warm against his neck as it had been the night before when she'd cradled him, his head on her breast. She was so little, she looked so fragile; but in her way, she was as strong as Marlow herself.

36

After spending the better part of the day tramping around The Fort, Jim and Stal Viat climbed back to Oulian's village, scouting out locations for the perimeter defenses Marlow had brought. He had hoped for heavy energy beams: it wasn't the first time he'd wished upon a star. What he'd gotten were small arms and perimeter shields.

"Commissioner Neave has sent us Aviva's test models," Jim told Stal Viat. "You should see the size of the shield installations on Aviva. Even the ones they just replaced are practically the size of a guest house."

His brother grinned. "I can't imagine it," he said. "Perhaps, tonight's dreams will show me. I suppose another reason for the size is that there are more people on Aviva."

"These models are old, but they're built to last," Jim reassured him. "Still, it might be better to test some installation that's less critical."

And that wouldn't be missed if a generator blew up.

"Why not the old trading post?" Stal Viat asked, with an uncharacteristically nasty edge to his voice. "Setelin's migrated the old data to the new machines. We wouldn't miss it."

Or Vortimer either, he carefully didn't add.

Jim shook his head. "Now that's something *I'll* have to dream on," he said. "By rights, the post belongs to the Commissioner. I'm pretty sure he wouldn't want it destroyed."

He still didn't share his brother's and his lover's conviction that the only safe Vortimer was a dead one. Even at the height of his prosperity, Vortimer had been a coward and a bungler. Defanged, he was capable only of petty mischief. And if a deserter and runaway could rise to love and respect, Jim had no right to deny Vortimer a second chance.

Stal Viat rested a hand on the generator he'd helped Jim carry. "You have a generous heart," he said. "I hope to learn that from you."

Jim flushed and turned away. He didn't want to see the younger man watch him as if he were a teacher and a hero; he wanted to deserve it.

He looked up at the sky. "I think," he said a little desperately, "there's going to be a storm. I see heat lightning."

Stal Viat glanced tactfully upward. A bolt of light sizzled across the sky some distance away, followed by a rumble.

"That's not heat lightning," said Stal Viat.

"You're right. It's not lightning at all. We have to get—"

Fast, unsteady footsteps brought both of them around, hands going to their sidearms.

"It's Iri!" Stal Viat exclaimed. "He was on duty today." Iri, who'd won a reader and four disks for winning the distance run in the games Jim had held to honor Cam Marlow, came pounding up.

"Sir . . . sir," he gasped, stumbling and dropping to his knees, "Setelin sent me. She . . ." he whooped for breath, then gagged. Stal Viat knelt beside him, holding him up. ". . . was listening in the—"

"Comm station," Jim said. "What did Setelin hear? Quickly, man!"

"It's Cantu," Iri said. "He's having trouble landing. Someone's chasing him." He doubled over, retching with exhaustion. Poor boy had probably sprinted the whole way upslope.

"I'll go," said Stal Viat. "Cantu's been my wingman since I learned to fly."

Jim opened his mouth to protest.

"When you first came here, who shepherded you down?" Stal Viat demanded. "I know these ships. Better than you do. They're little and tricky, and I will bring him home."

A word would restrain him. Jim didn't give it. Stal Viat

took off at a run. He'd alert Setelin, who could be trusted to close The Fort's gates and keep them closed.

"Get . . . get back!" Iri cried to Jim.

"I'm going to Oulian," said Jim. "And you're coming with me. Here, wipe your chin."

Stal Viat's mother would take the boy in charge. And Oulian had a communications link with Setelin: while Stal Viat tried to bring Cantu home and bar the door to any uninvited guests, Jim could mobilize defenses at The Fort as well as on the plateau.

By the time Jim aided a now-shivering boy into the village, it had all but emptied of women and children. "Get out of here, woman!" Oulian roared from inside his hall, his voice so deep Jim thought he felt subsonics.

"Don't you order me!" The thin, tiny woman who was Oulian's wife raced outside, as if that last blast had propelled her. She had a pack on her back almost as large as she, but she still managed a pretty creditable run. As she passed Jim, he shoved Iri toward her and saw her tug him toward the cave shelters.

Jim raced into the hall, where Oulian sat alone except for his usual guards. "My son—"

Oulian had called Jim "son" once or twice, but reserved that particular fearful tone for Stal Viat.

"He's gone to bring Cantu down," Jim said and saw the old man's face turn gray.

Why isn't it you up there? Never mind that Jim was necessary to coordinate defenses on the surface; never mind that Stal Viat had flown these ships for longer than Jim. For Oulian, Jim was the wrong person in the wrong place.

"Your son flew shepherd for me when I landed here, sir," he added, inadequate reassurance though it was. "With two of them, they even have a fighting chance against whatever it is. . . ."

Yes, and if Jim had moved faster in setting up the perimeter defenses, even now, he might be sitting at a weapons panel, preparing to fire from ground control. Damn.

"I must see," said Oulian.

Help me wasn't in his vocabulary. He waved away his guards.

"We should go to controls," Jim said. "Setelin, at The Fort, will brief us."

"I must see!" Oulian repeated. "My son is out there!"

"Here, sir," said Jim. He thought longingly of the better range, the screens—old, but serviceable—at the control center that had been his preoccupation for months and turned to one of Oulian's attendants. "Go to control, and get me the portable, will you? Run!

"I'll get you outside," Jim told Oulian. "We'll watch your son's victory together."

He flung an arm around Oulian and heaved him up. Oulian leaned against his shoulder, almost throwing him off balance. God, no wonder he couldn't bear his own weight for long.

"Victory?" he rasped. Terror for his only child, barely mastered, quivered in his voice.

"Yes, victory," Jim said firmly. "My own head answers for any harm that comes to him, I swear it."

Oulian came to a dead stop. The inertia of his immense mass made Jim stagger forward, but the old chief's hand clamped tightly on Jim's arm, steadying himself and warning Jim.

"I will hold you to that," he said. His words were more rumble than sound, counterpoint to the thunder overhead.

Jim shivered once, then levered his shoulder beneath Oulian's, pushing him out of the shadows of his hall and out under the gray sky.

Flares of green and red slashed through the cloud cover. Jim's head went up, his eyes straining for even a glimpse of Cantu's crippled ship or Stal Viat's, come to guide him home.

The wind, heavy with rain, whipped overhead. Oulian's attendant dashed back, carrying the portable comm installation and pressing it into Jim's free hand. Seeing him struggle to operate it one-handed, he took Oulian's arm, trying to shift some of the sick old man's weight off him. Deprived of Oulian's body heat, Jim was chilled through in a moment. That wasn't important: what mattered was trying to break through the interference—partly from atmospheric conditions, partly from jamming—and reach Cantu and Stal Viat.

"Up there!" called the second man, who ran out with an antique blaster and a blanket to wrap around Oulian. He tolerated the attention, his face turned to the hostile sky. Lights warred back and forth within the growling clouds.

"Cantu . . . Stal Viat . . . are you there? Do you copy?" Jim repeated.

The wind picked up again, dispelling one vast swath of curdled gray, and Oulian gave a roar.

Two tiny ships emerged. Hull plates on one of them were blackened, and wing damage made it list to one side as it flew, but that was Cantu's ship, definitely on a safe, almost a sane landing vector. There was nothing sane, however, about how close Stal Viat shadowed the crippled ship; he was practically wingtip-to-wingtip with it when a blast of fire separated the two vessels.

Even from here, Jim's nostrils twitched at the smell of ozone as energy seared through the atmosphere and punched into the lake below, which erupted in billows of steam.

"Report!" Jim ordered. "Do you copy? Did that last blast—"

"Unknown ship on approach—too fast! Cantu's ship can't take another hit. I've got to go back." Stal Viat's voice came through. Oulian gave a wordless bellow.

"Not alone you're not!" That was Cantu. Damned fool. Stal Viat was risking his neck, buying time for Cantu to land.

"Sorry, Cantu, but I'm commanding here, not you!"

Oulian barked out a laugh, then choked it off.

Stal Viat's ship banked and climbed fast, its two wing guns firing at their pathetic maximum. More slowly, Cantu followed.

"Men!" Jim shouted into the comm. "Consolidate your fire at the scoops."

The denseness of approaching atmosphere had to have

forced the invader to shut down all but a fraction of his engines' scoops. If they overloaded . . .

Jim heard hollow laughter coming through the comms, heard Setelin's frightened, angry voice trying once again to warn off *"hostile craft, stand down, repeat, stand down, or we will open fire."*

God, if they'd only had time to set up the perimeter shields!

Jim could feel his arm and shoulder muscles twitching as if he could hurl himself between his friends and their attackers.

The clouds gaped a little more. Now, he saw a ship a little smaller than *Blue Ridge,* its sides slick and battered with decades of too-hard use, turning to attack Cantu and Stal Viat. It was a miracle Cantu had gotten this far. It would be a bigger miracle if either of them made it down alive, seeing that neither was willing to abandon the other.

You won't get a better shot, Jim started to say, then fell silent. They'd be tranced out now in fighting pilots' concentration, awaiting a perfect moment that they were in a better position to see than he.

"Stay on target . . . at my word . . . half a point over . . . NOW!" Stal Viat shouted.

Four beams lashed out and coalesced on the invading ship's scoops. The ship's dorsal array exploded most satisfyingly.

Cantu's wordless cry of triumph hurt Jim's ears.

In the next moment, the rest of the ship blew in a wave of light and sound that blinded and deafened him. He hurled himself toward Oulian to help his assistants support him against the shockwave that sent everything that had not been fastened down blowing across the plain. He could feel the shudders that racked Oulian. *He's too old and sick for this,* Jim thought. *Stal Viat will kill me.*

Tears pouring down his face, Jim forced his eyes open long enough. Stal Viat had regained control of his ship already; Cantu still struggled with his, but was on target for a landing he could, at the very least, walk away from.

The enemy ship had broken apart. Its aft segment pinwheeled toward the lake, while sections of its wings and fuselage rained down on the forest. Good thing the ground was soaked, or they'd have fires to fight.

"Setelin to ships . . . Setelin to village . . ."

"Yes, Setelin!" Jim called jubilantly into the comm. "Our ships are coming in on target. Cantu, can you land here, or do you want to glide downslope?"

"The sooner I'm home, the better. Ask my wife what's for dinner, will you?"

Even to his own ears, Jim's laughter sounded almost like a sob. "Then, brothers, you're cleared for landing. See you at the field!"

Oulian jerked his head: mute command for his companions to aid him back into his house. He ignored the tears on his face.

Now, there was nothing stopping Jim from racing over to the landing field and joining what was going to be one hell of a victory dance the minute those two men landed. But the comm was crackling once again.

"Setelin reporting. Part of the hostile's still on course. . . ."

"That's only debris from the explosion," came Stal Viat's voice, tired, relieved, and jubilant.

"Negative," Setelin said. *"It's moving under its own power."*

The invader had escaped in a damned pod.

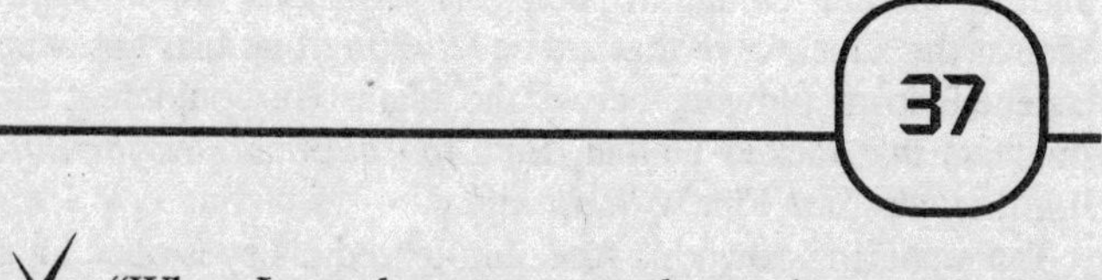

37

"When I ran the outpost, trade goods were there for the welfare of all," Jim heard Vortimer's voice whine from inside The Fort. "This man of yours wants to make himself a king."

"You sit in his house, you drink his tea, and you say that?" Setelin's voice was quiet but ice-edged. "I did not ask you here. And I want you gone before he returns."

"So it's greed with you, is it? Better than sex any time. I always thought you were a damn sight smarter than your mother, girl."

"Get out of here before I kill you as my mother should have!" Setelin's voice had lost the endurance Jim had always heard in it when she spoke to Vortimer. Now, it near set off echoes in the main hall. In a minute, her guards would come. She hated being watched and so far had managed to ignore it.

Damn. He'd tramped in the drizzle from The Fort to drink Melinkor's precarious tea and listen for hints that the Commodore was back. Cantu at his back glowered at every man in the place, and Stal Viat was asking every small holder and fisherman he could reach about strange splashes or explosions.

Jim had hoped for a hot bath, a quiet dinner, Setelin's sure hands rubbing the soreness from muscles that just didn't bounce back the way they used to. Instead, he had what he could only call in-law problems.

"Why should I leave?" came Vortimer's voice. "Ingrate though you are, I like seeing you rich and lovely and passionate. A lucky man, eh, your Jim?"

The very sound of Vortimer made Jim want to scrub his ears. He was a whiner, a cheat, and Jim believed with complete faith that he'd had more to do with the Commodore, now safely kicked offworld, than he'd ever admitted.

"But I come in need," Vortimer's voice took on the whine it got when he knew he was outmanevered.

"You," Setelin spat. "What can you need that I will not refuse you?"

"Not for me," said Vortimer. "But for a friend. A new friend . . . ahhhh, so that intrigues you. Not so proud now, are you? Perhaps you'll offer to trade now—over a fresh pot of the good tea, not this bitter stuff."

Jim turned quickly. He wanted to curse, horribly, the way he'd learned downbelow in half a hundred stations across known space, but if he gave way, at least four people within earshot would worry they'd offended him.

He strode into the hall and saw Setelin, making tea with dangerous efficiency. She straightened, turning with the refilled tea pot, and saw Jim. Even from the doorway, he could see how she sighed with relief, her eyes brightening.

"Hello, girl!" he called out, hoping to make her smile.

She set the teapot down at Vortimer's elbow and ran to him.

"I didn't ask him here. He came whining for free medications, one of the captain's new . . . personal diagnostic units . . ." she barely paused at the Alliance standard term.

Jim flung an arm over her shoulder—let Vortimer see how safe his former foster child was.

Vortimer poured tea for himself, refilled Setelin's cup, then rose and rummaged through the shelves for a third cup for Jim himself. He turned a nod of greeting into an obsequious bow.

"What are a few drugs to us?" Jim whispered so reasonably he knew instantly he'd have to apologize later. "Give them to him so he'll leave. If he stays much longer, we'll have to invite him to supper."

As Vortimer knew perfectly well.

"He says he has a new friend who needs help," Setelin whispered. "I don't like this."

Arm squeezing her shoulders, Jim walked her back to the chairs set by the fire. He tried to seat her, but she resisted until he dropped into the chair himself and let her perch on its broad arm. The fresh tea smelled as if it would warm him all the way down, but he really didn't want to drink with Vortimer.

"All this time, we've been trying to find out if anyone had survived that explosion," Jim whispered to her. He wanted very much to steal a kiss, but restrained himself. "And now the news drops into your lap. Don't be afraid. We have friends. Do you think Captain Marlow or Commissioner Neave would let us come to harm?

"You say you need the medication for a friend?" Jim demanded of Vortimer. "Where was he injured?"

"He wasn't injured," Vortimer parried. "He's sick. It's chronic."

"If he survived that ship, let him die," Setelin said. "He tried to kill Cantu and Stal Viat."

Jim squeezed her hand. "So fierce, are you? I think we need to learn what Vortimer wants to tell us."

Marlow had saluted him. After Havilland Roads, Marlow had given him a second chance, and another on Shenango's World, and another and another until, finally, Marlow's faith had paid off.

Could he do any less?

He wasn't half the officer or the human being Marlow was.

But he still had to try. Even if he never got to stand in front of her and report like an officer and a gentleman.

"Okay, let me have the whole story, and you better make it the truth," he told Vortimer. "Quickly. Because you don't have to live with Setelin, and I do." He grinned as he pressed her hand again and felt her dig her nails in. Oh, he'd pay for that tonight.

"I found the pod from the ship," Vortimer admitted.

"How many survivors?" Jim demanded.

"Just one. He's injured, he needs better care than I—"

Jim fixed Vortimer with the formidable stare he'd been on the receiving end of all his life.

"Are you sure? I have ways of finding out, if you're lying to me."

"Just one, I tell you!" Vortimer's voice grew agitated. His hand shook, sprinkling his grimy coverall with tea. "He's sick, I tell you. Coughing fit to turn himself inside out, and he's pale. Except for the blotches on his face."

Spacer's throat, obviously, and cancers like the ones Jim had seen on *Blue Ridge* crew. But he wasn't a straits-runner; none of *Blue Ridge*'s cousins would have fired on Cantu's ship. Still, Vortimer's refugee had spent a lot of time in badly maintained ships that traveled the No Man's Worlds.

"You think he's a pirate?" Jim brought his face close to Vortimer's. The man had come here drunk on the crude liquor brewed at the lakeshore: another reason Setelin was furious.

"Says he was an engineer. Kidnapped years ago. Says he overloaded the scoops and bailed."

It could have been. Men and women went missing portside every day. Hell, it had almost happened to him. An engineer would be of more use alive to pirates or scavengers than as spare limbs and organs and potential skin grafts. He'd be carefully watched on board, but if anyone could blow a ship and escape, it was an engineer.

"If he's that valuable, why wouldn't they treat him?" Setelin spat.

"You've traveled so much, you know best, missy?" asked Vortimer. "The man escaped his masters. The man is sick. I've appealed for help. After all, your boyfriend there's got such a reputation for helping. But this is my reward—"

Jim held up a hand. Anything to stop Vortimer from winding up again. "That's enough. As long as I'm here, every man and woman on this planet deserves a second chance. I'm giving you yours," he told Vortimer. "I'll believe you're telling the truth when you say you've come here to get help. So I'm going to give you your help. You can have the medications, the PDU—"

"I don't know how to use it," Vortimer said.

"He's lying again," Setelin hissed.

Jim turned and looked into her eyes. "Setelin, if what he says is true—if there's the slightest chance that what he says is true, could you forgive yourself if a stranger died in pain? I was a stranger here myself once."

Her eyes went wide and bright with tears. *You cheat,* she mouthed at him. More than ever, he wanted to steal that kiss, just as she perfectly well knew. Just as she knew he wouldn't.

Now that he'd won his point and she her more subtle one, she yielded. "I'll fetch the meds," she said.

"A kind hand to tend my friend," Vortimer commented. "Thank you. He knows how gentle your hands can be," he called at Setelin's back as she headed for her dispensary.

"Stop tempting fate," Jim told Vortimer. "Next time you provoke her, I won't intervene. But she's not going within half a klick of that warren you call a home without me."

"THIS WAY. OF COURSE YOU'LL REMEMBER THIS PASSAGE." Vortimer tossed too-eager words over his shoulder at Setelin, who turned back to watch Jim, as he adjusted the shoulder strap of the portable diagnostic unit. The corridor, carved out of the living rock face, was narrow, and he had to turn so that the equipment would fit.

"Come in, come in."

With an astonishing lack of tact or perhaps because it was still the cleanest place in the cave, Vortimer had settled his alleged guest in what had been Setelin's room. Seeing the stranger lying on what had been her bed made Jim stifle a growl and press closer to her. The man was pale, except for the evil blooms spotting his face and hands. Blood had trickled from one corner of his mouth and dried there, and he breathed shallowly. A coughing jag from a rotten case of spacer's throat wasn't anything you wanted to provoke. His eyes were shut, and their lids looked thin, bruised.

"It's damp in here," Setelin said accusingly. "You could at least give him warm steam to breathe. He's probably strained ribs or broken them. Did you strap them?"

"I'll check," said Jim, setting down the PDU and unkinking his back. Until he'd patted the stranger down for weapons himself, he wasn't letting Setelin near him. The idea of her bending in close, reaching around the stranger to support his strained ribs . . .

"I'll start the water," Vortimer offered, making Setelin raise an eyebrow at his back as he vanished from the room.

In that moment, his guest blinked open his eyes, ran them over Setelin and around the room, then shut them again so quickly Jim might have thought he'd imagined it—if he hadn't been waiting for just such an expert, appraising glance. Two things were certain: he didn't trust this man one bit and if Setelin had seen the man's expression, she'd have had her knife out.

"I know how this unit works, I think," Jim told her. "Why don't you go and check on—"

"Yes," she said. Her mother's grave, untended for all this time, or left to Vortimer's uncertain care. "I brought offerings," she added, foraging in her carryall for the golden leaves Jim had seen her leave on the grave the first time they'd met.

Opening the diagnostic unit, Jim attached its leads, then sat back on his haunches, Exquemelin style, while lights flashed and shimmered on its readouts. Once or twice the man flinched as injections shot home. Long before the war, chemo, administered in advance of surgery, could wrest remissions from the disease, half-understood and crudely treated. The drugs in the PDU were much stronger.

Jim leaned forward to read biosigns. Yes, body temp was up, way up, but nothing to worry about unless the red lights flashed, and the PDU would take care of that, too. The man would need to be stripped and sponged down, and he was damned if Setelin was going to do it. Not after the way he'd sized her up.

Jim tried to remember when *Blue Ridge* might possibly arrive. Its crew had plenty of practice taking care of their own injured; they'd know what to do. Jim could put the matter into Neave's hands. After all, if the stranger really were a poor, sick engineer kidnapped by pirates, he'd be glad to assist Neave in making investigations. And if he wasn't, he was Neave's and Becker's rightful prey.

He felt a gaze on him, harsh as a solar flare.

"You don't have to pretend you're asleep," Jim told the stranger. "I know you've talked to Vortimer. Feeling rotten?"

The man gagged, coughed, then collected himself. "Here." Jim tore open a towel and let him wipe his own face before he made a long arm and reached for a half-filled glass. He sniffed it.

"Oh, it's clean enough," the man rasped. "Just wasn't thirsty earlier. Now, what's in this thing I'm hooked up to?"

"Mostly painkillers and interferon derivatives," Jim said, supporting the man while he drank. He couldn't feel any weapons on the thin body resting against his shoulder, which meant precisely nothing. "I'd say you're too far gone for the PDU to cure you, but it should be able to force you into remission long enough for us to get you offworld."

"Yeah, yeah," said the man. "That's what they all say. Neat job, by the way, of getting the girl and the turncoat out of here."

"That turncoat," Jim said, bemused that he was actually defending Vortimer, "not only plucked your precious butt out of a crashed pod, but pleaded for your life. My . . . my wife was all for deciding you were a pirate and—"

The man laughed, a skeptical rattling noise Jim didn't like the sound of at all. Setelin would know better, but Setelin . . . no.

He'd taken pains to send her off. She ought to have the brains to stay away.

"Spicy little thing. Nice work. We'll keep this quiet, won't we? Honor among thieves, eh?"

"You told Vortimer you were an engineer," Jim parried. "But I don't recall what you told him your name was."

"I didn't."

"You're going to tell me."

The man lay back against the pillow. "I feel like hell," he said. "Can we have this conversation later?"

"I brought the water." With consummately vile timing, Vortimer bustled into the room, his arms laden with things that clinked and steamed and threatened to tip over, scalding everyone. "And I told her I was serving tea."

Point to you, you bastard, Jim thought at Vortimer silently, then glared down at the stranger, who was now showing signs of attention to the tea completely at odds with his earlier exhaustion. *And you . . . don't think you've gotten more than a breather out of this.*

"Leave the PDU in place," he said. "I'll talk to you tomorrow. And I'd better hear some answers I can believe."

He turned his back on the two men who watched him, a united front for now, and collected Setelin. As he and Setelin walked back toward The Fort, he took her hand, and clung to it like a lifeline.

He'd have traded everything but his regained soul simply to fall into bed beside her, pillow his face on her shoulder, feel her deft hands rub his temples, and listen to her voice, so sharp with others, so gentle with him. He could tell her anything, he knew he could. And he'd tell her the whole story, too, if only this were the right time.

Instead, he spent the night on guard.

As dawn came, black shadows against pale clouds, he was shaking. He only wished it were from exhaustion.

38

The trading post's battered door slammed against the cliff wall, as Jim strode inside. He held his blaster, fully charged, in his free hand. Behind him, confused but appropriately grim-faced, were the guards he'd borrowed from Setelin. She'd been glad enough to rid herself of their surveillance: if she'd only known why Jim had wanted them, she'd have sent half The Fort.

The rat-faced trader sat beside his guest, his body virtually writhing with goodwill.

The man's sparse hair, barely darker than his skin, had been roughly slicked back over his skull. He'd made some attempt to depilate, or gotten Vortimer to do it. His face, stripped of beard now, showed signs of healing. The largest open sore had closed, while two of the small ones were simply red marks, shocking on the spacer-pale skin. The blotches beneath, though . . . deadly, Jim thought. Could Aviva's physicians cure metastatic cancer?

And did he really care? *Maybe I can send a distress call to* Blue Ridge, *tell them to come early, wash my hands of this problem.* He could just see explaining that to Marlow.

When she'd left here, she'd *saluted* him. He couldn't betray that. Not again.

"Out!" Jim ordered Vortimer, who toppled two teacups and trampled one in his haste to obey.

The stranger had pulled himself up until he was almost sitting up. Sweat beaded his face from the effort, and he breathed heavily.

"Let's have it," Jim said. "You can lie to him, assuming you bothered. But I'm the authority here, as much of it as you're going to see. Let's have your name." He brought the blaster up under the man's chin, prodding his face upward so he had to look into Jim's eyes. He could see his face reflected: flushed, angry, resolute.

"My name?" the man asked, his voice astonishingly self-possessed.

"I took the Commodore out of the picture. It's a cinch you're not Amaranth: she's two meters tall. And Waerloga's missing a hand. That leaves—"

"And I was getting such a good impression of you, too," said the . . . he wasn't a man. He wasn't even a pirate. Jim could have guessed from the start. This was the wrecker named Hinksey Brown. "My very own angel of mercy. Although not quite as angelic as the pretty young lady who followed you here yesterday. Where is she, by the way?"

"Safe," Jim bit off the word.

Hinksey Brown chuckled and shrugged. *We'll revisit this issue,* Captain Heikkonen would say and do just that, when you least expected it.

"You going to shoot me now?" He barked out a laugh, then doubled over coughing.

Jim steadied him and wiped his mouth, then held a cup for

him. He could wash his hands when he got home.

"Right now, you couldn't get out of this room," he said. "You'd better rest while you can."

"No rest for the wicked," said Hinksey Brown.

Jim rose. Dammit, he was in control here; he didn't have to spar. "Then fake it," he said, and left the room, the cave, and the plateau for the cleaner air of The Fort.

"I DIDN'T LIKE THE WAY HE LOOKED AT ME," SETELIN TOLD Jim and Stal Viat. She had refused a perch on the arm of Jim's chair, preferring a chair of her own. Wise in her ways—if not wise enough, never wise enough. If he lived a hundred years, he knew this meant she disagreed with him but meant to fight fair. "We all know what the Commodore did, and Melinkor helped him. And you say this one's worse?"

"If he's as sick as all that," Stal Viat said, reaching out for a triangle of flatbread that he dragged through the remnants of yellowing *vetris* paste, "he's not going anywhere. And he's certainly no match for you."

He laughed, then lazily dodged a mock blow.

"You agree with him!" she glared at both men impartially.

"Hold on there," Stal Viat said. "I've seen this man's face in my dreams. Not the sort of thing you want cluttering up your mind, I can tell you."

"What did you—" Setelin's voice almost shook.

"I can't say for certain," said Stal Viat. "When I dreamed of my brother's Captain Marlow, I knew that was a true dream because she turned and took my hand, and gave me the finest gift I have ever received." He turned and smiled at Jim.

"There was nothing clear about my dream this time. But—"

"Would you agree with me that he—that every man—deserves a second chance?" asked Jim. He fought to keep the entreaty out of his voice.

God, please let Stal Viat agree. Let him say yes, Brown deserves the same chance as any other man. That would tip the balance, and Jim could finally confide his whole truth to his best friend.

He leaned back in the chair that had been his since he came to live at The Fort. He could see his face in the polished dark wood, which reflected treasures—the firelight, the sparkle in Setelin's eyes, the warmth of Stal Viat's smile.

"I can't quite say that, brother," Stal Viat shook his head. His hair was shaggy, too. *I've been pushing him too hard; he needs to rest,* Jim thought, even as he sighed at opportunity lost. "I don't like some of the things I've been hearing in the nearby villages. And my dreams have been . . . troubled. I can't quite remember. My parents always ruled in accordance with our laws. If we break them, we play into Vortimer's hands, certainly. And if this man is even worse—"

"What does your father say?" Setelin's voice was sharp.

Stal Viat leaned over, warming his hands at the fire that heated the tea. "He says he is old. That he doesn't understand this new world, these new people. That he and my mother will tend our people as they always have, while I serve as their eyes and ears for these new things."

Setelin shot a glance at Jim. God, of course she knew he'd spoken with Oulian about this; she knew him better than he knew himself, he sometimes thought.

Jim made himself laugh. "You got off easier than I did, brother. I had to promise that, if anything happened to you, my own life would answer."

Stal Viat grinned with a young man's fearlessness and grasped Jim's shoulder.

"My mother has two sons," he said. "And nothing's going to happen to either of us. Or to you either," he added, with a tug at Setelin's long hair.

"You're both too trusting," she snapped, twisting away.

She wanted Hinksey Brown dead. It was the easiest way out. But Jim was sick of expedient solutions. It looked so easy. All he had to do was tighten his hands around a dying man's throat. One twist and he could keep what he had: life and honor, a home, maybe children, if all kept going well.

But you had to grasp your reward with clean hands or you spoiled it.

Besides, where there was one wrecker, there could be others. Hinksey Brown had betrayed his ship.

But where there was one ship, there might be others, too.

Stal Viat yawned, then ducked his head apologetically.

"You're worn out," Jim said. "I've got to take better care of you. Of all of us. I think it's high time we were all in bed," he said and rose.

But before he slept, he went to the comms and coded a message to *Blue Ridge*. His compliments to the captain. No, the situation wasn't urgent. But if they could step up their schedule through the Straits, he'd be vastly in their debt.

That was discretion, not cowardice.

Oulian didn't truly understand what lay beyond his world. He couldn't spare Stal Viat or Cantu to fly word out; what's more, the idea itself might alarm them, or their people. But Jim would sleep more soundly knowing he'd taken every precaution possible except the one from which his reborn soul shrank—killing Hinksey Brown.

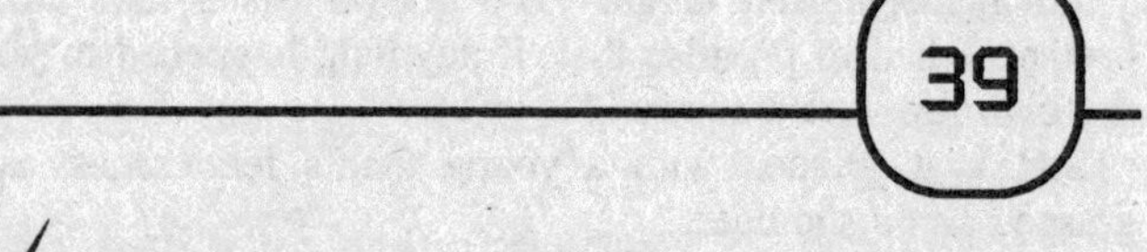

39

Jim smiled at the play of light and wind on the leaves. Several floated free of the low-hanging branches onto the stream whose bank had seemed such a perfect place for him and Setelin to go off together. This spot wasn't so far from The Fort that they couldn't get back quickly, but it was far enough away that they could snatch an afternoon together and pretend it would always be this peaceful. He leaned back, stretching himself on the cool ground cover until his overtired muscles relaxed.

Time to look on the bright side, such as it was.

Brown had entered remission. Vortimer, speaking for once without that whine in his voice that made Jim want to kick him, reported that the man had been eating and trying to walk. Next time Jim visited him, he'd try to talk to him about second chances. He'd seemed willing to listen the last time, and Jim could—at the least—endure him for that. As Marlow had endured Jim.

Stal Viat reported no trouble, anywhere among Oulian's people. And he'd heard from *Blue Ridge*. So: he had his life back and more than he had lost.

He drew in a deep, slow breath after years of feeling as if he was gasping for air. The breeze tasted better than the finest wine he'd ever drunk. The tension in his scalp released, the muscles along his jaw relaxing, leaving him almost dizzy with relief. He hadn't felt this young in . . . not even when he'd *been* young.

He caught Setelin's sidelong glance. For too long she'd had to be lover and caretaker both. Time now for her to relax, too.

Grinning, he reached over to her plate and stole a berry, a crimson juicy thing that reminded him of the strawberries, from Old Earth stock, that his homeworld had exported before the war. He pretended that he was about to pop the berry into his mouth.

"*I* wanted that one!" Setelin, mock indignant, fell rapidly into his playful mood. She shouldn't have to humor him as if he'd break. Not any more.

"Did you?" Jim laughed and dangled the berry on its stem in front of his mouth. "Then come get it."

The trees' lowest branches would seclude them. The ground cover was soft and fragrant. Even trying to persuade her—outside and in the daytime! he could hear her object—would be enjoyable. And who knew? The way his luck was shaping, he might even succeed.

Deliberately, he bit into one side of the berry. Setelin launched herself at him, laughing, her mouth glancing off the berry and onto his own. Laughing into her parted lips, he pulled her down, feeling the fruit squash between their faces. They nuzzled each other, licking it off, laughing breathlessly.

Oh God, for all his graying hair, he was as young as Setelin again. He tangled his hands in her hair and kissed her. Her open mouth tasted of fruit.

A roar, a rumble in the air, shook the ground underfoot, tumbling them onto their sides. Rocks began to clatter from the slopes of the plateau. He threw himself over her. She'd been laughing too hard to hear the falling rocks and mistook his action. When she tried to fling her arms about his neck, he pinned them down, protecting her with his own body until the tremor subsided. A few branches—small ones at that—slapped against his back.

Even before the ground stopped trembling, he leapt up and pulled her to stand beside him.

Abandoning the leaf-covered remains of their sunlit afternoon, they tried to run back to The Fort. Aftershocks turned their passage into a kind of drunken stagger. These weren't natural quakes. Anyone who'd spent time on Shenango's World knew what those felt like. There'd been an explosion, a big one.

Jim had appropriated Melinkor's tech, so this couldn't be Melinkor, setting off some long-hoarded tactical explosive. But Brown . . . Brown who had eaten their bread, profited from their medications, professed himself willing to listen to Jim . . .

The bastard had lied to him. It had *all* been a lie.

Setelin tugged her hand free of a grip that had become punishingly tight. *You're hurting the wrong person, Jim my lad. Again.*

"Sorry," he muttered on a gasped intake of breath.

But there was more fear than pain in her eyes. "I swear, if he and Brown are in this together, I'll kill both of them," Jim told her.

"Find them first," she gasped.

Search parties. Defense. Talk with Stal Viat, assuming he'd

still speak with Jim. And oh God, Oulian, who'd been ill all summer.

Imagine a man hailed out of hell, climbing out of the fires, shaking the last of the embers from his back, raising his face to the intoxication of cool, crisp air, only to turn at a shout from the Pit and fling himself back.

What if, after all, it was impossible to change your nature? Impossible to change your fate.

What if you really only got one chance?

Right now, such as he was, *he* was all the chance this planet had.

By the time they reached The Fort, the gates were closed. Well done, he thought, even as he shouted for them to open.

The massive leaves cracked open, just enough to admit one fool and the woman who loved him when a voice made them whirl round. The guards reached for their weapons.

"Wait! Help me!"

"It's Iri!" Setelin said. "He's covered with blood."

"Wait!" Jim called, but Setelin darted away from the guards and out into the open toward the boy. No one could outrun Iri, but he wasn't running now. He staggered up against Setelin and secure in her clasp, fell to his knees retching.

"Get Stal Viat's flier ready!" Jim ordered. Bile rose in his throat, as if he could vomit all his errors out. *How could you be so stupid? You* wanted *to believe!*

He ran toward Setelin, who knelt over Iri, holding his head, sheltering him with her warmth.

"Breathe, dear heart," she whispered. "Breathe. Now, you can tell me, what happened?"

She shot a glance at Jim as she ran her hands over the boy in a quick, expert examination. Iri could hear. He wasn't bleeding from lips or ears or nose. He couldn't have been that close to the blast.

"Let's get him inside," Jim whispered. At her nod, he picked Iri up, cradling the boy, much to his surprise, against his shoulder.

"The trading post," Iri said. "I was going there—"

"Name of God, why?" The boy flinched away from what was almost a howl. "Stal Viat put it off-limits to you."

"We knew you'd want us, all us boys, to keep it under observation for you. Something we could do, without bothering you when you've been so worried. It was my turn," Iri said. "I thought I saw someone coming out, so I moved in closer. I can move without making any noise. Everyone knows that."

If Jim hadn't had his arms full, he'd have torn his hair out. A pack of boys, longing for manhood, adventure, some damned-fool way or other of impressing him—him, of all people!—taking their lives in their hands. The boy broke off, looking down, paler and more frightened than he'd been a moment before.

"Don't be afraid of me," Jim said. "I'd have done the same thing myself. Tell me. You got to the trading post—"

"I didn't!" Iri said. "I got to the rock walls, you know where . . ." His eyes flickered at Setelin.

So the boy had reached her mother's grave. "And then?"

"I saw something lying there. . . ."

"And you went in closer, of course. . . ."

"It was Vortimer," Iri said, coughing. A guard ran up with a cup of water, and the boy gulped at it while Jim tried not to dance with impatience. "He says . . . sorry, sir . . . 'Bastard stuck a knife in me, and now he's gone.' I put a pressure bandage on him . . . that's why my shirt's torn, see?"

"I taught Iri first aid myself," Setelin said.

"So you left him?"

"He told me, go, bring help, it's too late for me. So I ran, I started climbing downhill, and that was when things exploded."

The child was lucky he hadn't been killed or swept away in a rockslide.

"Found a cave . . . rocks went over the lip of it. . . . When it stopped, I could only think to get here quick as I could." Jim carried the boy into the main hall and set him down.

"Setelin, lend me your blaster again, will you?" Jim asked.

"I'll be back and put you to bed," she promised Iri, then ran to fetch the weapon Marlow had given him, the best they had.

"Flier's ready, sir," a guard reported. His voice was calm, his manner crisp, but a muscle ticced at the corner of one dark eye.

Setelin would shut the gates and keep them shut while he was gone. She knew how to hold this Fort as well as they. Better: the only time her trust had been abused was when she trusted him.

Jim took the blaster from Setelin, belted it around his waist, and started for the door.

"He's probably bled out by now," Setelin cried after him.

"Then I'll bring him back here for burial," Jim said and closed ears to her protests.

THE FORT SHRANK SWIFTLY TO A CHILD'S TOY AS JIM'S FLIER rose. What a devil's game Hinksey Brown had been playing! Where Jim had seen Exquemelin as a sanctuary, Brown must have seen him as a fool in a drunkard's dream of honor on a world much too good for the likes of him to hold. Marlow had been right.

But Marlow had forgiven him. Didn't that mean he too had to try?

Not when others look to you for protection.

His scanners, such as they were, swept the area. Too bad Brown's ship had been destroyed. Jim would have enjoyed blasting him out of the sky.

Far before he wished, he was setting down on the trading post's ill-kept landing field.

"Vortimer!" If Vortimer were conscious, he'd at least try to make some sound, wouldn't he? And if all of this was a trap, well, Setelin kept the blaster fully charged.

His spine prickled, expecting fire. The wind roared, driving dust and grit into Jim's eyes. He backed into cover just as the wind died.

"Over . . . here . . ."

He raced toward Setelin's mother's grave. No one there; not even a wilted offering of bright leaves.

"Where are you?"

"He . . . re . . ."

Jim leapt and rolled, bringing up in the shelter of a squat bush with wide black-green fronds that offered good cover. The hot tang of blood hit his nostrils, and he followed it, his senses keener with self-reproach.

He found Vortimer propped against a boulder half-buried in the ground. The pressure bandage Iri had put on him was soaked through.

As Jim crawled on elbows and knees through the ground cover, Vortimer yawned, then chuckled.

"So the boy found you . . . picked a bad time to spy!"

"I knew I shouldn't have left Brown with you."

"Took the flyer," Vortimer said. "Didn't know I had one, did you? Kept it secret, even from her. Not so smart"—he gulped air, then fought to continue—"Brown found it. Used some tech I've never seen before. You've got to get out of here."

Jim swore at the extent of the trader's blood loss. "I told Setelin I'd bring you back."

"Waste of time," Vortimer said.

"She knows what she's doing," Jim interrupted. "Come on, brace yourself. I'm going to lift you, and it's going to hurt. You can yell all you want."

But Vortimer held up a hand. "Brown tried to talk me into going shares with him. Same arrangement Melinkor had with the Commodore, he said. He blew his own ship, he said. Didn't want to share with a whole crew, but he needed one man, just one downworld. I'm not an idiot, I want you to know I told him. If he could turn on his crew, why'd he bother keeping his word to me? He laughed at me."

"Iri said he stabbed you. Why the devil—"

"Nothing else to use. When I saw the way he was going, I locked up the sidearms. Didn't want . . . wanted to do something right . . . just one thing . . . last thing I ever do, but one . . ."

Vortimer's glazing eyes lit with some of his old malice.

"Almost funny, you know? All Setelin's fancy codes . . . bastard had a little toy that bypassed them. Like picking a kid's lockbox. But I got the last laugh. No flier . . . he had to take just what he could carry, an' he's still not that strong."

The trader shut his eyes. He was going fast. They'd never last till they could reach The Fort.

"Left a whole lot of tech. Now the door was open, I dragged m'self in there . . . set the whole lot of it to blow . . . gave myself two hours to get away. I got out far's the grave when I realized . . . wasn't goin' anywhere. Ten . . . nine . . . eight . . . you've got maybe five minutes to clear out. I'd use 'em if I were you. Some people down there . . . think a lot of you." Another gulp. A thread of blood trickled from the left side of Vortimer's slackening lips. "Get out! What d'you want to be, a hero?"

Jim shut his eyes against a wave of vertigo—black space, stars, sensors showing the approach of an ion storm—all he had to do was jump, and he'd be safe.

Not again. Never again.

"I said . . . get out of here!" With the last of his strength, Vortimer plucked Jim's hands away and ripped off the sodden bandage. "Get the bastard for me!"

He fell back against the rock, his mouth falling open, his eyes rolling up.

Gone.

And now it was Jim's turn to go. Snapping off a salute, he fled. Too bad he couldn't bring the man back to The Fort for burial: just one more broken promise to his account.

Hurling himself into the flier, Jim took it up before he snapped the safety webs about him. Not two minutes later, the entire shelf blew.

The tiny craft bucked and yawed, fishtailing over what felt like half the sky, but he wrestled it back under his control. This wasn't a time to die.

40

A storm kicked in, lightning dancing over half the horizon. Just Jim's luck they missed him every time. He made the approach to The Fort blind and on instruments and lurched through dense horizontal rain and stormwrack into the Hall. Even protected by its thick walls, he could hear branches smacking into walls like tiny explosions. It was the ion storm on *Irian Jaya* all over again.

No rest for Jim in the teeming hall. People rolled up the hangings and rugs of gentler times, piled furniture against the walls. Others lugged in supplies, trailed by children who broke free of their parents' control only to be herded back into the corners where shadows danced against the storage racks. Messengers came and went, a tidal flow that broke against the composure of Setelin and Stal Viat. Setelin sat in her usual chair before the fire, her clever fingers busy making lists. Stal Viat, a list in his hands, leaned against her chair. Neither spoke loudly, but even at the door, Jim could feel the calm eddying out from them into the storm.

"Over here, brother!" Stal Viat gestured, and Setelin looked up, her mouth relaxing in a tiny gasp of relief. Did she really think he wouldn't come through the storm? Or that he'd flee?

Jim walked through the hall, and people, looking at him, fell silent and let him pass.

Setelin ran over to him and let him put his arm around her, hold her, like an old man clutching his cane.

"Dead?" she whispered up at him.

"Vortimer set off the old trading post. Died better than he lived," Jim whispered and drew her even closer.

Behind them, Stal Viat cleared his throat.

"We've had a call from Father," Stal Viat told Jim. "He wants to see us."

"It's a wonder he got that message through," Jim said. "Is he well?"

"Better before this explosion," Stal Viat said. The lack of reproach in his eyes was worse than blame. "But he wants to see us, Mother said."

So, the explosion, the knowledge of betrayal hadn't brought on another stroke. At least, Jim wouldn't have that on his conscience. Hating himself, he asked, "Can it wait? Weather isn't fit to fly."

"I took the call," Setelin said. "Something in her voice. I think you ought to go now."

Stal Viat grimaced. "I've climbed in worse. One good thing. If we can't fly, neither can anything else. We may as well put the time to good use."

Setelin stirred under Jim's arm.

"You stay," he said. "We need someone reliable to handle comm in case there's word from *Blue Ridge* or Brown. To hold things together." The cliché, old as Earth, was "hold down The Fort." If Jim tried to laugh now, he'd run mad into the storm. As opposed to just into it and up the side of a damned mountain.

She pulled free and met Jim's eyes. "You know you're the best one for the job," he told her. "Everyone trusts you."

The big dark eyes filled. A better man would have had the right to kiss the tears away. Wrong: a better man would have seen to it that Setelin did not need to weep. *She* had never failed at her duty, though, and she did not fail now.

She cast an appraising glance at the organized turmoil in the hall, then made herself smile. "Come back soon," she said.

And when Jim turned at the door for what might be his last look at her, she even managed to smile again.

JIM BRACED HIMSELF AGAINST THE RAIN AND WIND FOR THE next step upslope and sprawled instead onto the blessed flatness of the plateau. He laughed at the splash he made, reached over, and grabbed Stal Viat's shoulder as he emerged over the crest of the hill. The younger man sank to his knees, his head down, gasping until he caught his breath. Runoff from the squall had made it feel as if they'd been climbing up a waterfall. Jim looked at the mud-covered Stal Viat, started to laugh again as he wiped the mud and sweat from his face, then choked it off. His cheeks burned, but from shame, not effort.

"I'm too old for this," Stal Viat started to say.

"Your father had a reason for dragging us out in the storm," Jim said. "Let's find out what it is."

He levered himself up on arms that were going to ache a hell of a lot worse two hours from now, assuming he had two more hours, and wobbled toward—no lights shone in Oulian's hall to promise a welcome, hot drinks, and instant offers of dry clothing.

"Blackout," Stal Viat said, with some satisfaction.

"Come on."

Exposed as the plateau was—*Oh God, we've got to get those people under cover!* Jim thought—the wind had slackened, and the rain was tapering off. Fog still hid the slopes, but he could see how the sky was dividing into darker and lighter strata. The darker layers were dissipating: in the lighter ones, he could begin to see stars.

Splashes came out to meet them, Oulian's usual guards, come to grip Stal Viat by arms and shoulders, draw him with them. Apart from Jim, he realized.

You should have thought of that a long time ago.

Stal Viat paused and gestured for Jim to catch up so they could go in together.

The windows had been blackened so no light escaped, but inside Oulian's hall were, finally, the light and heat for which Jim's body longed. The first time he'd come this way, he'd been reeling with exhaustion, with panic, and they'd let him steam in the warmth and then sleep himself out.

Now, Oulian's wife ran forward to greet Stal Viat. She had a generous heart; even now, she spared a quick smile for Jim, whom she'd always called her other son, before drawing both of them to the huge chair where Oulian sat, his hands squarely planted on his knees. Since his illness, he'd gained even more weight. His sallow face gleamed in the firelight, but his deeply shadowed eyes were unreadable.

Stal Viat hastened to his father's chair, kneeling at his feet in the archaic greeting that had always been a matter of silent, loving affirmation between father and son. Now, Oulian laid a hand on his son's head, smoothing back the matted hair. When he spoke, though, it was to Jim.

"There has been a call. From the *new* stranger."

Jim hadn't been a stranger here since he'd produced his tokens from Amory Eliot Neave.

"I listen and obey," he said, adapting the phrase he'd heard Oulian's guards use.

"This stranger—" Impossible to set bounds to the contempt, the fury, and the fear in Oulian's low voice.

"Hinksey Brown."

"He has set himself up as Lord in the town by the Silver River Crossing."

Two rivers met there, before joining to plunge three hundred meters in a spectacular waterfall. It was a rich site, and a beautiful one. Melinkor was said to have fled there. If those two allied, a potential Situation had just turned exponentially worse. If he accepted Brown as an ally . . .

"And I can no longer fight," Oulian said, his hands going slack on his knees.

"That is what you have sons for!" Stal Viat said.

Oulian's eyes burned into Jim's.

"Brown killed Vortimer," Jim forced the words out a mouth that was the dryest thing about him. His clothing had begun to steam in the warmth from the fire. No one offered him a blanket or a robe. "The old trader tried to stop him, and he answered for it with his life. As I will answer if harm comes to your son, or any of your people. *Our* people, you used to say. Has that changed?" Dammit, he was too old for his voice to crack like that.

"I have your word," Oulian said.

Jim inclined his head and fought down the lump in his throat. "Now," he said, "if you have the call codes for Silver River, let us speak with this stranger of yours."

Jim's oath must have won back some of the trust Brown had made him forfeit; because Oulian didn't protest when Stal Viat lugged the antique comm unit into the hall and accessed Silver River's codes.

Brown's face appeared onscreen. He looked younger, less ill, as if his recent murders had assuaged some hunger. Not sated, Jim was afraid. And, for all his appearance of health, he stared at Jim and Stal Viat with the unspeakable hatred of the fearful dying for the young and healthy.

"So you felt the blast, did you?" he asked Jim. "My sensors show another one. Too big for an aftershock."

"That was Vortimer," Jim said. "He lived long enough to make sure what you left at the post was no longer a threat."

"Rotten timing," said Brown. He rubbed his face where shiny pink flesh had replaced an open sore.

Abruptly Jim was furious. He hadn't trusted Vortimer, and he'd despised him, but the old trader had died like a man and a soldier. "He took you in. He risked asking help for you from people he thought would spit at him. How could you turn on him?"

"You're a fine one to talk, aren't you, Mister . . . "

At the sound of the surname he hadn't used for so long, Jim almost dropped the cup he held. His blood roared in his ears. His temples felt too tight. He was back in the dark, on the hull of *Irian Jaya,* scalding in the clumsy suit, breathing the reek of fear.

"Oh yes," said Hinksey Brown. "I'm quite aware of who you are and who you used to be. Isn't as if you ever really tried to hide. Now, let's clear the natives out of here and speak like honest men."

Stal Viat laid a hand on Jim's shoulder, restoring him to himself.

"The honest men here can damned well hear anything we

have to say," Jim replied. Stal Viat had blinked, but otherwise did not turn a hair at Brown's words.

"You really do put on a good man-of-honor act, I'll give you that," Brown said. "Quite the hero, turning the local heir into your sidekick and taking up with that pretty little thing. You didn't always have it this good."

"My friends and I still control off-world trade," Jim said. "What are you going to do when you run out of medications? Any more smart remarks and I'll let you go hunt for herbs in the woods."

Brown grinned, showing yellowed teeth. "Can't a man joke? I don't get much fun out of life these days."

"What do you want out of it?" Jim asked. "Look, you want tech? I can get you tech. I can get you offworld. I've got powerful friends on Aviva, and there's a ship coming—"

"*Blue Ridge* is no friend to me," Brown said. "Even if it comes when you whistle. Smart little bastard, aren't you? What makes you think I'm going to let the likes of you lord it over your own private kingdom?"

Jim shrugged. "It's not mine. If it's anyone's, it's his." He gestured at Stal Viat.

"Besides," Jim made himself continue, "you betrayed your ship. What can you match against *Blue Ridge?*"

"Don't you go all holy on me about abandoning ships," Brown replied. "You want to see my hand? Fine. Ante up."

For a long moment, Jim just stared at Brown in the flickering screen.

The wrecker flung himself back in his carved chair, spurned his cup, reached for a pitcher, and drank, spilling liquor down his chest. "There he is! Thinking, I'll bet you, what can I use to pay off this bad, bad man? Tech? Isn't a piece of tech here that's not a relic. I own this place, mister. And I own you."

He was being maneuvered, herded toward a cliff, Jim realized, but he spoke the words he knew Brown wanted to hear.

"You're bluffing."

"Am I? By now, I've got bombs planted all along the perimeter of this . . . this river-rats' warren." He leaned to one side, briefly out of Jim's view.

"Another bluff."

"That was the first stupid thing I've ever heard you say," Brown replied. "Aside from the sermons about second chances. Bring him in!" he ordered to someone out of range of the commscreen.

Two guards wearing necklaces of spent cartridges dragged Melinkor toward Brown and braced him there.

"Old enemy of yours, I believe," Brown said. "Want him?"

Jim shrugged and glanced at Stal Viat. "If that's what you're making an ally out of, I think you're making a mistake."

"Smart bastard, as I said. Melinkor only thinks he's been my ally. I'll grant you, he was useful getting me in here, but now . . .

"You've heard a lot of stories about me," Brown remarked to Jim. "Some are even true. But some . . . I'm a practical man. And when I don't need things anymore, I discard them."

He coughed, pressed a hand to his chest, sliding it inside his tunic as if to ease some ache within. But when he withdrew his hand, he was holding a blaster every bit as deadly—and as fully charged—as the one Jim now carried.

He gestured the men holding Melinkor to stand back a step or two. "I don't want to be caught in the backwash," he explained amiably. "And you deserve a good view."

"Brown," Melinkor said. "Captain . . . sir . . . don't do this. . . ."

"This dirtworlder thought he'd be my master," said Brown. "So he brought me inside. Not his first mistake. First mistake was that detonation. Oh, mind you, I can work around it. But I don't like mistakes."

Melinkor twisted in the guards' arms. Seeing Jim, he cried, "We've been enemies, but tell him, tell him I haven't deserved—"

The front of his shipsuit and jacket darkened as his bladder and his knees gave way. Only the guards' reluctant grips held him upright.

Brown gestured with the blaster barrel for them to stand away, and Melinkor toppled into the puddle he had made.

Jim gripped Stal Viat's hand hard. *Don't give anything away.*

"There's no need for that," Jim said. "I believed you."

"A minute ago, you called my bluff. Call me a liar, will you? You'll have to learn better if you're to be my second-in-command," said Brown. "Besides, he's made a mess. That's *two* mistakes he's made. Have to think of the troops; can't tolerate this lack of discipline, now can we?"

He raised the blaster and fired. Melinkor, sobbing, looked up in time to see energy lash out, engulfing him in a column of fire.

Brown set down the blaster and drank again, emptying the beaker. He tossed it aside and gestured as a gray-faced woman ran toward him with another one. Picking up the blaster, he pretended to sight down its barrel at the woman, who fled in silence.

"Just joking," said Brown. "But please do believe me that I am not joking when I say that, if *Blue Ridge* has any ambitions to arrest me, I will blow this kennel into orbit with less compunction than I killed your friend."

Stal Viat leaned forward into the screen.

"I told you to get rid of the natives," Brown said to Jim. "I'll warn you once, mister. I don't tolerate mistakes. I should add that I'll expect you to carry out my orders promptly when you're my—"

"My father is chief here," said Stal Viat over Brown's words. "He's authorized me to negotiate. Name your terms."

"Name my terms," said Brown. "So, you've been learning. I'll name my terms, all right, son, but to the man you call Jim. I won't even mind that you don't leave the room while he's dickering."

Sweat gathered in Jim's palms. Below Brown's field of

vision, he wiped them off and felt his hand clasped by Stal Viat's.

"As my brother said, Brown, name your terms."

"I want the planet," said Hinksey Brown. He coughed rackingly, spat, and drained his mug, which was rapidly refilled.

"You're drinking too much," Jim told him, leaning forward. "Sooner or later, you're bound to get a reaction, all those drugs in your system. Could be lethal."

"That wouldn't solve your problem," Brown replied, wiping his mouth.

"Got your bombs on a dead man's switch, have you?" Jim asked, keeping his voice level. Thank God, Brown held Stal Viat in contempt, but Jim knew he was listening to every word and already making plans.

"Wouldn't you just like to know?"

"I was an arms officer. Nothing wrong with my tech background. I can guess."

"Can you? I mean it. I want your friend there to step down. When his father punches out, I want to step in. And I've got a place for you, provided you toe my line."

Oulian's decline this past season—what Vortimer hadn't told him, Melinkor probably had. Damn, damn, damn.

"My friend will outlive you, Brown. And there's a hell of a lot of people in Silver River. You can't hide from all of them."

"That's what I want you for."

"As if they'd trust me if I joined you. That stuff's rotting your brains, that and the drugs."

"Level with me," Brown asked. "What's your price? Your *real* price?"

Despair made Jim curl his lip.

"Brother!" Stal Viat shouted. "I'm getting a transmission from Setelin. She says she's gotten a fix on something entering the system—probably *Blue Ridge.*"

Blue Ridge—or a rider—wasn't due for another month or so. If that. Jim suppressed a grin and flashed Stal Viat a thumbs-up where Brown couldn't see.

"He's bluffing!" Brown said.

"Your turn to decide if you want to put your money where your mouth is," Jim said. He leaned back. *I've got all the time in the world. Bless Stal Viat. Bless him.*

"Changes things, doesn't it?" Jim sensed advantage, scented wavering, and pursued it. "Come on, man. You can't fight that ship by yourself. Trust us again. We'll get you help. More meds, when the ones you've got run out. Hell, if you want, I'll go back with you and be a character witness."

Brown laughed. It passed into a paroxysm of coughing that left him gasping, hunched over in his chair. He looked at the half-empty beaker, then back at the screen.

"You're losing it, aren't you?" Jim said. "You blew your ship so you wouldn't have to share. You've killed two accomplices here already. You've got Silver River mined. And for what? So you won't die alone? You don't have to die at all, if you play this right."

Brown seemed to be listening. Stal Viat stood in the doorway, murmuring instructions to the men and women who clustered around him.

"We can get you offworld," Jim went on. "Ships may not be what you're used to, but they're good enough to dodge *Blue Ridge,* and we can warn them off if you don't do anything stupid, like blowing Silver River. You've probably got allies somewhere, and if you don't, you can still make do for awhile. What about it?"

"How about that sharp little piece you live with?"

Jim swallowed fury. "I wouldn't, if I were you. You'd have to sleep sometimes, and she likes knives. Better deal with me and Stal Viat. Think about it. You won't get a better offer."

He turned away from the screen, using his shoulders to block Brown's view of Stal Viat, who jerked his chin toward the door.

Jim knew what that meant. Someone had to go to Silver River and evacuate the place. At need, Stal Viat could probably identify and deactivate a bomb—he could read up on it on the way over—while Jim kept negotiations going.

He turned back to face the screen. "Brown!" he called the wrecker's attention back from the bottom of his cup. "We really need to talk about this."

"*You* need to talk about this," said Brown. "You talk too damn much. You do it on purpose. Me, I let tech speak for me. Four hours, and then I start activating my perimeter defenses."

Four hours. Say it took Stal Viat an hour to power up and fly to Silver River. Maybe more. Given Brown's offworlder tech and paranoia, he'd want to approach as stealthily as possible.

Keep yourself safe, brother.

"What do you think about my offer?" Jim asked. Stal Viat knelt for his parents' blessing, then raced outside. The rotten flying weather would help him slip through Brown's scans.

Assuming it didn't crash him.

"Not much, if it's the best one you've got. You don't have the winning hand here, mister. Haven't had it since . . . Havilland Roads."

"Rehashing old memories'll get you nowhere," said Jim. "Look, I'll give you the best ship we have. I'll even throw in the PDU and meds enough to keep you in remission for a year." The PDU was valuable; if they didn't have it, some people might not last out the year, but they'd have died in any event, and if they could get Brown offworld, he could keep the body count down. Maybe.

"Best offer I can make, Brown," Jim persisted. "I'd take it if I were you."

"Why?" Brown honestly sounded as if he wanted to know.

"*Blue Ridge* is coming. Sure, you might take it out, but *Blue Ridge* is part of a fleet, and its people have long memories. And I've got friends offworld, friends who sent me, who send out *Blue Ridge* and her cousins when there's need. If you harm any of us, do you think they'll ever give up?"

"What's it to me if I blow you all into Jump?" Brown said. "Last month, I was dying."

"Today, you're not. Maybe a dying man wants to take the

planet with him. But the meds have given you your life back. Face it. This is one world you're not going to get. Take the money and run, as they used to say."

"Did they?" asked Brown. He took a deep breath, held it, exhaled. Took another. Didn't cough. He nodded, half to himself. "What assurance do I have you won't rig the ship to blow once I leave atmosphere?"

"My word," Jim said.

Brown just laughed.

Keep talking, Jim wished him. *The longer you talk, the better the chances for Stal Viat.*

"You want to inspect the ship?" Jim asked. "I'll fly it over myself. Hell, I'll take its weapons systems offline so you don't have to worry I'd fire on an unarmed city. I'll make myself hostage for its good behavior."

"What if I accept? Would you go with me?"

Jim made himself laugh. "God, wouldn't that be a joke? You'd be crazy if you think you could trust me to be your exec after all this. Better run solo. At least, you know what you're capable of."

"Yes," said Brown. "That I do." He paused, looked at the liquor flask, and shook his head. "You can bring the ship," he conceded. "But I'm not making any promises."

"I don't expect them," said Jim. *Or trust them.*

41

Oulian had glared shrewdly at Jim as he reassured Stal Viat's mother. His chin dropped onto his chest, and he dozed.

He hadn't lied to Hinksey Brown. The flier whose acceleration shot him back in his shock webs was indeed their finest ship. There was a finer, but everyone considered it the personal property of Stal Viat, who'd taken it to Silver River.

Clear air on the comm. Setelin probably wasn't speaking to him. If he lived, he'd make it up to her. He'd promised her. He'd promised Oulian on his life. And he'd even promised Hinksey Brown.

Sooner rather than later, he was going to have to betray someone again.

The tiny cockpit enclosed him, sheltering him in red and green and white shining grids. Outside, the sky darkened from evening gray to the perpetual black of space as he left atmosphere behind. It would be so easy just to keep on going.

But Marlow had saluted him. Stal Viat trusted him. Setelin loved him. And he was sick to death of retreating.

He snatched a moment to look out at the clusters of stars and glowing gas that made up the Straits of Aquila. Then, he arrowed down again, activating the comms.

"You're late," Brown's voice was slurred.

"I took her up for a test run. Do you like what you see?" Jim asked. He was dropping out of heaven now. Lights glowed on his panels; outside, the hull gleamed like a hearthfire; and the darkness around him was thickening into clouds.

Static broke up Brown's sated chuckle. Damn shame to turn a ship this sweet over to someone who'd probably overdose himself within three days because he was too drunk to dial his own meds.

Jim's hands sweat. Navcomp told him he was coming up on Silver River. Deceleration pressed him back, and he found the pressure perversely comforting.

"Coming in to land," Jim said. "You can scan me. Weapons ports are sealed and weapons are offline. And I'm unarmed."

Truth, if you didn't count his wits, his unarmed-combat training, and his desperation.

"THAT YOU, HERO?" Brown's voice crackled in his ears. *"I'm sending you landing coordinates. Forget the landing field; got a better idea."*

I don't like that at all, Jim thought. *But just let me get in close enough . . .*

He brought the flier down in a broad spit of land defined by a curve in the river and marked out by torches. Neither it, nor the lush ground cover, slightly smoking now from the landing, were silver now, but dark.

Jim snatched up a handlamp before activating the miniature sliding platform that dropped him softly onto Brown's improvised landing field.

He raised it, peering through the rainy damp for a thin man whose skin bore the shiny patches of recent healing.

But the first face he saw belonged to Stal Viat.

In the white light of the handlamp, his friend's face was gray with sweat, except where it shone with tears or snot. His lips were split and puffy. Blood, black in the shadows, dripped onto his shipsuit. He looked older than Oulian and a hell of a lot sicker.

And he stumbled toward Jim the way a boy who knows that what he's broken is past mending runs toward his father—*make it right, you can make it right!*

Jim caught him around the shoulders and held him hard. The stink of fear was in his sweat, his poor fastidious brother. Stal Viat let his head drop onto Jim's shoulder, leaving a bloody mark. He sobbed only once, then pulled away.

"Brother, what's wrong?" Jim asked.

"Don't call me brother," Stal Viat said. He raised a battered hand to his face, trying to scour it. "I failed. His tech was better. He caught me. I talked to the headman, tried to get everyone to clear out, but they were moving . . . so damn slowly . . . so I thought we haven't got much time, maybe I can disable the charges. I was on the second one when he caught me."

"Never mind that!" Jim said. "Did you get them out?"

Stal Viat began to pant, then gagged. He crouched, and put his head between his knees, sick with his failure.

"Heads *up,* hero!" said Brown, strolling forward.

He grabbed Stal Viat's shoulder and prodded his chin up

with the muzzle of his blaster. The red of a full charge glinted off the fresh blood that dribbled from Stal Viat's torn lip.

"Your *brother's* attempts at stealth were pathetic," Brown remarked to Jim. "I had him on my screens practically the minute he took off."

Stal Viat dropped his head in shame.

"I doubt it," Jim snapped. "I've inspected Silver River's tech. I don't care how good you are; there's no way in hell you could have upgraded that setup in the time you had."

Brown shrugged. "Well, you know best, I'm sure. Thing is, I caught your young friend here making a jumble of one of my explosives."

"You and whose army?" A cold breeze was blowing. Stal Viat was shuddering with the chill and reaction from the kind of epic fuckup that makes men whimper in their sleep in the dreadful pale hours before dawn. Jim drew closer to his friend, trying to work off his jacket one-handed.

"Don't move," said Brown. "My bodyguard's got you covered." He gestured expansively. In the circle of light cast by Jim's handlight, he saw faces he remembered.

"Of course," Jim agreed. "They traded Melinkor in on a bigger bully. My congratulations."

He should have known. It was Heikkonen of *Irian Jaya* all over. Men like Heikkonen, men like Brown, always found people who were willing to go along, willing to sell their tiny souls for a tinier bit of bestowed power.

"You going to take them all with you when you leave?" Jim asked. "I brought the ship. Check it out."

"I don't need it," said Brown. "I've got his. Over there."

Stal Viat stiffened. "What happened, brother?" Jim asked in an undertone. "Did he tell you that unless you brought in the ship, he'd kill everyone here?"

Stal Viat nodded, then swallowed hard. "The children."

God, you could parcel out your soul in tiny deal after squalid deal when all you ever wanted to do was some good. Stal Viat had never hurt a soul in his life, never wanted to hurt anyone, and this is what happened to him.

"I'm guessing Brown shot them anyhow, to teach you—and this prize lot of fools—a lesson."

Stal Viat leaned forward till his head rested on Jim's shoulder. "Just five."

Only days before, he'd complained that his dreams had fled him. He'd be lucky if he never dreamed again.

Brown laughed, the low, sated laugh Jim had heard as he'd taken off.

"The gospel according to Brown," Jim said. "Robbing people is good. Running things—why, that's really good. But destroying things—cities, people, souls—by God, that's a job for a *real* man. Especially a man with the fear of death on him. I'm telling you, Brown, the meds in that ship are clean. You can take them and go. Get out of here."

"Not quite yet," Brown replied. "I've got one more thing to do."

Pulling a remote out of a sealed pocket, he bent over its glittering lights. A red square lit, gleaming in the center of the panel.

"NO!" Jim shouted. Letting Stal Viat stagger, he launched himself at Brown.

The wrecker's bodyguards plucked him out of the air and flung him on the ground. He felt two ribs snap.

"Yes," said Brown, and squeezed his thumb down on the glowing light, as if caressing some unwilling captive.

Fire exploded all around them, and the ground rocked. The guards went sprawling. Jim, used to explosives, fought to his feet first.

Quietly, he walked toward Stal Viat's ship, then paused. "You say you loaded the PDU on this one and the meds with it?" Brown asked, pitching his voice to carry over screams from beyond the field as well as Stal Viat's sobs.

"That's what I said."

"Thanks! Don't think I've simply demonstrated my power before moving on," Brown added. "I'll be back. With my own people."

He had a full charge in his blaster; Jim could see it; but

instead of firing, he walked toward Jim's flier, activated the hatch, and sealed himself in.

"Back up!" Jim shouted. If Brown didn't jib at blowing up Silver River—and God knows how many people had stayed in their homes—he wouldn't think twice about torching every man on this field.

The former bodyguards cut and ran. If there were any survivors, Jim wouldn't bet any money at all on the guards surviving past dawn. If the decision were his to make, he'd watch as the survivors took out their rage, their grief. . . .

He waited for Stal Viat to lay a gentle hand on his arm, to remind him of the law. He waited for the ground to crack open and swallow Brown the way his father said miracles happened sometimes. He loved his father. But he hadn't believed in those stories since he'd jumped ship.

The flier, with Brown at the controls, screamed upward. If only Setelin hadn't been bluffing—had she?—about the approach of *Blue Ridge*. Without recognition codes, the trader was likely to see the flier as hostile. And act accordingly.

"We've got to stop him," Stal Viat muttered beside him. "Got to. I've got to."

"You've got to get back," Jim said. "We'll get Setelin to look at—"

"Look at me? I can never look my father in the eyes again!" said Stal Viat.

His eyes flickered toward his ship, and he went very still—gathering strength, Jim thought. He tensed, preparing to restrain his friend.

"Let *me* go," he said. "I'm a better gunner."

"You gave your word not to fight him," said Stal Viat. "Besides, you never could figure out most of my modifications worth a damn."

He started toward his ship. His reflexes, which Jim had always envied, were shot to hell. Even with those modifications, he'd be no match for Brown in a scramble.

Maybe he had no intentions of engaging in a scramble. Or in any kind of fair fight.

Overhead, Brown's trajectory was just another spark from the fires that turned the ruins of Silver River red.

Jim staggered after Stal Viat, grabbing him by the shoulder and turning him around. "Don't do it," he begged. "Think of your father, your mother. They live for you."

"They're old," Stal Viat said. "They'll understand. I failed. If I ever dream again, I know what I'll see, and I can't, I just can't. What good can I be for any of them?"

"Brother . . ." Jim, who had never asked for anything, held out his hands to his friend. "You can live with these things. You can live through them."

"Can you?" asked Stal Viat. "Is that what you've been doing all these years? I honor the choices you made. But I'm not as strong . . . not as . . ." he shook his head, starting to reach out as if to take Jim's hand, then turned the motion into an uppercut that, even weakened as he was, sent Jim sprawling. He felt another rib give way.

"Come back, you damned fool!" he shouted.

But Stal Viat had broken into a stumbling run, was standing on the flier's ramp, was mounting into its cabin. He raised his hand to Jim in the salute he'd seen Marlow give him.

Even now, Jim could run after him, fling himself on the ramp before it closed. He could even clutch the flier itself. Stal Viat would never take off if it meant immolating the man he had always called friend and brother.

Or would he?

It didn't matter. Jim had seen the expression on his battered face. It was the same despair that drove men into any vice that offered a nibble of oblivion, that drove them to cycle themselves out airlocks, or turned able spacers into wreckers. Cut off from his dreams, his self-respect, Stal Viat looked over his life and . . .

"No!" Jim screamed again as the flier took off, accelerating so fast that ribs must have broken in the initial liftoff.

At least, here at the last, he hadn't said the unforgivable thing. He hadn't reminded Stal Viat that Jim had promised on his own life that Oulian's soul would live.

He stood and watched as the ship dwindled into a streak of fire chasing another streak of fire.

"Fly free, brother," Jim said. He brought his hand up in salute.

He let the tears stand on his face as he walked back to his flier. In the morning, someone would have to come out here, organize the survivors, identify the dead, and begin the work of rebuilding. Someone else.

He activated comm.

"Hello, boy!" It was Setelin's voice, almost unrecognizable with relief.

Scanners showed two ships, one trying frantically to evade, the other at ramming speed.

"Hello, girl," Jim answered softly.

The ships' vectors merged. Jim glanced away from the explosion that set the sky ablaze.

Sleep well, brother.

"Jim?" Setelin's voice was soft as she assembled pieces of the deadly puzzle. He heard the little choke of breath that meant she'd solved it.

She had known Stal Viat all her life. At least, she had known what made him grow up into the gentlest soul of Jim's acquaintance. And she'd been spared making the decision that spared Stal Viat a lifetime of guilt and bad dreams.

"I'm coming home," Jim said, after too long a pause.

He heard a sigh, almost a sob, then dead air.

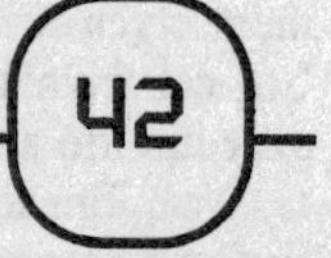

42

Setelin's hands shook as she began to unfasten the shutters covering the window of the room they'd shared. She stilled them and tried again, her hands fumbling as if she had become forty years older overnight.

Silvery light and morning air filtered through the shutters, along with Cantu's voice. Over the clamor of messengers, workers, and frightened children that immediately filled the room, Jim could hear Cantu bellow all the way from the main hall. He paused, and there was instant silence before the noise started up, if at a less-frantic pitch. Cantu sounded like he had matters in hand. Just as well.

Poor Cantu. After Setelin's cry of "Get away from us!" when Jim had come in looking, he was certain, like death warmed over, Cantu had taken up the burden of damage control. Freeing Jim to begin to unwind the skeins that had been his life. Starting with an explanation—the whole story—to Setelin.

Hell of a note to abandon these people without leadership. At least, they'd have Cantu . . . afterward; the man who should have led them was—at least Stal Viat had as clean a death as Jim could contrive. Cantu and Setelin would miss him. Would miss them both.

He walked over to the window, mildly surprised when it hurt that Setelin backed away from him. He had never meant to hurt her. He should have stayed away from her in the first place.

He drew a deep breath. How strange: he could still enjoy the freshness of the air, which last night's storm had left so crisp and cool it felt like wine in the throat. He'd be able to take the flier back up to the plateau. Just as well: he wasn't sure he had the strength to make the climb, and there was every chance he'd fall and his broken ribs would puncture a lung. That was as good a way to die as any, but it wouldn't keep his promise to Oulian. *On my own head.*

Setelin drew in a deep breath, then another. The light glinted on her dark hair and pooled around her on the floor. God, how he'd always loved watching dawnlight creeping up her bare shoulder, and he'd missed his last chance to see it. His last chance to hold her.

But what else could Jim have done? Flown in from the wreck of Silver River, with news that his best friend was dead when he could have stopped him, and then taken his woman to bed? Only a wrecker could have done that, and Hinksey Brown was dead. Killed by Stal Viat.

It was time, not for love, but for truth.

Setelin turned back toward him, and Jim rose.

"Your captain tried to tell me once," she said. "She said, 'He's not good enough.' I called her a liar."

Jim shook his head. "I wanted to tell you the whole truth. You and Stal Viat." His voice was hoarse, and the pitcher was empty. His eyes stung, his ribs ached like fire, and he expected he'd have one hell of a fever if he lived long enough.

"You could have trusted us," Setelin said. "We knew you grieved for something. Why else would you have come and given yourself to us?"

Abruptly, her quiet, her control abandoned her, and she ran to him, clasping him in her arms. So tiny; so strong. Jim forced himself not to flinch as she jarred his ribs. He closed his arms around her in his turn, lifting her up until he felt her face, and her tears, against his neck.

"I could never bring myself to tell you," he whispered against her hair. "It was my cowardice, not anything you did wrong."

Setelin stirred in his arms, and he set her down.

"So you see now why I have to give my life back," Jim explained. "I told Oulian, if anything happened to Stal Viat or any of his people, I'd answer for it."

Setelin's dark eyes dilated, and her mouth opened, a square of horror.

"No," Setelin said. "No. Oulian will forgive you. You're all the son he has left."

"There are some mistakes that cannot be forgiven," Jim said.

He stepped out of her arms and began to remove his jacket. Each movement sent jolts of pain through him. "I'm going to need your help," he said, pressing a hand to his chest. "Strap me up, will you? I don't want Oulian to see me hunched over and sick. I don't want his pity. Just let him keep his side of the bargain."

"No!" Setelin cried. Tears had begun to roll down her face. "I know who you are. I know what you are. You're *mine*!"

There was a clean shipsuit in the chest by the bed they hadn't slept in that night. Moving very carefully, Jim opened the heavy lid and bent to retrieve it. A rib sent jagged fire through his chest.

Setelin held her fists to her face, trying to force back the kind of sobs Jim hadn't heard since their first night together.

Jim reached for his medikit and injected himself. That was a waste of painkiller his people would need, but he couldn't risk being seen to flinch. Awkwardly, he began to wind bandages tightly about his ribs.

"Forgive me," he said softly. He hadn't meant to ask, but his need forced it out along with the rest of the truth.

"Never!" she cried passionately. "You yourself said some things cannot be forgiven."

"So I did. But it makes our parting even more bitter than it needs to be," he replied.

His ribs as tightly bound as he could manage, he struggled into the clean shipsuit. Thanks to the strappings and the painkiller, the effort made him gasp only a little. He sealed his suit, straightened his jacket, collected Marlow's blaster, checked the charge, and pocketed it.

It might be more merciful to spare Oulian, who was old and sick. But Jim had been heartsick long enough. And he had a promise to keep.

He cast one last look at Setelin and turned silently to go.

"Wait!" She ran after him and flung her arms about him. Oh God, something in the feel of her breasts, her belly . . . *don't you dare even think about it. This is no time for beginnings.*

"I won't have it said that *I* left *you*," she said, and walked with him out the door.

The last twist of the knife but one.

* * *

JIM'S PEOPLE FROM THE FORT WERE WAITING FOR HIM AT the airfield. They pressed forward, silently looking at him, then stepping aside.

Last of all them, Cantu came up to Jim. "Your flier is fueled and ready," he reported.

When in hell had his exec found time not just to have the thing fueled, but washed?

Jim reached out to clasp Cantu's hands in his own.

"I've served Oulian my whole life," said Cantu. "And I tell you, he is not a man who'll do murder."

Trust Cantu to know about the promise Jim was about to redeem.

Jim shook his head.

Cantu pulled Jim close for a hug that felt gentler than it looked, the first time he'd ever presumed. "*Blue Ridge* is coming," Jim whispered to him. "Get Setelin offworld. Her and . . . my son."

Cantu set his forehead on Jim's shoulder and sobbed.

"That won't help," Jim said. "One request. Obey me, for once in your life, will you? Look after things for me. Look after them." He pointed with his chin at the silent people who filled their eyes with him.

Cantu backed away. His shoulders hunched as if he just realized the weight of the burden that Jim laid on him. Jim looked beyond his shoulder and saw Cantu's wife in the crowd. A sensible woman. She'd pull him through, and he'd do just fine. Cantu would be better off without him: his own man, and a fine leader.

Taking Setelin's hand, Jim climbed into the flier.

"Better let me pilot," Setelin said.

"Good try, love," he whispered. "But I'm not letting you run away with me."

He turned to the controls to give her time to wipe her eyes. By the time he'd fastened his safety restraints, she was calm again.

* * *

SEEING JIM'S FLIER APPROACH THEIR PLATEAU, OULIAN'S people emerged from their houses and circled the field.

"What do they think they're doing, exposing themselves like this?" Jim muttered. "Anyone at all could be at the controls."

"They know," said Setelin. "They know how you fly. How Stal Viat . . . flew."

She unsnapped her webbing, and, before Jim could protest, his own, then stood aside to let him leave the flier first.

Overhead came a whir of wings and the song of a dawn-bird, brilliant green against the silvery foliage. That, and the sound of his footsteps and Setelin's, and his own harsh breathing, were the only sounds Jim heard.

People stared at him in silence, as they had at The Fort. He'd seen before how quickly a man can become an outcast. But the morning light glinted off the tears on their faces. They parted ranks to allow him to walk toward Oulian's house, then closed in behind him.

Of all the houses on the plateau, only Oulian's still had blackout gear on its doors and windows. The door was closed, rejecting what had happened.

I'll just wait here till I starve to death.

As he stepped forward, ready to rap on the door for entry or push it open himself, Oulian's wife opened the door. Her hair was unbound like a skein of yarn tangled by a wicked child. She wore none of her usual ornaments: just the drab shift and jacket of a poor woman's mourning.

"Must he pay this price too?" she asked Jim.

Setelin gave a little sob and ran to her.

She pulled Setelin into the house. Jim followed. The only sound he could hear was his slow, steady footsteps.

A circle of torches in the darkened hall marked where Oulian lay back in his chair of state, surrounded by his agemates, relatives, and friends. There seemed to be fewer of them than usual.

Jim managed not to flinch at the effort he sensed it took

Oulian to draw each breath. His friend's father's skin was the color of clay.

Near him lay a pile of gear: Stal Viat's second-best helmet, a red cap or two, a knife that the heirs in Oulian's line had probably carried since the First Ship had landed. They didn't even have a body to mourn over or to bury. Jim glanced at Stal Viat's possessions, then looked away.

"He came—" whispered an old man scarcely fatter than the carved stick that propped him up.

"He's taken it upon his own head," another man said, more loudly.

Jim turned toward them. "Yes," he said. "Upon my head."

He stepped forward to stand before Oulian. Setelin was already there, kneeling at the old man's right side, her now ringless hand covering the hand that dangled from the heavy arm of his chair.

Oulian's features on that side seemed blurred, as if a careless thumb had smeared a waxwork.

Jim waited awhile for Oulian's good eye to focus on him. It stared him down.

"I am come in sorrow," Jim said.

Taking the blaster from his pocket, he stepped forward, laid it on Oulian's lap, and waited. "I am come ready and unarmed," he added.

The big old man swept Marlow's blaster off his lap with what he held in his good hand—one of the weapons Neave had given him so long ago. He tried to speak, but between the stroke and his sobbing, his words turned into an inhuman moan.

He struggled to rise, then sank back panting until his attendants helped him from behind. Something metallic rang as it dropped onto the stone floor. Involuntarily, Jim glanced down as the ring that had been his talisman rolled beneath his foot.

Oulian tottered on his unsteady feet, making his attendants sway. Setelin darted in to stand at his right hand once again, her slight strength balancing the old man's faltering bulk.

Again, he opened his mouth to speak and uttered only gobbling noises. Tears rolled from his good eye. Even the weak one glittered with fury and heartbreak.

Stal Viat's mother sobbed. "Can't you spare him this?" she cried again.

Am I cruel in this too? Jim asked himself.

No more cruel, he thought, than Stal Viat, dying because there were some dreams he could not face.

Jim let his eyes meet Oulian's until he was sure the old man who'd been a father to him understood. *As I did for Stal Viat. End the dream.*

Oulian's hand tightened around the ancient weapon. Its charge gleamed like the eye of a serpent. Recoiling, Oulian let it fall.

Tears ran down Setelin's face. She wiped them away and picked the weapon up again. Shuddering at the touch, she fitted it into Oulian's shaking hand, then closed his fingers around it.

She did not look away. Clinging heavily with his left arm around the shoulders of an attendant about the age of Stal Viat, Oulian lifted his right arm deliberately and looked Jim in the face again.

There was rage in his good eye. Rage and grief. And beneath all of them, pity. He struggled for breath and words. "Dream of peace," he said, his voice miraculously clear, before his hand tightened on the weapon.

Peace came faster than the pyre.

Epilogue: Aviva

"Arrival date confirmed. Don't even think of Bachelor Officer's Quarters, Neave says. I've been at the Residence since I left Blue Ridge, *and I'll pick you up."*

Jones' last transmission came through right before I boarded the shuttle to take me downworld. Big of Jones to offer me Amory's hospitality, but I'd expect nothing less of either of them.

I glanced down at the mourning band some atavistic urge had made me wrap about the sleeve of my uniform. Since Jones' first message, I couldn't get Jim out of my mind. Damn the man. How dared he wad up love, reputation, honorable work into a ball and toss it onto the pyre for a crime he'd long since expiated?

Time after time, I'd told myself Jim hadn't just been a fool, he'd been a romantic, egotistical idiot. A cruel idiot at the last, who forced people who'd loved him to give him his death and abandoned the good he could have done for an impossible code of conduct.

He'd been one of us. And now, ironically enough, he'd become the standard we must all try to uphold, after all these years of failure. There's selfishness in honor, but I was damned if I could blame Jim this time. At least, not more than fifty percent of the time I thought about it.

"Captain!" I heard Ryutaro Jones call. "Cam!"

There he was, underneath the lotus pilasters of the station's high ceiling, lounging against the checkpoint with his usual insolent ease as the usual security contingent came glowering up, prepared to chuck him out and take him into custody if he so much as complained.

Business as usual. For the first time in weeks, I actually found myself smiling. I moved forward to wave away security, but a uniformed man forestalled me.

"Stand down, sirs, if you please," rumbled a deep voice. That voice too I recognized: Murad, Neave's security and Jones' usual nemesis.

Talk about improbable alliances! I could feel my smile widening into a grin, pulling unfamiliar muscles taut.

Jones rushed forward, flinging his arms around me. I saw strands of gray at his glossy temples, almost as many as on my own. On him it looked good; on me, it was old and tired.

Disengaging myself from Jones and his usual flashy bronze and pewter jacket, I nodded to Murad.

"Warrant Officer."

"Captain," said Murad, rising to the salute with his prosthetic hand. "Please to come this way."

Still a stickler for protocol. Then, reaching for my duffle from where I'd set it down beside me, Murad actually by-God smiled at me. "Good to see you back, sir," he added.

Jones and I followed his broad back out to Neave's groundcar without a word. Usually Jones talked my ear off.

Instead, as Murad sealed us in, he poured me fresh water and let me stare out the darkened windows as the car purred away from the station. Since my last visit, they had sealed Aviva's shield generators and extended the plantings. The fresh dark greens eased my eyes. A few days, maybe longer, in the humidity of a planetary environment, and they wouldn't hurt anymore.

And what about the rest of me? Not just the aches and pains, but the exhaustion, the shortness of breath, the sudden faintness. I made myself not think about it. I'd had plenty of practice at that lately. Denial. Wait till CMO Ankeny got a hand on me. Or one of Aviva's physicians.

Amory himself was waiting for me outside, leaning against one of the entranceway's pillars, a book in hand. He didn't just hand me out of the groundcar as if I were an honored guest, he stepped forward fast, and pressed me close.

Keeping an arm around my shoulders, he turned back toward the Residence. "Come and see who's here!" he told me, as he gestured for Murad to perform his usual disappearing act with my duffle. He even managed to make his words sound jovial, a host promising a guest a fine time.

I knew better.

Jones had already told me. When *Blue Ridge* actually did make orbit around Exquemelin some weeks after Jim's death, Jones had been aboard. Maybe he did have an assignment for a story on the straits-runners, and maybe he was acting as Neave's agent: sooner or later, most of us in the No Man's Worlds seemed to. But if *Blue Ridge* had reached Exquemelin with one passenger, it left with two, and Jones had yet another of his damn stories-of-a-lifetime.

"How is Setelin?" I asked Neave, close at my side.

"Dr. Marx—you remember Dr. Marx—says she's doing just fine. Physically, that is. She's depressed, though, and until—" He fell silent.

"Will she see me?" I asked. I'd looked wreckers in the face with less fear than I felt about confronting the fierce girl. She'd called me a liar once, defending the man she loved; I didn't want to see her now she'd lost him. But evading her was beyond contempt.

"When I asked, she just shrugged. Let's settle you in your rooms first, shall we?" asked Neave. He took my arm. The ring that had been Jim's talisman glinted on his hand again.

He saw what I was looking at and sighed. "Setelin refuses to wear it."

I could feel myself relax as the door opened on the familiar guest suite. Home again. Immediately, I glanced at the table to see what sort of flowers had been set out: this time it was the faience bowl with one blue lotus, so fresh and delicate it took my breath away. Neave followed my gaze and smiled.

"You always did like them best," he said.

Murad had set my gear down on the bed. It looked cheap and shabby against the subtly toned heavy silk covers. If I touched them, they'd probably snag.

"I see you got rid of the hospital bed," I couldn't help commenting. "What's Dr. Marx say about that?"

"He's been preoccupied with Setelin," Neave said, from his discreet vantagepost in the open door. "Oh, she's quite well physically, but . . . you'll see."

I straightened my jacket and ran my hands through my hair. Not quite gray, the mirror told me. For all that it mattered.

"Well," I said on a shaky breath, "no time like the present. Where is she?"

Neave took me down the long corridor and out to the atrium where we'd once drunk ourselves as giddy as adolescents on ice wine, then rushed around in a squall carrying in bottles and glasses, and damn near tumbled into bed together. At our ages.

Well, Neave had always said you had to reach for your reward with clean hands. Clean, meaning "empty."

I remembered the high silent walls with their carvings; the restfulness of the water, in its wide-rimmed basin; the lotus floating on the surface, a haven of rest, even for Jones, who was making a bad job of relaxing by a table that held a pitcher of reddish juice and glasses.

An awkward distance away, Setelin sat beside the fountain, stiffly upright in a wrought-metal chair. One small hand cradled her belly, the other, ringless now, rested on the arm of the chair. Maybe five or six months along, from the little I knew of such matters.

She wore a long white dress like the ones I'd seen on Exquemelin. Its folds pooled at her feet like carvings at the base of a pillar. Her dark hair lay on her shoulders, as well-ordered as the rest of her. Even the great black snapping eyes seemed subdued.

"Setelin," Amory said as gently as a father. "Do you remember Captain Marlow?"

I stepped forward into the breach, forcing a smile. "I was a guest in her house, Amory. I should hope she would."

"He's left me," Setelin said.

There was only one "he" in all the worlds for her, I knew.

"My mother warned me. They always leave. He asked me to forgive him, but I will not weep. Not one tear."

Her eyes were clear, but something in them ached like a bloodless wound and, like such a wound, remained unhealed.

"It would have been easy to die with him," she added. "I had my hand on the blaster. Oulian could not have stopped me." Her face twisted, then froze into stubborn composure.

"Let your grief out," I urged her. "It's bad for the baby."

She glanced down at the swell of her stomach as if it almost bored her. "He kept *his* promise. What right did he have to make it? I begged him to stay with me. And I swore on my mother's grave that I would not die weeping. And now, with this . . . this . . ." she raised her hand as if prepared to strike at her belly, then touched it gently, "I don't dare die at all."

Jones rose and placed a glass at the fountain's edge. She inclined her head in thanks, but didn't move to take it.

"Oh my poor child." I had never spoken that way to anyone in my life. "Did he know? Did you at least have time to tell him?" I came forward and, sitting on the edge of the fountain, took her little icy hand in mine. I patted it, then released it, thinking that she'd replace it on the arm of her chair. Instead, she let it drop, listless, in mid-air.

"For what, Captain?" Setelin's eyes blazed, melting through some of the glacial isolation in which she had wrapped herself. "So he'd know what else he was losing? I gave him all I had to give. And in the end, the best thing I could give him was mercy," she whispered harshly.

"And for forcing me to that," she continued, "I will never forgive him. Never."

"But you must have forgiven him somewhat to come here, here to his old life," I said. "He wanted so to be forgiven. We all do. And he was . . . almost happy here."

She turned her head to one side, the shadow of the animated, charming way she had always listened to Jim, or argued with him. "Was he?" she asked. "I came here because I wanted the child—*my* child—to live without being part of someone else's dream. I have dreamed it will be a son."

"Is that what you want?" I asked.

"I would rather die childless than have a daughter of mine die weeping," she said, final as a judge.

"What will you tell your child about his father?" Jones asked.

"That he was a great fool." She sighed so deeply I expected her ribs to crack.

"His folly, as you call it, saved a world," Jones said. He looked over Setelin's bowed head at me. "I'll show you my report, that is—"

Neave nodded permission.

She rose and went to Neave. "Sir, the physician said that I must spend part of each afternoon outside. I have done so, and now I am returning to my rooms. Please excuse me if I am not at dinner. I am quite tired."

Without a backward glance, she left the atrium.

Neave raised his eyebrows at me and shrugged. "That went about as well as I had a right to expect, Caroline. Still, I'd hoped—"

I shook my head. "You thought, because I was a woman who . . . cared for Jim, that poor girl and I could grieve together and I'd have some sort of wisdom for her? Oh, Amory. I'm not a woman to her. I'm one of the things, the *them* that stole her love away." Tears prickled at my eyes. "That poor child."

"She's got years, yet," Jones erupted. "My God, how can she live that way? What kind of a life can she give that child?"

He'd risen and was pacing the atrium, back and forth, like a captain on the bridge. *Oh-ho,* I thought, *is* that *how things are?*

For Jones' sake, I hoped not. Flexibility was not high on Setelin's list of virtues. And I'd had a bellyful of romantic young men. Or men not so young.

But Jones always had had the best survival instincts of anyone I'd ever known.

"Ryutaro, I told you, as long as she wants, she's welcome

here. We'll find someplace other than the guest house for the next group of *Blue Ridge* crew."

Jones started up, to follow Setelin. I raised a hand, then let it drop. He was a grown man: what would I warn him about, anyway?

"Don't worry, Caroline." Neave's voice was composed. "Aaron—Dr. Marx, I mean—says Jones sits with her for hours on end, talking about everything in the worlds. At least, she listens. Meds would lift that depression, but she's refused them. Maybe once the child is born."

He was old enough to take the long view, that there are few things that cannot be outworn, or outlived. But Setelin had lived with Jim.

"Jones can talk anyone around," I said. Half-agreement.

I glanced over at Neave, who was collecting glasses and replacing them on their proper tray. "Doesn't look like much of a night for ice wine, does it?" he asked with a rueful glance.

Oh, we were going to be one hell of a jolly house party. I'd have felt sorry for Neave if I weren't suddenly as tired as Setelin myself.

I should never have come here. I should return to my ship. I could probably talk Tom Ankeny around just one more time into fudging my medical report until, maybe, the mercy of an accident would spare me from having to decide what to do once I was no longer fit to fly. But a downworld physician like Aaron Marx—he'd look at me with those bright, merciless eyes, and discuss "other options."

The damn thing of it was, Neave probably knew precisely how my mind was working. Knew, and wouldn't interfere. After all, he had his standards, too.

"If you'll excuse me," I said. "Setelin had *one* good idea. I'd like to rest before dinner. That Dr. Marx—"

"Caroline, you know I've told you to consider this place . . ."

Home.

I mumbled thanks like the greenest ensign on a courtesy

call and stumbled from the atrium in the most awkward retreat of either of my lives.

Once inside the comfortable quarters I realized I did think of as my own, I sank onto the bed, so much more comfortable than the bunk back on board *Gavroche,* snagged the silk spread with my rough spacer's hands, and cried.

SETELIN'S WITHDRAWAL, IT TURNED OUT, MEANT THAT DINner was informal. Long ago, I'd gotten used to Neave's dining room, with its shining table and lamps, the orderly harmonies of the music he liked, and his deliberative courtesies over food and wine: they were natural to me now, but I was just as glad to dispense with them and fill a plate from the sideboard as though this were breakfast and I was about to walk five kilometers with Aaron Marx.

Marx, of course, raced in at the last minute from the guest house, muttered an apology for his lateness, and ate with his usual efficiency. My God, didn't they feed doctors at Aviva Memorial? Apparently not as well as Neave did; Marx must have jumped at the chance to play Residence Physician some more.

He shot me a "later-for-you" look before stoking himself with a second plate, stacking it neatly, and seating himself by the French doors. This time of year, darkness came early. I could see our reflections: Jones and Neave, exerting themselves to play out the roles of good guest and cordial host; me, silent; Marx, crackling with his usual energy and, yes, his peculiar brand of kindness.

He was giving me time, I realized, to make the decision that he would not shrink from if my courage failed. That itself was a test: was I captain enough to know when another captain could serve my ship better than I could?

To know when I could no longer serve adequately?

Even Jim had learned that the moment came when you could no longer flee, evade, or deny.

An accident would be easier, I thought, if only it didn't

hurt *Gavroche* and scar my crew the way Ragozinksi's suicide years ago had damaged me.

If I couldn't be a ship's captain anymore, what the hell was I? And what would I do?

I drew my attention back from the discomfort of my thoughts and distracted myself with the wine, fragrant with the scents of apples and honey. "A little sweeter than I prefer," Neave had pronounced it, then added, "but I didn't think we were up for anything too demanding."

I'd learned to understand exactly what he was saying. And I agreed.

Setelin, poor child, must be having culture shock. On top of grief and pregnancy. No wonder she seemed blighted by an early frost. Let her feel everything she had to feel, and she'd run screaming into the night.

Murad would, of course, find her and bring her back. Neave would impart his particular brand of common sense and wisdom. And, if Setelin were wise—and nothing I had seen of her convinced me otherwise, except, perhaps for her folly in loving Jim—she would thrive.

Meanwhile, Neave waited.

"Jones—very well, Ryutaro," said Marx, raising his head from dessert, "I've got to thank you for your help in exchanging medical libraries back on Earth."

I set my glass down with too little regard for its finely turned stem.

"Don't blame me," Jones said. "Neave's made the match; I'm simply the one who's getting to untangle all the bureaucracy."

"You're going to Earth?" I asked. "After all this time?"

Jones laughed. "I got an offer from HWN—HomeWorldNet. I was all set to turn it down. *Blue Ridge* asked me to fly with them again and promised a stopover on-station. No outsider's ever been on one of their trading outposts, but the captain promised I could meet the grandmothers who run the whole tribe. It'll wait, Neave told me. If I hook up with Home-

WorldNet, I can tell a whole lot more people what's going on out here."

And Neave and Abram Becker can make political capital out of your stories, I thought. Old age and treachery.

I raised my glass to Neave. "Well done, Amory." Then, I was sober again.

"What are you going to do with—" I gestured, reluctant to speak Jim's name.

"Let the dead be dead," Jones said. "Poor bastard deserves his privacy, after all these years. The way I figure it, the sooner I go, the sooner I can come back. That's right, you go ahead and laugh, Cam. If you'd told me, after the war, that I wouldn't scamper back Home—even if it was a home I couldn't remember—I'd have said you were suffering from freezer burn."

"You'd have been right," I said. "Remember?" I almost forgot to fear the way Marx raised his head, as if scenting some discovery he could use against me and my medical history.

"Damn place has gotten into my blood," Jones said. "Oh, go ahead and laugh. You probably knew it all along."

"I hoped," Neave said. "I've got to admit you were a particularly unprepossessing, bratty youngling. But you've shaped up well. But I don't agree it's a good idea for you to rush through your HomeWorldNet contract. It's worth doing well."

"And Jim?" Jones asked.

"Not forgotten," said Neave. "I'm making inquiries back on Aven for next-of-kin. Beside Setelin, of course. And *Blue Ridge* and her sisters will keep an eye out for wreckers stupid enough to try to move in on Exquemelin. By the time your story breaks, there'll be no one left to hurt."

"You don't think the bastard deserves privacy?" Jones asked. He was arguing the losing side, and he knew it. I leaned forward to watch the final blows.

"Jim spent his whole life trying to cleanse his name," Neave said. "Someone's got to finish the job." He drew a deep breath, and his eyes went vague. When he spoke again, his voice had that faraway, resonant tone that meant he was drawing another one of his texts from memory. " 'What a wounded name, things standing thus unknown, shall I leave behind me!' "

Jones raised his glass. "I've got it! 'Absent thee from felicity awhile/And in this harsh world draw thy breath in pain to tell my story.' "

"So you found more than buried bones in my library, did you?" Neave asked, returning Jones' toast.

"Yes, sir: buried treasure."

Neave rose and clapped Jones on the shoulder. "And that's why you're almost the only person I'd trust to tell this story. The other . . ." He raised his head and looked at me. I shivered a little from the force of that glance.

"What about you, Caroline?" he asked. "Someone's got to go and keep Jones honest. And I've got a few errands—that is, Becker and I do—that would get a better reception from Earth Alliance if you ran them rather than even as estimable a journalist as Mr. Jones."

My next assignment, if I took it. Neave was offering me a way past a negative medical fitrep. Judging from the deliberate blandness of Marx's face, I thought it was one that had been discussed with him. Probably, if I felt like checking, I'd find Tom Ankeny'd been in on it too.

They were spiders, those two old men, catching all of us in their nets and draining us. Some, like Jim, died of it. Others, like Jones, thrived. And I?

Maybe Earth was far enough away that I could break free. Assuming I wanted to.

Marx rose and touched Jones on the shoulder. "I'm going to check on my patient," he said, excusing himself. "Are you coming?"

"It's the thousand nights and a night all over again," said Neave. "Jones talks at Setelin till he's hoarse, and, if he's lucky, wins a faint smile. Talk therapy, but in reverse."

"As long as it works," Marx said. "I'll take any port in an ion storm."

He prodded Jones, who rose hastily and followed him to the guest house.

Leaving me alone with Amory Neave. I'd sat across this table from him times out of mind. But now he seemed a stranger to me.

"You set this up," I accused him.

"Nothing of the kind," Neave said. "Caroline, you're as much a realist as I. I saw it on your face when you greeted Marx: this year, or next, you know you're going to have to retire."

"What do you expect me to do?" I asked, deliberately striking back. "Sit on a planet and grow old?"

"Grow old along with me? The best is yet to be?" he asked whimsically. Another of his damnable quotes. "There are worse things you could do, as I found out when I asked the same question. But for you, there are better things. Jones is going back to Earth to tell the people there what it's like out in the No Man's Worlds. He's young enough to be a bridge between the two cultures, and I think he'll do well.

"But you, Caroline. You can show them by your own experience. We have no better ambassador."

Thrust and parry. Counterthrust and riposte. I waited a beat. "I hope you're using the term metaphorically," I said at last.

"If you wish." Neave inclined his head formally. This wasn't the man who'd become my friend over the years, I realized. This was the player, the gray eminence, I'd initially feared. And been right to fear.

Then, he made himself smile. The familiar, friendly intelligence returned. "Besides, I really do need you to keep an eye on Jones. I've been keeping logs all these years, writing up—"

"So you were writing your memoirs after all!" I exclaimed.

"A disease of academics," he said ruefully. "Chronic, I'm afraid. I'm trusting the files to Jones. But I'm trusting Jones to you. Will you accept?"

"We could send Murad to keep an eye on him instead," I suggested, and joined him in laughter.

"Caroline—"

"I'll go," I said. "What's left for me? I'll go and play star captain and dine out . . . and then . . ."

Neave drew breath more quickly than I had ever heard him. His eyes fell to his hand, on which he wore the ring Setelin had brought back to him.

"And then . . ."

It would be a long trip. No telling what we'd run up against, from Tokugawan minefields to ion storms to any one of the countless enemies I'd made since resurrection. Not to mention some particularly nasty Jump transits. Just going straight to Earth and turning around could take years. And if I did it right . . .

I'd be older. Neave would be . . . older than I, but he was the sort who aged well.

And he was waiting for my answer.

His face was smiling in a way that would make it hard for me to leave. He would stay here, with his writing and his study and his politics. He would help to build this world. He'd even take an interest in raising Setelin's child, and Jim's. And he'd wait for me to return and take my place, like a keystone in a bridge, in the painstaking edifice of home he'd built.

I met his eyes and nodded. Yes, even to the questions he hadn't asked. "I'll go," I said. "And if I live and last out the trip, I'll come back. To this place. To you. After all, this is the only home I've got."